THE RESILIENCE DUET

BOXED SET

AMANDA SHELLEY

ISBN
E-book: 978-1-951947-25-5
Paperback: 978-1-951947-27-9

Editor: Sue Soares
SJS Editorial Services
https://www.facebook.com/sue.soares71
Proof Reader: Julie Deaton
Deaton Author Services
http://jdproofs.wixsite.com/jddeaton
Cover Design: Amy Queau
QDesign
https://www.qcoverdesign.com

Visit my website at
www.amandashelley.com

RESILIENCE

BOOK ONE OF THE RESILIENCE DUET

CONNECT WITH AMANDA SHELLEY

Want to be the first to know about upcoming sales and new releases? Make sure you sign up for my newsletter as well as connect with me on social media and your favorite retail store.

Website:
www.amandashelley.com
Newsletter:
https://geni.us/AmandaShelleyNL
Facebook:
https://www.facebook.com/authoramandashelley/
Instagram:
https://www.instagram.com/authoramandashelley/
Twitter:
https://twitter.com/AmandShelley
Reader's Group:
https://www.facebook.com/groups/AmandasArmyofReaders/
Amazon:

http://amazon.com/author/amandashelley
Goodreads:
https://www.goodreads.com/author/show/19713563.Aman
da_Shelley
Book Bub:
https://www.bookbub.com/profile/amanda-shelley

ABOUT THE BOOK

Samantha never saw Enzo coming.

As the dust settles from her divorce, her life is full. She doesn't have time for distractions. She's too busy running her own company and checking off numerous items from her kids' demanding schedule to have a life of her own.

Then he walks into her kitchen with his breathtaking green eyes and a mischievous grin. He's there to surprise his father - her contractor, but his presence makes everything off kilter.

Enzo's perfectly content with his adventurous life as an elite rescue pilot, until a harmless prank turns on him. Instead of surprising his father, he finds his world thrown off course by the beautiful woman with a sexy smile, wicked sass and the mouthwatering ability to keep him on his toes.

With his limited time on leave, is she worth the risk to his heart?

1

SAMANTHA

I WAKE by hearing the kids moving about. Glancing at my clock, I realize my alarm was never set. *Shit!* I frantically dash out of bed, grateful for the alarms in each of their bedrooms. Maddie is already dressed and eating cereal in the kitchen. I hear Declan in the shower, and Frankie is dressed and watching cartoons. The bus will arrive in thirty minutes, so I dash into the kitchen to finish putting their lunches together.

"Frankie, have you eaten breakfast?" I ask as I make my way past her.

"Yeah. I had Lucky Charms. Can I have PB&J for my lunch today?"

She always has PB&J. Does she think I'll suddenly forget? "Sure thing, sugar. Do you want an apple or a banana today?" I say in my best morning voice.

"Apple. Can you slice it? Oh, and Ava wants me to come over today after school. Can her mom take me to ballet and you pick me up?"

Ava is Frankie's best friend. Thankfully, I already planned this with Ava's mother so I could be here if my contractors are able to start the kitchen remodel this afternoon. "That's the plan, Stan. I'm going to pick you up from ballet first then we'll grab Dec and go to Maddie's match. We'll grab dinner out tonight since I don't know if we can cook at home with the contractor coming."

"Okay, Mama. Sounds good." Frankie takes her lunch and puts it into her backpack. Though she's my youngest at eight years old, Frankie has been the most resilient of my three kids. She has somehow found a way to accept our new "normal" and has adjusted to the recent changes in our family with ease.

Declan, my ten-year-old shouts from the stairs, "Hey, Mom, did you wash my practice uniform for soccer? It's not in my bag."

Crap. I must have left it in the dryer. I'm so off my routine this morning. I holler, "Check the dryer," up the stairs so he can get it himself.

"Thanks, Mom. Got it." I hear drift through the house a few seconds later.

Maddie removes her earbuds as she gets up from the table to put her dish in the sink from breakfast. "Hey, Mom, you're going to make it to my match tonight, right?" Maddie is a freshman and managed to make the varsity volleyball team. She doesn't get a lot of playing time, but I wouldn't miss it for the world.

"There's no way I'd miss it, Mads. I'm picking everyone up and we'll be there on time. Promise."

She comes over and gives me an unexpected hug. "I know,

Mom. I'm just not sure if Dad will make it, so I want to make sure you're there."

"Don't worry. Even if he can't make it, I know he'd want to be there." I glance to the clock and find they have five minutes to make it to the bus. I holler for everyone to hear, "Okay, guys, time to get going! The bus will be here any minute. Maddie, so will your ride."

I rush each of them out the door and realize I have less than an hour to get ready to meet with the contractor. One of the benefits of owning my own business is I can work from home today. I'll have to fit reviewing a manuscript in at some point. Who needs sleep, right? At least I can do most of my work with my laptop or e-reader if I'm just reading for content. I can work from just about anywhere. Before I shower, I start the coffee pot. It feels like I will need an extra dose of caffeine today.

I'm just settled at the breakfast bar with my coffee and my computer, ready to check emails and review my calendar, when I hear a knock at the door. Lorenzo Harper, my contractor, greets me. He's an older man but has kept himself in great shape over the years. His dark hair is thick and barely showing any gray, just a little around his temples. He has a warm smile on his face that lights up his green eyes.

"Morning, Samantha!" he greets me warmly. "Are ya ready to show me what needs to be done around here?"

"Thanks for coming, Lorenzo," I eagerly welcome him into my home. "I can't wait to get things started!"

Lorenzo has done some work for us in the past. He's the guy who comes out to write the bids and sets everything into motion for his crew, then manages it as the project continues, even though he may have multiple projects going on at once. He has been in business for years and is nearing retirement age, but he's not ready for that to happen anytime soon. He claims he's a people person and knows how to get the job done right. I walk Lorenzo around my kitchen, family room, and dining room, discussing the final plans for the changes being done. He verifies the timeline for how long everything will take. He's already been to my home, and we've discussed the project on the phone, so the proper permits have been filed and the renovation should begin shortly. I know when it's finished, I'll be more than happy with it.

When we're done touring, Lorenzo opens his computer and taps out a few things. A few minutes later, he stops and looks at me with a huge grin. "Well, darlin', you're in luck. One of my crews just finished a job early and we can be over here as soon as tomorrow to begin demolition. We'll start in the kitchen so we can get it back to functioning for you as soon as possible. You should only be without your appliances for about a week or so if your order comes in on time."

Relieved he can get started right away, I nearly hug him. "Sounds great. While the crew is here, I'll work from home and try not to get in your way."

Lorenzo gets up to leave. "I'll see you tomorrow morning then. You'll have to empty out those cupboards since we'll be starting there." He grins ruefully as he knows it will take me some time today to clear those out.

"It's a good thing I've bought boxes then, isn't it?" I smile back at him.

After spending the day packing up my kitchen, I pick up Frankie from ballet and Declan from soccer practice, then rush to Maddie's volleyball game. Realizing we only have about ten minutes until Maddie's match starts, I speed into the parking lot at the high school and the tires screech as I come to an abrupt stop in the first open spot I see. I quickly unload everyone and briskly walk across the parking lot, stopping dead in my tracks when I see Devin, my ex, helping a pixie-like woman out of his car. He places his hand on the small of her back and escorts her to the gymnasium. He doesn't see me at first, so I have a moment to school my features before I meet who I assume is Aubrey, his new girlfriend.

Unfortunately, I don't get much of a chance to pull myself together because Frankie notices her father immediately. She squeals, "Daddy!" as she rushes toward him. I see Devin startle, his body instantly frozen in place, but eagerly turns and scoops her up into his arms for a gigantic hug.

Our divorce has had its challenges and not all of us are as eager as Frankie to greet one another. I straighten my back, lift my chin, and make sure to have a smile on my face as I do my best to greet him warmly. Devin still wants to have an active role as a parent, so I do all I can to keep things positive. I've never been one to hold onto grudges or play into bitterness; I simply don't have time for that. Hopefully, one day I'll be able to have a real conversation with him again that doesn't feel forced.

"Hey, Devin. Maddie will be so happy you're here for her match." I somehow manage to make my voice sound smooth and unaffected by him.

An indescribable emotion flits through Devin's eyes for a moment before he replies. "Yeah, I'm glad I could make it. Aubrey and I just got back into town from a business trip." He politely smiles in my direction before gesturing to the blonde beside him and states, "Aubrey, this is Sam. Sam, this is Aubrey."

For a split second, Aubrey looks a little nervous as she looks me over, but quickly recovers by sticking out her hand and saying, "It's a pleasure to meet you. I've heard lovely things about you." A slow smile spreads across her face, as I instinctively push my hand out to meet hers.

I can't help but look at Devin to make sure my ears weren't deceiving me. Not that he makes a habit of bad mouthing me, but I have to say, I'm surprised. *Well, at least he hasn't been a complete asshat, I'll give him that. I guess things could have been much worse.* I inwardly shrug. I briefly look to Devin with a flash of surprise before I remember my manners. "Nice to meet you, too."

Aubrey then turns to Declan and asks encouragingly, "How was your soccer game last weekend? I heard you scored in the last game."

Declan quickly tries to gauge my reaction. He's very aware of my feelings and has become a bit protective of me. I give him my best supportive smile and he sighs. "Yeah... it was amazing. I scored from the backfield with only a few minutes to go. We'd been tied, so I got the winning goal." He looks pointedly at his father before adding, "Sorry you missed it." I inwardly cringe at his disappointment.

"I'm sorry, too, bud," Devin states sincerely as he ruffles

Declan's wavy brown hair. "I'll be there tomorrow night. You know how things go with the business. I had to fly to New York to pitch that new ad campaign. I'm pretty sure we nailed the pitch, so I won't have to leave town again for a few more weeks." Devin puts his arm around Declan and pulls him in for a side hug.

Devin owns his own advertising firm. He's worked hard over the years and has made a name for himself. He has quite a few employees who usually do the traveling, but occasionally, there's a client for whom he needs to do the pitch. Travel was never a problem while we were married, until one day it was. He didn't meet Aubrey until after we were divorced, so I shouldn't have any animosity toward her, at least in that regard.

Before anyone can say anything else, Frankie exclaims, "Let's go watch Maddie! Dad, you can sit with us, right?" She suddenly looks at me to see if it's okay.

Great. Just what I need after a long day. I quickly remind myself that once again, this isn't about me. I refuse to be one of those parents who spars with her ex. You know, the ones who are bitter and vindictive and leave a wake of destruction in their path, caring nothing about the effects their rancor has on those they love, especially the children. My self-respect, not to mention my love for my children, won't let me behave that way.

Maddie doesn't expect to start the match, being a freshman. We find her sitting on the bench after the National Anthem is sung. But the smile that crosses her face when she realizes we've all arrived is priceless. By the way she keeps rubbing her hands up and down her legs, I can tell she's nervous since this is only their second match. She ends up getting to play during the second and the third sets, as setter, and does her best to help her team pull off a win. When she approaches us after the game, her smile is infectious.

"Hey, Mad-dog," Declan announces as she heads toward where we're seated in the bleachers. "Way to go out there!" He lifts his hand for a fist bump. He bursts with pride for his sister's success.

I can't help the way my heart flutters when I see the two of them supporting each other. Sure, they can also shriek like banshees when they really get into it, but overall, they really do care about each other. I sneak a glance at Devin who meets my eye and winks. *Yeah, we did something right.* His pride shines, too.

"Thanks for being here," Maddie says, gesturing to all of us. I can't help but notice her quick glance in my direction before hugging her dad. She knows things can still be tense between us, and having Aubrey here is new to our family dynamics.

"Amazing save out there." Aubrey smiles as she pats Maddie on the arm to congratulate her.

"Thanks. I didn't think I'd get that last dig, but somehow I managed." Maddie beams with pride for her accomplishment during the game. "Can we stop and get something to eat on the way home? I'm starving." She looks at me before glancing at her dad and Aubrey.

"Sure thing, Mads," Devin exclaims. Then he turns to me. "Want to join us, or should I drop them at the house after we get a bite to eat? I'm thinking pizza sounds amazing just about now." He rubs his stomach then beams at each of the kids before looking at Aubrey, then me for our reactions.

As awkward as this might be, I'm thankful I have the excuse of the remodel to politely decline. There's no way I want him back, but I'm just not ready to go out to dinner with Devin and his new girlfriend.

On the drive home, my mind whirls with thoughts of this evening and how far things have changed between Devin and me over the last couple of years. There wasn't just one thing that led to my decision to ask for a divorce. It was a multitude of things, compounding over time, which resulted in the demise of our marriage. The stresses of daily living, both at work and at home didn't help matters, but such is life. Everyone experiences those things; Devin and I weren't any different. The problem was when things became broken, it wasn't me to whom Devin turned. We tried to work things out, but nothing seemed to change. Eventually, when I realized how little I felt toward one act of betrayal or another, I knew it was time to pull the plug. I could no longer let the fear of the unknown keep me from doing what I knew was best. Obviously, my "give a fuck" had been broken and I no longer had any fucks left to give. Here I am at thirty-eight, starting over.

2

SAMANTHA

BY THE END of the next day, my kitchen is no longer
recognizable. Lorenzo's crew brought in drop blankets to cover
my furniture that hadn't been pushed into the garage. The
walls have been stripped of the cupboards and all the
appliances are gone. The carpet has been ripped out and the
wall being removed is set to go in the morning. With all the
banging and people moving about, it's difficult to get much of
my own work done.

Tonight, the kids will be at Devin's. He saw the state of my
kitchen when he picked up the kids and offered to take them
tomorrow night, too, starting the weekend early since it's his
time for visitation anyway. The kids are excited to be there
since we can't cook here. They begrudgingly ate hot lunch
today at school, but I know they're looking forward to their
cold lunches for the rest of the week, courtesy of Devin. After
they left, I went out and got dinner for myself, then settled in
for the evening to catch up on some much-needed reading.

About noon on Thursday, Lorenzo returns to check on his crew before they break for lunch. He checks on their progress and is in the middle of a phone call for another job when an unfamiliar man walks in with a guy I recognize from the crew.

This new man immediately grabs my attention. He's well over six feet tall, with short, tousled, dark-blond hair. He's easily in his mid-thirties. He has an athletic build and a mischievous smile that makes his familiar green eyes sparkle with delight. *If I'm being honest, he is like sex on a stick. No man should look that good.* He's clearly up to something, but it's hard to tell from my vantage point in the hallway. When he notices me, he quickly motions for me to stay quiet by placing a finger over his lips and winks as he stalks up behind Lorenzo. As soon as Lorenzo ends his phone call and turns around, the stranger embraces him in a gigantic bear hug, nearly lifting Lorenzo off his feet, which is no small feat; Lorenzo is just slightly smaller than the size of this man in front of me.

"Hey, Pops!" The stranger chuckles.

The look of utter shock and then bewilderment quickly transforms Lorenzo's features. He quickly returns the hug with an UMPH and a muffled chuckle. "What the fuck are you doing here, son?" As soon as he's released, Lorenzo steps back to fully assess his son. Then without a word, pulls his son in for another tight embrace, patting him on the back like men do. "I... I... can't believe you're here." Lorenzo gathers his wits and remembers where he is, looking around the room, still in a daze.

While keeping an arm around him, Lorenzo spots me and beams. "Samantha, this is my son, Enzo. The last I knew, he was stationed in Germany, not due to come home for a few more months." Then he looks pointedly at Enzo. "Everything all right?"

"Yeah, Pops, it sure is!" Enzo beams back at his father. "I just got leave and thought I'd surprise you."

"Well, you sure as shit did!" Lorenzo chortles, still looking amazed and bewildered. "Did you see your Ma yet?"

"Yep. I stopped there first thing this morning. She told me where to find you. Need a hand?"

"Well, I might, but not today. Today, I'm going to knock off a few hours early and catch up with you... if Samantha doesn't mind." Lorenzo looks at me with a grin on his face, but a question in his voice.

Who am I to begrudge the man seeing his son. I know I would do the same. "I wouldn't want it any other way. Have fun!"

"Thank you, Samantha." Enzo looks at me with appreciation, then gives me a once-over. "I appreciate your understanding. I know Pops doesn't usually like to cut out on work." He looks around the room, assessing the project at hand. "I'll be sure to give him a hand to make up for it later."

I can't help but chuckle. "No worries. Your dad's helped me out a lot over the years. I know he'll enjoy every moment he gets to spend with you."

Before they leave, Lorenzo shows him the rest of the project. I go back to the living room and attempt to work on the manuscript I had planned to read today. For the first time in forever, I seem to be a little distracted though. I find myself reading the same paragraph over and over again, as I steal glances at Enzo. *Gaahh! Why am I letting him do this to me?* Sure, he's unbelievably gorgeous. He's muscular, but in a way that shows he's active, not a gym junkie. He has a presence about him that completely draws my attention. I have no idea the last time I felt this drawn to anyone, including Devin when we first started dating. There's just something about that man I can't get out of my mind. If I'm being honest, it's a little unnerving.

I steal glimpses of Enzo as they walk through my home. Who wouldn't look at a man like that? One time, he catches me in the act. *Crap!* He nods his head at me once, with a smile forming on his lips and a twinkle in his eye. Even though the man is breathtaking, I scold myself for staring. What the hell has gotten into me? I'm being utterly ridiculous. I'm not a schoolgirl easily distracted by the captain of the football team. I'm a grown woman, for God's sake, with kids and responsibilities. Being a single mom, I have no business getting caught up with thoughts about a stranger. It's not like he would ever be interested in me. Besides, he's going to leave, and I'll never see him again, *except in my fantasies*, but those don't count.

God, how long has it even been? Just the possibility of connecting with someone again has turned me into a bundle of nerves. Maybe I should consider dating again? But if I end up acting like this, I'm better off single.

3

―――

ENZO

WHEN I ARRIVE at Pop's worksite, my mind is entirely focused on surprising him. But I can't help but notice the sexy brunette in the hallway as I make my way to him. Her alluring smile and chestnut eyes almost distract me from my mission. But I manage to catch Pops off guard. He always was one for surprises growing up, wanting to get one in while he could, and I couldn't pass up this opportunity.

As Pops shows me around Samantha's beautiful home and explains what he has in store for it, I find myself glancing in her direction more than I should. When I catch her doing the same, a smile spreads across my lips. It's a spontaneous reaction, happening before I could put any thought into it. Pops quickly points out something else, and I'm back to having my attention focused on him.

I'm relieved to be home. I just spent thirty straight hours traveling from Germany. I had a few long layovers, then I snagged the last jump seat from New York City to Portland.

Being in the Air Force has its perks. Though it feels strange to let another person sit in the cockpit. Surprisingly, I managed to sleep most of that leg of my trip, so I'm still alert and ready for action.

As Pops and I make our way toward the door, I glance at Samantha one more time. She nods with a sheepish grin and tucks her shoulder-length hair behind one ear. A slight blush spreads across her face and she immediately has my full attention. *What would make her do that?* Upon further inspection, I notice she isn't wearing any jewelry, at least not on her fingers. As an airman, my life may be wild and full of adventures, but a married woman is a 'no-fly zone' no matter my level of attraction to her. Samantha has a natural beauty about her that draws my attention to her further. She's wearing little makeup, jeans and a dark-blue shirt that hug her curves perfectly. Samantha's shy demeanor and sexiness is a contradiction, making the selfish bastard in me want to get to know her further. But knowing there's an expiration date on anything that could transpire, I know there's little that can happen.

"So, what do you have in mind for today, son?" Pops pulls me from my thoughts.

"Well, I just got into town and could use some lunch," I mention, rubbing my stomach. I had surprised Ma earlier and, of course, she wanted to cook for me, but she was on her way to meet some friends for lunch, so I insisted she go with them, knowing we will have plenty of time to catch up. "Why don't we leave my rental car here and hit that diner only a few blocks away? I can come back for it later."

While we're waiting for our orders at the diner, Pops finally asks the question I've been waiting for. "So... have you decided if you're going to retire?"

He knows I need to decide within the next few months about whether I'm going to be in for four more years. I've already been in nearly twenty years and am eligible to retire, thanks to Running Start, a program which allowed me to graduate from high school with my associate's degree as well as high school diploma through a local community college. From there, I worked my ass off, when I wasn't deployed, to get through college and into flight school as soon as I possibly could.

But by the time I retire, thirty-eight still seems young and I love to fly. I could go into the private sector, but there's something to be said about flying helos for special ops, as opposed to civilians. I'm licensed to fly a variety of aircrafts, but I'm just not sure about the direction I want to go. Flying has been my life for the better part of forever, so as long as I'm airborne, I'll be a happy man.

"I'm still keeping my options open," I say with a sly grin. "That's part of the reason I'm on leave. There's a few opportunities I want to check out before I finalize my decision."

"Have you ever thought about settling down, son? I know that didn't work out for you years ago, but you're not getting any younger. I could use some more grandbabies and so could your ma," Pops teases.

I laugh. My younger brother and sister have already given them five grandkids. "Like you don't already have enough. You can't even move across the room on Christmas morning, there are so many kids under foot."

He doesn't know much about the details of my past, but I'm sure he can put two and two together. He doesn't have any expectations, but he likes to ask every now and then. I was almost married once, but while on deployment, I got a 'Dear John' letter and haven't given serious relationships much of a thought ever since. The Air Force has been my life. It's much easier to live in the moment, enjoying one day at a time. Besides, being the perpetual bachelor has had its perks. I enjoy women as much as the next guy and being a pilot hasn't left me lonely. Who am I to complain?

Pops sighs and is distracted by our meal arriving. We both dig into our BLT sandwiches and fries while Pops fills me in on what I've missed over the last few months. He updates me on my sister Erin and her two kids as well as my brother Zane, his daughter, and two boys. I feel like they're growing like weeds and I need to try to get to know them better while I'm here.

After we finish eating, we make our way across town to check in on the other sites his crews are working on. As he shows me around, I can't help but be impressed. His craftsmanship and dependability are the reasons he stays so busy. Pops isn't yet sixty years old and I can't even imagine him slowing down. My old man is still fit and in his prime. His employees, as well as clients, have nothing but compliments to give him. I aspire to be the man he is one day.

It's nearly six when Pops drops me back off at my rental car. He and Ma have tickets to a show she's been dying to see.

Not wanting my surprise visit to be an imposition, I insist they continue with their plans, knowing we'll have plenty of time to catch up in the coming weeks. Since the street is full of cars, Pops pulls in to drop me off from an open spot just down the block, so that he's not late. As it is, he'll barely have time to make it home and change before he and Ma must leave for the theater.

Just as I put my hand on the car door, I see the striking woman from earlier exit her house and lock the door. I can't help but take in her sexy curves and natural beauty. I catch her eye, and a grin spreads across my face. Without even giving it much thought, I find myself being pulled to her. By the time she makes it down to her car in the driveway, I'm only a few feet from her.

"Hey." My voice comes out thicker than expected, but I quickly recover. "Thanks again for letting Pops spend the afternoon with me. I really appreciate it."

A smile pulls at those kissable lips as she replies, "It's not a problem. Your dad would want me to spend time with my family if they'd just gotten into town." She fidgets with her keys and suddenly appears nervous, looking anywhere but at me.

"So where are ya off to?" My curiosity gets control of my mouth before I have the chance to think about it. When my brain catches up, I shake my head in disbelief. *Great. Stalker much.* I seem to be in the mindset of a teenager, rather than a man of my thirties. I've met beautiful women from all over the world, but can't figure out for the life of me, what it is about this woman that has me wanting to go out of my way to talk to her again.

"I'm on my way to grab something to eat. I think I might try the new Thai restaurant that just opened down the street." She points in the direction of the place as if I'm supposed to know where it is. "It's supposed to be good."

My mouth waters and my stomach has impeccable timing as it completely roars at the thought of my favorite food. I can't control the chuckle that escapes. "Obviously, Thai's my favorite. I'll have to try it while I'm here on leave." I can't remember when I'd last eaten decent Thai food. It doesn't help that it's been hours since Pops and I ate.

Samantha fidgets a little more with her keys. Then her head tilts to the side as if she's weighing a decision. I have no idea what's making this utterly attractive woman hesitate. Suddenly, she closes her eyes for the blink of a second, squares her shoulders, then pins me with rich mahogany eyes that nearly take my breath away and says, "Want to join me?"

4

———————

SAMANTHA

I HAVE no idea what just came over me. I squeeze my eyes tight for just a moment so I won't have to see his immediate reaction to my utter absurdity. He appears to be the type that's used to being propositioned, but I'd just ejected out of my comfort zone and am spiraling out of my mind as I force my eyes open to await his answer.

When I open my eyes, I see complete amusement spread across his sexy, rugged face. He's developing a five o'clock shadow, and a small dimple peeks at me from his left cheek. I swoon at the devastatingly handsome man before me.

Damn, Enzo's one of the sexiest men I've ever laid eyes on. He possesses me with a gaze that's right out of the pages of a magazine. The kind only models with airbrushed faces can portray. I know. I look at the beautiful faces of said models on books I assist in publishing on a regular basis. *But God help me, it's even better in real life.* I know that look. It could mean one of two things. A, he thinks I'm a complete nut job, or B, he could be interested. *Ha! As if!* I haven't been on the receiving end of a magnificent gaze like that, in ages. So, he must think I'm out of my mind. Great! What was I thinking?!?!? I haven't asked anyone out in my entire life. Sure, I have had business meetings with attractive people, but I've never asked anyone I've just met to dinner. That's what I get for getting married in college.

I'm just about to prattle on and make some excuse for why he probably wouldn't be interested when he surprises the ever-loving hell out of me and simply states, "Sure. I'd love to."

I let out the breath I didn't know I'd been holding and shake my head in disbelief. Asking a man out, is by far, one of the most uncharacteristic things I've done. Sure, I'm confident in myself. I'm at the top of my game when it comes to getting things I want at work. I know where I stand. But, since I haven't dated much since high school, this is a little unnerving, especially since I just met the man. I'm not sure what possessed me to be so forward, but I smile at myself in awe, still a little shocked I just blurted out what was on my mind, rather than keep it as an amazing fantasy, like I usually do. I've been single for over a year, but never just put myself out there with someone I'm this attracted to. It seems as if my girly bits might just be dusting themselves off.

Suddenly, he seems to be waiting for a response of some sort, so I quickly regain the brain power I still have control over and will myself to say, "Would you like me to drive?" I jingle my keys between us.

He shrugs then looks at his car parked on the street in front of my house. "I suppose I could ride shotgun for a change." His glorious green eyes shine with mirth. There seems to be some hidden secret I'm not privy to, but based on the devious look on his face, I hope to find out more about it soon.

We fill the short ride to the restaurant with small talk, discussing what his dad is doing to remodel my house as well as how happy he was to spend the day with his father. The ride itself takes less than ten minutes before we pull into the parking lot. I'm thankful to have driving to focus on, a reprieve from ogling the ridiculously gorgeous man next to me. Surprisingly, there weren't any awkward moments or nervous gaps of silence, as I'd feared. Enzo has this natural presence that puts me at ease and I feel comfortable around him instantly. Maybe that's why I asked him to dinner in the first place. Who knows what I was thinking? I just hope I don't regret my bold move later.

As we exit the car, he immediately comes to my side and helps me with my door. When we walk toward the entrance of the restaurant, my nerves flutter even more as he places his large hand on the small of my back to lead me in. Feeling his strong warm hand causes a mixture of emotions. For as much as my nerves feel like a twitching cattail in a room full of rockers, Enzo is a calming presence as well.

As we take our seats we're handed our menus. We spend a few moments in silence perusing what the restaurant has to offer. Once I decide, I place my menu aside and look up to find his beautiful green eyes focused in my direction. A slight upturn of his lips has that ridiculously sexy dimple popping out again. *Yikes! Please God... give me coherent thoughts,* I plead internally.

"So, have you decided, Samantha?" Enzo asks in a deep tone I can't help but be entranced by. I notice his menu is off to the side and his entire attention is now focused on me.

"It's Sam," I say hesitantly. "Only my parents call me by Samantha. I met your dad through them and never thought to correct him. But yes," getting back to what he had asked, "I'm going to have the broccoli and chicken with peanut sauce. It's one of my favorite Thai treats."

The greenish-gold specks in Enzo's eyes sparkle as the corners of his lips pull into a smile. "Well, Samantha is a beautiful name and it's quite fitting for you. I'm going with the cashew nut chicken. What would you like to drink?"

He picks up the drink menu and looks it over. When the waiter arrives, I decide on a glass of wine since the kids aren't with me tonight, and he orders a beer.

"So how long are you on leave for?" I ask, remembering bits of conversation with his dad. I know he's in the Air Force and he has been in it for quite some time.

"I actually have the next six weeks off." He takes a pull on his beer before adding, "I can't remember the last time I was home for so long. Usually, it's just a couple of weeks at a time."

The way he curves his lips around the long neck of the bottle has an interesting effect on me. One I haven't felt in forever. It may be the wine, or Enzo himself, but a sudden warmth spreads over me and makes my nerves flare all over again. *Calm down,* I chastise myself. *It's not like you've never been on a date before. But it has been a long time since you were this attracted to anyone,* my inner voice reminds me. *And he's H-O-T. When was the last time you ever felt this way about anyone, including Devin?* I ask myself. My libido has been dormant for way too long and I have no idea how to handle it.

"That's exciting for you," I add after finishing a sip of my wine, trying to keep my thoughts under control. "You seem close with your dad. Will you spend a lot of time with your family?"

He nods, but we're interrupted by the waiter bringing our delicious-smelling food. My mouth waters at the thought of tasting it. I quickly grab my fork and take a bite. My mouth explodes with flavor and I can't help myself when a little moan escapes. I glance up at Enzo and see his gaze darken. *Great, now he thinks I'm a freak.*

Suddenly embarrassed, I cover my mouth and speak when it's cleared. "Sorry. I haven't eaten since breakfast. With the construction, I forgot to eat lunch today." I wave my hand in the air, trying to dismiss my savageness.

He glances at his watch. "Do you make a habit of that?" he teases. "It's after seven. You ought to be starving by now. I ate around noon, and you heard my stomach rumble." He chuckles lightly.

"No." I motion to myself. "I obviously don't skip many meals. But with no kitchen, I just hadn't gotten around to getting out of the house yet today."

He gives me a full assessment before he adds, "You certainly don't have room to miss many more meals."

The way he says that has me squirming in my seat. I'm dumbfounded at his remark. I work out when I can, but a regular regiment isn't really on my schedule. With work, three kids, and my taxi schedule in the evenings, I'm lucky to fit any time in for myself. I usually try to fit in a jog a couple of times a week, but sometimes even then it's difficult unless I go first thing in the morning. But the way he looks at me makes me think he might appreciate the efforts I do make.

I shake my head and dismiss the comment with a laugh. He hesitates for a moment before picking up his fork to take a bite of his own food. For the next few minutes, each of us are consumed with the savory food that's before us. Eventually, Enzo breaks the silence.

"So... what do you do when you're not hanging around a remodel?"

"Well, I'm a commissioning editor for a small publishing house in Portland." Enzo looks interested, so I continue to explain my job since most don't know what it really entails. "Basically, I find books worthy of print. I work with authors and keep them on track and stay within budget. Since it's a small company, I also assist in the basics with editing from time to time when the need arises. Usually, others do the nitty-gritty of that aspect. But when a project calls to me, I sometimes like to see it to completion." I smile when I think of some of the amazing projects I have worked on over the years.

"It sounds like you love your job," Enzo observes. "I can tell by the look on your face while you're talking, it's something you're passionate about." He forks another bite into his mouth as he waits for my response.

I sigh, and a smile spreads across my features. "Yeah, I'm actually part owner of the company. My best friend Lexi and I started it after college and have built it from the ground up. We remain small because we both like to stay involved in the entire process and help undiscovered authors reach their dreams. We have quite a few full-time and part-time employees, but neither of us wants to become part of the impersonal corporate conglomerates like the bigger publishing houses. Some big names have come through our doors. Once we discover new authors, our attention to detail and the ability to match them to the right market allows us to compete with the bigger houses, but on a smaller scale."

"That's impressive," Enzo adds as he leans in and rests his forearms on the table, giving me his undivided attention. "It's nice to see people's goals pay off for them. That must be quite rewarding."

Nodding, I reply, "Yes, it certainly is, but enough about me. What is it that you do exactly?"

He nods his head and shrugs hesitantly. "Well, I don't really talk about the specifics much, but I'm actually a pilot. I mostly fly the PJs, that's the Pararescue men in and out of their missions. For the past ten years or so, I've been working with those teams." He stops for a moment then shrugs. "There isn't much I can't fly. My job is to get the teams there and back safely and I do what I can to make that happen."

His voice sounds somber at the end. For some reason, he sounds quite humble when he says this. Sure, he exudes confidence and I'm sure he has a cocky side to him as well, but it amazes me at how that side of him slipped away as he explained his job. He shows a great sense of pride in his abilities, but he isn't pretentious in the slightest. I have no idea what it specifically entails, but from the look on his face, I'm not sure if he can or should go into further detail with me. But all the same, I'm in awe of his service and skills.

"Wow, that's incredible," I whisper. "Have you been in Germany long?"

"Well, for the last couple of years, I've been based out of Ramstein Air Force Base, but my missions have taken me all over the world. My hope is to be stateside again soon." Enzo locks his gaze upon mine before continuing. "I'm actually home this time to feel out a few offers and decide whether I'm going to stay in." He shakes his head before adding, "I'm not even sure why I've told you all of that. I haven't even mentioned it much to my family, so if you can, keep this between us while I decide?"

The way he says it makes me think I might be seeing more of him in the future. This pleases me to no end, but it's a little unnerving at the same time. I can't believe how much I'm enjoying my time with Enzo tonight. I don't remember the last time I've enjoyed a man's company like this, apart from Devin when things were happy in our marriage.

I nod in agreement, my heart full of understanding. "That definitely is a lot to consider." I find myself reaching across the table and patting his forearm. Before I can pull my hand back, Enzo grasps my hand lightly and holds it on the table. The spark of electricity that zooms through me catches me off guard. I can sense Enzo feels something as well because he holds my gaze for a long moment before saying another word.

"I've actually been in for nearly twenty years. It's kind of hard to imagine what life would be like without being a part of a unit." Enzo looks as if he's a little lost in thought at the end of this statement. I can tell it's a decision he won't make easily.

"That's truly amazing. Thank you so much for your service and dedication!" I say with sincerity.

"I don't know any other way." He grins humbly, then shakes his head as if dismissing a thought. "Over the years, there have been many stories to tell. Some worth repeating, while others are unmentionable. I've traveled the world, though not in the way you would traditionally think. Not a lot of sightseeing done on this job. But it pays off when the mission is successful, I get to help bring someone home."

"What would you do if you weren't in the Air Force?" I ask as I let go of his hand to take another sip of my wine.

"That's the million-dollar question." Enzo quirks a smile, making his dimple pop again. "I could stay in, I could go into the Air National Guard because it's based here in Portland. Or I could go into the private sector and continue with missions much like what I currently do. I have a few meetings lined up. I've already been propositioned by a couple of ops teams, but I need to see if the fit is right." Enzo gives me a knowing nod and I shake my head in agreement.

"It's always good to have options," I weigh in, not really knowing how to respond. I take another bite of my chicken and a sip of wine.

Enzo takes another bite as well before taking another pull on his beer. "Enough about work. What do you do outside of work, Sam?"

Suddenly, I think of my kids and my recent divorce. I guess I should be as straightforward with him as possible and break the news to him about my kids. I know from experience as well as what my friends have told me, that kids are sometimes a deal breaker for guys in general, especially sexy airmen like him. I might as well rip the bandage off before either of us get too invested. I love my kids and I'm proud of them. If he reacts poorly, I'd rather know up front. It's unlikely we will even see one another with him only being here temporarily *Geesh, Sam. Get a grip.*

"Well... I actually spend a lot of time being a glorified taxi to my three wonderful children." I smile and shrug dismissively. I inwardly cringe, hoping he won't react wrong because we seem to be hitting it off well. For the first time since my divorce, I want to consider a second date. However, my kids are my life, so if he doesn't respond well... he can suck it.

To my surprise, he grins sheepishly before adding, "I saw their pictures at your house. They're beautiful. What are their names and ages?" he asks as he leans forward and pats a hand on my forearm, sending a zing of electricity shooting through me.

Of course, I'm a proud Mama so I dive into telling him all about Frankie, Maddie, and Declan. I tell Enzo their interests as well as characteristics which make each of my kids unique. Enzo prods me with questions as he gets to know them better through our conversation.

After a few minutes of letting me fawn over my kids, I ask, "So what about you, do you have a family of your own?"

A dark cloud crosses his features before he shakes his head and dismissively states, "I love kids and at one point, I wanted some of my own. But it wasn't in the cards for me." He has a far-off look in his eyes, as he continues with, "Ever since I've kept my life focused on my job." He's silent for a heartbeat before his mood lightens. "Besides, that's what my nieces and nephews are for."

There seems to be a story there, but I won't push it. Maybe someday he'll tell me more, but since I just met the man, there's no way I'm going to push this issue now. Instead, I change my tone to match his and tease, "Well, you must date a lot." I eye him up and down with a grin on my face, trying to get a read on him.

He sighs, and the side of his mouth turns up as he states, "Well... I don't really date a lot, but yes, I've had relationships. Some have lasted longer than others, but nothing permanent."

I'm not really sure how to take that, but for some reason, he doesn't come across as a complete serial dater. The more we talk, the more I want to get to know him.

We spend the better part of the next hour making small talk and just enjoying each other's company. When the check comes, Enzo grabs it before I even know it's here. I try to put up an argument and attempt to pay since I asked him, but he won't hear it. He insists on paying. As we get up to leave, he once again puts his hand on the small of my back and leads me to the car. The zinging sensation I experience is almost indescribable and I'm not really ready for it to end.

"Are you okay to drive?" he asks as we approach my car.

"Yes." I appreciate his concern. I only had the one glass and had finished it at the beginning of our meal.

When we get back to my house, I feel a little awkward. As the evening went on, the dinner we shared felt more like a date than any I had been on. Since my divorce, my best friend Lexi insisted I date a few times. There were even a few orchestrated setups, but I had never been that into it. Enzo seems different. I can't put my finger on it, but everything about him seems to spark my senses.

I'm not sure what to do next as he gets out and walks me to my door. Once again, he leads me with his hand on the small of my back. His touch sends a bolt of electricity through my entire body. It's as if there's a live wire connecting us and I have no desire to shut it off.

When we get to my door, he brushes a stray strand of hair behind my ear. I gaze into those delicious green eyes and get completely lost in Enzo for a moment. In a gravelly voice, Enzo whispers, "I had a great time." His hand lingers on my cheek as he says, "If it were any other night, I'd find a way to get you to invite me in because I'm nowhere ready for my time with you to end. But..." he hesitates, like he's forcing himself to say the words, "I just got back into town today and I promised Ma and Pops I'd be home when they returned from their night out. It's the only way they'd go out this evening. Is there any way we can continue this evening another time?"

He completely entrances me with his stare. The determination shining through his green eyes to get me to agree with him not only sets me on fire but leaves a swarm of butterflies taking flight in my belly. I haven't felt this much of a pull toward someone in as long as I can remember. I'm so lost in him, I forget to respond.

He gives me his wicked grin, pulling out that lickable dimple, and rests the hand that had brushed my hair away from the base of my neck. "So... what do you say, Samantha?" Enzo whispers smoothly.

5
____

ENZO

I FEEL LIKE A COMPLETE ASS. I'm so into Samantha my pants have shrunk about three sizes since she asked me to dinner in the first place. I'm sure she thinks I'm a complete tool for ending things so abruptly. *Meeting my parents?* What a dumbass thing to say. I'm thirty-seven years old and I haven't used Ma and Pops as an excuse to leave since I was in my teens. But I know, with every fiber of my being, if I were to go inside, I wouldn't be leaving anytime soon. I promised my parents I'd be there when they got home... and if there's anything redeeming about me, I'm a man of my word. Besides, she's a mom and who knows where her kids might be?

Christ, what is it about Samantha? I usually steer clear of women like her. She's the epitome of a long-term commitment in the making. *Huh? This should scare the shit out of me.* But there's something about her I'm not ready to walk away from. *Yet, anyway.*

As my hand reaches the base of her neck, it takes

everything in my power to keep from completely devouring her. I'm dying for just one taste. Which I will have before I leave as the chemistry between us is almost palpable. But first, I need her to say yes. "So, what do you say, Samantha?"

She takes in a deep breath. Her gaze locks on mine and for a moment, I have no idea what her response will be. This is so unnerving. I've never had to work to get a woman to agree to see me. Suddenly, she seems to gather her thoughts and I hear her whisper, "Sure. I'd love to."

Relief washes over me and before she can even finish her thought, I find myself pulling her face toward mine. I bend down, closing the distance between us. My lips crash onto hers, releasing some of the pent-up chemistry we've been flirting with all night. As my tongue sweeps across her lips, they part, and I feel as if I've died and gone to heaven. If she tastes this sweet, with just a kiss, I can only imagine what it'd be like to taste elsewhere. When she brings one hand to my neck and fists what little hair I have at the back of my head in her other, I feel as if she has just set off an inferno inside me. If I don't end this now, I won't be held accountable for my future actions. Something primal has been lit and there is no telling how this night will end. After a few more moments of completely devouring her delicious mouth, I pull back, attempting to regain control of myself and the situation.

"So..." I kiss her once more, soft and feathery, trying to keep my tone light. "What are your plans..." Another amazing kiss. There is no way I'll be able to wait to see her again, "... for..." quick peck, "tomorrow?"

She pulls back with a pant, looking me in the eyes. "Um...

I'm working again from home. The kids are with their dad through the weekend." She leans up, brushing my lips with a kiss, seeming just as eager as I am to keep her body in contact with mine.

"Great!" I say, realizing my wait might not be as long as I'd feared. "Can I pick you up tomorrow afternoon?" Like a magnet, I'm pulled to her. Before she can answer, I sweep down across her lips, kissing her once more. Her body is addictive and I haven't had enough, but I force myself to pull back.

"Sounds good," she says breathlessly before reaching up on her toes for another kiss.

I nearly lose myself in the moment, but when she lets out a deep moan, setting my nerves on fire, I'm also brought back to reality. I need to slow things down. I pull back for good this time. I've been with my share of women, but no one, and I mean no one has *ever* made me feel the way Samantha does. I pluck her keys from her hand, then unlock and open the door for her. She steps in and I wait for her to put in a security code. I briefly kiss her once more before whispering, "Until tomorrow," in a huskier voice than I recognize. Then I turn and painfully walk to my rental car.

The next day as I drive to meet Riggs, the owner of one of the security firms, I can't get my mind off Samantha. I make a hasty decision and pull into a parking lot. Before I know it, I'm dialing the restaurant from last night to place an order for delivery. Knowing her home is in shambles from the construction, I don't want her going hungry again. Besides, her beautiful smile keeps playing on a constant loop in my mind. Maybe she'll think of me and smile again.

With that task complete, I continue driving. As I arrive, I'm not surprised to see an unobtrusive brick building that looks more like a warehouse. It's in an industrial area. If I were an untrained observer, it appears like every other building around. What my trained eyes show me is that Riggs owns this entire area. There are likely dozens of cameras on my approach and I would be willing to bet the clarity of those images could even describe the freckle on my inner wrist. I saunter up but before I reach the door, it swings open.

A man about my age and build dressed in black cargo pants and a matching t-shirt approaches me with an outstretched hand. "You must be Harper." His grip is firm and no-nonsense like, though his facial expression is a little hard to read. But like most of these situations, I'm sure he's sizing me up as much as I am him. "I'm Boone, Riggs sent me to meet you. He's on a conference call and will be with us shortly."

I nod, following him through the door. We enter a small reception area. There is a desk with a computer and phone set up. Most would just assume a small business was running behind these doors. Boone continues to walk and motions for me to follow. We turn right, down a hallway. It quickly becomes quite evident, this isn't a normal office suite. Placing his palm on a scanner, he waits for a door to open. After going down another hallway with no other points of entry, we reach another door. This one is steel and from the looks of it, thick. Boone scans his retina, then I hear the whoosh of locks.

We enter the next area and it's as if we've entered a tech

geek's wet dream. There are monitors everywhere. Along one wall are all sorts of electronic devices. Some I've seen and used before while on routine missions, while others I have no idea what their intended uses are. A couple of men sit at monitors using code and completely locked into their task at hand. Along another wall are cabinets from floor to ceiling. I keep my well-trained mask in place to not give any of my thoughts away as we move toward another room at the back of this one.

We enter a conference room with a large table and about twenty plush rolling chairs around it. There's obviously long meetings held here if they go to such measures to have comfortable chairs brought in. I guess that's a perk of moving to the private sector. Boone gestures for me to sit as he says, "I'll let Riggs know you're here. Have a seat and I'll be back in a few. Can I get you anything to drink?"

"I'm good. Thanks," I reply, taking the seat closest to me.

With that, Boone exits, and I'm left in this enormous room by myself. Upon further scrutiny, this must be their tactics and operations room. The walls itself are stark white and as I turn around, I see a huge flat-screen monitor on the wall behind me as well as multiple smaller screens along each side of the middle one. There's also another door at the other end.

I'm not left with much time to myself before Boone and Riggs join me. My military training and manners have me standing to greet them. I shake Riggs' hand as he greets me. "Good to see you've made it."

"Glad to be here. It's been a while since we last met up." His team had helped with one of our missions about six months ago. After experiencing first hand my flight abilities out of more than extreme conditions, he'd told me to come talk with him when my contract with the Air Force was up. At the time, I brushed him off, but now as that date could be a real possibility, I'd be a fool not to keep my options open.

"Let's cut to the chase." Riggs lets out a breath as he folds his over six-foot broad body into a chair. "I've done my homework and know we'd be a good fit for one another. I've seen your records and they stand for themselves. I've also witnessed firsthand what a badass you can be in any cockpit. Are you here to tell me you're finally going to take me up on my offer and join my team?"

His bluntness catches me a bit off guard. I thought this would be an interview, not a formality. Riggs has always been known for his matter-of-factness. I shake my head and chuckle. "I'm seriously considering it. I have four more months on my contract with the Air Force, but I feel too young to completely retire. It doesn't hurt that your home base is close to my family here in Portland either."

His eyebrows raise as his head tilts knowingly in my direction. "Family is important. If you work for us, that's where you'll be when we're not out on a job. Don't get me wrong, sometimes there is little time between getting the call and wheels. They can also last a few weeks at a time. Usually, we're home within a few days. Trust me when I say, compared to what you're doing, the compensation's worth it."

He knows exactly what I'm looking for. This is by far the oddest of interviews I've ever been on. Can I even call it an interview? It seems more like he's interviewing for me now.

I place my hand on my chin, letting my fingers rub against

it as I contemplate his offer. It'd be nice to get a place of my own and not be gone for months at a time. I could spend more time with my parents and get to know my nieces and nephews. Perhaps someday I'd even settle down and have a family of my own now that I'm not moving every couple of years and distance won't be an issue. An image of Samantha's beautiful face flashes before my eyes and I shake the thought away before it takes any merit. *Christ, I just met the woman yesterday.* She has no business being in my thoughts today. Besides, she has a family and a life of her own. *What in the world would she want with an Airman who is always away on a mission?* But... if I could stay in one place long enough... ENOUGH! *Get back to your interview, dumbass.* I feel the pull of a slight smile spreading across my face for letting my mind wander and being so stupid. Hopefully, Riggs and Boone will take it as I really like the possibility of being at home.

"What would the terms consist of?" I ask, knowing I'd be a good fit for this operation. I've already met and worked with many of the men and a few women working for Riggs. I also know I'd be an asset to his flight crew with my skill set. I think it's time to get the logistics taken care of, so I can make an informed decision for my future.

A smug smile forms on Riggs' face. His dark eyes crinkle in the corners, the only sign showing his age. I know he's near forty, like me. Riggs hands me a small packet of papers. "I took the honor of drawing this up, in case you came to your senses."

Once again, I'm taken back by his bluntness. I begin looking through the papers. It's essentially my contract. It discusses my salary, compensation, benefits, and even an additional retirement package. When I look at the numbers, my eyes widen slightly. There's even a huge signing bonus. Taking a few moments to let everything sink in, I realize there's some perks working in the private sector, especially for a job I'm currently already doing. This opportunity could be hard to pass up.

Trying to contain my eagerness, I place the papers back on the table and coolly ask, "When would I have to let you know?"

Riggs and Boone both smirk at each other before glancing back at me. Just as I think Riggs is about to comment, Boone states, "You take your time. Enjoy your leave and let us know in the next couple of weeks. We know you can't start until you are done with the Air Force, so we're in no hurry to know the answer."

Riggs adds, "If you'd like, we're having a barbeque at my place on Saturday. You can stop by, visit with the rest of us, and get a real feel for the men and women you'd be working with. Feel free to bring a friend. The families will all be there. My wife would have my ass if I didn't tell you about it."

I laugh. I can't help it. The man before me is as gruff as they come but the moment he mentions his wife, he's a walking contradiction. There's a lightness to his features I can only hope to experience for myself one day. Knowing I shouldn't pass up the opportunity to get to know the team I'd be working with, I reply, "Sure. Just give me the time and address and I'll be there." Besides, after what he's shown me, it's highly unlikely I won't be taking him up on his offer. I want to meet with another buddy of mine before making my final decision.

After my meeting with Riggs and Boone, I drive toward my parents' house. But before I go too far, to make the phone call that's been weighing on my mind, I pull into a nearby parking lot and find my buddy Carson in my contacts and hit dial. We served together for many years and when I told him about my meeting with Riggs, he told me to call afterward. His deep voice greets me, "Hey, Harps! What's up?" I can hear music in the background and he sounds slightly out of breath.

"Not much, just finished meeting with Riggs." I shake my head, realizing the entire process was merely a formality, rather than an interview.

"Awesome. So... are you going to finally play with the big boys?" Carson teases. He's been working with Riggs for the past five years. I know if I join their team, I'll be with good people. I met Carson shortly after I enlisted in the Air Force and we've been friends ever since.

"I'm thinking about it," I nonchalantly say, to evade giving a direct answer. "I still need to talk with the CO at the Air National Guard before making any major decisions."

A low chuckle comes across the line before Carson says, "I hear ya. So, how'd you like Riggs and Boone?"

I try to figure out how to put my experience into words. Before I can say anything, Carson interrupts, "So did they act as if it were a done deal?"

"Um... yeah, actually they did," I reply. "I'd thought it would be more like an interview of sorts, but it was almost as if everything were just a formality. It's definitely the strangest job interview I've experienced."

"Ha... that's how they roll. You've already worked with us. They know you'll click with our team." He takes a deep breath and lets it out heavily. "Besides, they know if they make you a lucrative enough offer, you'll have no other choice but to sign with us. I know you love what you do, or you wouldn't do it. Why not do the same thing, making a shit-ton of money while you're at it? The best part is you'll be able to work with yours truly and see my handsome mug every day," Carson teases. "Fuck, you know you love me, Harps."

I shake my head and can't hold back my laughter. "Yep, that might just be a reason NOT to sign," I joke. "I know you snore like a boar in heat and all sorts of other crazy-ass shit about you." I continue to smile as some of my favorite memories with Carson flash into my mind. The thought of some alone has me in stitches again.

"You know you love me, Harps, even if you won't admit it!" Carson taunts as if he doesn't know I'd lay down my life for him or any member of my team. It's just the way we are. "So, what are your plans for the rest of the weekend?" Carson asks, changing the subject.

Once again, Samantha's beautiful face fills my mind. But I quickly divert my thoughts to answer his question. "Well, I will probably just hang with my parents and see my family. Riggs invited me to a barbeque at his place on Saturday, so I will make an appearance there as well."

"Good to hear. If you want to come out Saturday, a couple of us are going to head out to McMenamins'. You're welcome to join us. My buddy Todd's girlfriend always brings a few friends along. The more the merrier."

"I'll keep that in mind," I say noncommittally, but then amend my thoughts once another flash of Samantha's sexy smile and wicked sass fill my mind. "But I wouldn't count on it. I'm pretty sure I'll be busy."

Why the hell would I want to spend a night with a stranger? I may not be into long-term commitments, but I don't juggle women either. I'm sure as hell not stupid enough to walk away or blow any chance I have with Samantha. I have no idea what's gotten into me, but there are some things I just don't do. I haven't been able to banish her from my memories, and with any luck, she'll still be up to going out again tonight and make some more.

"Suit yourself." Carson chuckles then adds, "Listen... I gotta run. I'll see you Saturday. Oh, and for what it's worth. I think it'd be an honor to work with you again. I hope you make the best decision, for you."

"Don't worry, Cars, I will." I add before ending the call.

I glance at my watch. It's now a little after three in the afternoon. I contemplate where to go next, but those rich mahogany eyes keep calling to me and a decision is quickly made. *It is the afternoon.* Since I didn't think to get her number like the dumbass I am, I guess it's only fair I show up to see her, like I promised. I point my car in the direction of the sexy woman I can't seem to get off my mind and wonder what the hell she's doing to me.

6

———

SAMANTHA

ALL MORNING, my mind keeps replaying my time with Enzo, as if it's on a loop. I find myself lost in thought as I touch my lips, recalling his taste. I can't remember when I'd ever been kissed so senseless. He managed to unhinge me in just mere moments with that sexy wicked mouth of his. *Fuck, that man can kiss.* I thought I'd burst into flames on the front porch and the neighbors would have to call the fire department. I might be incinerated if I were to experience more than just his delicious mouth.

I've tried over and over again to read the manuscript I'd started yesterday, but my mind keeps wandering back to Enzo. The construction crew is busy at work, so I do manage to get some work done. Thankfully, I'd read most of it yesterday and don't have as much to do today.

Around noon, I'm pleasantly surprised when I answer my door and find take-out from last night's Thai restaurant being delivered. There's no note, but I know it must be from him.

Who else would send me chicken and broccoli with peanut sauce? It makes me a bit giddy to know he's thinking of me. I wish I could call and thank him, but since neither of us thought to exchange numbers, I'm left with wondering if he'll show up today like he said. I'll admit, I've had my doubts. I keep trying to pass everything off this morning as if last night didn't matter, but now that I sit on my back porch eating my favorite Thai food, I know without a doubt he will be showing up today. *Though I wish I knew when.*

Around three-thirty, while the construction crew is still hard at work, I hear the doorbell ring. Not knowing who it is, I quickly rush to answer it. Pulling open the door, I'm greeted by the devilishly handsome man who's taken over my thoughts throughout the day. His short, dark-blond hair is messy on top and his gorgeous green eyes glint as if he holds all the secrets in the world. A slow smile spreads across his face, revealing that delicious dimple on his left cheek, instantly making my knees go weak. His dark blue t-shirt stretches heavenly across his broad defined chest. I'm at a loss for words as I take in my spectacular view.

"Um, is this a bad time?" Enzo asks, shaking me from my thoughts.

I shake my head to clear my suddenly lust-filled thoughts away. "No, not at all. Please come in."

With all the noise coming from the kitchen. I motion for him to follow me through the house to the back patio. I've created my own private oasis in our backyard, as I love to be outside any chance I can when the weather is decent. It's covered, so I can even be out here in the winter months or enjoy the rain, as only true Oregonians can do, while curling up with a great book. Lounge chairs and patio furniture are set out so I can entertain in our big backyard as well. When we finally reach my intended destination, I turn to face Enzo. "I... uh... didn't know when to expect you," I admit sheepishly. "I wanted to call and thank you for the fantastic lunch, but we forgot to exchange numbers last night."

"I'm glad you liked it." He reaches for my hand and I realize the zing of electricity from last night wasn't in my imagination. It's still there and back in full force. "I didn't want you going hungry again today. Mind if we sit?" Enzo's green eyes gesture to the double chair next to us.

"Sure," I say, guiding us to the oversized chair. From this spot, we're guaranteed not to be overseen by any of the crew working on my house, unless they come out to join us for some reason.

Before we reach our destination, he tucks one strand of hair behind my ear with one hand, while he continues to hold mine with his other. He lightly brushes a kiss on my cheek as he asks, "How was your day, beautiful?"

"Fine. They're making a lot of progress on the house. I managed to get some work done earlier." *Well, at least I tried to work... when I wasn't thinking about you!*

He pulls me down next to him on the chair as he states, "It was a grave oversight for not getting your number." He digs out his phone from his pocket. "Please, let's rectify this now, so it won't happen again. What's your number?" A sly smile pulls at his lips, making me catch my breath.

When his eyebrows raise at my hesitation, I quickly regain

my thoughts and rattle off my number. Seconds later, I receive a text notification. Grinning, I smirk at Enzo. "I take it that's from you." I leave my phone unchecked, laying on the table next to us. I don't need to see his number since he's right in front of me. Shaking my head at his thoroughness, I ask, "So what did you do today?"

As Enzo tells me about his day, I can't help but be entranced in his deep timbre and sexy tone. If he were a narrator for one of the books I promote, I could listen to him read the phone book all day long and still be completely satisfied. The man just exudes sex and confidence, and I find myself more entranced with each thing he says. He tells me about having breakfast with his parents and catching up with his sister and her kids earlier this morning. Her children sure know how to keep everyone on their toes. Enzo's enthusiastic expression while explaining how he had to chase a half-naked toddler out the front door has me nearly doubling over. He ends by telling me about the most interesting interview I've ever heard of. I'll admit I'm a little shocked at Riggs' approach, but overall it sounds like an opportunity worth considering.

Enzo surprises me by changing the subject when he asks, "I know this is short notice, but do you have plans for tonight?" He eyes me hopefully, awaiting my answer.

"Well…" I say sadly, "I've been waiting around to see if a guy I went to dinner with last night is going to show up. You see, he forgot to ask for my number. I wasn't sure if or when he would get here," I tease mercifully. "What do you have in mind, maybe you'll have a better offer?"

Enzo lets out a deep belly laugh at my sass. "Well, if you

think it's a better offer, I was going to see if you wanted to grab a bite again tonight. We could go to a restaurant I enjoy each time I'm home... but if you're waiting for that fool, I understand. Only a complete tool would walk away from a beautiful woman like you and not at least score her digits."

"Hmmm." I pretend to think it over for a bit. "Decisions, decisions!" In a sing-song voice, I add, "He was kinda cute and a fairly decent kisser." I put my hand on my chin, pretending to contemplate a decision.

Enzo grabs me around the waist, pulling me closer before growling, "Cute and decent?!?! *Those* are definitely two words I've never been described as..."

Suddenly, I'm pulled closer. I feel his warm breath on my lips. My body begs to close the gap. To taste what I haven't been able to get out of my mind all day. But my inner sass continues to shine, as I innocently say, "Would you prefer handsome and fair? I think I might need another reminder. It's been a while. I may not have judged you accurately." *Who is this woman that has taken over me? I have NEVER been this bold or flirty in my life. What is this man doing to me?*

Without even a second of hesitation, Enzo's hand engulfs my cheek and pulls my lips toward his. The lightning bolt which struck between us last night seems to have set off an inferno. His tongue slides across the seam of my lips, parting them, just as he had done last night. The fierceness of his kiss and complete consumption of my mouth makes my body hum like nothing I've experienced. I can't seem to control my actions because before I know it, one hand grips his short hair while the other cups his chiseled face. I find myself pulling him closer to me, if that's even possible. One of his hands slides to my waist and rests on my hip above my jeans while the other remains at the base of my neck, guiding my efforts to reciprocate this passionate kiss. Hours... days... an eternity could have passed, and I wouldn't have been any the wiser to anything that wasn't Enzo. When he breaks the kiss, *all too soon*, I'm surprised to find I have nearly crawled into his lap and I'm panting as if I just sprinted a marathon.

"Holy shit, woman, what have you done to me?" Enzo growls as he looks into my eyes, his hands firmly keeping me in place.

A furious blush spreads across my features as I realize what I've just done. I try to avert my eyes, but he won't have it. He pins me with his glorious green stare, *which are now several shades darker* and whispers, "Do you still think I'm cute and decent?" This sends a shiver across my entire body as it fights its carnal reaction to this man.

As if his touch and kisses were a truth serum, I blurt out, still regaining my breath, "No... definitely sexy and all-consuming."

7

———

ENZO

HOLY FUCK, *what's this woman doing to me?* She has me panting like a randy teenager, fogging up the back windows of his parents' car. I have no idea what just happened between us. It took everything, and I mean EVERYTHING in my power to put a stop to it. I'd heard a saw turn on from the crew working inside, which brought reality crashing back. She's somehow millimeters away from finding out just how much of an impact she has on me, too. I shift her a fraction of an inch away from my raging hard-on but hold her in place because I have no desire to let her go. The sheepish smile spreading across her face is one I'd kill for to experience over and over again.

"Do you still think I'm cute and decent?" I growl in a whisper to keep the crew from hearing me.

When she responds with, "No... definitely sexy and all-consuming." I nearly lose it. I couldn't keep my mouth off hers if she was the last drop of rain in an impending drought.

I crash my lips onto hers once again to experience that delicious taste of sugar. This time I'm mindful of a potential audience because I don't share. Period. And if this continues any further, we're at risk of being exposed in more ways than one.

When I feel as if I might internally combust or *have an experience I haven't had since I was a teenager,* I force myself to put on the brakes. It's harder than fuck to say no to this irresistible woman nearly climbing in my lap, but somehow, I manage.

"Hey, sugar," I say as I steal one more taste from her delicious lips. "We'd better slow things down a bit, or we might just put on a show," I tease and kiss her softly once more, lightening my touch.

She suddenly pulls back, shaking her head as if she just became aware of our potential audience. "Oh my goodness... I... I... I've never done anything like this." She starts to pull away from me, but I can't let her go entirely.

I place her next to me, continuing to hold her hand. Her cheeks are pink and mortification settles on her features. Fuck, she has no right to feel this way, so I assure her, "You've got nothing to be embarrassed about, Samantha. You've done nothing wrong." I glance down at the evidence in my lap and smirk. "In fact, I have firsthand knowledge of just how right you feel."

She glances down at my now severely tight jeans and slightly gasps. She covers her face with her only free hand and mumbles almost to herself, "That's what I get for going years without so much as kissing a man... ugh... how embarrassing. I nearly mount him in front of his father's work crew..." she says something else, but I can't quite catch it all.

I'm stuck on the amount of time she said... Years?!?!?! What the ever-loving fuck is this incredibly sexy woman going years without so much as kissing a man for? I must clarify this, because obviously, I've heard her wrong. "Um... did you just say years? Without so much as a kiss?"

"Yes," she squeaks and squeezes her eyes shut. "This is so embarrassing. Just forget I ever said anything." She tries to brush the thought away by waving her hand in the air.

No Way. There's no way I can let this go. She can't really be serious? Before I give it much consideration, my previous thoughts come crashing out of my mouth, "What the ever-loving fuck is an incredibly sexy woman, such as yourself, going years without kissing someone for?" This catches her attention. She immediately opens her eyes to stare at me.

"You think I'm sexy?" she whispers as she shakes her head in disbelief.

"Umm... you have no idea, sweetheart," I say but she's still looking at me with denial. I'm a man and must prove myself, so I grab her hand. I place it on the bulge in my jeans, giving her direct proof of just how sexy I think she is. She gasps a little but doesn't move her hand as it clasps around my now even larger erection. "Is that proof enough?" I raise an eyebrow at her as my dick decides to give her his own salute. This causes her to blush and immediately pull her hand away.

"Why?" I say quietly. "Why is it that you haven't been kissed in years?" I'm still dumbfounded by this revelation.

She pulls in her lower lip and chews on it with her

perfectly sculpted teeth as she tilts her head to the side, as if she's weighing a decision. Then I pin her rich mahogany eyes and she seems to give in. She lets out a deep breath, pulls another quick breath in, then quickly rambles,

"Because...my husband cheated on me three years ago... and I haven't kissed another man since." she says all in one blur of a sentence.

"Excuse me?" I ask in both disbelief as well as for a confirmation of what I think I heard.

Much slower this time, she closes her eyes and whispers, "Because... my husband cheated on me three years ago... and I haven't kissed another man since."

Fuck... what an asshole. She has no right to feel ashamed of anything she has done tonight. I squeeze her hand, waiting for her to look at me. After a few moments, her eyes finally meet mine. "Samantha," I say to make sure I have her attention. "Samantha sweetheart, you have absolutely nothing... and I mean NOTHING to be ashamed or embarrassed about. I completely reciprocate your feelings and I'm just as into kissing you, trust me. If it weren't for the fact there are people just on the other side of that door," I point to the French doors we came through, "there would've been nothing except you stopping me from taking just what I wanted. But you should know, I don't share."

Samantha's beautiful eyes widen at my boldness, but they darken a few shades as well. "But, it's just so embarrassing. Sure, I've dated a few times since my divorce, but I've never just kissed anyone the way I attacked you just now." She peers at the ground as she finishes that comment. "What is it about you?" she whispers aloud in wonder.

Once again, I'm caught in confusion and need clarification. "You mean to tell me that you've dated other guys, but haven't been kissed since your divorce?"

She shakes her head no and I can't help but ask, "Why?"

"There wasn't any chemistry. It didn't feel right to kiss someone just for the sake of kissing them." She peers at me through narrowed eyes as if I should understand, yet a glint of sass from before shines through her expression.

"Woman, that's definitely their loss. I'm honored to have you devour me," I tease. "In fact, I'm so honored, feel free to kiss me anytime." I pull her to me, kissing her senseless one more time before releasing her. I'm not sure how long it lasted. All I know is I didn't want it to end. "You're a FUCKIN' AMAZING KISSER and I only hope you'll devour me like that as often as you can!" I wink at her before giving her a peck on the nose. "Please, baby, practice on me all you want!"

"I'm sure it'll be a hardship." Samantha's beautiful eyes shine with mirth. "I suppose. If you insist." She boldly leans in, brushing her lips against mine. When she pulls back, she shows no sense of embarrassment. I'm relieved.

"So, dinner? Are you interested?" I ask, trying to regain control of my body. *Maybe if we talk about something else, I'll be able to move before too long.*

"Yeah. Sounds good." Samantha straightens her clothes and brushes down her hair. As my eyes rake over her, she appears as if she's been thoroughly kissed. Her beautiful lips are slightly swollen, her cheeks pink, and her eyes are slightly dilated. *This is definitely a look I want to see on her again.*

I glance at my watch and realize it's too early for dinner. But the thought of taking her to one of my favorite places comes to mind, so I say, "Why don't you go and freshen up. Grab your things and tell the crew to lock up when they leave. I'm going to make a call and then we'll head out." She eyes me suspiciously but doesn't say anything. *She's good with surprises. That's good to know.*

"Just wear what you have on," I tack on as an afterthought. There's no need for her to change from that scrumptious loose tank and sexy-fitting jeans. Besides, it's still warm for September and the weather is perfect for what I have planned.

As soon as she's through the door, I stand to adjust myself. *God, that woman has an effect on me.* I call and let my parents know something's come up this evening, so they shouldn't expect me. I also pull up a few websites to help me make my decision for what to do later tonight. *I can't honestly think of when I've gone to this much effort for a date.* Usually, I keep things casual and low key. But Samantha is special. I still can't believe a woman as sensual as she is hasn't kissed anyone else in years. I shake my head in disbelief. How on earth does someone go that long??? Geesh, I consider a dry spell a couple of months... but years? All that untapped energy. I can't believe I'm the lucky bastard she wants to let it out with.

8

———

SAMANTHA

I RUSH INSIDE FEELING a little dazed from my brazen move on the patio. *What in the world was I thinking? I wasn't.* It felt so amazing to be caught up in the moment, I hardly knew what to do with myself. *God, the way he made me feel!* First thing's first. Go upstairs and freshen up. Then talk with the crew to let them know they will need to lock up when they leave.

I nearly sprint up the stairs as soon as I'm out of view from anyone. I rush into my bathroom to find a woman I hardly recognize staring back at me in the mirror. My face is flushed, my lips are swollen, and my hair looks as if I have been thoroughly fucked. This isn't that bad of a look on me. *God, how long has it been?*

Suddenly, another thought fills my mind, leaving me a bit apprehensive as I stare at my reflection. Crap. Enzo is only home on leave. This isn't permanent. Am I sure I want to do this? My hormones must get the best of me because they're screaming *"Hell Yes,"* as my mind weighs the decision. Why do I have to be so logical all the time?

After a few moments of hesitation, I look at myself in the mirror and say, "Stop it! You deserve every moment with that man downstairs. He's gorgeous and makes you feel sexy, why not have fun and enjoy it? What's the worst that can happen?" Decision made.

I take another moment to calm myself. I glance at my clock then do my best to tame my wavy, yet tousled hair. Luckily, it only takes a few minutes to get it under control. I opt to leave it down around my shoulders. I quickly brush my teeth and throw on some lip gloss. I rush to my closet to reach for my light-blue leather jacket to bring, should it get cold later. I have no idea what Enzo has planned. But it should keep me warm enough. *He did say, not to change.* I shrug at myself in the mirror one last time before peering down at my sandals in my full-length mirror by the closet. *This will just have to do.*

It isn't even ten minutes before I'm back out on the patio, excited to see Enzo once again. Just seeing him has my body fully humming like before, even though he's standing feet away from me. When I walk outside, he glances up from his phone, an enormous smile slowly spreads across his devilishly handsome face. Of course, that dimple on his left cheek chooses this moment to pop out. I feel myself go weak at the knees. *Jesus, Samantha, get it together. You've been on a date before. Yes, but it's been an incredibly long time,* I quietly remind myself.

"Samantha," he growls in a deep timbre that has my heart picking up its pace. "You. Look. Amazing." He stands and closes the distance between us with little effort. He reaches out, grasping my hip to pull me in closer. He shakes his head slightly before whispering, "What you do to me..." the words trail off as he brushes his lips quickly across mine.

The grinding shrill of a saw is heard from inside and he steps back slightly, still keeping his hand resting on my hip. "Are you ready to go?" Enzo asks in a lighter tone.

I can't help the laughter that escapes my mouth as I take in the scene. I had suddenly forgotten what was on the other side of the doors. "Sure. Let's go."

Not wanting to be stopped by the crew for any reason, I allow Enzo to take my hand in his as I direct him to the gate on the side of the house. When we reach the driveway, he tugs me in the direction of his SUV. Effortlessly, he opens the passenger door and waits for me to get settled before closing it. I sit back and relax into the soft leather seats as I watch him privately take the few quick strides to make it around the front of his vehicle. This man sure is a sight to see. His green eyes twinkle with awareness as he catches me blatantly pursuing him from head to toe. *Busted... again! Gaaahhh! He must think I'm a nut job.* I need to get a hold of myself... or become stealthier.

By the time he enters the car, I have control of myself. I place my purse on the floor of the SUV and fold my jacket over it. He gives me another panty-melting smile, sexy dimple included, before he quickly buckles, adjusts the mirrors, and backs out of my driveway.

Enzo drives out of my neighborhood and approaches the freeway. He glances in my direction with one hand on the wheel, the other resting on the center console comfortably. His dark-blue shirt stretches across his chest to perfection. For a moment, I'm at a loss of what to do or say, but I do my best not to show my thoughts, *because that would get me into trouble.*

His chiseled jaw flexes as he smiles in my direction. I'm forced to stop my ogling and respond when he says, "I hope you don't mind. I haven't been home in a while and I absolutely love the Gorge in the fall. I thought we'd take a trip out there and have dinner."

"Sounds good. It's beautiful this time of year." I try to tear my eyes off him and look out the window. *If I don't stop staring... this will get awkward.* I pretend to take in the scenery around me instead as I gather my wits.

"So, last night you told me about your kids and work. I want to know more about you. What do you like to do, for you?" His deep voice fills the car and has my entire body humming once again.

Without even thinking, I burst out laughing. "Ummm... that's my life. I try to do a few things for me like run a few mornings a week. I hang out with a few close friends occasionally when our schedules allow it. Sometimes, we meet for drinks or get pedicures together, if I don't have the kids. My best friend Lexi and I see each other at work. Right after my divorce, she was my rock. But she has a life of her own, too." I shake my head when I realize my life isn't all that interesting. "What about you? What do you do when you're not flying?"

"I manage to keep myself out of trouble." He chuckles softly to himself. "Honestly, my life has been the Air Force for a long time. I spend a lot of my time working off base, which doesn't give me much time to be at home, wherever that happens to be. I love to hang out with my buddies because our off time is spent preparing for the next time we're back in the air. We're tight. We work hard and play even harder." A deep laugh escapes before he adds, "Well, I guess we have to be, our lives depend on each other." He suddenly goes quiet and his eyes appear distant, so I let that conversation go.

After a moment of comfortable silence, Enzo glances in my direction and an enthusiastic expression spreads across his features. "So, have you been to Multnomah Falls lately?" he asks as we leave the hustle and bustle of the city behind us. "I haven't been in years. Do you mind if we stop by?"

"Not at all." The fall leaves will be a spectacular sight to see with the waterfall in the background. I try to remember the last time I visited the state park along the Columbia River. Hmmmm... I've been so busy with work and the kids. I don't even want to think about the last time I went for a drive without a specific place and time to arrive. I miss feeling this relaxed. I stretch and let my muscles fall further into the seat. I take a deep breath and realize I could get used to this. I peek at Enzo, trying not to be too obvious about my intentions. *I could get used to this view, too.*

Enzo smiles at some unknown thought and I find myself blurting out, "What are you thinking about over there?"

He shakes his head to clear his thought but gives me a sideways glance with a lopsided smile. "I was just thinking about one of the last times I was out this way. My brother Zane bet me I couldn't beat him to the top of the trail. So of course, we had to race. Even as adults, we're still competitive. Zane thought I might be getting soft in my old age." He chuckles aloud as he shakes his head once more. "I still managed to smoke him." His voice now mischievous.

I look down at the sandals I'm wearing. "Uh, I might not be wearing the right shoes to race to the top." I give him a questioning look and he immediately brings my mind to ease.

"Oh, I'm not planning on hiking to the top, or a race, Short-Stuff." There is a wicked gleam in his eye as he continues, "Just maybe getting out and looking around a little."

Short-Stuff? "I'm five-foot-seven. Since when is that considered short?" I'm never referred to as being vertically challenged. "Not all of us are six-foot-four gargantuan beasts," I tease in return. "Besides, if I had my running shoes, you just might be on."

He clears his throat, suddenly looking slightly humbled. "Um, actually I'm six-foot-six, not that it matters. But relax. I'm not here to race you, sweetheart. I just want to relax and enjoy the view."

He grins once again, and his smile has me losing my thoughts completely. *Wait! Six-foot-six?!?!? He's almost a foot taller than I am. No wonder I feel like a bit of a dwarf around him.* But still, I'm by no means considered tiny or short for that matter. I shake my head, trying to regain my thoughts.

"I thought we could kill some time there for a while before dinner at one of my favorite places. You couldn't believe how much you miss the Pacific Northwest when you're gone. Sure, Germany is beautiful, but it isn't home. Not that I spend much time there anyway."

From his comment, I can tell he must be out on missions a lot. "You seem to travel more than you're home."

He shrugs his shoulder. "I go where I'm needed. I've been flying a lot throughout Europe and the Middle East, occasionally to Africa and South America. If there's a hostile area, I've been there. But it's not like I get to be a tourist. I get us in and get out as safe as possible. My team depends on me. Most of my view is from the cockpit, not on the ground."

"Wow. That has to be stressful." I try to picture myself in his shoes. I honestly can't.

"It's not that way all the time. Sometimes it's a lot of fun. The team I work with is tight. We're like our own family, so it isn't a hardship," he reassures me.

I can't help but wonder. "Will you miss it if you retire?"

He gives it serious thought before answering, "Not really. If I work in the private sector, I'll be working with great people, too."

He takes the exit on the left of the freeway and we suddenly enter the parking lot for Multnomah Falls. It's between the east and west bound lanes on Highway 84, which always feels weird to enter. Enzo pulls into a place close to the pathway, to cross under the freeway. This beautiful September afternoon has brought on a few visitors to the state park, but not as many as there would be in the summer or on the weekend. Before I can even get out, he's at my door, opening it for me. He reaches for my hand with a god-like smile, making me tingle in places I've thought were broken. His strong grip on me sends that ever-present electricity zinging through me when I'm near him. I reach for my purse but opt to leave my jacket. It's still quite warm so it won't be necessary.

He keeps his hand linked with mine as we walk toward the tunnel. I can't help but feel my heartbeat quicken as he rubs my thumb with his. It's as if we've been holding hands naturally for years, rather than just knowing each other a couple of days. As we walk, I notice a tattoo peeking out from his dark-blue sleeve between us. I can't quite make it out, but I'm now more than curious as to what it might be. Thankfully, I have some social grace and realize it might be awkward if I point it out, so I do my best to ignore it. But with each flex and movement of his arm, I'm more and more intrigued. At least when we get through the tunnel, I'm distracted from my ogling by the beautiful view of the tree-filled hill ahead of us.

"Magnificent, isn't it?" Enzo's husky voice breaks the silence and my reverie.

The colors are so vibrant, a gasp escapes as I nod my head at its beauty. I take in the rich reds, burnt oranges, yellows, and greens variegated throughout the magnificent hillside. The waterfall sporadically reveals itself as we walk along the path no bigger than two people side by side. Off to the right, a stream swiftly moves past us along the way. Finally, I see the bridge to get us to the visitors center and the falls itself.

As we follow the trail, the viewing area for photo ops of the falls quickly appears. It's a beautiful place to stop and admire the view. Enzo leads me to the handrail at the center of the platform. Since there are only a few people hanging around off to the side of the center, I don't hesitate to follow him. He pulls out his phone and uses the full force of that sexy dimple as he grins. "I want to take a picture of this gorgeous view." I immediately attempt to step out of the way, so I don't obstruct the view. He looks at me knowingly, pinning me to my place. "Um, you're part of the view, Samantha." He shakes his head as if I should have figured that part out, then motions to the spot he originally had me stand.

I return to the railing and raise my eyebrows. "Only if I get to take some of you, too." I reach for my phone in the pocket of my jeans.

Enzo laughs loudly. "If you insist. Though I won't look as beautiful as you." He rolls his eyes, and with a teasing tone, boldly states, "Get over there and pose, woman, before I put you there myself."

After a few shots of me, I dig out my phone and insist we trade places. I manage a few pictures of him before my arm is tugged, forcing me closer to Enzo. He places his closest arm around my shoulder, holding his phone so he can snap a selfie of us. He pulls me so close, I must place my hand on his chest to keep my balance. Glancing up at him, I realize I'm a goner. His hypnotic green eyes capture my attention and I can't help but get lost in them. He grasps me tighter and I gasp at the sudden closeness, as I involuntarily react to his movement. I stretch up on my toes, making our faces closer for the photo, while not taking my eyes off his. He briefly closes the gap with a peck on my lips as he holds out one arm with his phone. I barely register the phone is still taking pictures. Suddenly, a man next to us clears his throat.

"Um, would you like me to take a photo of the two of you?" he asks, trying to be helpful. Eyes darting between the two of us, he's about sixty years old, with kind eyes and graying temples. His wife is behind him, waiting to see if we want his help.

"Sure thing." Enzo chuckles as we focus our attention on him. He backs up and snaps a few pictures as we both beam at the camera.

He hands Enzo back his phone as he gestures to it. "Did they turn out?"

Enzo sweeps through the photos quickly. "Yes, sir. Thank you so much." He reaches out to shake the man's hand. Then Enzo motions for the woman behind him to join us. "Can we return the favor?"

She steps forward without hesitation. "That would be lovely. I absolutely love the falls in autumn." Enzo takes the woman's camera, snapping quite a few shots. He tries to get as much of the background in them as possible. When he's finished, the couple thanks him.

"No problem. You have a great evening," Enzo tells them, as they turn and walk down the path toward the visitors center.

9

ENZO

AS I HAND the camera back to the couple, I thank them once again before they leave.

"Come on, Samantha." I grab her hand to walk up the path to the next bridge. "Let's go take a picture from there," I say, pointing at the bridge high above us. I'm not really one to want my picture taken, but she's breathtaking, with the sun shining on her and the fall leaves behind us. Her sexy sass and wicked smile make me want to completely devour her, but since we're in public, I'll just enjoy her company. We walk hand in hand further up the path as I do my best to adjust my pace to hers. She's by no means short, but with being a foot taller, it's something I'm conscious of. We should reach the bridge in a matter of a few minutes, but when I see a turn in the path completely obstructed by the eyes of others around us, I pull her to a stop.

Unable to wait any longer, I growl as I tug her closer to me. "What you do to me," comes out as a growl and my lips are on her within a fraction of a second. I crush my mouth onto hers. My tongue darts out and parts the seam of her luscious lips. Her mouth is heaven. Ever since we were in her backyard, I've been wanting to get another taste of her deliciousness. Keeping an awareness of our surroundings, not willing to let things get out of control, I keep our kiss brief. Well, as brief as I can before I force myself to pull away. I graze her lips once more before standing to my full height, trying to casually adjust myself as I brush a light strand of hair back behind one of her ears.

Samantha's eyes darken as they regain their focus, which is gratifying. I know the effect she has on me, but it's nice to know she might feel the same. I shake my head, trying to regain my thought, but the look on her face brings a huge smile across my face as my heart thunders. What is it about this woman that I can't get enough of? I've *never* had such an instant pull, not even Vanessa and I was about to marry her. This is how it should have been. Dodged a bullet there!

WHAT. THE. FUCK? *Why am I thinking about marriage?* I just met this woman for CHRIST'S SAKE! She has kids, a family, and a life I barely know anything about. I'm more the type of being "Mr. Right Now," not "Mr. Right," and certainly not "Mr. Forever." But I need to know more about her and figure out this connection we share.

I hear a group of people coming up the path. Before they get to us, I pull myself out of my own head. "So, are you ready to keep walking?" I gesture in the direction of the bridge. She pulls away to continue our walk, but I just can't seem to let her go. I grab a hold of her hand once more, absentmindedly stroking her thumb with mine. I've never really been a touchy-feely guy. But Samantha is like a magnetic force set on high, and I can't fight the pull.

Conversation flows easily as we walk along the path. I tell her about the time my parents took us here when I was a teenager. "One time, my mom nearly had to bribe us to get one decent picture from this bridge." I point at the spot we stood, fondly remembering the experience. "None of us wanted to even be here, let alone stand together for a picture. My brother stood off to the side, barely in the picture, refusing to smile. My sister glared at me because I had done something to annoy her and I was doing my best to just take the ridiculous photo and get it over with. It was the early 90s, so there was big hair, flannel shirts, and hiking boots on every one of us. The total grunge look, now that I think about it. Ma was ticked." I laugh again at the memory. "I don't remember what she said but the look on my dad's face made us all comply with her wishes, immediately. It was a horrid photo, but in the end, we'd made her happy. She still has it hanging in the family room." I shudder at the thought, but the sound of Samantha's laughter has me willing to tell her more embarrassing stories if I continue to get a reaction like that.

Of course, she, too, has stories about trying to get her three kids together for one photo. I burst out laughing as she explains one of her favorites. Frankie's nearly running out of the screen, Declan's pouting, and Maddie smiling like a trooper. When she mentions it's framed in her home office, I'm dying to see it. It must be hysterical, but from the sense of contentment on her face as she recalls the memory, I know she cherishes it.

When we make it to the bridge overlooking the waterfall, Samantha and I take in the beautiful view of the Gorge itself. As far as the eye can see, the magnificent Columbia River is lined with trees of varying shades of autumn colors with steep reddish-brown cliffs of weathered basalt far off in the distance. Once again, I can't control my need to capture the beauty before me. As if on autopilot, I find myself pulling out my camera to capture this moment with her. The more I've gotten to know Samantha, I find she's so modest and completely unaware of the exquisiteness within her. At the same time, she's bold and confident in some ways, sassy the next, and I love that I never know what she's going to say or do. I'm doing my best to keep my distance, but as I get to know more about her, I find myself losing the battle. My intrinsic need pulls her in for another kiss, but I force myself not to get carried away. We *are* in public. Throughout our entire time at Multnomah Falls, I find myself touching her in some way as if I can't let her go. *What kind of spell has she put on me?*

Later, as we drive further up the Gorge, I hold her hand casually across the console. Our conversation easily flows from one subject to another. I'm about to ask her another question when her phone rings. Samantha quickly pulls it out of her pocket, checks the caller ID, and mouths, *Sorry,* to me as she answers, "Hey, Maddie. What's up?"

From her side of the conversation, I can tell her daughter's just checking in. The sense of pride Samantha shows for her daughter is unbelievable. I admire the fact she stops whatever she's doing to give her full attention to Maddie. They talk about an upcoming dance and at one point, Samantha promises to go shopping for a dress later this week. Once that's settled, they chat about Maddie's plans for the weekend.

After a few minutes, Samantha's voice changes when she talks to her youngest daughter, Frankie. Frankie's obviously excited about something because I can hear her enthusiasm burst through the phone. Though, I have no clue her reason for such excitement because Samantha can barely get a word in edgewise. But as she listens, the smile which spreads across Samantha's face is infectious.

Eventually, her voice becomes more businesslike, causing me to glance her way to make sure she's okay. From her side of the conversation, I hear. "Hello? ...I'm not really sure. The place was still torn apart when I left... No... They won't be working on the weekend, so it looks like it might be early next week... Are you sure that's okay with you? I can still pick them up from school to drive them to practice. Yes... I think that'll be best. Okay. See you Monday afternoon. No, I'll get them something to eat along the way. Thanks, Devin. I'll talk to you later."

When she hangs up the phone, she turns to me with an apologetic tone in her voice. "Sorry. That was my girls and their father. We needed to make arrangements for next week, so everyone's on the same page." Samantha's face fills with an expression I can't read before she groans, "Ugg, I miss them like crazy, but with my house under construction, it's what makes sense. They love homemade breakfasts and cold lunches, so it's easier this way. Besides, Devin's always been a fantastic father so the kids will enjoy spending the time with him." She lets out a heavy sigh. "He'll keep them until

Monday when he drops them off at school and picks up Declan from practice like usual." She lets out a deep breath before adding, "They usually return Sunday evenings," as an explanation for the change.

"Do they stay with him often?" I ask, not knowing what else she might be thinking as she stares out the window.

"Usually it's just Wednesday nights and every other weekend, unless either of us goes out of town on business. We try to co-parent as much as we can. He helps with the daily drop-offs and pick-ups. The kids' schedules are so crazy, it's impossible to manage alone. It's not easy, but Devin and I try to get along for our kids' sake." Samantha takes a deep breath and seems to steady herself before adding, "Believe it or not, Devin actually only lives about five minutes away, so our kids can ride the bus to either house depending on where they need to go." She tucks her hair behind her ear and looks out the window as I continue to drive.

I can't imagine getting along so well with an ex. From what she told me earlier, she was the one cheated on. Samantha must make a tremendous amount of effort to make this happen. I don't think I could do that. The woman next to me must be a saint. I glance over at her in awe once again. Samantha has so many facets to her, it's a miracle she's still single. Devin was an idiot to let her go. She's smart, sexy as hell, and an amazing mother. Everything I learn about her just keeps drawing me in further. What the hell could've been so wrong for him to look elsewhere?

Trying to keep my voice indifferent, I say, "It's obvious

you're a great mom who loves her kids. Not a lot of people would put forth the effort you do. Your kids will appreciate it."

She looks taken back by my compliment. She shrugs before letting out a deep breath. "Some days are easier than others, but I wouldn't have it any other way. We both chose to have the kids. Just because one of us chose a path that didn't involve the other doesn't mean our kids should be the ones to suffer. Maddie, Declan, and Frankie are the best things to ever happen to me. I can't imagine my life without them. Sometimes, I wonder what life would have been like if I hadn't gotten married in college, but then I wouldn't have them in my life." She smiles at her realization.

As I glance over in her direction, I can tell she means what she says with conviction. The love that flows from her eyes is unmistakable. Her positive attitude and an outlook on life, in general, amaze me. Most women would be evil and vindictive toward their cheating exes, but not Samantha. She handles it with grace and dignity. Just one of many traits I'm quickly coming to admire about her. "I can't wait to meet them," comes out of my mouth before I give it any thought. *Wait? Did I just say I wanted to meet her kids? That could be a cluster fuck...* but when I think more about it, my nerves calm. They're a part of her and from what I can tell, she's amazing.

We pull off our intended exit in Hood River. I take the necessary turns to make our way to the part of town overlooking the waterfront. I manage to snag a place to park along a side street. I get out of the car to help Samantha with her door. It's a bit windier here in the evening, so I suggest she take her jacket. I grab a hoodie from my "go bag" in the back of the SUV. I never am far without it, even when I'm not on duty.

The magnetic force sizzling between us makes it so I cannot keep my hands off her. I guide her down the sidewalk with my arm around her lower back. Instead of resting my hand in the middle of her back, I find it comfortable to rest it on her outside hip. This settles her closer to me. I take a huge breath, inhaling the delicious scent of her hair. It's a mixture of honey, mint, and something that's entirely Samantha. It's intoxicating, making me wish I hadn't driven so far to take her out for dinner. Being in public has its disadvantages.

We walk down the sidewalk, peering into shops along the way to the restaurant. She stops at one storefront to admire the dress on the mannequin. It's a sleeveless, green lace dress. The top seems to wrap around itself, while the bottom flows out like an A-line. I only know that type of dress because I had a sister growing up. *Not that I have a clue about much else.* I just remember my mom and her endlessly talking about how flattering the shape was.

"Why don't you try it on?" I suggest when I see the longing in her eyes. As she turns to face me, she seems a little confused by my suggestion.

"No, it's okay. I'm just window shopping." She glances at me sheepishly as if she doesn't know what else to say.

"It isn't a problem to stop in. That would look gorgeous on you," I suggest. *What the hell has come over me?* I'm never one to purposely choose to shop. In fact, everything I own can be grouped into two categories, military issued or bought on a brief trip to a department store. I'm not one to browse, or even indulge in fashion sense. It's for function only that I even bother. But for some reason, when I saw her eyes light up, I picture her in that dress. Now I want to see if the real thing does my fantasy justice.

"Are you sure? It seems weird to shop on a first date. I don't want to bore you." She chews on her lower lip and I can't help but want to free it with my teeth.

"I never say anything I don't mean," I huskily growl at her, fantasizing about those luscious lips. "We're here. If you want to try it on, go for it." *I certainly wouldn't mind seeing your sexy curves in that dress.*

She bites that lip some more and I nearly lose it. "Okay..." she whispers. "If you insist."

We walk into the small shop and a saleswoman quickly helps Samantha get a dress in her size. I browse a little while she's trying it on, but stay near the dressing room, hoping to get a view of her. My prayers are answered a few minutes later when she steps out of the dressing room.

Damn! Her curves fill out that dress perfectly. As she walks toward me, my mouth suddenly goes as dry as the Arabian Desert. I must pick my jaw up off the floor and smack my head against a wall to form any coherent thought. She smiles shyly and gives a quick spin. The skirt portion of her dress nearly does a Marilyn Monroe impression, but nothing indecent. The only indecent thing about it is my thoughts and how I wish I could get her out of this spectacular dress. Or just going back into that dressing room would do, too.

"What do you think?" she asks, wanting an honest opinion.

I clear my throat, trying to gain the capacity to speak. When I finally find my voice, I growl, "It belongs on you."

Her face blazes with the perfect color as if she's never received a compliment before. "Thanks," she whispers.

It takes everything in my power not to devour her on the spot. Eventually, I regain control of myself and say, "Go change, I'll have the saleswoman ring it up."

Samantha looks at me questioningly before she turns to head back to the dressing room. While she's in there, the saleswoman asks if there is anything else we need. I ask her to point me to the area for accessories. The saleswoman assists me in finding some handmade jewelry, which is made locally. I pick out a necklace and a pair of earrings to match. I have her ring them up and place them in the bag. To speed things along, I also ask her to ring up the dress as well. When Samantha arrives, she hands the dress to the saleswoman but has no idea about the accessories I bought her. A flash of irritation crosses her face when she finds I just purchased this dress for her. She starts to put up a fight.

"Get over it, beautiful. My plan is to take you out tomorrow night to reap the reward of seeing you in that exquisite dress." I raise an eyebrow, challenging her to question me. I can't help but chuckle when her mouth opens like she's about to rip me a new one, quickly changes her mind, then attempts again.

Finally, her spit-fire self comes through. "What makes you think I'm going out with you tomorrow night?"

"I have my ways of convincing you," I tease as I pull her in for a side hug and kiss the top of her head. I reach for the bag and lead her out the door. "Besides, who says I'm letting you go tonight?" I let her ponder over that as we walk out the door to the restaurant.

10

———————

SAMANTHA

HE BOUGHT ME A DRESS. *He bought me a dress? Why on earth would he do that?* I'm perfectly capable of buying my own dress.

His words keep cycling on a loop through my head. *"I have my ways of convincing you. Besides who says I'm letting you go tonight?"*

What the hell does he mean by that?

I know I'm completely attracted to the man, but to go all alpha-male, is it really necessary? Yeah, sure, my panties just burst into flames, but to be so brazen and bold? Heaven help me if he follows through with his threat. I can't remember the last time I even had sex, let alone thinking about having it. *Before I met him, that is.* Yep. And there he goes, bringing that delicious dimple into the mix and... BAM! I might as well not be wearing any underwear, for all the good they're doing me. My jeans will have a wet spot in them if he keeps this up. Oh, who am I kidding? If we weren't on a public street, I'd be climbing him like a tree. Holy hell, this man is pure sex on a stick.

As I glance at him, I notice his five o'clock shadow makes him look even more scrumptious. He has the perfect amount of scruff for running my fingers along his strong jawline. He slings an arm over my shoulder while carrying my bag in the other hand. His masculine scent sends my body into overdrive. I do my best to keep my emotions under control as we walk together along the sidewalk. But my mind is reeling. I can't imagine where he's going to take me so I can wear my new dress tomorrow night. *Slow down, Sam. You haven't even gotten through tonight, you need to get through dinner first. Yes. That's it, focus on dinner and just take it one step at a time.*

As we arrive at the restaurant, I pull myself out of my head, focusing on the fact I need to concentrate on the here and now. Not of the possibilities to come. *Oh, but those possibilities...*

There wasn't a wait, so once we're seated we spend a few minutes to peruse the menu. I can barely concentrate on the words in front of me, as Enzo has yet to release my hand from across the table. The electricity zinging between us makes me feel like a fixated teenager, staring at her first crush. I'm grateful for the interruption when a perky waitress arrives. She explains the special tonight and I'm easily sold. It's steak with grilled asparagus and a side dish unique to the restaurant.

When the waitress leaves, I do my best not to ogle Enzo. I force myself to think of something to say to keep from staring at him like a fool. Focusing only on his gorgeous green eyes, I find myself asking the first thing that pops into my mind aloud, "Tell me, if there was a book made about your life, what would the title be?"

Enzo seems a little taken back by my question, but soon appears to be giving it some thought. Eventually, a slow smile spreads across his face and I brace myself for the full force of his scrumptious dimple. Slightly shaking his head, he lightly laughs. "I have no freaking clue." He lets out a deep sigh, leans back in his seat, and gazes up at the ceiling as if he's still pondering my question. His jaw juts out and his lips purse. His hand that isn't holding mine reaches up to scratch at his chiseled jaw. Finally, after a long moment of thought, he chuckles once loudly and sucks in a deep breath. "Maybe... Man on a Mission?" His eyebrows rise along with his shoulders, awaiting my response.

There are so many ways I can take this. Yeah, he's a pilot in the Air Force, and then his comment from the boutique comes to mind. My face immediately feels as if it will burst into flames from the last realization. Thankfully, I don't have to respond because we're interrupted by the arrival of our food.

After we have both taken a bite, Enzo clears his throat. "So, what about you? What would the title of your life be?"

He catches me mid-bite, so thankfully I have time to think about it while I clear my mouth. Phrases like Derailed and Matronly Mom pop into my mind. But then I consider Enzo's glorious greens which stare back at me, filled with such intensity, my mind heads in a different direction. Now the phrases Bound and Determined, Rejuvenated, Revitalized, Hot and Horny come to mind and I smile. *There's no way I'm telling him that last one.*

I shake my head to rid my thoughts from going into the gutter. "I don't know, nothing I'm thinking of really describes it."

"Well..." His deep, husky voice rumbles. "Why can't you make it up as you go? Nothing says you must let one thing define you. The more I get to know you, the more facets I'm enamored with." He takes his hand to brush a strand of hair back from my face. As he places it behind my ear, a shiver runs through my spine. He blows me away when he continues with, "I think resilience is key to your success. You're a single mom of what sounds like three amazing children. You're career oriented and you overcome obstacles that get in your way. You are strong, fierce, and from what I can tell, loyal. Not one title would justify your life. At least, as I've come to know it."

Holy Crap. I just met this man, and he already knows me better than Devin ever did. I stare at him a little dumbfounded at my revelation. "I—Ummm... I don't know what to say," I whisper as I bring my hand to cover my chest. I feel my eyes prick with tears, but I blink them away as fast as I can. "No one's ever said that about me before."

"Was I wrong?" Enzo's deep voice questions. "I—Uhh... hope I didn't offend you. I consider myself to be a great judge of character. It's a necessity in my line of work. That's just... well, I tell it like I see it." He clears his throat and holds my gaze as he awaits my response.

The look in his eyes slays me. The thought he could have

offended me is crazy. That was the nicest, sweetest compliment I could've ever received. "No. Thank you." I stare into the great depths of his eyes much longer than I should and they smolder. I finally add, "I appreciate the compliment."

He eyes me dubiously before he lowly growls, "You'd better fuckin' believe it. You're unlike any person I've ever met." Seeming to be taken back by his own words, his eyebrows suddenly rise to meet his forehead. He appears to recover, then smiles with the full force of his dimple at me.

All I can do is stare at him in return. That's it. I'm in complete shock and unable to mentally process anything else at this moment.

The waitress returns and interrupts my gawking. "Can I get you two anything else?" She briefly smiles at me and then turns her attention to Enzo. His eyes remain on me while he shakes his head no.

"No, thank you," Enzo mumbles.

Thank God, for the interruption. *What in the world has come over me?* I've received compliments before. It's not like I live my life completely devoid of them or anything. I rack my brain to think of something else to say to get the intensity of our connection to turn down a few notches. What do people talk about when they're first dating? Sports! He's a man... and it's a subject we have yet to talk about.

When the waitress saunters away, I ask, "So... do you follow any sports teams?" *Gaahh... could that sound anymore forced?!?!*

Enzo finishes the food he'd just placed in his mouth before smiling back at me. "I'm known to watch a game now and then. I like to watch the usual, football, hockey, and soccer if I get the chance. Though it's been a long time since I've seen any in person. What about you?"

"Well, I love to watch football. I'm an avid fan of the Seahawks. I try to go to a game each season, but mostly I just yell from my couch." I laugh at my revelation. "I'm a huge fan of Russell Wilson."

Enzo gives me a mischievous smile. "They're my favorite team, too. I'd love to catch a game while I'm home on leave." He takes a bite of his steak and chews it before adding, "They've had a good run lately. I hope this season continues the way it's started."

"Do you watch the games in Germany? Or do you just keep up on STATs?" I ask, thinking it must be hard with the time difference and all the traveling he does.

"Well, I don't always see them live. But I enjoy it all the same. Sometimes, I just keep track of the score."

"They play Monday this week," I casually mention. "You're welcome to come over and watch the game with me. I'll have to leave at some point to pick up Declan from soccer, but you're welcome to hang out. I must warn you, though. I might be known as being part of the twelve that makes noise," I tease, then realize what I've just said.

Shit, Sam... that's a sure-fire way to scare him off. Meeting your kids after just three days? Talk about baptism by fire! I can't believe I just asked him that! I immediately close my eyes, not wanting to see his response.

"Can I bring pizza and beer?"

My eyes go wide, and I feel my mouth take the form of an

O. I stare at him blankly, not knowing if I've really heard him right. *He wants to meet my kids? WOW! Okay. This will be a first, but I can handle it, and they will, too. Who am I kidding? I have no idea how they will react, but I deserve to have a life.*

"Is everything okay, Samantha?" Enzo's deep timbre pulls me out of my panicked state.

I briefly shake my head, regaining my thoughts. "Yes." I inhale deeply and let it out slowly. *I might as well be honest. Here goes nothing.*

"Just to give you a warning, my kids have never met anyone I have dated," I quietly state. When I look up, I find a bit of surprise on Enzo's features. I immediately backpedal. "Don't get me wrong. It's not like I've dated a lot of men, or hardly any for that matter, but this is new for me."

"I can't say I've ever met anyone's kids before either." Enzo's eyes hold my gaze in place as he adds, "But I'm looking forward to it. After all, it's just football and pizza. It's not like we're getting married or anything. Your kids are a part of you, so they can't be too scary. They're past the biting stage, right?"

I laugh at the sudden seriousness I'd brought to our situation and realize he's right. It's just football and pizza. Enzo puts me at ease without even knowing it. For that I'm grateful. "I'm pretty sure they are. They might fight or bicker, but you should be pretty safe," I tease. "Frankie grew out of that stage a couple of years ago."

The rest of our meal goes by effortlessly. By the time we finish, I've learned more about his nieces and nephews, and the various stages they had gone through. I almost spit my drink laughing when he tells me about the time his nephew gave himself a hickey with the vacuum cleaner in the middle of his forehead. It's evident from the way he talks about his family, Enzo's an amazing brother and uncle. As we leave the restaurant, Enzo takes my hand in his and we walk hand in hand to the car.

11

———

ENZO

ALL THROUGHOUT DINNER, I can't take my eyes off Samantha. Not only is she stunningly gorgeous, but she doesn't seem to comprehend the hold she has on me. She is fun, witty, and keeps me on my toes. I never know what she is about to say. When she goes deep into thought or is unsure of how to say something, she tends to pull her lower lip in and nibble on it until she could come up with something else to say. It takes all my effort not to reach over and tug that luscious lip out from the capture of her perfectly sculpted teeth, *though I'd rather do it with my own teeth. Fuck! This woman could be my kryptonite.*

As we walk to the car, I find myself completely drawn to her. I hold her hand in mine, with her purchases in my other. A cool breeze has picked up this evening, so Samantha is now wearing the light jacket she brought. I assist her in putting it on and once we're outside, I'm assaulted with her scent and force myself to keep from taking her immediately.

"Do you want to go down to the waterfront?" Samantha asks as we reach the car.

It's easier to drive to it, so I suggest, "Yeah, why don't we get in and drive down?"

Within a few minutes, we're down by the river. There are a few other people out enjoying the remains of this beautiful fall evening. On a hot summer day, countless people are down here. Most will be windsurfing. Now there are only a few die-hards in wetsuits enjoying the evening breeze. The shore is fairly empty, but I guide her further away, wanting to be alone with her.

Our conversation flows with ease as we stroll along the river's edge. We talk about how delicious dinner was. Never having it far from my mind, I mention how I can't wait to see her again in the dress I bought her. Just thinking of how she looked coming out of that dressing room makes me want to devour her. It doesn't help when color fills her face as I reveal my thoughts. The desire flowing through me makes me want to surprise her like that again soon. I shake my head at the preposterous thought. *This is so unlike me. When have I ever invested this much into someone in such short of time? Never.*

When we get further down the shore, we stop to take in the view. As Samantha admires the beauty of the Columbia River and the Gorge around it nearing sunset, I enjoy my view of her. Her mahogany hair blows lightly in the wind as it's pushed back from her face. The fading sun brings out lighter streaks of color throughout and illuminates her beautiful face. She lifts her head and takes a deep breath, seeming to relax.

After all too short of time, she catches me watching her. Her smile nearly takes my breath away.

"It's so beautiful here," she whispers.

"Yeah, it sure is. Can't get much better than this," I huskily growl. Without any thought, I find myself stepping forward to embrace her. My arms fold around her waist as I nuzzle into her neck. It's like she was made for me. Her body fits perfectly with mine. No other woman has made me feel so unhinged. I've never met anyone more addictive. I'm drawn to her like a moth to a flame. I pull Samantha to me so her back is against my chest. Taking a deep breath of her heavenly scent, I kiss her neck lightly, just at the crease of her shoulder. I feel a slight shiver pass through her body, so I must be having some effect on her, too.

Before I know it, she turns around. Her arms drape around my neck. Having everything else around me fade into the background, I pull her to me and close the gap with my lips, needing another taste of her. One hand glides to the back of her neck beneath her hair while the other remains at her lower back. Her hooded eyes may be the death of me. The spark that ignites as soon as our lips touch could incinerate me on the spot and I could care less. Without another thought, I deepen the kiss with pressure from my hand at her neck. I'm rewarded for my efforts as I seem to have set off a magic switch inside her. She nearly climbs me and I'm thankful for my years of working out and quick agility. Effortlessly, I put my hand under her ass to pull her up to match my full height, so we are not thrown off balance. Her glorious legs naturally wrap around my waist and I remind myself not to get carried away. The small moan that escapes her mouth as her hands run through the back of my hair, nearly has me finding the first available flat surface to take her on. But I manage to keep my control. *Barely*.

To keep my composure, I reluctantly break off the kiss. Instead, I pepper kisses down her neck, continuing to hold her close. Her legs squeeze me tighter as if she's trying to find some release as well. I kiss her once more, though it's not as consuming, and slowly lower her back to the ground.

"Wow," she whispers as she looks into my eyes. "How do I always seem to lose all control when I'm around you?" The look on her face tells me there's no shame in her words, just wonder and awe. A sense of warmth spreads over me.

A slow grin spreads across her face when I clear my throat and say, "Trust me. You're not alone."

Knowing movement is the best course of action to keep from letting things burn out of control, I take her hand and walk back toward the parking lot. "Let's get back to the car before I get too carried away." By now, the sun has nearly set, and dusk is settling in. We can still clearly see where we're walking, but it won't be long before it's dark.

It doesn't take long until we're back in the car. Before I can drive the distance back to Portland, I kiss her one more time. Her hands wrap around my face and it takes everything... and I mean *everything* in my power not to take her right here. Eventually, I pull away from her and start the car, although my body curses at me and I regret this decision.

There is a sexual charge that could fuel the car if we could harness it, as we drive back to Portland. It doesn't take me long to reach over and take her hand in mine once again. I need to touch her, caress her, just be close to her. *Who the hell is this woman? I don't remember being so touchy-feely before.* In fact, I'm usually the one to keep things at a distance. I wouldn't say I'm being clingy. I'm just quickly becoming addicted to her. It's like I can't help myself. *What the hell, man?*

So far, we've kept our conversation light, but suddenly Samantha catches me off guard when she asks, "How exactly are you still single?"

"Um... what do you mean by that?" I give her a confused glance to see what she's thinking.

She sighs. "Never mind." Then shakes her head. "I didn't mean for that to be said out loud." From the lights on the dashboard, I see her face turn chagrin. Then she mumbles, "Gaahh... what is it about you? It's like I have no control over my thoughts or actions."

I laugh aloud. "Samantha. You've got no idea the effect you have on me. It took all my effort not to take you in this car once we got back to it from the river."

"No way!" She shakes her head in disbelief.

"You have no idea," I grumble and adjust my jeans. "You're magnificent. I could feast on you for days."

She's quiet for a few moments. I fear I've offended her. "Everything okay?" I ask, needing reassurance since I can't quite read her expression in the dark.

Her voice turns sultry as she replies, "Yes. I'm fine. You've just got me thinking..." she trails off.

"About..." I prompt, needing to know what's on her mind.

God, I hope I haven't offended her.

"What it would be like..." Her voice is barely audible.

She's killing me. Literally. I might even wreck the car because all my blood supply is traveling south while I'm supposed to be driving the car west. After another long moment, I ask, "What, what would be like?"

Thankfully, I see her peek over at me. Then I see her brazen smile as she straightens her back to face me directly. "Like... what being with you would be like. It's been so long... until I met you, I thought I'd never feel this way again. You have me nearly attacking you... AGAIN... in public no less." She shakes her head. "The funny part is I would have been totally on board with your train of thought... and I have NEVER done anything like that in my life!"

"What do you mean?" *I NEED to hear it. I NEED to know so I can be completely sure. I want nothing more than to pull this car over and have my way with her.*

"I've never had sex anywhere remotely public." She makes a weird noise with her throat, somewhere between a laugh and a snort before she adds, "I haven't done much outside my bedroom in so long I can't remember." Then she full out laughs. "And I can't even remember when the last time would have been. For all I know, my lady bits have shriveled up and died."

"Fuck, beautiful, you're killing me," I growl. When I see an exit ahead, I don't even think before I pull off, leading us to who knows where. I'm barely aware of the fact that it's a side road leading to the middle of nowhere. I don't even care. My only goal is to get to a place where I can park this damn car and not be bothered by anyone.

I know there must be a god when I see a turn-out that's half hidden by trees on one side. I quickly slam the car into park. Before I know it, I have unbuckled my seat belt and am reaching for her. She must read my mind because without hesitation, she's grabbing at me across the seat as well. Our mouths fuse together and we kiss passionately for endless moments. The electricity zinging between us is indescribable. It's like I can't get enough, no matter how hard I kiss her or caress her. I part her lips and delve into the depths of her. Samantha has me nearly losing control within moments.

I must get closer. I tear at her jacket and have it removed within seconds. I slide my hands up her smooth skin as I bring her loose tank over her head. Her body ignites when I unclasp her bra as I continue to kiss her. She sheds it quickly and I growl when I finally reach her magnificent breast with my hand. I tweak and pull her dark nipple with my thumb against my forefinger as I knead her flesh with the rest of my hand. Her nipple pebbles magnificently as if it were made for me. Wanting to give equal attention, I switch sides and assault the other one with the same intensity. Within moments, she lets out a sound I don't think I will ever forget.

"Fuck, Samantha. I need more of you," I moan as I let go with one hand and recline my seat before pulling her over the console to be on top of me. I scoot up the seat to give her more room in front of the steering wheel. Gone is the shy girl from before, replaced by a woman who knows her needs. She eagerly straddles me as a low growl escapes and grips tightly onto my shoulders.

Loving this new angle, I pull one ample breast into my mouth as I tease the other with my hand. Her skin is delicious. The scent that makes her uniquely her has me completely entranced. I lick and suck each delicious bud in my mouth to get more of those addicting sounds to come out of hers.

When she moves along my hardened length, digging my zipper into my full erection, I reach for the button of her jeans to open them. "Oh, Enzo," comes out on a harsh breath as she seeks a release I know she needs. I take a moment and reposition us so that I can get my hand between us while enjoying her nipples the entire time with my mouth.

When my hand finally reaches her slick, wet center, I'm rewarded with her fisting my hair and guiding my mouth back to her delicious breast. Loud moans escape each of us as I nip, pull, and tug, making her addictive nipple taut and fully extended. My tongue slides across its peak as my long fingers find what they have been searching for. I curve my finger and give it a 'come hither' motion into her front wall and the gorgeous woman before me nearly screams.

"What are you doing to me?" she moans breathlessly, so I continue my efforts in full force.

"Oh, Enzo... there... right there." Her head falls back, giving me easier access to her heavy, erect breasts. I press my thumb across her clit, massaging it for mere seconds before she detonates.

"There you go, beautiful," I growl. "That's it. Give me all

you've got," I whisper into her ear as I nip on her lower lobe. "I wanna watch this all night long."

Now any woman coming apart is a beautiful sight to see, but when Samantha comes apart, it's more than I can even comprehend. I nearly embarrass myself and come right along with her in my jeans, but I manage to hold on. *Holy Shit! I have no idea how much longer I can hold back. I haven't felt like this since I was seventeen.*

As she comes down from her glorious high, she kisses and sucks on my neck. Soon, she buries her face in my shoulder and I hold her tightly in place. Though she seems unaware, her ass rests squarely on my straining erection. I do my best to ignore it and pray it doesn't try to start a conversation with her on its own. Right now, this is about her and nothing else matters. After a few moments of stillness, I break the silence with a rough whisper, "You okay, beautiful?"

A soft sigh escapes before she answers, drawing out the word, "Perfect."

I push her back slightly, cupping her chin to have her look me in the eyes. "Are you sure?"

The utter sincerity almost slays me. "Just blissed out at the moment..." Her smile is infectious. "Give me a minute. I'm sure I'll manage to move soon." She rests her head back on my shoulder as her body remains slightly limp. "Sorry to squish you..."

I readjust her so she sits on my lap, rather than on her knees, by swinging her legs across the console. "Take your time, Samantha. I'm not going anywhere." I rub her bare back in slow circles and take another deep breath of her delicious scent, feeling mostly content. *Well, except for the fact that my erection has yet to stop making his presence known. Maybe if I think about car crashes, pre-flight checks, anything except for this beautiful woman before me, he will disappear or at least give me some reprieve.*

After a few minutes of listening to nothing but our breathing returning to normal, what she said before this all began hits me and I let out a low laugh. "I guess your lady bits haven't shriveled up and died. They felt pretty fucking amazing to me." *And he's back.*

Samantha buries her head in my shoulder. "Gaahh... Enzo. Why can't I have a filter around you?!?! I swear it's like I can't contain anything. Are you sure you haven't slipped me some truth serum or something?" She laughs, trying to make a joke of it.

"I wouldn't have it any other way, Samantha," I say with all honesty. "Please don't ever hold back."

I notice a light in the far distance and reach for her shirt. Pointing in the direction of the oncoming car, I suggest, "We'd better get you dressed." She immediately scoots over the console and puts on her shirt, sans bra. Before I can say anything, she stuffs her bra into her purse. She buckles up, acting as if nothing has happened, before she innocently asks, "Ready?"

I can't take it. I pull her face to meet mine and kiss her thoroughly once again. I completely devour her mouth and I can't help it when my hand snakes under her shirt to cup her ample breast. The moan she lets out is satisfying and I can't help but grin. "Samantha, you're incredible," I whisper as I kiss across her lips. The interior of my car suddenly becomes illuminated with the passing of the vehicle I noticed earlier. I pull back, placing my hand on her thigh, and put the car in gear. It's going to be a long ride to Portland. My body is on fire and I want to be inside this woman before the night is through. Samantha gives me a knowing look and places her hand over mine, showing me she feels it, too.

12

SAMANTHA

THE RIDE back home is quiet. I'm lost in my head as Enzo drives with his hand on my leg. My body is still tingling from earlier. As I sat on Enzo's lap, I couldn't help but feel his length under me. I'm dying to know more about that part of him up close and personal.

I haven't had an orgasm like the one he gave me, ever. It's been so long since I've even had another person involved. Thank goodness, for my battery-operated boyfriend, or I'd be certain parts of me had withered up and died. Oh! My! Freaking! God! I can't believe I told him that. I seriously about died when he mentioned it. I was sure I'd only said that in my mind.

As we enter the city, Enzo breaks the silence, "What are you thinking about over there, beautiful? Your face keeps going from serious, to happy, to mortified, to something I can't entirely read. You're killing me over here." He squeezes my thigh he's been holding on to since we left.

Not really sure what to say, I go with the truth. "Just taking it all in."

"And you're sure you're okay?" he asks hesitantly. "That we're okay?" he rephrases. "...you're not upset with me, or anything?" I'm slightly shocked at the uncertainty I hear in his voice. Since I've met him, he's oozed confidence and his vulnerability is my undoing.

"No," I implore him. "I'm perfectly fine. I was just thinking about how I couldn't wait to get you home where we won't be interrupted by anyone... and there goes my lack of a filter. What is it about you that seems to have me misplacing it?" I tease, trying to shake off my mortification.

Enzo's deep baritone voice hypnotizes me when he says, "Oh, Samantha, we're just getting started. I have plenty I want to do to you, too."

My jaw drops, and my cheeks burst into flames as I think about what he might have in mind. Thankfully, we're only a few blocks from my house, so I won't have to wait long.

The moment he puts the car in park, he's out of the car, bounding to my door to get me. He reaches for my hand and we're at my front door within seconds. Thankfully, I have my keys ready, so we don't have to wait long to get inside.

The moment we shut and lock the front door, Enzo's mouth is on mine. I drop my purse and keys on the table next to the door before throwing my arms around his neck. Effortlessly, he hoists me up so that my legs snake around his waist and I'm propped up against the door. Every nerve ending is on fire. I want him more than I've ever wanted anyone. Each touch, each caress, and each kiss send electric pulses across my entire body. I. Want. More. I need more. I pull at his shirt because I'm dying to explore that sexy body beneath his clothes. Thankfully, he gets the hint and removes it over his head with only one hand.

"Only if yours goes, too," he huskily growls into my ear.

I gasp as I take in a deep breath. Enzo is sexy with clothes on, but shirtless... I may expire on the spot. Holy Hell! The man has thick, broad shoulders, with a few tattoos scattered over his chest and upper arms. I recognize the Air Force symbol on the upper part of one arm. I also see some that I would love to know the meanings of, but not now. Now, I'm going to lick each. And. Every. Muscle, across his delicious abs. I was convinced people only obtained sculpted bodies like this through Photoshop. He has a V traveling down his lower abs. You know, the kind that makes smart women drool and do and say stupid things.

"You can't be real," I moan as he reaches for me again. I could care less that being up against my door isn't comfortable. All I care about is the fact Enzo grasps my shirt and pulls it over my head in one swift move that I can't even begin to comprehend.

"You'd better fucking believe I'm real," he growls. Instantly, his mouth is back on mine and I'm devouring all that is him.

Finally, we're skin to skin. Chest to chest. The contact feels absolutely amazing. His lightly covered chest hair assaults my hardening nipples and I can't help but let out a soft groan. *I want this man. No! I need this man.*

"Bedroom," I moan as I break our kiss.

"Next time," he growls as he sets me down and unbuttons my pants. I try to help him by kicking out of my shoes as he pulls the length of my jeans down. He manages to grab my underwear in one tug, and now I'm standing in my living room in all my naked glory. I have no time to get embarrassed or think about anything other than him. He reaches into his wallet and picks something out before he drops it on the table beside us. When I realize it is a condom, I reach for his jeans. He brushes my hands aside as he unclasps them himself. With his boxer briefs in tow, they drop to the floor and he steps out of them. He kicks them aside and I'm in awe of the glorious man before me.

He's utter perfection. He catches me as I lick my lips. I'm about two seconds from dropping to my knees to get a taste of him when he takes a step toward me. He kisses me fiercely as he guides my hand to him. When I wrap my hand around his length, he moans. After only a few tugs, he pushes my hand away and says, "Condom." He hands it to me and I roll it on him. He tugs it down further than I had, in a practiced motion, then he grabs my hands and places them above my head against the door. He devours my lips, kisses my neck, and uses his other hand to pull my body close to him. I feel his entire body against me and I almost explode with my eagerness. He dips a hand down to spread me open, taking my own juices to drag them up and rub along my clit.

"Oh! My! Fucking God!" I almost scream as I feel my body work itself up. I have never had multiples but with this man, I could only hope.

He slips a finger into me for a few strokes. Then he adds

more, stretching me wide. Just when I think I'm about to go over the edge, he stops, and I groan my frustration.

"Not yet, beautiful. I want it to be with me." With one quick motion, I feel him lifting me at the waist and placing me on his thick length. My legs naturally close around his waist and my back leans against the door behind us.

"Samantha," he growls as he slowly pulls out and reenters me, giving me time to adjust between each thrust. "God! You feel amazing!"

After I've completely adjusted, I urge him to pick up the pace. "Faster…" I moan my needs as I grasp his body tighter with my legs and clench down with my inner muscles. He grasps my hips with both hands. So hard and controlling, I know I will see bruises in the morning. *But. I. Don't care!* He pistons in and out of me and I lose myself completely. Being with Enzo is complete and utter bliss. He reads me like a book and has a secret code to get me to detonate in record-breaking time.

As the tingles form at the base of my spine, I let him know. "I'm close. So close, Enzo," I draw out his name as he ratchets up his pace even further. Suddenly, I feel one of his hands loosen his grasp on my hip and slide under my ass. His fingers slide along my backside and suddenly, I feel pressure in a place I've never felt before. He doesn't enter but massages it, putting pressure on me. It's an unbelievable sensation and once I get past the unique feeling, I find myself barreling over the edge into the most explosive orgasm of my life.

I hold on for dear life as Enzo continues until he reaches his release only moments behind me, with a long thrust and a loud groan. His release only spurs me on and I feel for the first time in my life what it's like to experience true multiple orgasms. *And I thought the last one was the best! Holy fucking hell! This man is a god! I have only read about this in books, never actually experienced it. What else have I been missing out on?*

For a long while, he holds me in place against the door. He rests his forehead against mine and stares into my eyes. When our breathing returns to normal, a lopsided smile appears on his face. Even after the out of this world experience I have just had, when his dimple appears, my insides clench, causing us both to groan.

"Samantha," he whispers. "I don't know what you think you've been missing out on, but I guarantee I'm willing to help you find it."

I can't help but roll my eyes. "Once again, I can't believe I said that out loud. But I've never experienced anything like this in my life." I might as well own this.

"Me neither, beautiful. Me neither," Enzo mumbles as he kisses my lips softly again. After a few minutes, he says, "Um… I need to take care of this." He points down at our joined bodies. I can feel him hardening again and I grin in surprise.

"Already? Holy shit! You're a god," I mumble.

"No… just Enzo." He grins impishly, but his face morphs into seriousness. "I'm sorry, Sam, I need to change the condom." He squeezes me tightly as he embraces my body once more. Then he lifts me off him and I feel a sudden loss.

"The bathroom's right there." I point to the door down the hallway.

"I'll be right out," he says as he takes off the condom to tie it.

While he's in there, I quickly gather our clothes, placing them in a pile. I'm about done when he reenters the hallway. "You didn't have to do that." He gestures to the pile of clothes in my hands.

I shrug. What can I say? Old habits die hard.

When I finally get a look at him in all his beauty, I almost have to pick my jaw up off the floor. He's utter perfection. His body is ready for me again and just the thought of it makes my mouth water. "Upstairs?" I gesture.

"Show me the way, Samantha," he growls as he picks me up and throws me over his shoulder.

"I can walk, Enzo!" I pound on his back, until I get a glimpse of his glorious ass flexing as he climbs the stairs and all the fight in me dissolves. I can't help myself when I reach down and slap his ass.

"Hey, now!" Enzo warns.

"Oops, Sorry!" I laugh. Who the hell am I? I haven't ever smacked anyone in my entire life. "I couldn't help it." As I glance at his ass once again, I find myself reaching to cup his scrumptious cheek in my hand. "I've never been a butt girl before." I chuckle loudly at my realization.

"Oh, Samantha. What am I going to do with you?" Enzo chuckles as we enter my room and he sets me in the middle of my bed.

AS I STRETCH and open my eyes, I find my body is stiff and sore in places I'd forgotten existed. Flashbacks from the night before cause a blush to creep over my body. I can't help but sigh as I remember each lick, touch, or moment of intense pleasure Enzo gave me last night. Just the thought of the things we did makes me want him all over again. *But there is no way I can go again.* I'm going to be lucky if I can walk. I feel an arm snake around my waist which pulls me back against his hard length. *Hello, Hardness. Good morning to you, too.*

"Good Morning, beautiful," Enzo's deep sleepy voice whispers in my ear.

"Morning," I hoarsely whisper. I roll over and I'm met with the greenest eyes I've ever seen. His now reddish-blond scruff is sexily displayed across his jawline. His dimple makes an appearance and I forget any coherent thought I was about to say.

His hand glides from my hip up to cup my face. "Sleep well?"

"Yes," I whisper, nodding my head.

"What do you have planned today? Wanna get some breakfast?"

"That would be great. I'd offer to cook... but that's not an option," I tease as my hand reaches for his chest.

"What are your plans for later today?" Enzo's deliciously sexy morning voice asks.

I need to think for a moment. He's all too consuming. I'd love nothing more than to stay right here all day. I can't even imagine the last time I've had a night as spectacular as this. But reality must rear its ugly head.

Before I can get my train of thought clear in my head, Enzo's mouth is on my bottom lip. His teeth pull my lip free from the confinement of my teeth as he growls, "I've been waiting all night to do that."

Confused, I pull away and look at him. *Not that I mind his teeth on me but what in the world is he talking about?"* I raise an eyebrow at him, awaiting an answer to my unasked question.

He huskily whispers, "You pull in your lip when you're in deep thought. I've been wanting to release it with my teeth since last night."

I purposely roll my lip into my teeth and pretend to contemplate something. But I'm not very successful because before I know it, he has my lip captured with his teeth once again. But this time, he parts my mouth and quickly devours me with a kiss. He rolls me onto my back and straddles me in an instant. He kisses me as he makes his way down my body. Before he has a chance to explore me too far with his hands, I break the kiss and moan. As much as I want everything this man has to offer, I can't have him again. *I may never walk again properly as it is.* I groan in utter dissatisfaction, "Ugh... Enzo, I want nothing more than to continue this train of thought... but I do want to be able to walk again. Last night was more than I've had in the last five years combined." I give him an impish grin before adding, "Please take mercy."

A satisfied expression crosses his features. He bends down and kisses his way up my body. When he gets to my ear, he pulls lightly on my lower lobe with his teeth. Then he whispers sexily in my ear, "I'm sorry you're hurting, beautiful.

I'll make it up to you." He slowly extracts himself from me. I cry out, not wanting him to leave. "Do you have a tub in that bathroom of yours?" he asks, standing at the edge of my bed completely naked, distracting me from his question.

I stare. I can't help it. I feel my mouth part and jaw drop. The next thing I know, I see him smirk and cover himself. *Wait! Don't move. Let me enjoy the view.*

"Samantha," he chastises. "You can enjoy the view all you want, but let's get you into the tub first."

I quickly close my mouth and squeeze my eyes shut. I cover my face with one hand as I pull the sheet up with the other, hoping I can disappear into the bed.

Before I know it, the sheet is ripped back from me. Strong hands approach me from the side and snake under my back and knees. The air swooshes around me and I smell the heavenly scent of Enzo before my body collides with his chest. I peek one eye open to see what he's doing, and he lets out a deep belly laugh, shaking my entire body. "No reason to be embarrassed," he rumbles. "Let's get you into a warm bath."

He sets me on the floor and reaches for the faucet. As soon as I hear the water, I realize I have other business to attend to. *I have had three kids after all.* "Um... Enzo. Do you mind giving me a moment?" I look up, not wanting to ruin the moment, but I also don't want to do a potty-dance, like a three-year-old. "You can come back in a moment." I glance at the toilet longingly before looking at him for his response.

His wide smile slays me with his dimple. "No problem. Take all the time you need." Without another word, he leaves the bathroom, shutting the door. *God Bless This Man.*

It takes us a lot longer to get ready than I would on my own. It doesn't help that Enzo joins me in the bathtub. Once he gets me all relaxed, he somehow manages to rile me up. Then, of course I must devour every part of him. *And I mean every part.* He tastes just as delicious as I imagine he would. I have no freaking clue as to when I last felt so bold or sensual. Even with nearly twenty years of marriage, I've never experienced anything like this. I know he'll be leaving soon and this will end in disaster. But for once, I'm going to enjoy this moment, as if I may never get it again. *Hell, I don't recall ever having it before. This man is one of a kind, a temptation like no other and I have no idea how long this will last.*

13

ENZO

AS WE SIT down at a local diner for breakfast, I can't help but feel relieved when Samantha orders a full meal. Not that I make a habit of getting breakfast with many women, but I absolutely hate it when they order only yogurt or fruit. That's like ordering only a salad for dinner. I want a woman who eats, not pretends she's a rabbit. How in the hell will they survive in life on only tidbits of food? I maintain an active lifestyle. I must eat to sustain my energy. Who wants someone who just stares at me while I eat during a meal, as they move the food around their plate, but never really eat it?

After chewing a bite of my buttermilk pancakes, I ask, "So what are your plans for the rest of the day?" I wasn't going to invite anyone to that barbeque this afternoon, but I don't really want my time to end with Samantha.

"Ummm..." She pulls that fucking lip into her mouth as she thinks. "I have Declan's soccer game at three and that's about it, why?"

Well, the barbeque is out. Maybe I'll be able to pull a plan out of my ass and get to see her in that sexy dress again. I still can't believe I bought her that dress. It's not like I care about the money. It's more about the fact I have never, in my life, done that for anyone. I don't think I've even taken my sister shopping. Though if she needed one, I would gladly buy her a dress. *Who the hell buys a woman he just met a dress, anyway?!?!* I do, apparently.

"What do you say to going out later this evening?" I suggest as I fork some hash browns into my mouth, trying to be nonchalant.

"I might be up for that," she coyly states as she cocks her head to the side, showing me that sass I enjoy so much.

"I'll make sure the occasion will suit your new dress." I place my hand on my chin, acting as if I'm contemplating world peace. I really need to move boots, if I'm going to find anywhere decent to take her this evening. Maybe one of my buddies who owns an upscale restaurant will help me out. Shit. I didn't bring home any dress clothes. I guess shopping will also be on my list of things to do today.

Samantha's eyes light up with delight and a slight blush spreads over her. I can't help but be in complete awe of the woman before me. If this is all it takes to cause that look, it seems I will be investing in multiple new shirts today. "Would you be available by six?"

"Yes, I should be home before five," she states, then continues to eat a piece of bacon that she had been holding. "It won't take me too long to get ready."

BY THE TIME I drop Samantha off, it's almost noon. I know I won't have much time, so I google to find what I'm looking for and head straight there. It's a big and tall store, specializing in suits with an on-site tailor. I know they will have what I need, and I can get in and out without much fuss. Besides, if they need to make any alterations, I can always come back to pick it up later this afternoon.

Thankfully, there is a salesman who is quickly able to measure me and help me find an entire suit that fits within about thirty minutes. Their tailor is available and tells me it should be ready to pick up within a few hours. I even managed to pick up a few shirts in different colors and a new pair of shoes that looked sharp but are still comfortable. My usual wardrobe is entirely function over fashion, old habits die hard. But knowing how Samantha will look in her new dress tonight, I need to step up my fashion game for our date.

I don't even hesitate as I swipe my card at the cashier. I'm pleased by the little amount of time I had to spend shopping. Besides, what do I really spend my money on? What's the use in having it if I never get the chance to spend it? I may not wear this suit often, possibly never again, but at least I'll have it if it's needed. Not only that, Samantha deserves a nice night out.

I glance at my watch and realize I still have plenty of time to pick something up for the barbeque on the way to Riggs' home. I should still make it there on time, too. For someone who avoids shopping like the plague, at least I'm efficient.

As I sit at a red light on my way to the barbeque, I pull up a buddy of mine from my list of contacts, who owns a prestigious nightclub in Portland. I did him a solid a few years back while we were on a mission. I'm hoping he can do one for me in return. I know there's always a waiting list for people to get a table at his restaurant, but maybe he'll give me a break and fit us in tonight. If not, I'm sure I can find something else. My main mission is seeing Samantha in the gorgeous green dress. The best part might also be the fact I will get to see her out of it, too.

Fuck! Now I'm thinking about Samantha's sexy curves and everything else about her.

Thankfully, before I'm too far out of control, I'm interrupted by Rowan's gruff voice. "Holy fuck! Has the world come to an end? Is this really Harps?" Before I can say anything, he laughs as he continues, "To what do I owe the pleasure?"

I can't help but grin as I greet him, "Hey, Ro! What's up, man?"

"Not much, just about to head to work."

"About that..." I start, but then realize I'm not sure how much I should divulge.

"Yes?" he drawls out and I can hear his sarcasm drip through the phone.

I might as well just get to the point. "Look, man, is there any way I could score a table at your place tonight? I know it's incredibly short notice..."

Before I can say more, he interrupts with, "I could

probably work it out... for how many?" By the end, I can hear the humor in his voice.

"Just two," I say nonchalantly.

"Hmmm... I see."

"You see what?" I ask, not getting what he's hinting about.

"Well, since you willingly ask for favors, I take it there must be someone special," he induces, as if I've been holding out on precious intel.

I can't spend years working with someone and not know his tells. Sleeping in less than desirable conditions for days on end will do that. I can play this two ways. I can feed him a line of BS, or I can be straight with him. Not being one to put up with much shit, I keep it simple. "Yeah. I have. I want to take her to a nice place like yours. Do you think you can make it happen?"

"Only if I get to meet her," he hedges. "Your game is usually at the local dive bar, so I'm interested in who you've met. Especially since I know you haven't been stateside for a while."

"Hey now," I defend myself. "I don't usually go to dive bars."

Rowan lets out a belly laugh. "Relax. I know. I was saying that to get your goat!" He takes a deep breath. "Seriously, if you want a table, it's yours. I'll put your name on the list with the hostess. Text me when you're on your way and I'll make sure a table is ready for you."

"Thanks, man. I appreciate it."

We spend a few more minutes catching up before disconnecting. He tells me how business is doing, and I tell him about my leave, as well as the decision that lays ahead of me. He doesn't ask about Samantha, but I'm sure he's waiting on that for tonight. Knowing Rowan, it will just be a matter of time.

We disconnect just as I get to Riggs' house. The driveway is long and filled with vehicles. Most are some form of 4x4 or SUV. Upon further inspection, they're also nondescript, but high end all the same. I find a place to park, ensuring I won't get blocked in. There's no way I'm going to be late to pick up my suit or Samantha. Approaching the house, I hear most of the noise coming from around back and the side fence is open, so I head in that direction.

Carson is the first to greet me, "Harps! Glad you made it."

He lifts the hand he's holding a beer within greeting, as he breaks from the small crowd he was talking with to meet me in person. When he gets closer, he shakes my hand with one arm, pulling me closer to pat me on the back with the arm he's holding his beer with. "Nice to see you, Cars!"

"Same here, Harps! Same here." Carson steps away and points in the direction of the food tables. "Are you hungry? There's plenty of food over there."

Motioning to the bag I'm carrying. "Thanks. I'll just add this to it."

He follows me to the table. "So how have you been, Harps?" In a lower tone, he asks, "Make any decisions?"

"Not yet. I like the thought of being near Portland though." Once again, a flash of Samantha's beautiful face comes to mind. "I'm meeting with the CO at the Air National Guard later this week."

"Are you sure you want to switch over?" Carson asks, giving me a knowing look. He and I both know I wouldn't be doing what I am currently, and it'll affect my years of service, but I'd be guaranteed to be stationed here in Portland. More than likely, I'm going to take Riggs up on his offer, but I'm not making any decisions yet.

Carson introduces me to many of the people I'd be working with. Each welcome me eagerly and have nothing but good things to say about working on Riggs' team. I'm pleased to discover I know most of them already. I know I'd be a good fit. I just don't know if I'm officially ready to retire from the Air Force altogether.

Riggs and his wife, Stella who also happens to work for him, make quite an impression on me. He's exactly like I expect, what you see is what you get. But he has a soft side for his firecracker of a wife. It's evident as the day is long that he loves her above all else. She may be petite, but I've no doubt that woman can pack a punch. She's quick as a whip, and if you're ever on her bad side, I'm sure her tongue lashing would be impressive. She's in no way a bitch. The woman has a heart of gold, but I can tell she knows her shit and won't be afraid to put you in your place. She's such a spitfire. It's pure entertainment watching her keep Riggs on his toes. That itself is a sight to behold. I thought the man was unflappable. Stella is true to her stereotype of being a redhead. But from what I gather from the guys around here, it's best to never mention that fact to her face. Together, they're quite the dynamic duo. Both badasses of their own right, but each bending just slightly to fit each other perfectly. It would be an honor to work with them.

I keep an eye on my watch as I enjoy the gathering of what could become my closest friends. These are good people. Even if I don't take the job with Riggs, I'm sure they'll be people I see often. I feel right at home as I relax and enjoy my afternoon.

AS I WALK into Ma's kitchen that afternoon after picking up my suit, I'm greeted with her warm hug. There's never a loss of affection growing up in our house. Ma may be a petite woman, *well, almost anyone is compared to me,* but she knew how to keep us in line.

"So, what've you been up to, love?" she says as she kisses me on the cheek I've lowered toward her. I take a seat on the barstool next to the counter she's working at. The kitchen smells delicious.

"I'm just stopping by to check in before I head back out this evening."

Eyeing the garment bag I've hung on the back of the stool next to me, she gives me a knowing grin. "And I suppose that," she says, gesturing to the bag, "has something to do with the fact I won't see you until tomorrow, either?"

I'm thirty-seven years old. I've lived on my own for the better part of the last twenty years. Traveled all over the world. I'm in the Air Force for crying out loud, but she can make me feel sixteen all over again.

Never being one to lie, I say, "More than likely."

The knowing twinkle in her eye pierces my heart. Ma is the best mom one could ever ask for. "So, you've found someone special." She doesn't ask. It's said like a fact. Which I guess she's right. The woman has always had her Spidey senses from the time I could walk.

I hesitate for a moment, trying to figure out what to say. Samantha is special, there's no doubt about it. But I've just met the woman a few days ago. From the glimmer of hope in Ma's eye, I don't want to squash it if it doesn't work out, so I go with the truth. "It's still very new."

"Lorenzo Dean Harper, you can pull your BS with your buddies. But I know you, remember? So, spill it. Who is she?" And there it is, the BS radar that could have grown men groveling on their knees. I could be held prisoner by hostiles and they couldn't get the truth from me, but one raised eyebrow from Ma... *SHIT, I knew better.*

I cough and run a hand through my hair, taking a moment to look any direction but at her. Never being one to cower, I finally come to my senses and nod. "Yeah. There is someone, Ma. I just met her, so don't get your hopes up. I wasn't lying when I said it's new."

"But she has you buying a suit..." There it is. That cocked eyebrow reaching further away from her hazel eye. The woman should have been an insurgent interrogator. There would be no world secrets with her seeking the truth. She missed her calling in life.

I can't help the lopsided grin that takes over my face. I shake my head as memories of Samantha come flooding back to me. I try to keep as nonchalant as I can, but that would almost be as effective as raking leaves in a hurricane, around my mom. I stick with simple. With her, less is always more.

"Apparently..." I shrug dismissively.

"Correct me if I'm wrong, but the last time you actually bought a suit to go out with a woman was in high school, right?" She taps her finger on her chin as if she's trying to remember for herself when the last time was.

Hell, I don't even remember. She might be right.

"Ma, it's not like I've never bought a suit since then," I say in my defense. "It's not that big of a deal."

But of course, it is. I usually just wear my dress uniform for special occasions. Not that I purposely choose to wear that often either. Only when I'm forced to or strongly encouraged is my usual rule of thumb.

Ma interrupts my thoughts, "Enzo, I really can't remember you wearing anything but your dress uniform other than at your sister and brother's weddings," she states, not making accusations, just recalling memories.

A slight chuckle escapes. "You're right, Ma, me neither. But I had to class it up a little to go with her dress." Damn, what a dress it is, too.

And then I see my mistake. Simple as can be... but epic at the same time. I just opened another can of worms that my mom won't let rest until I give her the entire scoop. Yep! There it is... the eyebrow. She doesn't even need to talk. It's like she has subliminal powers to make me tell all. Dammit to hell.

Before I know it, I tell her all about my date with Samantha last night. Well, the very G-rated version. She can draw her own conclusions as to where I've been all night. She may have powers for being "all knowing," but there are some things I just don't share with my mother, not that I'd share them with anyone else, for that matter.

Ma doesn't seem to get overly excited or really say much for that matter. She just listens as I tell her about taking Samantha up the Gorge to have dinner. She chuckles when I tell her about finding a dress. I do get another brow raised when I mention that I paid for the dress, but luckily, she doesn't press me about it. She knows as well as I do that this entire situation is very uncharacteristic of me. Since Vanessa, the type of girls I've dated in the past usually didn't hold my attention past the first date, if you can even call some that. I'm sure Ma's given up hope of me ever settling down, figuring that ship had long since sailed.

Eventually, I excuse myself to get ready for my date with Samantha. The word "date" sounds weird to think about. *But what else would you call it?* Usually, I just casually hang out or meet up at a restaurant. Not since high school have I gone to this much trouble. But the thought of Samantha's gorgeous smile reminds me there is nothing I wouldn't do to see it again.

By the time I return downstairs, Pops is still not home and Ma's waiting in the family room reading a book. I didn't exactly divulge the fact Samantha is dad's client. I'll cross that bridge when I get there. He being gone makes it easier to keep that bit of information to myself for a while. *This is still very new.*

As soon as I walk in the room, Ma lets out a slight gasp. "My, don't you look handsome!" A knowing smile spreads across her face as she stands up to inspect me further, making me feel as if I'm back in high school going to prom.

"Thanks, Ma," I say as I bend down to kiss her goodbye. "I'll see you later."

Traffic is light, and I get to Samantha's house with plenty of time to spare. I glance at my watch and see it's five thirty. It's a habit, being early is considered on time, being on time is considered late in my book. Years of being in the Air Force will do that to you. I even stopped by a flower shop on my way here to pick up a bouquet of dahlias for her since she mentioned they're her favorite. It doesn't hurt that they're in full bloom this time of year. I knock on the door to her house, but there's no answer. Her car's in the driveway, so I know she's here. Maybe she's in the shower. I take a seat on the bench next to her door and send her a text, letting her know I'm here.

14

SAMANTHA

FROM THE TIME Enzo dropped me off, I've been running non-stop. As much as I've wanted to bask in the delicious memories of last night, I force myself to stay busy. I throw in some laundry and shower again. This time, I take extra care with the razor and blow-dry my hair so it'll be easy to style when I return from Declan's game. I also flat iron it, knowing I won't have much time later. Not wanting to look too done up, I keep things casual for the game. Before leaving, I switch over a load of laundry to the dryer and pack some extra snacks for Frankie and Maddie during the game.

I rush to the field, armed with my snacks and chair to watch the game. I make it there before Devin and the kids, so I choose a spot on the sideline to take a moment and relax. To pass the time, I pull out my e-reader to keep my thoughts occupied. *But that, of course, is an Epic FAIL!* Enzo's been on my mind since the moment he left and I'm more than eager to see him again this evening. Eventually, I'm able to get into the manuscript I'm reviewing for a chapter or two before I'm nearly knocked over by Frankie and her infamous hugs.

She sneak attacks me from behind, as she screams into my ear, "Mama, I've missed you! Is the kitchen done yet?"

"Not yet, Sweet Pea," I say as I pull her around to sit on my lap for another squeeze. "I've missed you, too." We sit like this as she tells me about her morning with Devin and her siblings.

Just as she's in the middle of some story about eating the biggest pancakes ever, Devin, Aubrey, and Maddie come to sit down beside us. I give them a nod in greeting, as I do my best to keep up with Frankie's explanation of her cooking breakfast.

I notice Maddie deliberately sits next to me while Devin and Aubrey set up their chairs on the other side of her. Declan is with his team warming up for the game. Maddie seems distracted by someone she's texting, but overall, she looks content. *Just another day at the soccer fields for us.*

Frankie's still talking a mile a minute, but suddenly I hear, "...so then Aubrey said I could have the next one. Mom, it was almost bigger than my plate..."

Wait. What? Aubrey was there for breakfast? I try not to let my reaction show. *I guess things are more serious with her than I expected. I'm not sure how I feel about this. When did Devin start having sleepovers?* But then my mind goes to my evening last night. Memories of Enzo and his delicious body replay on a loop. Suddenly, I'm not the least bit worried about Devin because my mind is filled with all thoughts of Enzo.

After a few more glorious memories flashing through my mind, I take a good look at my kids. They each really look okay. *Well, no different than normal.* They seem to be fine with what's going on between Aubrey and their dad, so I guess I could be, too. *Besides, it's not like I want him back. That ship has sailed, caught on fire, and sunk.* I think for the first time ever, I'm really not jealous of Devin and his relationship. *Huh, that's an interesting thought.*

When Frankie finishes telling how syrup got everywhere, and Devin made her take a shower, I take a moment to check in further with Maddie. "Hey, Mads, how are you?"

She looks up from her phone and smiles. Genuinely smiles. "I'm good, Mom."

I can't help but tease her, "So... what's got you into such a good mood?" I gesture at the phone in her hand.

A slight blush crosses her face. *There must be a boy involved. She never blushes like this.* "Well, you know I'm going to the dance this Friday..."

"Yes. I remember you telling me about it." I wait for her to go on. I've found it's usually best to wait for her to divulge information. I get a lot further with her if she thinks it's her idea to share.

"Well, at first, I was just going with a bunch of friends. But then Soren Silva, you know the junior I told you about. The one that plays lacrosse... well, he asked me to be his date instead."

A date. My daughter wants to go on a date. Okay. I knew this time would come, but it's still hard to let her grow up. She's still my baby. We told her she could go to dances, but dates? Well, I knew it would happen eventually... just hoped it'd be later.

I try to be as nonchalant as I can when I respond, not to give my thoughts away. "So, what did you tell him?"

She sheepishly looks at me, then glances at Devin. "Um, I told him I'd have to ask my parents. I'm talking to you first, because well, you know how Dad can be. If you don't think it's a good idea, there's no reason in even telling him." She starts to speed-talk by this point. "So, what do you say, Mom, can I go? Can I tell him yes?" By now, she's nearly bouncing in her seat.

"How exactly would you be getting there?" I ask, trying to stall for time. I need more information before I can say yes. I know I started dating at her age, but it feels different being on this side of the scenario.

She suddenly looks even more nervous than before. "Um, he's had his license for about a year. He makes the honor roll every term and he's never been in an accident. I know, I asked. I even asked his brother to check." She still has a pleading look on her face.

"That's nice, honey. But I'd at least have to meet him before I make a decision."

"Mooommmm! That's so not fair," she protests, but Devin cuts her off.

"What's not fair?" He raises an eyebrow in question to me.

I, in turn, look pointedly at Maddie. I won't lose her trust by spilling the beans to her dad. She can tell him if she really wants to go on this date, though I'm sure he won't make it easy on her.

I can't help but be proud of her when I see her turn toward him, sit up taller, and say, "I was asked to go to the dance on Friday, by Soren Silva. I'm asking Mom if I can go."

Hmmm... this boy must be someone worthy if she's telling Devin so openly about it.

Devin's eyes go a little wider, but that's the only sign he shows of being unprepared for our conversation. "And... what did your mom say?" He glances in my direction.

Maddie lets out a little sigh. "She said she has to meet him first."

Knowing Devin, I can tell he's holding back a smile as he keeps the solemn look on his face. "Well, that's not unreasonable, Mads. I would like to meet him, too."

"Daddy..." She puts her hands over her face as if she's suddenly embarrassed. *I don't blame her really.* Devin's been putting the fear of God in her ever since she looked like she might notice boys. She knows he'll do something to completely embarrass her, or at least he's been threatening to do so, for as long as I can remember. She also knows I won't let him get away with too much, *but a parent has rights.*

Attempting to put her out of her misery, I state, "How about we invite him out to dinner one day earlier in the week? Then we can meet him and not have it be a big deal when he picks you up for the dance."

"Mom, since his practice usually gets done around mine, do you think we could make it less formal and just let me introduce you when you pick me up?" She gives me a pleading look.

I look to Devin since we're trying to co-parent the best we can. He gives me a slight nod. "Sure thing, sweetheart. Why don't you have him plan to meet us Tuesday evening after practice? Then I'll take you dress shopping if all goes well."

She hops out of her chair to give me a hug. "Thanks, Mom, you're the best."

Not letting her get away with anything, Devin states boldly, "I still reserve my right to meet him, too. *Before* your date. I'll be there when he picks you up."

I must hold in the chuckle that wants to escape. *Dad's will be dads!*

"I'll be there, too!" Frankie chirps in, not wanting to be left out, making us all laugh.

Thankfully, for Maddie's sake, Declan's game is about to start, so our attention is soon diverted from her to the game. The team they're playing is a tough one. The score has stayed at zero for both sides for quite some time. Finally, Declan assists in the first goal, and the crowd goes wild! Sure enough, at one point in the game, he does that new maneuver where he flips as he throws the ball in, giving me a near heart attack. *But at least it looks cool, right? Don't worry, poor mom's over here having palpitations.*

After the game, I wait to congratulate Declan on his win. As his team huddles afterward for a talk with their coach, the sidelines pack up the gear they brought to make room for the next game. I stay near Devin, Aubrey, and the girls. Aubrey and I make small talk while we wait. It still feels a little forced, but it's a lot easier than last time. I guess the shock factor is over. Devin does his best to remain respectful to each of us and breaks in to contribute to our conversation.

Within a few minutes, Declan runs over. He high-fives or fist bumps his sisters, Aubrey, and his dad before reaching me. I'm lucky, I get a hug. "Great game, Dec! I'm so proud of you," I say as I squeeze him tighter.

"Thanks, Mom!" His smile stretches clear across his face and his arms remain wrapped around me for a while longer. Then he looks up mischievously. "So, did you catch that new maneuver I learned?"

I tickle him on his side as I say, "Yeah, thanks for the near heart attack, Dec. I've always wanted to go to an early grave! If I get gray hair, it's because of you, squirt!"

Declan laughs and tries to pull away, but I'm still quicker. I continue to dig my fingers into his side, tickling him where I know he's weakest. Right under the armpits. *Yep! A mother knows best.*

"Enough... Enough," he pants, still trying to squirm away.

I give him mercy by letting go. "Way to go out there, champ. You're pretty impressive!" I wink to let him know just how proud of him I am. His grin in return is priceless.

We spend the next few minutes talking about his game. I make sure the girls know I'll be picking them up after school on Monday since Devin usually picks Declan up for his practice. I still can't believe Maddie's going on her first date. With our spectator gear in tow, we head to the parking lot. Each of the kids gives me one last hug before they get into Devin's car with Aubrey. It's never easy to say goodbye, but with my plans for this evening never being far from my mind, I'm eager to get home all the same.

By the time I get home, it's nearly five o'clock. I know it won't take me too long to get ready, but I still want to look my best for Enzo. *When was the last time I've had the opportunity to put this much effort into a date?* Knowing how the night will end, I opt for taking another quick shower, taking care to pull my hair up, so it won't get wet. That was the point of using my flat iron earlier.

Before getting dressed, I take the time to apply my makeup and put the final touches on my hair. By the time I'm ready to exit my bathroom, I check my phone to see the time. Crap, he's here already. I send Enzo a quick text to give him the combination that unlocks our door, telling him to wait inside for me.

I rush out to my room to retrieve the dress out of the bag. I'd forgotten to hang it up last night. Thankfully, the material isn't the kind that wrinkles easily. I can't help but feel flushed when I recall how preoccupied I'd been when we arrived. *Though, I wouldn't have stopped to hang the dress up for a million bucks.*

I take the bag to my bed and pull out the dress, ready to inspect for tags needing to be removed. As the dress is freed from the bag, a small wrapped cluster of tissue falls to my bed. Curiosity has me forgetting the tags for a moment to see what this could be. As I grasp the tissue to pick it up, I feel there's something in it. It's lightweight but has a square shape, like a cardboard tag of some sort.

As I take care to unwrap it, I'm shocked to find a matching necklace and earrings to my dress. I know I didn't pick these out. This is all Enzo. My heart melts a little. These are just what I would've picked out to go with it. The man has good taste. *This must be too good to be real, right? What man picks out accessories? How in the hell has he stayed single for so long?!?!*

Suddenly, I'm in a hurry to see Enzo. I quickly put on the dress and earrings, *after removing the tags, of course.* I grab a pair of my favorite black heels as I clutch the necklace in my hand. *I think I'll ask for his assistance in putting this on, so I can get to him quicker.*

As I quickly descend the stairs, I notice Enzo is pacing at the bottom. There's a bouquet of dahlias on the sideboard that wasn't there before. I can't see him entirely, just his backside. But when he turns as I approach, I'm completely awestruck.

OMG! Enzo is pure perfection in his stunningly gorgeous black suit and light-green shirt, sans tie. It's cut to precision. It lays perfectly across his broad shoulders, forming the perfect inverted triangle. His muscular form is sexier than I've ever seen. Even the models I use for covers have nothing on him. If I wasn't eager to find out what he has planned for me this evening, I'd say to hell with it and drag him upstairs.

"Hey, beautiful," his sexy voice calls to me. "You look exquisite. My memories of you in that dress didn't do you justice."

I quickly close the distance between us and meet him at the bottom of the stairs, as I reply, "You're not so bad yourself, handsome."

He grins shyly, and that delicious dimple makes an appearance, making his sexy smile reach his potent green eyes. *Yep, this is the perfect combination to make a grown woman go weak in the knees and lose all train of thought. God, what Enzo does to me is unbelievable.*

Remembering I still have the necklace in my hand, I hold it up and ask, "Can you help with this?" I force myself to turn away from him, lifting my hair off my back to keep it out of the way.

Before I know it, I'm enveloped with the scent that's entirely Enzo. His strong, muscular arms, hidden behind that magnificent suit come around, placing the necklace near my collarbone before clasping it in the back. As soon as he's done, he embraces me with those welcoming arms while snuggling into my neck. His breath on my skin makes me tingle in all the right places. He kisses me once at the base of my neck, then places his hands on my hips to turn me to face him.

"Hi," I whisper, as I'm still caught in his trance.

"Hi yourself, beautiful. Are you ready?" He matches in a whisper.

"Just let me get my coat and purse, and we'll be on our way."

Reluctantly, he lets me go and I walk to the hallway to get my burgundy knee-length trench coat and my purse. It's still warm, *or at least I feel warm,* so I opt to just carry it. When I turn around, I see Enzo's outstretched hand waiting for mine. I eagerly take his as we walk out the door. I can't wait to see what he has planned for this evening. With the way he looks in that suit, it could be a food cart downtown and I'd be completely satisfied just to be in his presence.

As we drive over the Fremont bridge, I take in the cityscape and all that is Portland. Dusk is nearing on this magnificent, clear, fall evening. The twinkling of lights from below never fail to entrance me. As we take an exit, Enzo drives us further into downtown. Before I know it, we're in a parking garage and he's leading me out onto one of the busy streets.

Figuring we're about to go to one of the street-level restaurants, I readily follow his lead. I'm a little surprised when we enter a lobby to one of the many high-rise buildings lining the streets. I eye him skeptically when we enter the elevator and he presses the thirty-sixth floor. A group of people who are dressed up like us also enter the elevator, so I don't get the chance to ask Enzo what he's up to. He pulls my back flush against his body, as we make room for the crowd. The ride to the top is silent between us since other couples are having conversations around us. My body instantly hums by the nearness of Enzo, though I do my best to ignore it. *We are in public.*

When we reach our floor, I'm surprised to see we've arrived at a waiting area. There's beautiful art hanging on the walls around us, along with a sculpted silver sign hanging above a hostess stand that reads "Allure." The script is done beautifully, leaving me very intrigued as to where Enzo has taken me. We wait our turn to get to the hostess. From what I can tell, there's going to be a substantial wait. But when Enzo gives his name, we're immediately ushered right back to an incredibly dressed table overlooking the Willamette River and the twinkling city of Portland. A gasp involuntarily escapes as I take in this incredible view. I almost forget I'm supposed to be finding my seat. I'm too busy staring out the window at the miraculous view.

Enzo pulls me out of my trance when he steps around me to pull out a chair. He places his hand on the small of my back as he ushers me to my seat. He assists me in scooting back into the table before taking a seat across from me. By the time he sits, I realize my jaw is hanging open as I stare at him in disbelief. The waitress says something, and he replies, but I have no idea what it entails. I'm too lost in thought. Finally, he gets my full attention with a raised eyebrow when he asks, "Problem, Samantha?"

Re-gathering my wits, I blurt out the first thing I can catch from the swirling thoughts in my mind, in a whisper, "Come here often? Isn't there a month-long waiting list for this place?"

Enzo's only response is to grin sheepishly.

I wait for an answer, but my mind reels out of control. *He must have already made reservations here when he knew he was coming home. Just whom did he plan on taking here?*

Before my thoughts get too out of control, he shakes his head. "No, this is my first time actually."

I give him a look that clearly says I'm not buying it. "And..."

He clears his throat, looking around nervously. "I... might know the owner."

Tension I didn't realize I had been holding on to suddenly releases. "Oh."

Well, there goes that theory. What the fuck had I been thinking? And where did that sudden pang of jealousy come from? I seriously had no right to jump to that conclusion. He's given me zero indication there's been anyone else. I guess old habits die hard. He shouldn't have to pay for Devin's sins. *Thank God, I'd managed to keep my filter in place for once.*

When I don't say more, he adds, "Ro and I go way back... I called in a favor."

Before I can say anything, a man in a suit approaches our table. He looks much too classy to merely be a waiter, but he commands my attention just the same when he blatantly states, "Ma'am, what on earth are you doing with this tool?"

"Excuse me?" I blanch, then glance at Enzo who now has his head in his hand, shaking it slightly, looking very embarrassed.

The man stands straighter and clears his throat and with a straight face says, "I said, what are you doing here with this tool? You are the most beautiful woman in this room, and you came here *with him?*" He points at Enzo, who is now rolling back his shoulders as if he's itching for a fight while keeping his hand over his eyes blocking his full reaction from me.

I push back my chair to stand as I quietly hiss, not to draw too much attention, "What business is it of yours whom I come with? The man you just insulted I might add, could kick your ass in a New York minute." I point my finger at his chest and step closer. "He's served our country for the past twenty years, and he's *anything* but a tool!" By the time I finish my rant, I turn my head toward Enzo to find he of all things is nearly rolling out of his chair with silent laughter.

"You're right," the bastard before me states. "She's special." His icy façade melts and he roars with laughter.

Between gasps of air, Enzo coughs out, "I... told you... she was." Enzo stands and is suddenly hugging the man before us. "It's good to see you, Ro!" Then he lowers his voice and says, "I can't believe you just pulled that shit. I thought this was a high-class establishment." Enzo pats him on the back then looks at me, holding out his hand. "Samantha, I'd like you to meet Rowan Evans. We served together before he got out and decided it was time to change in his boots for fancy loafers. Rowan, this is Samantha O'Reilly."

Rowan doesn't give me a chance to say anything before he pulls me into a hug and whispers, "Keep this one on his toes. He deserves it." I can't help but laugh and feel more at ease.

"I'll keep that in mind," I reply as he releases me and gestures for me to return to my seat.

"Seriously, it's good to meet you," Rowan says apologetically as he grabs a chair from a nearby table to join us. "I was just messing around with Harps. That man can prank like the best of them. It's good to finally get one over on him. I didn't mean for the joke to be on you, too. Sorry."

I glance at Enzo and the gleam in his eye is infectious. I can't help but let my guard down and enjoy the moment. Man, I was really riled up. I don't know what came over me. It's not like Enzo couldn't defend himself. *He's six-foot-six for crying out loud.* But that was a good prank... he got me good. I decide to let Rowan off the hook. "It's all good."

"So where did you kids meet?" Rowan finally asks.

"We're not here to play twenty questions, Ro. Thanks again for getting us a table tonight. I appreciate it."

"Yes, thank you," I add.

"Any time. I had to meet the woman who turned this sorry

bastard's head enough to get him to call in favors." He shakes his head in disbelief. "And after you handled that stunt I just pulled, I know you're worth it."

I can't help but blush. I really was about to cause a scene. I don't get to say anything before Enzo reaches for my hand across the table. "She totally is, man. She totally is."

Rowan stands and places the chair back at the table next to us. "Well, I put your name on the list upstairs at the club as well. Feel free after you leave here to go up and use a table in the VIP section. Dance the night away and enjoy!"

Enzo once again stands and reaches his hand out to Rowan. "Thanks again, man. I really appreciate it." He dubiously looks at me and states, "You might just get me out on the dance floor yet, Ro. We'll see..."

After Rowan excuses himself to go check on something on the other side of the restaurant, our waitress soon comes over to tell us the daily special as well as hand us our menus. We're quiet for a few minutes while we look over the selection. Everything looks amazing and I can't help but grin as I take in the entire ambiance of the restaurant. Enzo really did well in choosing this place. It's spectacular.

After the waitress comes back to take our orders, Enzo breaks the silence with, "You handled him like a champ, Sam. I can't believe he tried to pull that on you." We both laugh at the memory, but Enzo grips my hand in his before continuing, "You really are an amazing woman. Thanks again for coming out with me."

"Enzo, I still can't believe you pulled this off with so little notice. Though I must warn you, I haven't danced outside my house in years. I might not be the best of partners, but I'd love to check the club out if you're willing. I don't think I've been to a club since college." I bite my lower lip as I try to recall the last time I've danced, other than at a wedding.

"Then we'll check it out." Enzo shrugs as he squeezes my hand. "I might have been known to throw down a move or two back in the day."

"Bring it on, Enzo. Bring it on," I tease.

AFTER WE FINISH our dinner and even have dessert, we end up going to the club upstairs. As we enter the wide hallway from the elevator, I realize the club is decorated as well as the restaurant below us. Art hangs as well on the rich blue walls that lead to a room at the other end. Music you can dance to greets us, the bass pulsing like a heartbeat. As we make our way into a large room, I take in the space around me. The bar stretches across one entire wall, with several stations set up for multiple bartenders. It has modern gray-stone masonry as the entire wall behind it. There are tiered shelves behind the fogged-glass bar that has blue backlighting. Those shelves must be filled with every type of alcohol imaginable. The countertop of the bar itself is reflective and every color imaginable reflects from it. There's an obvious VIP section, with plush seating and tables, up the stairs with an incredible view of the enormous dance floor. Patrons are strewn all throughout, and everyone seems to be enjoying themselves. A deejay is set up in one corner and a stage in the other, filled with musicians.

Enzo guides me to what must be the VIP section. He gives his name to the gorgeous woman in her twenties standing at the podium before the section and she escorts us to a large lounge chair with a table in front of it. Before she leaves, she takes our drink orders as well. I order a lemon drop and Enzo orders a beer of some type. He slides down next to me and places his arm around my back as we wait for our drinks. For a few moments, we take in the atmosphere around us.

Finally, Enzo breaks the silence, "Well... what do you think?"

"This place is incredible. I thought I'd feel old and out of place, but I don't. People of all ages are out enjoying their evening." It's a relief to know this. I thought a club would mean it was for barely twenty-one year olds at a rave or something. I guess since this place is more upscale, everyone of all ages comes here to enjoy the evening.

Enzo chuckles in my ear. "Samantha, you're not old." His voice suddenly gets deeper. "In fact, you're the sexiest woman in this room. I can't wait to get you on that dance floor."

Just the thought of being in Enzo's arms has me shivering with anticipation. "Me neither," I softly speak into his ear. I finally give into the pull that's been between us all night and kiss him on the cheek. "Thanks again for this incredible evening."

"It's my pleasure, beautiful." Enzo grazes a quick peck on my lips before the waitress interrupts us with our drink orders.

I sit back to enjoy my lemon drop. It's the perfect

concoction for this evening. As I relax, I can't help but head bop a little as I sing along under my breath to a song I recognize. After a few moments, I realize I have Enzo's full attention. I immediately stop and take a large drink, almost getting a brain freeze, to keep myself from singing further.

"Don't stop on my account." Enzo sweeps a strand of hair behind my ear, so he can fully see my face. "I was rather enjoying the view."

Embarrassed, I shake my head. "Sorry. Got lost up in the moment. This is one of Maddie's favorite songs, so I know it well."

He takes a long pull on his beer. "It's a great song. Wanna go out there?" He gestures to the dance floor below us.

"Sure, why not." I shrug.

By the time we get down to the floor, one of my absolute favorite songs makes an appearance. The melodic start to Ed Sheeran's *Shape of You* begins. I pull Enzo out into the middle of the floor and dance like no one's watching. I can't help it. I feel the need to move when I hear this song. After a few bars, Enzo grabs my waist with one hand and pulls my body to his. He clasps his other hand with mine, and we move around the dance floor. *The man can dance.* He guides me effortlessly and even puts in a few spins at the appropriate moments. When the song gets to the chorus about the smell of bedsheets, memories of last night flood my thoughts. Enzo's now hooded eyes don't help with my suddenly lust-filled mind.

Enzo had left his jacket at our table with mine. His shirt sleeves have been rolled, so his muscular forearms keep flexing right along with the music. His shirt is open at the collar and I can't help but want to undo a few more buttons and feel his magnificent chest without the barrier of clothing. *But we're in a club, not my bedroom.* After dancing with him like this, I don't think I'll ever be able to hear this song and not think of the sexy man before me. I shake my head to keep my thoughts from lingering so I can simply enjoy the rest of the song. By the time the song ends, we're so in tune with one another. Maroon 5's song *Sugar* starts immediately afterward, and we can't help but dance to the beat, moving with the music. In fact, we stay on the dance floor for countless songs, just enjoying each other on the dance floor.

I soon find Enzo is pure magic and I simply cannot get enough. I laugh when I realize I haven't let loose like this in years. It's primal and our connection continues to grow throughout the night. Enzo is sexy as hell and the more I'm around him, the more I want him in every way possible. When I finally can't dance anymore, we head back to the table to reorder drinks. Though it's not long before we're out on the dance floor getting caught up with one another once again.

15
____

ENZO

FROM THE MOMENT I picked Samantha up, I've been dying to get my hands on her. It's not like I'm a randy teenager, but I haven't felt this way since my early twenties. She looks amazing in that dress. I wasn't kidding when I said my memory hadn't done it justice. By the time we get out onto the dance floor and she begins to dance, I nearly lose it. When she lets loose, she's the most beautiful woman in the world. She owns her moves and I can't help but want to sway right along with her. As I guide her around on the dance floor, I notice Rowan off to the side of the room. He gives me a knowing look that says, '*I never thought I'd see the day.*' I know, I haven't been out on the dance floor willingly in years. I quickly dismiss him and focus my entire attention on the sexy woman before me.

By the time we head back to her house, it's two o'clock in the morning. Neither of us drank much throughout the evening, as we spent most of our time out on the dance floor. I'm still cautious as I drive because others might not have made the same choice.

After dancing, the sexual tension between us is even thicker than last night, if that's possible. I can't wait to get Samantha home and refresh my memory of what she looks like out of that glorious green dress. The woman moves in heels as if they're just an extension of her. I might just have to insist she keep those on for a bit, but as beautiful as that dress is, it's gotta go!

Once again, clothes are flying as soon as we enter her house. Our bodies passionately entangle the moment the door is shut. I'd like to say we make it to the bed because I'm a gentleman, but it's just too far away. Being a man to use the resources around him, I find the stairs to be quite an effective tool. In a not so suave move, I hurriedly try to kick off my shoes and pants after grabbing a strip of condoms from my wallet. I end up falling to the stairs in a sitting position. Samantha takes this as an invitation and climbs me like a tree. I haven't even gotten my shirt undone.

Seeking to resolve the problem with my shirt, Samantha straddles me and slowly unbuttons it. Her soft, warm hands ignite a fire deep within me. She kisses my chest and each muscle as she makes her way down my abdomen. I'm going to burst into flames if she keeps at it. I can barely contain myself. I must fist the stairs to keep from directing her. When she gets past my navel, she stops and takes a good look at my straining erection that's begging to greet her personally. Not wanting her to feel obligated to go any further, I reach out with one hand and grab the side of her face to get her to look at me.

"Come here," I encourage.

"I'm a little busy." She smirks, letting that sass I'm quickly becoming to love shine through.

"Well... don't let me interrupt. I'll be right here when you're ready," I tease.

Without any warning, she cups my balls with one hand and gently massages them. With her other hand, she strokes at my base. All the while, just looking at my cock as it turns a darker shade of red. When a bit of precum makes an appearance, she surprises me by licking it free. Then she uses her tongue by rolling it around my tip, making swipes down my shaft and causing me to utterly lose my mind.

"Fuuuccckkk," I growl.

I'm trying with all my might to let her keep control of this situation, but I can't not touch her. I reach out to place my hand at the base of her neck, my fingers entwine in her hair, and I can't help but guide her head as her spectacular mouth slides up and down my cock. Between the massaging, stroking, and sucking, she creates the perfect rhythm that's unlike any I have ever experienced. My toes curl as the tingling at the base of my spine makes its presence. I don't know how much longer I can hold on, so I try to encourage her to stop.

"Come here, beautiful," I groan, needing a release.

She looks me directly in the eye as she continues without missing a beat and shakes her head no.

"Are you sure?" I pant. "I'd rather come with you." *HOLY HELL, I'm going to lose it!* She keeps her eyes on me, but she somehow manages to increase her effort at the same time. *OH. MY. FUCKING. GOD!!!!*

"Right there, beautiful… just like that!"

I can't help it when my grip goes stronger on her hair. My entire body is so taut, it could rip apart. When the tingling sensation at the base of my spine explodes throughout my entire body, I'm sure I let loose a string of expletives. She continues to keep up her efforts until I'm so sensitive I don't think I can handle any more. *Is that even possible?*

"Jesus, Samantha," I huff out. "That was unbelievable." She pulls off with a pop from my still semi-erect cock.

I pull her up to me and before she can say anything, I kiss her as if she's my last breath of air. Sure, I can taste myself on her, but like I give a shit. She tastes of the perfect mixture of the two of us. I pull her body further up mine, so I can stroke her core. Like expected, she's drenched. I slip a finger inside her and drag the wetness to her clit. I massage her clit with my thumb while I use my fingers to bring her more pleasure. Like in the car, I find that perfect spot and the sound she makes is all I need to know I'm on the right track.

After a few more moments, I realize I can't take it anymore. I need to taste her, too. I scoot down one step as I lift her body higher. I don't give her much time to think as I hoist her up even further. Her arms fall out in front of her and brace themselves on the steps above me. She protests when she realizes what I'm about to do, but the moment my tongue strokes between her outer lips, she suddenly relaxes. When my tongue and dexterous fingers find the perfect rhythm, she nearly screams. I use my middle finger to make the 'come hither' motion, pressing against that magical spot and her body trembles from the inside out. I swipe my tongue across her clit before clamping down on it with suction and she explodes beautifully on my hand.

When she comes down from her sated bliss, I lower her to my lap. She presses her ass right into my straining erection, but I ignore it for now. Her hands wrap around my neck as her face falls against my chest. This is the most content feeling in the world. Slowly our breathing returns to normal and she traces the tattoos on my chest.

"What does this mean?" she whispers as she traces my Pararescue tattoo. It's an angel holding a globe.

"That's my Pararescue tattoo. Everyone got some version of it when we became part of the team. Traditionally, it also has the words 'that others may live,' but I know the words, no need to repeat them." I shrug as if it's no big deal.

"Wow," she whispers as she kisses it softly. It's on my right pectoral. I have a few other tattoos but she doesn't ask for more information. She kisses me on the lips once again, but before things get too carried away she suggests, "Wanna take this upstairs?"

"Sure thing, beautiful," I say as I help her stand. I look around the entryway and see our clothes are once again scattered. I can't help but chuckle as I see the evidence of our passion around us. "We sure do like this entryway, don't we?"

"It seems that way." She shakes her head and laughs as she gathers her things. "Let's go upstairs."

Who am I to disagree. "I'll follow you, beautiful." *Anywhere. What the fuck? Where did that come from?* As soon as I catch sight of the beautiful sway of her ass, my thoughts are soon distracted. I quickly pick up my things and run up the stairs after her.

THE NEXT MORNING, Samantha is sprawled out across my chest. Her hair covers one of my shoulders and her face looks toward me. I can't help but draw circles on her back with the hand that's under her, as well as study her unique features. From this angle, I can see she has a slight dusting of freckles across her nose, as well as the way her eyes flutter from time to time while she's asleep. The sheet rests just barely over her hips and mine, leaving her on display for viewing. Never having been one to sleep in, no matter the time I get to sleep, I take this moment to fully enjoy all that is Samantha.

Her bedroom is entirely her. Off to one side, she has a reading area. There's a window seat with cushions, a soft, gray leather loveseat and an oversized dark-gray chair that has a cozy tan blanket on the back of it. That must be where she likes to sit the most. I can almost picture her with her legs pulled under her as she curls up with a book. There's a walk-in closet leading into a full bathroom on the other side. I know from personal experience she has a large tub, as well as a walk-in shower and double sinks. Across from the bed we're lying in is a large black dresser with pictures of her family displayed on top. The bed itself is a large black platform. It rests against the wall I'm leaning against. The headboard is built into the wall. It's well-padded and covered in black soft leather.

I glance at the clock on the table next to me and it reads

nine o'clock. I don't recall the last time I've been in bed this late, but then again, I think we were up until dawn. I try my best to just relax and let her sleep. Listening to the soft cadence of her breathing puts me deep into thought. I mull over my delicious memories of the past few days.

Has it only been four days since I've met her? I can't believe I'm here in her bed again. Fuck, I usually try to make a habit of being gone before morning, not trying to find ways to be back again. I've made a habit of keeping women at bay since Vanessa. There's no point in settling down if I won't be around long enough to see where it might go. I've always been upfront about that. It's always been casual or time constricted. When my next mission called, I always beat feet to be back with the Air Force.

But not with Samantha. With her, I've been completely enamored. And besides, who knows if I'm really going to be Air Force much longer? *That offer with Riggs is nothing to be taken lightly.* If I do take that job, I'd be guaranteed to be based here in Portland. Sure, I'd still have to travel and there'd be distance between us at times, but those will be for a few weeks, not months at a time. Samantha doesn't seem to be the type who would move on without telling me first. From what I can tell, she knows first-hand what cheating can do to a person. She waited three years just to kiss another man. Who knows how long she's waited to do more. *Ugg... I can't think about her and other men. Not going there.*

Something about Samantha completely draws me to her. I don't even have words to describe it. She's smart, funny, and caring. She's sexy as sin and completely in tune with my needs and desires. I can't recall a time I've ever been more satisfied. But it's more than just sex. With her, I want to go out of my way to make her smile. *She has me willing to put on a monkey-suit and dance.* When was the last time I've felt this way? *Never.* I think my mom may have been onto something, as well as Rowan. But there is still so much unknown.

From what I've gathered, Samantha is smart, independent, and is what I'm sure a wonderful mother. *Fuck, she has kids.* Yes, I'm a great uncle, but I have no idea how to navigate around being in a relationship with a woman with kids. This is uncharted territory for me. I'm totally out of my depth here. Maybe I'm not what she needs in her life right now. Maybe this is going too fast and I should slow things down.

Fuck. That. Shit, Dumbass! Just the thought alone of attempting to end things has my gut churning inside. There's no way I'm ready for my time with Samantha to end. I'll just have to take her lead and see where this goes. I'm set to meet her kids tomorrow evening. It could be a disaster and she might dump me on my ass. There's also that little bit about figuring out how to tell my dad that I'm suddenly very interested in one of his clients.

Four Days. I've only known her four days. It's not like I'm going to be proposing or anything. I just want to date the woman. That's all. Jesus, I need to get a grip on my emotions.

I look down at her beautiful face and see Samantha's beautiful mahogany eyes studying me. Before I can say anything, she asks, "What are you thinking about over there? World peace?"

What the hell do I even say? There's no way I'm ready to

repeat even a fraction of the thoughts bulldozing through my brain. I go with the truth. "Just about you, beautiful. Just about you." I bend down and kiss her on the forehead as I brush her hair out of her face.

"What time is it?" she asks as she stretches her body and yawns.

"Almost ten o'clock."

She snuggles back to my side, laying her head on my chest and her arm across my waist. "I don't remember the last time I slept in this late. But snuggling with you is something I could get used to."

Her stomach rumbles and I suggest, "What do you say to breakfast? Wanna get dressed quickly and come back to take showers later? Just put on something casual and I'll run down to my car and get something out of my bag."

She grins mischievously. "You brought a bag, knowing you'd be staying?"

I shrug. "Not really. I always have my "go-bag" with me. You saw it when we went up the Gorge. It just has everything I need, so I won't ever be without."

"That's very prepared of you," she teases as she tries to tickle my side.

"Hey now. If you start that, we'll never get breakfast. I'm starving, woman!" I roll her onto her back and tickle her until she's convulsing with laughter. Her naked body has me wanting to have her for breakfast instead, but when her stomach rumbles for a second time, I stand next to the bed and pull her in for a quick kiss. I keep it brief before turning her toward the bathroom.

"Go! Get dressed and I'll get my things." As she walks away with a sway, I'm dying to follow. I smack her on the ass and chuckle. "Don't tempt me, beautiful!"

She walks to the bathroom while I search for my pants and shirt from last night. We brought them upstairs, but they're combined in a pile of his/hers discarded clothes. I quickly put my pants, shirt, and shoes sans socks and head out to my vehicle for my things. I don't bother to look at myself in a mirror because I can already see that my clothes are rumpled, needing to be washed. I haven't done a walk of shame in years. Though with Samantha, if it doesn't tarnish her reputation, I'd gladly do it every day.

When I get to my car, I decide to just bring the entire bag inside, so I'm not going through it in the driveway. *I really need to do some laundry if I keep using this as my source of luggage.* When I'm back inside, I use the downstairs bathroom to get ready. I know if I go upstairs, we'll never leave her bedroom.

By the time I'm dressed, I realize Samantha has yet to come downstairs. Not wanting it to get in the way, I take my bag to my SUV. Then I go into the living room to wait for her. I have no intention of rushing her; she can take all the time she needs. I can hear Samantha moving around upstairs, but so far, no sight of her.

Suddenly, I hear the front door bang open. I look up in surprise to find Samantha's youngest, Frankie, running through the door. She's at a sprint, heading for the stairs when she stops dead in her tracks as she notices me. She doesn't say anything, just stares, doe eyed. *Well, this is awkward.*

I might as well break the ice. "Hi, you must be Frankie."

She nods but doesn't respond. Shit. *Now what am I supposed to do?*

I try again. "I'm Enzo. I'm a friend of your mom."

Before she can respond, two things happen at once. An unknown man approaches the wide-open door as Samantha hollers from upstairs. "I'll be down in a second. Just switching over some laundry before we go."

The man in the doorway has yet to see me and scolds Frankie. "Frankie, I told you to wait for me. I don't like it when you ride your bike so far ahead of me."

The man in front of me is about six-feet tall. He resembles the pictures of Declan, but an older version. He has dark-brown hair and appears to have kept himself in shape. He notices Frankie staring and turns his attention to me. *Well, this is one way to meet her family.* His look of pure shock is almost amusing, if it hadn't been for the fact his daughter just walked into a room with a stranger in it.

Before either of us say anything, Frankie turns to him as if it isn't a big deal. "Dad. This is Enzo. He's one of Mom's friends." She looks back to me before continuing. "I'm Frankie. This is my dad, Devin." Wow, what manners for an eight-year-old... and she saved me from having to introduce myself.

I step toward Devin with an outstretched hand. "Nice to meet you, Devin."

Truth being told, Devin still looks out of sorts. It takes him a moment, but eventually, his manners kick in. "You, too. Enzo?" he asks my name, questioning.

"Yes, Enzo Harper," I clarify.

Devin acts as if he's trying to solve world peace, he's

concentrating so hard. Then he whispers my name again before almost shouting, "Oh, I remember now. You're the contractor Sam has hired for the remodel. I'm surprised to see you here on a Sunday. Sam said you weren't working this weekend."

"I'm his son actually." I want to add that I'm not working. But I'm not sure how Samantha wants this to play out with her children.

"Well, it's nice to meet you." Devin seems a little more at ease.

Frankie tugs on her dad's arm. "Daddy, I'm going to get the ballet slipper I forgot. I'll be right back."

"Okay, Frankie. I'll be right here."

Well, at least he doesn't just make himself entirely at home in Samantha's house, though just waiting in the doorway is awkward. What the fuck am I supposed to say to him? Finally, after a few more moments of uncomfortable silence, I gesture to the couch. "Would you like to have a seat?"

He sits down and there is still silence.

Finally, he breaks it. "So, how much longer do you think the remodel will take?"

I laugh. "I have no idea."

He gives me a face that looks as if he's saying, 'what the fuck?'

Just then, I hear Samantha call as she runs down the stairs, "I'm starving, are you ready to g...?" She freezes when she sees Devin sitting across from me on the couch. She looks back and forth from him to me. She suddenly shakes her head as if to clear her thoughts and asks, "Devin, what are you doing here?"

"Frankie lost one of her ballet slippers. She's upstairs looking for it now."

"Oh..." Samantha still appears as if she's unsure what to say.

Devin stands and calls upstairs, "Frankie, did you find it yet?"

"It's under my bed. As soon as I get it out, I'll be right down," Frankie hollers from what I presume is her room.

"How in the world did she lose it under her bed?" Samantha grumbles. "She just wore those shoes a few days ago."

Devin laughs. "Will she be able to find her way out is the better question?"

"Who knows? That is her go-to place for cleaning her room. At least she knew where it was." Samantha then looks at me. "I'm sorry, Enzo. Have you been introduced to Devin?"

"Yes, we've met," I reply.

"So... he says he has no idea how long the remodel will take..." Devin eyes me suspiciously as if I'm not qualified to be doing the job.

Samantha's beautiful laugh fills the room. "Well, that's probably because it's his father doing the work, not him. Enzo is in the Air Force. He doesn't work for his father." She shakes her head at Devin's misconception.

Devin is back to looking more confused than ever. "Oh," is all he says for a moment. "Where are you stationed?"

"Ramstein Air Base in Germany," I reply automatically.

Devin puts his hand over his chin and scratches it before adding, "So, how long are you on leave for?"

"For the next month and a half," once again comes automatically. I'm used to that question, but not sure why it would be a concern to him. But then I eye the beautiful woman standing next to me and I'm pretty sure I can guess.

"I see..." Devin states.

Before anyone can say another word, Frankie comes barreling into the room. She rushes up to her mother and squeezes her tight. "Hi, Mama," is muffled, but can be made out.

"Hey, sweet pea," Samantha replies with a smile on her face. "Did you find your slipper?"

"Yep, it was stuck between the wall and my bed. I had to crawl under to get it." Frankie holds the slipper up proudly for all to see, making us all laugh.

"Well, we'd better go, Frankie. Everyone is waiting for us," Devin states as he turns her toward the door.

"Okay, Daddy, race you!" Frankie shouts as she rushes out the door.

I stick out my hand. "It was nice to meet you, Devin."

"You, too," he replies. Then he looks to Samantha before turning back to me. He appears as if he's about to say something about me being here but changes his mind. He clears his throat then states, "Sorry for the interruption." He walks toward the door. "I'd better run, or she'll beat me home."

"Goodbye," Samantha says as she follows him to the door.

He leaves without another word, but Samantha just stares at the door in silence.

I come up behind her and snake my arms around her waist. "Everything okay, beautiful?"

As if I have shaken her out of a trance, her body has a slight tremor. "Yeah, it is." Then she looks around at the entryway and suddenly giggles. "We'd better start using the deadbolt if we're going to continue using the entryway like we have."

I turn her so she's facing me. "If you say so..." I lean in for a kiss and then pull away. "Are you ready to eat?"

"Sure. Let's go."

16

SAMANTHA

DEVIN BEING at my house totally shocked the shit out of me. I tried to pull it off like it wasn't a big deal, but I'm not sure how well I managed that, or if my shock even went unnoticed. *What the hell had he and Enzo been talking about?* That look on Devin's face when he realized Enzo wasn't the contractor was almost hysterical. It seems it finally has dawned on him that I've met someone else. This is a first since I've never gone on more than one date with anyone. And I certainly haven't brought anyone home, but he can suck it. He doesn't deserve to know the details of my private life. He made the choice long ago not to be privy to that information. I've silently watched him move on. God, it feels so good to be on the other side in this situation. Meeting Aubrey was difficult for me, and she hasn't even been the first person Devin's brought around the kids. I can only imagine what is running through Devin's mind.

"What are you laughing about over there, beautiful?" Enzo

asks, breaking me out of my trance on the way to the restaurant.

I shake my head, not really wanting to divulge my thoughts, but I do ask the question I'm dying to know the answer to. "So, what did you and Devin talk about?"

"After Frankie came bursting through the door, he came in and seemed a bit surprised to see me in your living room," Enzo states matter-of-factly.

"Wait, they didn't even knock?"

"Nope, the door burst open, scaring the shit out of me, I might add. But before I could react, Frankie came barreling in. She was on a mission. As soon as she saw me, she froze on the spot. Wouldn't even say a word to me when I introduced myself."

"Okay…"

Enzo lets out a chuckle. "Then, when her dad came in, she introduced me like we're long lost friends. Your kid's a riot. I've never seen anything like it. She ran in and out like a hurricane. Does the girl ever slow down?"

"That's Frankie for you. She's a force of nature. You will never have to guess with her; she has no filter. Her heart is bigger than the ocean and she's as silly as they come." I can't help but chuckle. I love that girl more than life itself.

"I'm looking forward to seeing that," Enzo says as he turns into the parking lot.

Does this mean he plans on sticking around? Samantha, I chide myself, focus on the situation at hand. Let that be tomorrow's worry when he actually meets my kids again.

"Did Devin actually say anything to you?" I press again.

"Not really. He seemed interested as to why I would be there. He mistook me for my dad, and I didn't really correct him until you came in."

"Oh..." *So, I didn't miss that much.*

"There's nothing else to tell you, Samantha. No need to stay in your head about it." Enzo pulls into a spot and reaches for the back of my neck to pull me toward him. He lightly kisses me on the forehead. "You can always ask me anything."

I sigh. "I know." Not wanting to miss out on an opportunity, I reach up and kiss him on the lips before saying, "Thanks."

JUST AS WE'RE finishing breakfast, Enzo's phone must vibrate from his pocket because he suddenly pulls it out and looks at the screen. He apologetically looks at me. "Sorry, gotta take this."

"Hey, Ma," he greets warmly. He listens for a while before looking at me hesitantly and saying, "I'm not really sure... Yes... I know." He lets out a huge sigh. "Yeah, Ma. You're right. Sure. I'll see you soon." Before he hangs up I hear, "I love you, too, Ma," in closing.

Enzo looks as if he's contemplating something, but I'm not sure if I should press the issue or not. I decide to just finish my coffee instead. It has cooled but at least it keeps me from having to be nosy.

"So..." Enzo seems more resolved in whatever he was in

deep thought about. "What are your plans for the rest of the day?"

I try to remember if there is anything I must do this afternoon. "I might do some laundry, but other than that, it's wide open." I eye him closely to try to get a read on his thoughts. But there's nothing giving them away. "What do you have in mind?" I tease, trying to get a reaction from him. I have no idea what he has in mind, but I certainly wouldn't mind spending more time with him.

"Well..." He clears his throat and it miraculously becomes even sexier as he sits across from me at the table where we're eating. "I'd love nothing more than to spend the day with you." He clears his throat before he continues. "Actually, Ma just told me she's expecting me for dinner." He raises his shoulders and a slight grin makes his dimple pop. *Holy shit. It does it every time to me, my inner muscles clench in anticipation. What is it about this man?*

He pulls me from my thoughts when he continues, "She's invited my brother and sister's families over, too. Kind of a homecoming celebration of sorts." Enzo shrugs humbly and shakes his head as if he doesn't think it's worth the fanfare. "And..." he hesitates.

For the first time since I've met him, Enzo almost seems a bit shy. *What in the world has him behaving this way?* I manage not to say my thoughts aloud as I nibble on my lower lip to keep myself from blurting them out. I just raise an eyebrow and wait as patiently as I can for him to continue. *Though patient is the least I'm feeling about now.*

I'm about to give into my temptation by asking him to

continue when he suddenly pulls a hand through his hair and states, "She wants you to come, too." He looks apologetically and then as if he's bracing himself for my reaction.

What. The. What?!?! She wants me to come, too? How does she even know about me?

"She does?" I manage to say, as my thoughts hurdle at top speed through my head and I can barely catch one to keep a hold of.

Enzo looks a little chagrin. "Um... I might have mentioned you to her last night when I went home to change." He tries to brush it off like it's no big deal.

"Okay... what exactly did you tell her?" Mortification fills my mind. *His mother must think I'm a two-bit hussy since he's been staying over, and I haven't even known him a week.* I can't help when I shudder at the thought.

"Relax, Samantha. Breathe. Your mind is like a freight train that's lost its brakes on a steep incline." He laughs lightly before adding, "I can see your wheels turning ninety miles a minute barreling out of control."

I take in a deep breath and try to stop from letting my thoughts get out of control. He's right. I'm doing that. *How is it that he knows me so well already?*

He puts my mind at ease when he explains how his mom saw him come home with his new suit. She knew it was for someone special because he may have mentioned the part about getting me a dress, which sent her into detective mode. We both laugh when he gets to the part about his mom giving him a hard time about not having bought a suit since high school and the fact she missed her calling as an international interrogator. By the time he's done, I don't feel as mortified and am looking forward to meeting the amazing woman who raised him.

"Well, I guess I could go," I tease, then I'm hit with another thought. "What about your dad? Does he know about us?"

"Not that I know of. I guess we'll just be honest and tell everyone how we met that first afternoon when I went back to get my car."

"Are you sure you want me to meet your family? It's only been a few days," I try to explain my hesitation, but he gives me a stern look, cutting me off.

"Samantha." Enzo's deep voice sends shivers up my spine. "I have no idea where this," he points between the two of us, "is going, but what I do know is that I want to spend as much time with you as possible." *I feel the same way, but isn't it a little fast?*

"And... you're not just... horny?" I try to tease again, and he adamantly shakes his head with complete confidence. The emotion shining through his glorious green eyes pierces through me. I've never seen anyone with more conviction.

"You and I both know there's something else here or we wouldn't even be sitting at this table together. I don't know about you, but I've never felt this way about anyone. Ever." His declaration continues to slay me. The wall I've been holding up for so long cracks.

I nod my head in agreement. *It's true. I never even felt this way with Devin, and I was married to the man. I don't remember having feelings for anyone so quickly like this.*

Before I can say anything, he continues, "I don't know

where this will lead us. Hell, I don't even know where I will be living in four months, but I do know that while I'm on leave, I plan to spend as much time with you as possible to figure it out."

I can't do anything but stare at the beautiful man before me, laying all his thoughts out there. I'm in pure shock. No one's ever been that blunt with me before. I don't even know what to say. If I wasn't tongue tied, that is.

Thankfully, he continues as he runs a hand through that glorious thick, blond hair. "Fuck, I don't know what will happen. Your kids might hate me, or I might annoy you to death and you'll kick me to the curb." His dimple-wielding smile hits me again. "But I do know that I want to see where this goes." He stops and stares at me, trying to get a read on my thoughts. "So... what do you say? Are you willing to see where this goes?"

He hit everything in one fell swoop I could have used to argue against him. He mentioned the newness of our relationship and my kids. But, our connection is incredible. Maybe it's the lust-filled haze he keeps me in, maybe it's just the fact that it's all new and exciting, but there's something about Enzo that makes me want to see where this goes. So, I say the only thing that seems right, given our situation.

"Sure," comes out in a whisper.

"Come again?" He lowers his head to truly study my face. His glimmering green eyes look hopeful as they bore into my soul, taking my breath away. I nod my response again.

He cocks his head to the side, squinting his eyes toward me, willing me to say more.

Finally, after what feels like an eternity, I find my voice. "I'm willing to see where this goes, if you are."

Relief spreads across his features and he lets out a breath he had been holding. He reaches for his wallet, places some bills on the table, then he stands, holding his hand out to me. I take it as I stand, but he surprises me by pulling me in closer to him. He wraps his arms around me in an enormous hug, so I wrap my arms around his waist and melt into him.

When he releases me, he simply states, "Okay then. Are you ready to get out of here?"

17

———

ENZO

WHAT THE EVER-LOVING fuck was I thinking? After only a few days... days?!?! I just laid everything out on the line for Samantha. And she said yes? She feels our connection, too? A part of me is freaking the fuck out, while another part is riding cloud nine. I must get her out of the restaurant, I must get her alone to show her just how much she means to me. When I reach for her hand, and she willingly takes mine, everything just clicks into place. It feels so right.

Hell, I have no idea if we'll make it work. She has a family she must consider, too. It's not just about us. Am I even ready for something like this? Holy Shit. Family. Can I even be a stepdad? Do I even want to be? Wait! *I'm thinking about marriage?!?!?* I take a long, hard look at the beautiful woman before me and I reach for her hand. The moment her hand contacts mine, I realize for the first time since Vanessa, I'm willing to see where it might lead with someone, even if it means taking on an entire family in the process.

Not wanting to be apart from her any longer, I pull her into me for a hug and brush a kiss on the top of her head. "Okay then. Are you ready to get out of here?" I take her hand and lead her out of the restaurant.

I'D LIKE to say I spent the rest of the afternoon wooing Samantha and romancing her, but I just couldn't think about anything except being with her again. I drove directly to her house. I remembered to lock the deadbolt before I rushed her upstairs, lavishing her body the only way I know how.

About an hour before my mother was expecting us, Samantha sexily unwove herself from my body and insisted on taking a shower, alone I might add, to get ready for dinner. I reluctantly used the guest shower down the hall to get ready. I guarantee that we would never have left the house again had I stepped into that bathroom with her. She's so damn addictive.

We manage to arrive at my parents' house about twenty minutes before my mom said dinner would be ready. Samantha's quiet on the way over and I'm a little lost in my own head, too. I pull a hand over my freshly shaven jaw and scratch it absentmindedly, trying to remember the last time I brought someone home to my parents' house. Hell, I don't have a clue. High school? Vanessa? *Holy shit. I haven't brought home anyone since Vanessa, and that ended shortly after I enlisted.* Hmmm... this should be interesting to see how my family reacts.

"Contemplating world peace over there?" Samantha teases, breaking me from my trance.

I shake my head and a smile forms on my face. "Nope. Nothing that serious. Just taking everything in, that's all."

She cocks her head to the side to get a better read on me. "Everything still okay? You're not having second thoughts about bringing me here, are you? I could totally Uber it home or something if you'd rather I not come."

She looks as if her comment was serious. I'm not having any of that. "Samantha, if I didn't want you here, I never would've asked." I reach for her hand to bring it to my mouth for a kiss. "Get those crazy-ass thoughts out of your head, beautiful. You've nothing to be nervous about. Besides, I'd never let you Uber it home." I glare at her to show my seriousness. Then I add, "You already know Pops, and Ma already likes you. I can't promise you anything else from the rest of my family. They could go rogue at any moment, but overall keep in mind they're good people."

She takes in a deep breath before letting it out slowly. "Okay, I know," quietly escapes her mouth. "I just haven't met anyone's family since college. I guess I'm getting a little nervous." She shrugs as if it should make sense.

"Well, if it makes you feel any better, I haven't brought anyone to meet them in about that long either." I give her a side glance, pulling my mouth into a smile. "I'm not feeding you to wolves, Samantha," I attempt to tease.

Pulling into the driveway, I kill the engine. I keep a hold of her hand for a moment to make sure I have her attention. "We can leave at any time, I promise. If you don't feel comfortable, just say the word and we're out of here. I'd like to spend time with my family and let them get to know you. Time is precious, and I don't want to miss an opportunity to be with you either." I lean in and kiss her firmly on the lips. I must remind myself to not get carried away because the driveway's full of vehicles and I don't want anyone getting a free show. Knowing my family, I'd get the razzing of a lifetime if they witnessed anything as well. Thankfully, I feel her relax in my embrace. In all too short of time, I pull away to give her a reassuring smile. She audibly sighs, then gathers things from around her to go inside.

It turns out Samantha had nothing to worry about. As soon as we're inside, Ma greets her with open arms and Pops acts as if this is just a normal occurrence. I did see a slight eyebrow raise discreetly in my direction as to ask, *"So this is who you are spending your time with?"* But nothing is said aloud. I'm sure at some point he will ask me about it... but knowing Pops, it won't be in front of anyone.

Ma offers to take Samantha into the kitchen where the girls are visiting while they get dinner ready. The guys are outside with my nieces and nephews for the moment. Pops casually mentions that he'd like to show me something in the living room. I silently ask Samantha if she's comfortable going alone with my mother, but she just flashes a confident smile that nearly takes my breath away. When she's out of sight, my dad clears his throat, reclaiming my attention.

"So..." He keeps his face stoic, but I can see the gleam in his eye that tells me he finds this amusing.

"So..." I counter, not wanting to give too much away.

"It sure is nice to see Samantha O'Reilly again. I'm a bit surprised though. I didn't realize you knew her."

"It's still pretty new, Pops."

"I see..." he draws out, waiting for more.

Never being one to keep secrets, I launch into the story about how I met her outside her house after he dropped me off. Pops has a slight grin on his face the entire time I reveal everything to him. He bursts out laughing when I mention the fact my stomach rumbled just as she said she was going to dinner.

"No shit? You couldn't have timed that better if you tried, son." He leads me over to the couch in the living room. We can now hear kids somewhere in the house and adult conversations from the kitchen, both male and female.

"I know, right." I shake my head at the memory of my embarrassment.

"So, Ma says that Samantha has you taking her to a place fancy enough you needed to buy a suit," he presses on, giving away the fact he already knows everything, but just wants to hear it from the horse's mouth.

"The dress she bought was amazing and I didn't want to look like a dumbass next to her." The memories of her in that dress flood my mind, as well as the night we spent afterward. Holy hell, the woman is hot! She's smart, sexy, and does things to me that I have never experienced before. I admit, I've had my share of women, so that's saying something. Samantha O'Reilly sure is special.

I shake my head to clear my thoughts and get back to my conversation at hand. "Besides, I took her to Allure, you know, the restaurant and club my buddy Rowan opened a few years back. I couldn't go in looking like I just stepped off the airplane. I didn't bring anything home other than casual clothes."

"No. You couldn't," my dad agrees. "I'm more interested in the fact you've seemed to deem her worthy of bringing her around here." He gestures to our family in the other room.

"She's special, Dad. I'll give you that." I shrug. What else can I say?

"What about her kids? Have you given much thought about them?" He raises a good point and thankfully, I already know my answer because I told Samantha about my thoughts on her children earlier.

"Samantha is the type of person you don't let slip through your fingers, Pops." I'm a little shocked at my own wording. It's true, but at the same time, I'm not used to thinking that way about anyone. Ever.

"We're taking it slow..." When I think about these past few days with her, I amend my thought. "Well, one day at a time. I plan to meet her kids tomorrow. I'm going over to watch the Seahawks play tomorrow night. Who knows? They could hate me. She could get bored of me... and hundreds of things could happen, all making her want to kick me to the curb." I shake my head, hoping it doesn't go in that direction because that would suck.

"Kids are tricky, son, but I think you'll know how to handle it." He pats me on the shoulder. "If it's meant to be, it'll all have a way of working out." He stops for a second, looking as though he's thinking about something before he continues, "Does this mean you'll be taking a job around here then?"

"Ha… believe it or not, Samantha has little to do with my decision." My dad nods like he thinks I'm full of shit. Before he can say anything, I add, "I think I'm ready to be in one place, rather than moving every couple of years. I'm pretty sure I'm going to retire one way or another. I still have a meeting later this week with the CO for the Air National Guard. But, I'm ready to have a permanent home, regardless of which direction I go. It doesn't hurt that Riggs offered me a lucrative position with his team either. I still have a lot to consider, though."

"Whatever you decide, Ma and I will support you. I know she'll be relieved to hear you're at least strongly considering returning to Portland, that's for sure." There's suddenly laughter from the kitchen that draws our attention.

Pops beats me to my thoughts. "What do you say we go in there and find out what the ruckus is all about?"

By the time we enter the kitchen, the roaring laughter has me more than curious. I don't even get a foot into the room when a screaming, naked toddler comes barreling past me, trying to escape. Her hands are full of Cheerios and her body is doing the best she can to stay upright as her feet move faster than her torso. The grin on her face is pure bliss.

"Zoey!" my sister-in-law Ann hollers. "You get back here! I need to finish putting on your diaper and changing your clothes!"

Doing my best to help with the situation, I bend down and scoop her up into my arms, keeping her from her great escape. Quickly, I bring her up to blow a raspberry onto her belly, making her squeal in delight. "I think you're missing your booty cover, Zo! Let's get you covered up before you go traipsing across Granny's carpet."

"You do it, Zo!" she screams at me in her cute as can be toddler voice. "Not Mama!" She's still giggling as she says this. "Git my belly 'gain!"

Of course, I oblige. I give her another raspberry and reach for the diaper Ann's holding. I quickly get it in place. *Yep, I'm a great uncle. I do know how to change a diaper, and I know the severity of needing to put them on quickly and accurately.*

I'm kneeling on the floor, just having fastened the diaper securely, when the rest of my nieces and nephews come over to get in on the action of picking on me. Before I know it, they all dog-pile on me. I tickle them and do the best I can to keep the upper hand. They're like slippery fish and bursting with laughter. I love moments like this. *Of course, this is why I'm their favorite uncle.*

Soon, I hear Ma say, "I think that's enough. Who's ready to eat?" One by one, they all dismantle the pile we have created. Brandon, Riley, and Nick all rush to the dinner table, while Zoey and Isabel continue to climb all over me like little monkeys. Thankfully, their parents rush in and pick them up, so all I need to do is get myself upright and head to the table.

Samantha's beautiful smile nearly knocks me back on my ass. Her amusement over what she just witnessed is evident. She walks over to me to lend me a hand. Still laughing, she asks, "Want help?"

I reach out to take it, but not really using it to get the momentum to stand. The spark that shoots through me is completely electrifying. Without even caring about the present audience, once I get myself to fully standing, I find myself reaching under her hair at the base of her neck to pull her closer to me. It's as if I *need* to get my lips on hers, the pull is so strong. I give her a heated kiss, entirely caught up in the moment, but my obnoxious family quickly reminds me of their presence.

Several noises erupt at once. Everything from, "Ewww," to loud whistles to, "Get a room."

I pull back and see Samantha completely blush from head to toe. *Shit. I didn't mean to embarrass her.* "You okay, beautiful?" I ask, tipping her chin to make her eyes meet mine.

She looks around the room and shrugs as if that should explain everything and she pulls on her lower lip with her teeth.

I look at my family who all, except for the kids who yelled 'Ewww,' look at us with a mixture of awe and hope. My brother and sister's mouths are both opened so wide they could catch flies in them. Obviously, my behavior shocks them. But I don't give a shit. All I care about is the woman before me.

"Sorry if I embarrassed you, Samantha," I whisper, though I'm sure everyone can hear me. "But there's nothing to worry about. I've seen each of them," I look pointedly at my brother and sister and their significant others before adding, "kiss one another as well as my parents and it's not a big deal." I kiss her once more to prove a point. "I just can't help myself; you're irresistible." I shrug as if that should answer the unasked questions running through her mind.

When I pull back this time, she has a smile on her face, but not from embarrassment. "Oookkkaaay." She sucks in a deep breath to steady herself.

"Get used to it," I whisper as I take her hand in mine, leading her to the dining room table.

Dinner itself goes off without a hitch. My brother and sister attempt to bring up stories to embarrass me from my past, but I have no problem with it. I've dished out my share over the years. Payback is a bitch, but I honestly haven't done that much to be too worried about. My most embarrassing moments are secretly kept just that, a secret.

By the time dinner is complete, Samantha is well at ease with my family. My sister Erin, Mom, and Zane's wife, Ann, are all avid readers, so they have a lot to talk about. Samantha seems in her element when she talks books and authors. The passion in her eyes ignites a flame that will never burn out. I can see she loves her job and takes great pride in representing authors who are worthy of being promoted. When Erin mentions she has written a little since becoming a stay-at-home mom, I'm even a little shocked. I had no idea she was interested in publishing a book. She and Samantha set up a lunch date to discuss this idea further because Erin wants to know what the next steps are for getting her book out there.

When dinner is over, Pops shoos all the girls out of the kitchen so us guys can clean up. It's a tradition in our house. My parents raised us to be an equal opportunity family. If someone cooks, the other cleans. Ma didn't want us boys going off and not knowing how to fend for ourselves, so it's proven to work out well for all involved over the years.

I set into clearing the plates from the table and prepare

myself for the razzing I'm about to receive. My guess is that it'll be less than thirty seconds after the women and children leave that either Zane or my brother-in-law Nate will say something. I count in my head as soon as the room is just us guys.

They make it to eighteen seconds before Zane casually asks, "So, how is it you're back in town less than a week and you have a woman as hot as Samantha here for dinner?"

Before I can respond, Nate adds, "Since when did you ever bring someone to Sunday dinner?"

I pointedly look at Zane. "Dude, you're married. You shouldn't be calling Samantha hot." *She sure as fuck is, but that shouldn't be his concern.*

"Reality check, Enzo," Zane mocks. "I'm married… but not blind or dead. Samantha's hot by anyone's definition. Even Ann whispered that to me earlier."

I can't help but nod in agreement. I'd be lying if I didn't acknowledge that fact. But then I turn to Nate. "Ma asked her to come for dinner."

"Didn't you just get into town a couple of days ago?" Zane asks.

"Yep." I glance at Dad and he just smiles as he loads the dishes into the dishwasher. *The bastard. He knew this would happen.* It was inevitable the guys would give me a hard time. Might as well get this over with. I've certainly dished out my share of shit to them.

"So, how'd you meet her?" Nate asks with sincerity, no longer teasing me.

I chuckle at the thought. "Well, I actually went to surprise Pops and I happened to meet her. He's remodeling her kitchen. Pops and I went out for lunch and he showed me around his job sites. When I got back to my car, I ran into Samantha and we went out to dinner."

"You remember the rule Pops had about not messing with clients, right?" Zane chides.

I glance at Pops whose smile just gets wider by the minute. *Shit. I knew the rule. I'd never even thought of breaking it before. But fuck the rule. I'm a grown man and I'm not about to fuck up Pops' business. This is different. Besides, we're all adults.*

Pops interrupts before I can continue. "I only had that rule in place when you boys were randy teenagers. I had to keep you away from the daughters of clients or the Mrs. Robinsons of the world. Enzo's a grown-ass man. If he wants to date Samantha, I have no problem with it." Pops shrugs nonchalantly and I can't help but want to hug him. This will surely get Zane and Nate off my back.

"She's special," I sincerely state.

"No shit, Sherlock." Zane chuckles. "You haven't brought anyone home in nearly twenty years. We knew you aren't batting for the other side, too many rumors from your youth to dispute that, but I never thought I'd see the day you'd bring home someone like her. Are your manwhoring ways finally over?"

Offended, I bodily state, "I was never a manwhore. I just didn't see the point in settling down when I would never be in one place for long."

"So, does this mean you're going to be sticking around? Finally getting out of the Air Force?" Nate asks, sounding a little shocked. I look over to Pops, and I can tell he has kept my business mine.

"I'm thinking about it. I have a few weeks to decide whether I'm going to re-up or do something entirely different. That's part of the reason I'm home on leave. I'm here to make some decisions about my future." I tell them about my meeting with Riggs as well as the one coming up with the CO at the Air National Guard as we finish up with the kitchen before meeting up with everyone else in the family room.

18

———

SAMANTHA

BY THE TIME Enzo comes out of the kitchen, I feel completely at ease with his family. I love the way they joke and tease one another. I can't believe the way he kissed me in front of them. I'm not one for much PDA, but when a man like Enzo kisses me like that, who gives a fuck about my surroundings?

Sara, Anna, and Erin are all people I could become friends with easily. Their children are adorable. Of course, we have a lot in common: kids, books, and Enzo. *Though that last one is the one subject I do my best to avoid talking about. I don't want to give them any reason to think less of me since I've known Enzo for such a short time.* Thankfully, no one does or says anything to make me feel as if I don't belong here.

I can feel Enzo enter the room before I see him. My back is to the entrance, but the prickling up my spine is the sensation I experience whenever he's near. He comes to sit next to me on the couch, instinctively grabbing my hand to hold once he arrives. He kept his hand on my leg all throughout dinner. Like now, my nerve endings are spasming out of control. It's as if each nerve is a live wire, waiting to explode. It's taking all my energy not to climb him like a tree and have my way with him.

Eventually, we say our goodbyes. I promise Erin we will get together for lunch soon. She texts me her number so I can call and schedule something once I have my calendar in front of me. Enzo's parents each give me a hug and we make our way out the door, heading back to my place for the evening.

THE NEXT DAY, I awake in Enzo's arms. His delicious scent envelops me, and I swear, if I died right now, I'd go happy. As I recall each delicious thing he did to me, for me, and with me last night, I realize I can still feel the tremors of the after effects throughout my body.

I had to set my dreaded alarm today because I have the contractors coming, as well as meetings in the office I can't get away from. Fortunately, I still have some time before my alarm, so I decide to be a wake-up call of my own for Enzo. Let's just say he's more than satisfied with being awakened earlier than the alarm this morning. *That man is pure heaven!*

I make it to work on time, even with his help in the shower this morning. He left my house when I did, even though I insisted he could stay for as long as he liked. He didn't really tell me what his plans were for the day, but I know I will be seeing him tonight for pizza and the football game.

I can't stop thinking about him throughout the day as scenes from last night play on a loop through my mind. It's hard not to picture him as the hero of every story I read throughout the morning, either. He's absolutely mind consuming.

By the time one o'clock comes around, I find Lexi standing at my door. I apparently have been staring out into space because she actually knocks, which never happens, and her greeting is almost yelled, "Earth to Samantha! Come in, Samantha!"

I, of course, quickly snap out of my lust-filled stupor and jump out of my chair to greet her with a hug. She has been out of town for the last few weeks and I have been working from home as much as I could, so we haven't seen each other in a while. "It's so good to see you. How was your trip?" I ask as I pull away from our hug.

"Great. I had the best time in New England. The fall leaves were something to write home about." She looks around at my desk and then peers back at me. "So, what do you say to lunch? I skipped breakfast this morning for that meeting with Morgan. I'm starving."

Jay Morgan is our client who is about to launch a new mystery series. Fortunately, when we discovered him, most of his stories already had been written, so all we had to do was help him brand, edit, and get his series published. Then we will roll each book out strategically to get the optimal readership. Lexi is our go-to gal for that part of the process; she thrives on marketing.

Not even thirty minutes later, Lexi and I are sitting at our favorite Mexican restaurant. Our orders are in and Lexi is telling me all about the trip across New England. She'd always wanted to go in the fall to see the leaves change and she finally made it happen this year. Lexi and her husband Tim took a kid-free vacation since her high-school aged kids stayed with their grandparents to attend school. She even managed to tie it into meeting with a client in Vermont to keep from getting behind while on her travels.

I'm excited to hear all about her trip, but thoughts of Enzo keep flashing through my mind and I'm a bit distracted. I have no idea how Lexi is going to react, or even what I'm going to reveal for that matter. I have never been with anyone like Enzo. Nothing has ever been this fast or as intense... and the things he makes me feel. *Damn, that man is sex on a stick.* I inwardly groan as I feel my well-used muscles clench, just thinking about him.

Suddenly, Lexi stops talking and my attention is back to being on her, due to the silence. She stares at me for a moment. Her head turning to the side while her bright blue eyes scrutinize me. "All right. Spill it. What's going on with you?"

I've never kept secrets from her, but with everything being so new, I'm just not sure what I should say. I manage to get an, "Uh..." out before her face suddenly lights up like the Fourth of July.

She blurts out, "Oh, this has to be good. I haven't seen you this spacey since you were in college and starting to date Devin." Lexi pauses for a moment to look me over closer. "OH! MY GOD! You've met someone!" She nearly screeches at the end. Then, as if there is a God in Heaven, she lowers her voice before she continues, "You have that '*just been thoroughly fucked*' look about you." Sudden shock comes with her realization, but then I see curiosity wins out. "So... who is he, Sam?"

Yep. This is my best friend. The knower of all things Samantha O'Reilly. The keeper of my confidences. There's no stopping her once she catches hold of the possibility of a secret. When she sniffs something juicy out, she sticks to it like a dog to a bone. I might as well just come clean. There's no point in stalling. She'll find out anyway.

"His name is Enzo Harper," I quietly state as I pull my lip into my teeth to figure out what to say next.

Since this is Lexi I'm dealing with, there's not much chance of being able to think for long. "Annddd..." she prompts.

I can tell she's trying to keep her enthusiasm under control... but this is Lexi. She knows everything I have been through over the years. She's dying to know what has me acting this way. I hold on to her gaze as she penetrates me with a dubious smile. I finally concede and break the silence. "It's still pretty new..." Still trying not to give much away. *I wouldn't be her best friend if I didn't make her work for it a little.*

"But you've slept with him." It's not a question, but an assessment.

I want to hold out on the details, but this is my best friend. I can't keep secrets from her. Besides, if I'm being honest, I've been dying to dish out the details, so I can wrap my head around things. I burst out laughing at her attempt to pump me for more information.

I shake my head to clear my thoughts before giving in.

"Lex, there's just something about him. I don't know what to say. Ever since I met him, I can't get him off my mind." I shrug as if that should make all the sense in the world.

"How long have you been seeing him?" Lexi eagerly asks as her eyes fill with more excitement.

She knows me. She knows I don't date anyone and let things get serious. I'm sure she thinks I've been holding out on her. I can't wait to see her reaction to this. I casually state, "Thursday."

Yep, there it is, her eyes go wide, her mouth forms a perfect 'O.' Lexi never disappoints. "Come again?" She finally asks, a little weary.

"Thursday," I repeat.

"Samantha, *today... is Moonndaay*," she slowly exaggerates.

I smile and nod in agreement. "Yep."

"And you've already slept with him? Who the hell is this man with the magic mojo who got you out of the funk you've been in for years, *in just four days?*"

"Two days," I quietly correct her, but I quickly continue with other facts before she can respond. "He's the son of my contractor. He came to surprise his dad one day and later that evening, I ran into him. I ended up asking him to dinner Thursday and we've seen each other every day since."

"Wait... You, Samantha O'Reilly, the woman who rarely dates. Even if she does, never does anything but give a polite kiss at the end of the night, are saying that YOU asked a man out?"

I tell her about how we met on Thursday and went to Thai food together. Being my best friend, I give her all the details she will require to be satisfied. When I get to how Thursday night ended, she suddenly interrupts again, "Wait. You said only two days. As in, you slept with this man on Friday at some point?"

"I'm getting there. Be patient." I proceed to tell her about my lunch delivery and going up the Gorge for dinner. She seems really impressed with him when I tell her how he bought me a dress. She prods me for more information and nearly falls out of her chair with laughter when I tell her about the car after dinner.

"No WAY," she gasps. "You did *not* almost have sex in a car!"

I feel my cheeks heat and I own it. "You think *that's* hot, wait until I tell you about when we got home."

She's fanning herself by the time I finish explaining the rest of my evening. "Holy hell, Sam, that's HOT!"

I nod in agreement. What else can I say? Enzo has done things to me I've never experienced with any man.

"So, where did he take you to wear that sexy dress?" Lexi asks as she takes a drink of her margarita. She insisted we each order one after I began to tell her about what she's now deeming as my 'sexcapade.'

"Allure," I say nonchalantly, once again waiting for her reaction. She knows it's an exclusive restaurant and club. Now that I've been there myself, I recall her telling me about it once.

Her jaw drops, and before she can say anything I add, "He's friends with the owner." I tell her about my amazing experience there, too. Lexi is nearly crying when I finish telling her about the stunt Rowan played on me. Her laughter is infectious. I can't help but join her. Eventually, after our laughter dies down, I give her the sordid details of the rest of our evening and yesterday morning.

"I may never look at your entryway the same," she teases when I finish explaining my adventures of the evening.

"Neither will I," I gasp, before laughter makes its appearance again. "The man does unbelievable things to me. I'm telling you, Lex, he's sexy as hell and can read me like he was given his own personal instruction manual."

"So. What did you do yesterday?" Lexi asks as she eats a tortilla chip. "Well, after our unusual encounter with Devin and Frankie, we went to breakfast then eventually went to his parents' house for dinner."

"WTF?" Lexi nearly yells with a look of complete shock covering her face. "You've already met his family? Moving a little fast, aren't you?"

I can't help but feel a little shy and guilty when I say, "Well, I've kind of been monopolizing his time. I don't really blame them for wanting to see him."

"Sam," Lexi says sternly. "You've been with him for four days. How is that monopolizing his time? PLEASE tell me he doesn't have mommy issues or anything?"

"He's on leave. He actually just arrived on Thursday," I say as if it's not anything important.

She hedges with, "On leave from where?"

"Germany. He's a pilot for PJs... pararescue men in the Air Force."

"Only you would find a man who you connect to so well

and he lives halfway around the world." She shakes her head teasingly. "Sam, what are we going to do with you? Is this more like a rebound thing?"

I shake my head. "I don't think so. I've been over Devin for some time. Enzo is something else." I try to put my feelings for him into words, but too many thoughts go through my head at once to really grasp a definition of it all.

"But he lives in Germany. As in Europe. How will this work?" I can tell she's just looking out for me at this point.

"I have no idea, but I'm willing to see where it goes. Who knows what'll happen? Besides, there's a good chance he's retiring from the Air Force and moving to Portland when his tour is over."

"When will that be?" She looks sad.

"Um... he has less than six months to go and he's on a nearly two-month leave, I think." I try to figure it out in my head, but I realize I don't really have the specifics.

Lexi lets out a deep breath as if she finally found the information she's been waiting on. "Okay. Now it makes sense why you want to try it one day at a time..."

"For the past few days, it's been amazing to be wrapped up in our own personal bubble. But now that I'm away from him, I'm having other thoughts about him, too."

Lexi suddenly appears weary as she slowly asks. "Like what?"

"Well, for starters, what about my kids?" I start out slow with my reservations, but the more that comes to mind, the more rapidly I fire the questions to Lexi, never giving her the time to respond. "What on Earth am I going to tell them tonight? Do I not tell them much and let them jump to their own conclusions? Do I tell them that I'm dating him? Ugh… I've never been in this situation. What if they don't like him? I think he's wonderful. I've seen him with kids. Believe it or not, he's even sexier while playing with them, but if my children hate him, there's no way it'll work." I gasp when another thought hits me. "Lex, what about when he goes to Germany? Will he get bored with me and find someone else? What if…"

"Stop," Lexi firmly states. "Sam, you're going crazy with questions. You've only known the man for four days. You don't need to have all the answers right now. It's not like he's asking you to elope tomorrow or anything. Chill out. Relax." She places her hand on mine across the table and I feel myself relax and mentally thank her for pulling me off the edge of a cliff.

I take in a deep breath and calm myself further. "You're right. I need to calm down. I'm just so gun shy since finding out about Devin's infidelity issues. I completely trusted him, and it was a blow to find out about his affairs. I've never brought anyone around the kids and I'm just nervous."

"Oh, hon, you're going to be just fine. Anyone who can break through your barriers in such a short time must be worthy of meeting your kids," Lexi reassures me in only the way my best friend can.

"Thanks, Lex." I shrug and shake off the negative thoughts. "I don't know what I'd do without you."

"That's what I'm here for, Babe. Just keeping it real. I love you and can't wait to meet this devilishly handsome man that's got you so tied up in knots. He must be special, or you wouldn't have given him the time of day."

AFTER LEXI and I have our almost two-hour lunch break, I decide to call it quits for the day so I can pick up the kids. I drop by the grocery store to pick up some snacks for the girls after school. I can't wait for my kitchen to be finished so that I can just cook a regular meal again. Just as I am leaving the grocery store, I receive a text from Enzo and I can't help but smile.

Enzo: Hey beautiful, how's your day going? I haven't been able to stop thinking of you. I'm looking forward to seeing you this evening.

Holy Crap. What a way to start a conversation. The man sure doesn't mince words. Just the thought of seeing him again soon has me tingling all over. But what do I say in response? After a few minutes of thought, I finally tap out

Me: Me, too. I had a good day. How was yours?

Gaahhh... so lame. But it's already out there, what can I do?

Enzo: Great. Met with CO. Tell you more later.

Before I can respond, another text comes through.

Enzo: What kind of pizza do your kids like?

I'm curious as to how his meeting went, but I decide to wait for later, so I just answer the second question.

Me: Pepperoni or Canadian Bacon and Pineapple.

Enzo: What's your favorite?

Me: I usually just eat what they do, but I like garlic chicken or meat lovers as well. But whatever you like is fine.

Enzo: Any preference on drinks?

Me: You can just pick up what you like. I should have the drinks for the kids covered with what we have at home.

Enzo: What time do you want me there?

I want to say *now*. But instead I type:

Me: The game starts at 5:30. I should be home by 4:30, so any time you'd like.
Enzo: Gotta run. See you then.

I spend the rest of the afternoon in a lust-filled haze as I drive around taking the kids to their activities. My mind doesn't wander far from Enzo, but I manage to pick up Declan and Maddie from each of their schools on time. As I rush to feed Dec a snack so he can be at practice by four, I casually tell my kids we'll be watching the Seahawks game with a friend this evening. Neither of them gives much of a response, but then again, we're rushing from one place to the next and it's not like I haven't had people over for the game before. Just never a man I've been dating.

In the process of picking up and dropping off, I get a text from Maddie saying her friend Nicole will be dropping her off at home after practice. I'm relieved to have one less thing to do this afternoon. It takes a village to raise children and I'm thankful for all the help I can get. Usually, Devin picks up Declan at six from his practice, so I'll just meet him back at the house.

Before I know it, it's just Frankie and me driving home in the car. She's telling me all about her day and I contribute to the conversation the best I can. By the time we make it to our driveway, I've learned all about her friend's new haircut, what her dad made her for lunch, as well as a funny story her teacher told her about why it's important to learn how to read with punctuation. The amount of enthusiasm Frankie has for learning astounds me.

When we pull into the driveway, I notice Enzo waiting on the front porch. There's a bag of groceries next to him on the bench out front and he's looking at his phone. When he realizes we've arrived, he nearly takes my breath away with his greeting smile.

"Mama, isn't that Enzo?" Frankie asks.

"Yeah, honey, it is. He's here to watch the game with us," I remind her as I park the car.

Enzo greets me at my car door, by opening it. "Hey, beautiful, how was your day?" His husky voice sends shivers up my spine.

While Frankie's still in the car, he brushes a light kiss on my cheek, making me wish we could do more than that.

"Great. I had lunch with Lexi and I don't have to go back out to pick up Declan or Maddie tonight. They're both getting a ride home, so we can just watch the game."

"Fantastic. I ordered some pizza. It should be here around the time of kickoff." He closes my door and turns to greet Frankie, as she's finally managed to gather her things and climb out of my SUV. "Hello, Frankie."

"Hello." Frankie looks from me to Enzo, then back to me.

I remind her of our conversation in the car, "Hey, sweet pea, why don't you go inside and get your homework started, so we can watch the game in a little bit?" I gesture for her to move along and not doddle.

"Okay. I'll do my math. Then we can check it and read together," Frankie says without any fuss, thankfully. Sometimes she likes to procrastinate or play a while first.

As Frankie runs inside and closes the door, Enzo and I slowly make our way to the house. Enzo reaches for my hand to hold on the way to the front porch. Before we can get into view of any of the windows, he stops and pulls me in for a kiss.

"Damn, you taste good. I've been waiting for that all day." He keeps the kiss short, but it still has a lasting effect.

I reach up on my toes to kiss him once more before forcing myself to pull away. "Good to see you, too, handsome."

He lets out a slight groan and pulls away completely. He does lean back in to gruffly whisper, "I have no idea how I'm going to behave around you this evening. You've spoiled me this weekend. How do I refrain from touching you whenever I damn well please?"

"I feel the same way," I sigh. Then I look at the house. "We'd better get in there before she gets distracted and forgets to do her homework."

We walk to the porch in silence next to one another. He reaches down to pick up a grocery sack and we go inside. Just as we enter the door, I hear Frankie yell from the living room, "Mama, can you help me with this math?"

Since we don't have a working kitchen, I just tell Enzo to go put whatever needs to be put in the refrigerator in the spare one we keep in the garage. The rest can just be brought back into the living room since it's the only place we still have usable furniture and a TV. I point to the doorway off the kitchen so he knows where to go. He takes care of what's in his bag.

I settle down on the couch to help Frankie with her math. It's only a few minutes before Enzo returns and asks Frankie, "So, what are you working on?"

"Ugh," she sighs loudly. "I just have to do some multiplication and division." She points to the page she's working on.

"Want some help?" he asks, melting my heart just a little more. "I'm pretty good at math." He gives her a genuine smile and waits for her response a bit apprehensively. I don't think Frankie notices this though.

Frankie looks from me to him. She usually digs her heels in with me, so I'm so relieved when she eagerly accepts his help. "Sure, I guess so." *I can't believe she acts as if this is just an everyday occurrence.*

He sits on the couch and she scoots closer to him to show her work that's spread out all over the coffee table. She sounds so official and excited when she explains her homework to him. He has her read the directions at the top of the page to him then he asks her what she's supposed to be doing.

I sit back on the couch for a few minutes to watch. I'm quickly impressed with the fact Enzo has a natural way with her that makes her feel like math is fun, not a chore. He even teaches her a few tricks for how to do nines on her fingers as well as some basic chants to help her remember her facts like, "eight and eight, ate some more, eight times eight is sixty-four." She giggles and soon her homework is done. *I wish he would be here every night to make homework this easy.* Not that she's too difficult, but she seems to connect with him and didn't argue about the right way of doing it like she does with me. Sometimes, parents know nothing when it comes to schoolwork, according to the kids. I should know, I've been told many times. I guess it's just a rite of passage.

By the time they're finished, she is even eager to read her book she brought home. This never happens. I usually break it up and read before bedtime, so it doesn't become a fight. I'm shocked when she asks Enzo to read her *Magic Fairy* book with her. When she suggests, "How about... I read a page and you read the next, Enzo?" The look on his face is priceless. She crawls right up on the couch next to him, so they can both read the book together. He gestures to me for assurance and my ovaries nearly explode. The man is magic. *Apparently, I don't need to worry about Frankie liking Enzo. They seem to get along just fine. One down, two to go.*

She finishes her reading just as the game starts and the pizza arrives. Before I can even answer the door, Enzo is up and off the couch, paying for the pizza he had delivered. When he comes back from the door, he has at least three pizzas in front of him and a few smaller boxes on top. *Who the heck does he plan on feeding?* They all seem to be large pizzas. From the delicious aroma that fills the room, I can tell there must be a dessert pizza in the mix as well. When I count just how many things Enzo ordered, I see there are five boxes.

"Are you expecting company?" I exaggerate as I look around the room to see if there's more than just the three of us in the room.

Enzo looks as if he's a kid caught with his hand in the cookie jar. He's so damn adorable when he clears his throat. "Well, I didn't know exactly how much everyone would eat, so I just ordered one of each."

I can't help but laugh. "Um... the kids and I usually just eat one pizza, and sometimes there are even leftovers from that. This has to be over a hundred dollars' worth of pizza here."

"Well, since Maddie and Declan are just getting done with practice, I thought they might be really hungry. I know I always was when I played sports as a kid. Besides, I can usually eat at least half a pizza on my own." Enzo shrugs as if it's not a big deal.

"That's because you're six-foot-six and work out regularly.

If I eat more than a couple slices, I'm definitely going to have to go running in the morning."

"What time can I join you?" he suggests eagerly. "I haven't run since I've been home. Although I have been able to burn some calories in *other* ways." He waggles his eyebrows suggestively and I burst out laughing.

"Yeah... right..." I look over at Frankie who is completely oblivious to his suggestions. I can't help myself when I add seriously, "I usually run around six a.m. before I have to get the kids up for school."

"I'll be here," he whispers. Then, looking at Frankie, he changes his tone from deep and sexy to cool and kind as he addresses her, "I hope you're hungry. What kind of pizza do you want?"

Frankie eagerly helps us set up the pizza boxes on the coffee table. We put them in stacks on top of another, planning to pull from just the ones we need. Enzo pulls out some paper plates and a roll of paper towels from the bag he sat beside the couch. *The man thought of everything.* He tells Frankie there are containers of chocolate milk and juice staying cold in the garage fridge. Enzo and I burst into laughter as she pops off the couch and runs toward the garage to get a drink. I'm guessing she comes back with chocolate milk since it's her favorite.

Enzo doesn't waste any time while she's gone. He moves closer to me and plants a scorching kiss on my lips. Like usual, it doesn't take much from him to have my body become a sudden inferno. *Fuck, I wish we were alone. I want him to know my kids but being around him and having to control myself is torture.*

As if he reads my mind, he pulls away and whispers in my ear, "I know. I feel it, too."

The sounds of Frankie's feet making a fast track back to the living room has us pulling further apart. She has a container of chocolate milk in her hand and an enormous smile on her face. "Thanks, Enzo! Are you ready to watch the Hawks crush the Packers?"

Enzo's deep laughter fills the room. "Sure thing, Kid." To my surprise, she chooses to squeeze herself between Enzo and the other side of the couch. *I guess I no longer rate.*

"Um... Franks, do you think you should give him some room?" I eye the tiny space between the end of the couch and Enzo.

"Well, if you scoot over, we'll all have plenty of space," she states matter-of-factly, then shouts at the TV, "Way to go, Wilson!" as Russell Wilson, the quarterback for the Seahawks, just threw a long pass into the end zone for a touchdown. Frankie then cheers, and our conversation is forgotten, at least by her.

I look to Enzo and he just beams. Then he whispers in my ear, "Yeah, Sam, just move over so we can watch the game." He high-fives Frankie and we're glued to the TV until the next commercial break. Then he moves closer to me, so his entire leg presses against mine. Though the action might be innocent, the thoughts that swirl in my head about the sexy man next to me are anything but.

19

ENZO

SAMANTHA WASN'T LYING when she said she and her family are huge fans of the Seahawks. Both she and Frankie continue to yell at the screen, as if they're at CenturyLink Field. I don't think I've ever seen two girls so into football before. They cheer for their team as if they're playing in the Super Bowl right now. I can't help but find Samantha sexy as hell as she hoots and hollers at the television. I find myself cheering right along with them, enjoying every moment. In fact, I don't think I've ever had so much fun watching a football game before.

Within a half hour or so, two teenage girls come through the front door. From the pictures I have seen, as well as the resemblance to Samantha, I can tell which one is Maddie immediately. The girls are in deep conversation as they enter, but as soon as they see us here in the living room, they stop dead in their tracks.

"Uh, hi," Maddie says as she stares at her mother, Frankie, and me on the couch.

"Hey, Mads," Frankie greets.

Samantha follows with, "Hey, Maddie. Hi, Nicole. How was practice?"

"Good." Maddie still seems to be locked in place as she eyes me up and down.

Samantha takes notice and introduces us. "Maddie, this is Enzo Harper. Enzo, this is my daughter and her friend Nicole."

I stand to shake both of their hands, telling them it's nice to meet them. Then I gesture to the stacks of pizza still left on the table. "Care to join us for pizza?" I almost laugh when Maddie's eyes go as big as saucers when she takes in the number of boxes. *I guess I did go a little overboard. So sue me.*

"Are you expecting more people, Mom?" She looks to her mom for clarification.

Samantha shakes her head. "Nope. Just you and Declan. Thank goodness, Nicole is here. Maybe we won't have to eat pizza for a week." Before Maddie says anything else, the sassy woman next to me pins me with her beautiful mahogany eyes. "Apparently, Enzo thought we eat like savage beasts. He bought out the place." Her beautiful laughter fills the room as she motions to all the food.

"In my defense, I didn't want anyone going hungry." I hold my hands up as if to surrender.

"That won't be a problem, Mr. Harper. You bought enough pizza here for an entire army," Nicole adds with a grin as she eyes all the choices before us.

Okay. So... I went a lot overboard. I just remember my friends and I always being hungry. Wait. Mr. Harper? Since when have I become my old man? "Um, you can just call me Enzo or Harper. No need for the mister."

Maddie and Nicole look at me quizzically. They glance at Samantha, as if they're unsure of what to do. Before either of them can say anything, I cut them off and clarify, "Mr. Harper is my dad. Last I checked, he's not here. Enzo or Harper is what I respond to if you want my attention. My buddies usually shorten it to Harps. I'm used to all three since that's what I'm usually referred to. Twenty years in the Air Force will do that to you, I guess." I shrug as if this should explain everything. No need to go to such formalities.

Just then Samantha yells, "Go! Go! Go!" at the TV, as if it will personally usher Wilson into the end zone for another touchdown. *God, I love her enthusiasm.* Now we're all glued to the TV to see if he can score or not.

Nicole and Maddie sit on the other couch in the living room and watch the game. All of us are completely enthralled with the action on the screen. Hoots and hollers can be heard sporadically as we sit on the edge of our seats. The Hawks have stopped the Packers on the one-yard line and there's less than a minute until half-time. Rodgers, the Packers' quarterback, receives the snap and throws it to one of his wide receivers for a touchdown, but it's picked off by Sherman. Everyone goes wild. The screams that can be heard throughout the room are insane, considering they're coming from a mom and three kids.

When it finally quiets down, we notice Declan has entered

the house with his dad at his side. Declan seems to be in awe of the celebration that has taken over the room. He greets us, "What's going on?"

Maddie jumps up from the couch excitedly. "You missed it, Dec! Griffin got another pick and stopped the Packers from scoring!" He looks at the TV, which is now in a replay of the scene.

"Sounds like a good game," Devin states. He appears to be interested in the game, but I can't help but notice the brief look of surprise that crosses his face when he notices me here. He doesn't say anything, but I can tell he's not expecting to see me.

I decide not to make this any more awkward for him than necessary. "It's a great game. You're welcome to stay and watch. It's just about half-time and I've ordered plenty of pizza." I point out the piles of boxes on the coffee table.

"Nah, I think I'll head out so I can watch the rest of the game at home. Thanks for the offer," he sincerely states before turning to head to the door. Before he can leave, Samantha stops him.

"Hey, Devin, do you think you could keep Dec tomorrow after practice until I can pick him up from you? I'm taking Maddie shopping after her practice, so I won't be home until later."

"Shouldn't be a problem. Do you want me to pick up Miss Muffet from school, so you can just go with Mads? Tomorrow is when you're going to get the dirty deets on that boy Maddie is going to the dance with, right?"

"Dad," Maddie huffs out in complaint. "That right there is why you aren't meeting him first! You're horrible."

"Only doing my job, Mads. Only doing my job," Devin reminds her with a grin spread wide across his face.

I can't help but smile at their interaction. *God knows what I would do if I had a daughter who wanted to date. Heaven help me there.* I think if it wasn't for the fact Devin cheated on Samantha, I could see myself liking this guy. *But then again, his loss is my gain. If the fucker didn't screw things up with Sam, I wouldn't be here.*

"Who says I'm not going to give Soren the third degree?" Samantha perks up trying to get in on the ribbing.

"Mom. Not you, too. You're the sane one. The nice one. The one that doesn't make threats or embarrass me," Maddie reminds her sweetly.

Samantha looks very serious at me and says, "You know how to hide a body, right?" Then she looks back to Maddie and adds with a straight face, "I'm sure I could get some help if I needed."

All that can be heard from Maddie is a sudden intake of air.

Without missing a beat, I casually state, "I'm sure I could figure something out."

"This is insane," Maddie huffs. "Come on, Nicole. Let's go upstairs. It's only a dance; it's not like I'm going to marry the guy or anything. You guys need to give it a rest." She and Nicole each take another piece of pizza on a plate and head upstairs while the rest of us try to contain our laughter.

"She's ticked," Samantha says under her breath as Declan comes into the room and helps himself to pizza.

Frankie exclaims, "There's chocolate milk in the fridge out in the garage, Dec!"

"Awesome!" Declan puts his pizza down and heads to the garage.

"Well... I'll leave you to it," Devin states awkwardly. "Let me know if you need anything, Sam." Devin looks up the stairs and shakes his head in disbelief. "I still can't believe she's going on her first date this week. Time sure does fly."

"Yes, it does," Samantha agrees. "Don't be too hard on them when you come to meet him on Friday."

He grins dubiously. "I have rights as a father, Sam."

"Would you rather she sneak around?" Sam points out, raising an eyebrow. Devin slumps in defeat. "No... no, I wouldn't. I guess I'll talk to you tomorrow." With that, he shakes his head and walks out the door.

Sam and I both sit back on the couch. Frankie takes it upon herself to sit on the other side of me again. The girl hasn't left my side since I've been here. Well, except to get her chocolate milk. Which is a hit in this household. I'll have to remember that for future use. I'm just about relaxed on the couch when I look over and realize Declan is eyeing me suspiciously. Shit. I forgot to introduce myself. He's giving me a *'what the fuck are you doing here with my mother look.'* I immediately stand to rectify the situation.

I hold out my hand to him. "Hey, you must be Declan. I'm Enzo."

He shakes my hand firmly and looks me in the eye. "Nice to meet you." He then looks toward his mom.

"Sorry, honey, I forgot to introduce you. He's already met

everyone else and with the drama stunt your sister just played, I got distracted." Samantha then asks, "How was practice?"

"It was good. What's the score on the game?" He motions to the TV.

"21-7, Hawks," I interject.

Declan cocks his head to the side and looks me over with care. I notice him glance at his mother, then back to me. I want to ask him what's on his mind, but I'm not sure how to handle this. This is uncharted territory and I'm making it up as I go.

I finally break the scrutiny with, "So what position do you play?"

Declan smiles and tells me about his position as forward. He can play all positions, but from what I gather, this is where he shines. With the help of strategic prodding on my behalf, we have a real conversation that seems to easily flow. I glance from time to time at Samantha, and she just smiles in a way that could take a grown man to his knees. The pride she has for her children is evident.

When halftime is over, we all go back to watching the game. Samantha remains at my side as we laugh at commercials, joke with each other, and cheer for our team. Her touch is addictive, so I keep one leg along hers most of the evening. I know I can't have more now, but I like being close to her. The more I get to know Samantha, the more I find myself completely drawn to her.

WHEN THE GAME'S OVER, Samantha tells Declan and Frankie that it's time to get ready for bed. Nicole had left awhile ago and Maddie is still upstairs, having yet to resurface. Declan heads upstairs without an argument to take a shower and finish his homework. Frankie hangs around for a while longer. She doesn't seem to be ready for bed. She laughs and jokes around with me as easy as my nieces and nephews do. Finally, about twenty minutes later, Samantha pulls out the mom voice.

"Frankie, it's already past your bedtime. Tell Enzo goodnight and head upstairs. I'll be up in a few minutes to tuck you in."

For the first time all night, I hear a whine come from her, "But, Mom... I don't wanna go to bed."

"Sorry, Charlie, it's bedtime for you." Samantha comes over to her, cocks her head to the side, and places her hands on her hips. If she wasn't trying to be stern, I would burst out laughing. I give her a look asking if I should leave, and she shakes her head no. *Okay then. What should I do to help the situation?*

Frankie looks to me as if I can rescue her. "Can Enzo tuck me in and read another story with me?" She looks at me with pleading eyes and I can't help it when a small laugh escapes. She's fucking adorable. The eight-year-old extortionist. That should be her new name. Frankie's way too cute for her own good.

I look to Samantha for direction. She looks... a little shocked, if I'm correct in my assessment. Finally, she shrugs. "If Enzo is okay with it." I nod in approval. "But you," she looks to Frankie, "need to get upstairs, change into jammies, and brush your teeth. Enzo won't come up until that's done. And he will only read one chapter. Got it?"

Frankie looks as if she could jump up and down and scream with excitement. But instead, she shoots me a look and asks, "Will you really read me a story before bed?"

"Sure thing, kiddo. But do what your ma tells you first. Then I'll be upstairs," I reassure her.

"But you don't know where my room is." Frankie protests.

Samantha sighs. "Frankie. I'll show him. Now, scoot up the stairs, so he can come and read."

Frankie turns and runs up the stairs. It's finally just Samantha and myself. She comes to me and I pull her body close to mine in an all-enveloping hug. After a moment, I place my hand under her chin and turn her face to look at me. "You are amazing, beautiful." I lean down and kiss her gently on the lips.

I seem to have ignited the flame between us because she takes our kiss to a whole new level within moments. I do my damnedest to keep aware of our surroundings because there's no way in hell I want to have her kids walk in on us at this moment. Yes, I feel my arousal course through my body. Yes, I'm sure she wants it just as bad as I do. But I can't. Get. Carried. Away. It takes everything in me to pull away from the gorgeous woman before me. I hold her close for a moment more before letting her go. Well, almost. I'm still holding her hand.

She starts to walk toward the stairs, but I stop her. "Um... give me a sec," I whisper.

She looks at me questioningly and I can't help but show her what I mean when I adjust myself. *Jesus, what is it about being around her that makes my jeans shrink?* "There's no way I can go upstairs and face your kids in my condition."

The challenging grin conspiring on her face is the only warning I get before she walks over to me and feels for herself, just how much my condition is affecting me. "Samantha," I groan. "You're not helping."

She whispers, "Payback's a bitch. My panties have been drenched since before the game started." She leans up on her tiptoes and kisses me lightly. Then she turns and walks up the stairs. The sway of her ass has me wanting to follow her for an entirely different reason.

Suddenly, Frankie yells, "Enzo, are you coming?"

I wish. I grumble to myself. Samantha stops at the top of the stairs and almost falls back down them with silent laughter. She turns to me, shaking her head. "They always do have impeccable timing."

"Good to know," I try to grumble, but laughter wins out.

Samantha walks me to Frankie's door and tells me she's going to check in with the others after she discovers I'm going to be fine on my own with Frankie. As an uncle, I've told a lot of bedtime stories. I pull out all the punches and do special voices for the characters. Frankie insists on me sitting on her bed next to her, so she can see the words on the pages, too. She's wearing fuzzy pajamas with feet in them. The kind that looks way too warm to wear, but she digs them. She's lying on top of the soft purple quilt on her bed. As I look around her room, I see her walls are a light purple as well. That must be her favorite color.

"So, what are we reading tonight, kiddo?" I ask as I sit beside her, keeping my shoes hanging off the side of her bed.

"*The Twits.* I just got it from the library. Mama said I can only read one chapter with you, but they're really short. Can we just read for a while?"

I realize she's right. The first chapter is only a paragraph or two. It's about noticing beards. Now that I've read it, I can't help but think about how many beards I notice when I'm out and about. The next chapter has Frankie squirming when she realizes how disgusting Mr. Twit is. I can't help but laugh. I've never read this story before, but it's very entertaining. The part about how dirty beards can be makes me never want to have one again, not that I've ever worn one. Damn, that man is disgusting. Keeping morsels of food for later, never showers, and his being an all-around Twit makes me want to vomit. I flip the front cover to see when this was published. Wow. I wish I'd read this as a kid. I totally would've loved it.

After about fifteen minutes or so, I tell Frankie it's time for bed. To my surprise, she doesn't argue. Instead, she says, "Thanks, Enzo. I had fun tonight. Will you be back again soon?" She yawns heavily, and I take that as my cue to stand from the bed. She pulls her covers up closer to her chin.

The look she gives me floods my heart with emotion. There's complete trust and comfort. *I could get used to doing this every night.* I shake my head to clear my thoughts. I ruffle her hair and clear my throat to hide how she's affected me. "I sure hope so, Kiddo. Night."

"Night, Enzo," she calls to me as I walk to the door to turn off the light.

"Do you leave it open or closed?" I point to the door.

"Closed. I have a nightlight." She rolls over to face the wall as I close the door.

I don't get much further in the hallway when I see Samantha leaving Declan's room. She shuts the door and motions for the stairs. I make my way over and walk down. I can feel Samantha behind me. But I don't say anything until I'm in the living room.

"How is everything?" I point upstairs. "Was Maddie upset? She never came back down earlier."

"She's fine. She just had a lot of homework and was talking with Soren on the phone after Nicole left." Samantha shrugs. "She's just about done and is about to go to sleep."

"What about Declan?" I walk over to the pizza boxes and consolidate as many of them as possible.

Samantha helps me. We manage to get it all into two boxes. The kids devoured the dessert pizza earlier. "He just had me turn out his light. He will be sawing logs soon. He wears himself out at practice."

She gathers the full boxes as I gather the empties. "Let's take these to the garage," she suggests.

As soon as we rid ourselves of the boxes, I stalk over to Samantha, who's next to the fridge. "Thanks for inviting me over tonight. It's great getting to know your family." I pull her close to me. One hand is reaching for the nape of her neck while the other snakes around the small of her back.

"I should be thanking you…" She looks as if she's about to say something else, but suddenly seems distracted.

Samantha pulls in a deep breath as she locks her eyes with mine. "I've missed you," comes out before I can think about what I'm saying. I pull her even closer than before.

"Me, too." She willingly closes the gap between us.

Having lost all my restraint from earlier, I slowly consume her with a kiss. The contact alone has me nearly losing all my control. It doesn't help that she's reaching under my black t-shirt and scraping her fingernails against my abs. I take a step to the side, bringing her with me so that her body can be hidden behind the fridge, should anyone walk in on us.

I press her body up against the wall and one of her legs encircles my hip. I grab her ass to hoist her into the air, pinning her against the wall and my chest. This reminds me of the first night at her front door.

"Enzo, I can't wait any longer," Samantha practically pants. She pulls me back, devouring my mouth.

Thank fuck, she's wearing a skirt. I've wanted to reach under it all night and have my way with her. I inch it higher, running my hands up her inner thigh. When I get to the delicate fabric of her panties, I find them completely soaked. She hadn't been kidding earlier… had I only known. I would've found a way to help her out. I push them to the side and tease her. The quiet noises she makes let me know that I'm right on track. With little effort, I slide one finger inside, then quickly add another. I work her up until I know she's close to teetering over the edge by mimicking the motions of my mouth with my hand. The minute I change the position of my fingers to reach that perfect spot inside her, she detonates around me. I feel her inner muscles clamp down as spasm after spasm spread through her.

Each sensational tremor makes me want her even more. I pull my hand out from under her skirt to steady her as I reach for my wallet. And that's when I realize. FUCK!!! Fuckity, Fuck, Fuck! I knew I'd run out of condoms and I was in such a hurry to get over here, I'd forgotten one very important item on the list. Then I think it is for the best. I shouldn't be having sex with her while her kids are here. What the ever-loving fuck had I been thinking?

Samantha can tell there is something wrong and opens her mouth to ask, "Wha..." She slides down my body to put her feet on the floor.

"Nothing to worry about, beautiful. Let's see how quick we can make another orgasm rip through you." Making my entire focus be on her, I do my best to forget about my own needs for now. I drop to my knees and pull her legs over my shoulders. I hold her against the wall with one hand resting against her hip while I push up her skirt with my other to get to what I need desperately. *Shit, this underwear must go.* My hands find a seam and all that can be heard is the quick rip of fabric. Samantha gasps at my bold move. Within mere seconds, my mouth reaches the promised land of all that is Samantha. I make good on my promise of bringing her to another crippling orgasm quickly. I lick up every drop of her arousal as she comes down from her high.

As I set her feet on the floor, her legs almost buckle beneath her. I pull her down onto my lap and cradle her as both of our breaths return to normal. Having her in my arms is more than enough. I wish I could take her to bed and have her wake in my arms as I have for the past three mornings, but with her kids at home, that isn't an option.

Wait! When the fuck did I start wanting sleepovers all the time?

Since you met this amazing woman, dumbass.

As if reading my mind, Samantha sexily whispers, "I wish you could stay. I've gotten used to waking up with you."

"Me, too, beautiful. Me, too. But I'd better get going or I'm never going to be able to leave." I absolutely hate that I said that aloud. But it must be done. "I need to go home and take a very cold shower. I have very little self-control left. I know that kids can walk in at any time, as I've heard many embarrassing stories from my siblings about their own kids interrupting times like this." There's no way I'm going to compromise Samantha in any way, shape, or form. As much as I try to test my limits on a regular basis, I know I only have so much self-control.

Samantha sighs deeply with as much regret on her face as I feel. "I know."

"I'll be over here at six-thirty to go running with you tomorrow." There's no way I'm going to miss out on any time I can have with her.

We get up and I help her adjust her clothing. I notice she grabs her shredded panties off the floor and fists them in her hand. She kisses me gently one last time before I pull away. *If we keep this up, we'll be sleeping in the garage tonight.*

With all the resolve I can muster, I motion to the garage

door. "I think I'll just head out this way. I don't want to risk the chance of your kids seeing me still here. I wouldn't want them to get the wrong impression."

Samantha shrugs and gives me a nod of understanding. "I appreciate that."

With one last goodbye kiss, I whisper, "Goodnight, Samantha. I'll see you in the morning."

She walks me to the door and kisses me one last time before saying, "Goodnight, Enzo. Thanks for coming over."

With that, I leave. *Fuck! Being honorable sucks. My dick wholeheartedly agrees with that sentiment as well.*

20

———

SAMANTHA

MY DREADED ALARM goes off at five forty-five a.m. The only thing that gets me out of my all-too-comfortable bed is knowing I'll be seeing Enzo shortly. That sexy man made it so I could hardly walk up the stairs last night, as my legs feel like Jell-O. As soon as my head hit the pillow, I barely had time to contemplate what he'd done to me in the garage because I was sound asleep. Now that I think about it, I realize I hadn't returned the favor to him. He had made me blissfully climax twice and I didn't even offer to reciprocate. I know he didn't want to get caught, and neither did I, for that matter. I can't help but think I was a bit of a shitty girlfriend.

Girlfriend? Since when did I think of myself as that? Well, what else would I be? We agreed to see where our relationship would go, didn't we? Doesn't that make me his girlfriend?

I glance at the clock again and realize I have been daydreaming about Enzo for longer than I thought. I rush to the bathroom to brush my teeth and run a brush through my hair. It doesn't take long before it's in a high ponytail. I come back to my room and dress in a pair of running pants, tank, and a long-sleeved shirt with holes for my thumbs. I know it's still going to be dark outside, and there's no way I'm going to be cold. The shirt and pants have built-in reflectors in them, so I can be seen. I also grab my visor that has a built-in headlamp and flashing light on the back of it. *Always better to be safe than sorry.*

I rush down the stairs to put on my running shoes that I usually leave in the hall closet. Then I leave a note for the kids, should they get up before I get back. I'm about to grab a glass of water when I hear a quiet knock on the door.

It is just after six, so I know it must be Enzo. I'm learning to expect him to arrive earlier than he always says he will. *I might want to remember this for the future.* I feel like a schoolgirl with her first crush. My stomach has a thousand butterflies swarming inside as I walk to the door.

Without a word, Enzo pulls me in for a mind-shattering kiss. When he pulls back, he has a smile on his face that would sell millions of copies of romance novels based on that alone, if he worked in the book industry. *Damn! He would make bank in the modeling world.*

"No, beautiful. No one would buy a single copy if I was on the cover. You, on the other hand, might sell out within minutes."

Did I say my thoughts aloud? Again? Shaking my head, feeling slightly embarrassed by the comment I hadn't intended to say to him, I say, "There I go without my filter again."

"Thanks for the compliment though. That was one I've never heard before," Enzo teases. "Are you ready to go?" he asks as he gives my body a full assessment.

I take a moment to ogle him as well. He's in a black t-shirt that looks as if his muscled body is trying to escape. The hard planes of his chest are on display, thanks to the taut fabric. His black running shorts perfectly display his thick, muscular thighs. Upon further inspection, I realize he, too, has reflective strips throughout his clothing to be seen better.

"Wanna stretch in here or outside?" he asks as he glances upstairs to see if anyone else is up.

"Let's go outside."

We head out and begin stretching in my driveway. Before long, I put my visor on and we jog down my driveway and into my neighborhood. We run at a conversational pace. It dawns on me I never asked him about his meeting with the Air National Guard. *I'm a shitty girlfriend.*

"So how did your meeting with the CO go?" I ask as we round the corner on my block.

"Not bad. They don't have any jobs in the area I was hoping for and it would screw with my retirement. So, I won't be going in that direction." He shrugs.

Wanting further clarification, I ask, "What does that mean?"

"I'm leaning pretty heavily on taking Riggs up on his offer." It's still dark, so I can't see his facial expression clearly.

"Oh," I reply. We jog a few more paces in silence and I consider what his comment could mean. When I realize I don't have a clue, I decide to ask him. "Would it be much different from what you're already doing?"

"Not really. I would get to relocate and have a permanent home though. I'd still go out on missions, sometimes without much notice. My job would be to get his people in and out of locations safely. I might have to do other things to help the team, but transportation would be my focus."

"Is it safe?" I ask, suddenly working my lip between my teeth.

"That's what I'd be there for. To get everyone in and out safely. I'd be behind the scenes unless it was necessary for me to be out in the field. It would be a team situation with a lot more money and eyes on the game than what I'm used to." Enzo is quiet for a few strides. Then he continues, "You know, Samantha, I don't take risks that aren't necessary. I keep my head in the game and I do what's best for everyone involved. Is this job risk-free? Hell no. But I can promise you this. I'll do my damnedest to get back to you as often as possible."

Did he just make a declaration to me? Did I really just hear that?

"What do you mean?" I ask, wondering where he's going with this line of thought.

Enzo suddenly stops under a lamp post so I can clearly see the expression on his face. He sets his hands on his hips and says, "I want to move to Portland and really see where this thing goes between us. Before meeting you, I'd decided I didn't want to stay in the Air Force. I want a permanent home and not have to move every couple of years, but I'm not ready to give up flying entirely. I want to spend more time with my family. And… while I'm being honest, now that I've met you, I want to spend more time with you, too."

"I'd love that," is all I manage to say because my heart is fluttering out of my chest.

"Good to hear." He smiles smugly and his dimple pops. *I'm a frickin goner. This man's dimple gets me every time.*

Suddenly, I think of something that should've been my first thought. "What about my kids?" I whisper.

His eyebrows raise, and his smile turns into a smirk. "Uh… Sam… You're kind of a package deal. I know that. So, quit worrying."

A rush of relief I didn't know I was holding on to barrels through my body. He wants to be with me; he wants to see where it goes. "Okay."

"Okay? Is that all I get after baring my soul to you? Just, okay?" Enzo's lips quirk, so I know he's teasing, but there's a hint of seriousness that shines in his eyes.

I'm a little overwhelmed by his declaration, but relieved at the same time. *Who knew those few simple words would be such a big deal? My kids and I are a package deal for him.* Of course, I wouldn't have it any other way. Even though everything is still new, and I'm in completely uncharted territory, I look at the man before me and am stunned by the complete sincerity in his glorious green eyes. There's also a slight sense of vulnerability to him as well, so I clarify my thoughts, "Okay. I want to see where this goes, too. Besides, it'll be a whole lot easier to find out what happens if you're closer to me each day."

He steps closer to wrap his arms around me, pulling me

into an enormous hug. He smells so incredible, even after working out. Soon, Enzo pulls us apart enough to kiss me, showing the emotion of his unspoken words. But when he's done, he says, "Those are just the words I needed to hear, beautiful."

I can't help the laughter that escapes when I look around and realize our surroundings. *Here we are in the middle of the street, declaring ourselves to one another and the sun hasn't even risen yet. What will happen by breakfast?* I try to make light of everything by taunting, "You ready to run, hotshot?" I adjust my visor and run down the street faster than our pace before, but he catches up to me with ease. We keep this pace for a while, making it difficult to have any conversation, but I'm in the zone, flying high not only on endorphins but on the words from Enzo as well.

After a couple of miles, we slow back down to a conversational pace. Enzo lifts the end of his shirt to wipe the sweat from his face. I can't stop myself from gawking at his washboard stomach. Without even processing the words, I blurt out, "How in the hell did you get those?" I point at his stomach in disbelief. *Yes, I've seen his body before, but now that I'm working out with this man, I know he must do more than just run each day to get abs that look photoshopped onto his body.*

At first, he obviously doesn't know what I'm talking about because he asks, "My shorts?"

I laugh, I can't help it. "No, hotshot. Those abs." I point at them again while we run a little further.

He shrugs his shoulders. "I was born with them?" he offers, trying not to make a big deal of it.

I give him a pointed look to let him know I'm not buying it.

"Samantha, I work out regularly."

"Ugh..." I moan. "Please don't tell me you're actually a gym junkie?" Not that that would be a big deal, but I would feel like I need to step up my workouts and I just don't have a lot of time.

He stops running completely and bends down to place his hands on his knees. His body shakes and when he looks up at me, I can see a full belly laugh ripping through him. "Shit, Sam, you should have seen the look on your face. I don't spend much time in a gym. I do lift a little, but usually, it's more CrossFit and resistance type training. I don't need to bulk up. I prefer to be able to scratch my own ass."

That last comment has me nearly doubling over in hysterics. What a picture to paint in my head. Geesh! *What a smartass. He's got good looks and a sense of humor.*

"You don't appear to be the type that lifts in front of a mirror to see his progress on a daily basis." I take a deep breath to steady myself.

"Sam, most of what I do to work out involves limited space and time. I just fit it in when I can." He once again shrugs as if it's not a big deal. "Do you have a problem with going to the gym?"

Oh. My. Goodness. I'm a complete dork. I stop dead in my tracks when I realize how ridiculous I just sounded. I shake my head. "No, Enzo. I don't have a problem with going to the gym.

I was just teasing you." I look down at myself and shake my head, feeling a bit mortified. "I was just caught ogling you... and tried to give *you* a hard time for being the cause of it. You tried to pass off your hotness as not a big deal. But look at you! I could put you on the cover of almost any of the romance books I work with and you'd have an instant following." I raise my hand up and down as if to point out his hotness even more, but by the end, I can't help but close my eyes as I wait for his response.

He's shaking his head. Trying to contain a laugh as he says, "The look on your face is priceless... you didn't offend me. You looked as if you're completely mortified and have absolutely no reason to be. I just wasn't expecting you to compliment my body after all that we've done together." Enzo reaches out to grab a hold of me and pulls me close to his body. He perfectly executes a huge bear hug, but I can still feel tremors from his silent laughter. "Your lack of filter is definitely one of the many things I enjoy about you."

I let out a big huff but hug him back. He feels amazing against me. I don't even care that I'm sweaty and likely stink. I take a deep breath. *The man even smells sexy. This is so not fair.*

"What's not fair?" *he asks. UGGG!!! My fucking filter.*

I look up to him sheepishly. "Even when you work out, you still smell sexy."

"You're delusional, Samantha." I feel his body rock with another tremor of silent laughter. "I reek just like everyone else. Just give me time. I promise."

"If you say so..." I take in another breath and all that I smell is Enzo. No reeking involved. I wish I could bottle what I smell. I'd make a fortune... but then again, I wouldn't be willing to share.

We finish our run and head back to the house. The kids are already up and dressed, but still getting ready for school. Enzo asks if we have time to go out for breakfast, and after looking at the clock, I tell him, "Only if we drive them to school." My two younger kids are ecstatic and rush to finish getting ready. Maddie is also eager to go because it sounds better than a cereal bar, so she retreats to her room to finish gathering all her things for school. Enzo asks if he can use one of the spare bathrooms upstairs after getting something he needs from his bag outside. I rush upstairs and take a quick spin in the shower. In record time, we're all back downstairs, ready to go within fifteen minutes. I decided to just towel dry my hair because there is no way I would have had time to dry it this morning. Enzo offers to drive and we all pile into his rental SUV. He takes us to his favorite diner not far from my house.

Conversations flow easily all throughout breakfast. The waitress overhears me telling the kids there won't be time to dilly-dally as we eat, or we'll be late for school, and without even asking, I hear her put a rush on our order. Thankfully, our food is out with plenty of time to eat leisurely. Maddie opens up and I can tell she's excited to go shopping this evening for the dance on Friday. Declan and Frankie chat Enzo's ear off and I can't help but smile at how eager he is to hear what they have to say.

We drop the kids off at their respective schools with plenty of time before the arrival bell rings. Enzo brings me back to my house and as we approach, we can tell his dad's crew is up and running for the morning. With any hope, things will be back to normal before too long. "Would you like to come in? I have to be at the office later for a meeting, but you're welcome to stay for a while."

He puts the car in park and peruses the driveway and trucks lining the street. "Um... Sure. I'd love to. I guess I could go see how Pops is doing." He points to a truck that must be his father's.

We head inside through the front door and the sounds are evident that progress is being made in my kitchen. No one sees us approach or hears us, due to the noise I'm sure. Lorenzo Harper has his back to us, and when the sound of a saw stops, Enzo makes our presence known. "It's about time you got out of bed, Pops."

Lorenzo turns around with a huge grin on his face. "I was surprised to find you gone when I left this morning actually."

Enzo looks over to me. "Wanted to get a run in. Samantha works out before the kids go to school. Then," he points around the room to the beautiful kitchen for an explanation, "we took them to breakfast. We just got back now."

"Busy morning, 'Zo." He winks at me and says, "Nice to see you again, Samantha."

"Nice to see you, too," I reply. "You guys are making a lot of progress."

"We should be done taking out the floors by the end of the day. Your current tile is being stubborn in some places." He points to a spot where men are chipping as we speak. "Then with that wall removed..." He points to the wall in question where two other men are working on it since the floor around it has been removed. "We hope to be ready for floors tomorrow."

"Wow, you do quick work." I marvel at the amount of work that needs to be done beforehand.

"Need a hand?" Enzo asks.

Lorenzo looks around at his crew. "Naw. We've got it covered. I was just popping in to check on everything. I'll let you know if that changes. You just enjoy your time off." He gives me a wink and then walks over to help one of the guys from the crew hold a new piece of drywall they're replacing under my new bay window. From across the room. Lorenzo hollers, "I'm going to head out to another site in about thirty minutes if you want to join me."

"Sure, Pops, sounds like a plan." Enzo smiles then turns toward me. "Do you need to get ready?"

"Yeah, I'm going to head upstairs to finish getting ready for work." I motion for the stairs. "You're welcome to come visit with me while I do."

Enzo's eyes turn a darker shade of green and the look on his face is evident of his intent. "Sure, sounds good." The playful mirth dancing in his eyes and sexy smile give away his intentions.

AS I SIT at my desk later that afternoon, I can't help but contemplate the events of my morning. After Enzo and I went upstairs, we made good use of my bathroom counters. I had every intention of just getting dressed and ready for work. But knowing that we won't have much time alone together this week, we made good use of our time alone. Thank God, my bathroom is the furthest from the crew working downstairs.

As I leaned forward to put my makeup on in the mirror, he came up behind me and whispered in my ear how sexy he thought I was. One thing led to another, and the next thing I knew, I was pushed forward over my counter, the skirt of my dress was around my waist, and my panties were easily discarded. It was H-O-T! I watched Enzo's intense gaze through the mirror as he showed me just how sexy he thought I was. Our connection was so unbelievably strong, the house could've caught on fire from our combustible chemistry alone. When we were done, he helped me clean up, then he cleaned himself. *Always the gentleman.*

Once he was put back together, in all his usual perfection, he kissed me goodbye and went downstairs. I, on the other hand, stayed upstairs to make myself look presentable once again. It was a lot faster without his sexiness distracting me. But, I missed him all the same.

I made it to work and met with my client as I was supposed to. All went better than I expected, and we should see some amazing returns on our efforts. Now, I find myself staring out the window and daydreaming about the man who is starring center stage as my real-life fantasy. I know I should be working, but the manuscript I'm working on is another contemporary romance and when the scenes get sexy, my mind shuts off to all things, other than Enzo. *God help me.* I need to get my work done at some point.

When I realize I can't concentrate on the words in front of

me. I pick up my phone and call Enzo's sister. I try to keep it as professional as possible, telling her my available time to meet with her early next week. She eagerly takes me up on my offer and we agree she will come into my office to meet one afternoon.

When I hang up, I notice a text came through from Enzo while I was talking.

Enzo: Hey, beautiful. How's your day going?

Me: I just got off the phone with your sister. I'm meeting with her next week. How are you?

Enzo: I can't stop thinking about bending you over that counter this morning.

I can't help the blush that creeps over me. He must be a mind reader because our sexy scene has been playing through my mind on a loop all morning. *What the hell do I say to that?* I go with the truth.

Me: It was incredible. I won't deny that it has been on my mind, too.

Enzo: What are you doing now?

Me: I was just going to finish up with a manuscript, then grab something for lunch.

Enzo: Want some company?

Me: I'd love some.

Enzo: I'll be there in 20.

I'm about to ask if he needs the address when another text comes through.

Enzo: Make that 5. I'm closer than I thought.

21

———

ENZO

EARLIER THIS MORNING...

AFTER I LEAVE Samantha this morning, I head out with Pops to look at a few job sites. On our way to the first one, he asks me how things are going with Samantha. Of course, I tell him the truth. I've never felt this way about anyone else. We also talk about my job possibilities again. I tell him I'm heavily leaning toward the job with Riggs. He makes the situation crystal clear when he asks, "What's holding you back from making your decision?"

I really can't come up with anything. I think long and hard about it while Pops picks up an order from our local hardware store. It's just for a small tool, so I stay in the truck to ponder my thoughts. Every pro and con for each of my potential choices make it that much clearer that I want to be in Portland. I've wanted to retire from the Air Force, and I've wanted to go to the private sector, rather than stay in the military, so I have control of my future. If truth be told, Samantha did have an influence on my decision as well. The thought of leaving and going back to the single life after experiencing what I've had with her makes me shudder.

I've been dating for the better part of the last twenty years. I've never, and I mean *never*, come across a woman who has captured my interest the way she has. I know it's still new. I know she has a family and there will be a lot of obstacles in the way, but I have zero desire to walk away from her at this point. She may get annoyed with me and chuck me to the curb, but for now, I need to see where this goes.

By the time Pops comes back out to the truck, I've made my decision. Pops must see it in my eyes because the grin on his face becomes infectious. He lets out a deep chortle. "So, you've made your decision." *The man does know me well. But then again, that's my dad for you.*

"Yep, I'm going to take Riggs up on his offer," I state eagerly.

"I figured as much. I didn't see you staying in the Air Force much longer, after seeing you with Samantha this weekend and again this morning." He seems to think for a moment, but then another smile spreads across his face. "She sure is something."

"You can say that again, Pops. The more I get to know her, the more I fall for her. I can't honestly say I've ever felt this way about anyone, including Vanessa."

Pops lets out a low whistle. "That's saying something."

"You may as well make it official and let everyone else in on your decision, Son. Why don't I drop you back off at

Samantha's? You must have some important phone calls to make. No need to keep anyone waiting any longer." *Damn. The man sure doesn't mince words.*

"Are you sure, Pops? I can hang out with you today if you'd like."

"Son, you do what you need to do. I'll be here. You can always hang out with your old man another day."

"Thanks, Pops." I give him a knowing look.

"Anytime."

When we get back to Samantha's house, I'm disappointed to have missed her before she left for work. But we both have things we need to do, so I'll have to catch up with her later. Not wanting to waste any time, I make my calls from Samantha's driveway.

First, I call my CO in Germany. It's still early evening there, so the timing is right. He had asked to know when I make my decision. I can tell he isn't surprised with my choice. Most people don't make it twenty years, let alone stay in longer these days. He seems happy for me and is looking forward to seeing me when I come back until I officially retire. Knowing the crew I work with, there will be a lot of ribbing coming my way, but it'll all be done in good fun. It does feel weird to know I only have less than four months to work with them now. They've been my life for so long, it will be strange to not have my team with me. The fact I have over a month left of leave makes this all seem even more surreal.

My next call is to the CO at Air National Guard. I don't owe him anything but my decision, so there's no hard feelings.

He understands I've committed twenty years to being with the Air Force. Being thirty-eight allows for me to have a civilian retirement as well.

My next call is to Riggs. He wasn't expecting my decision so soon, but I can tell he's pleased. He's going to email me my contract to sign, as well as all the paperwork necessary to fill out as a new hire. I tell him I will get on it today and get it back to him within the next day or so. We talk about my potential start date and I tell him I will have to get back to him on that. I mention that I will need a couple of weeks for my move back from Germany as well. Overall, things seem to be falling into place, making it evident this is the best decision for me.

By the time I finish my calls, there's only one person I have left to tell. I look up her office on my phone and find the address. I realize I know exactly where it is, without even having to get directions. I shoot off a quick text to her.

When I arrive at her office and walk to the entrance, I can tell she has established herself and has done well for herself, as it looks upscale. As soon as I open the door, I see a receptionist to one side of the office suite. She looks to be about twenty-five, dressed professionally with straight strawberry-blond hair, pulled into a high ponytail. She locks eyes with me for a second, acknowledging my presence before taking a breath to greet me with, "Hello, how can I help you?"

"I'm Enzo Harper, here for Samantha O'Reilly."

She appears to be looking over a schedule but before she says anything, I hear another woman approach from the hall behind me. "You're Enzo Harper?" A mixture of shock and awe fill her voice.

I turn to find a woman in sky-high heels, black pencil skirt, and a blue top staring at me wide eyed through quirky red glasses. Her curly brown hair has a life of its own as it spirals in all directions. From the expression on her face, it's clear she's heard of me. And then it all clicks. "You must be Lexi."

"Correct." She beams. Without having a chance to react, Lexi closes the distance and embraces me with a hug as she loudly states, "So nice to finally meet you. Samantha has told me wonderful things about you." *Okay, she's a hugger, who squeezes the life out of you,* leaving me slightly stunned. When she's about to let go, she whispers, "But if you hurt her, I will hunt you down."

I can't control the laughter that bubbles out of my mouth as she releases me. "That's perfectly fine with me, Lexi, since I don't plan on hurting her. Nice to meet you, too."

She gestures for me to follow her down a hallway, to where I assume Samantha is. I can't help the smile that spreads across my face when I spot Samantha about to walk through another door. "Hey, Samantha," slips out without a second thought.

Needing to be close to her, I close the gap between us and kiss her cheek as she whispers, "Hello."

She appears in a daze for a moment but when Lexi clears her throat, Samantha suddenly shakes her head and remembers where we are. "Oh, Lexi. Have you been introduced to Enzo?"

I turn my attention to Lexi who darts a mischievous grin at Samantha before turning her attention to me. "Yes, we met in the lobby." The woman knows more than she lets on. "What do you the two of you have planned for today?"

I run a hand through my hair as I answer, "I came to take Samantha to lunch."

Lexi beams in my direction. "Well, isn't that nice? Don't let me stop you."

"You're welcome to join us," I offer. It would be nice to get to know some of Samantha's friends.

She sighs as disappoint fills her face. "I'd love to, but I have a meeting across town in about an hour."

"Maybe next time," Samantha offers.

"Absolutely!" Lexi declares. "So, Enzo... are you enjoying your time on leave?"

I can't help but smile when I look at Samantha. "Yes. I've gotten to spend time with my family as well as get to know Samantha so far. As much as I don't want to go back to Germany, I can't wait until the next few months are over, so I can be back in Portland permanently."

Samantha's jaw drops, and I hear Lexi gasp. Neither of them says anything for a moment.

Lexi's the first to break the silence. "So, you've decided to retire, huh?" Obviously, she and Samantha talk, but I'm surprised she knows all the details.

"Yep. Twenty years is enough. I met with Riggs again this morning and they should email my new contract this afternoon." I'd planned to tell Samantha this bit of information during lunch, but I can't contain my excitement.

Finally, Samantha finds her voice, "That's amazing!" She throws herself in my arms and I hug her for all I'm worth. I'm so relieved this is her reaction.

When we pull apart, I explain, "After our run this

morning, I had time to think about it more and it was an easy decision for me to make."

Lexi interrupts with a sly comment before I can continue. "You and Enzo went running this morning?" I can tell by the look on her face that she's jumped to the conclusion that I stayed the night.

Before she can get any more out, I set her straight. "Yes, I met her this morning at her house to run before taking her to breakfast."

At first, Lexi looks confused, but then she must remember Sam's kitchen is in shambles. "Oh, right. Her kitchen is a wreck."

"Yes," Samantha interjects. "And he even took the kids with us. The man seems to be a glutton for punishment."

I love her kids and I don't want her thinking otherwise. "Your kids are no punishment, Samantha. In fact, I think they're quite amazing."

"Thanks. I'm glad you think so," she responds with pride and my heart melts a little. I can't believe how much I enjoy her family. It's hard to believe I've fallen for all of them in such a short time.

"Well, I need to jet if I want to be on time." Lexi turns and surprises me with a hug. Lexi is a hugger apparently and her sheer strength takes me a bit off guard "I'll see you two later. Have fun this afternoon!" With that, she turns and walks to her office.

"So, you're really retiring?" Samantha asks when we're finally alone. Her eyes scrutinize me to gauge my reaction.

"Yep. I really am." I smile with delight at the thought of

being able to spend more time with the beautiful woman beside me. "The timing's right, the offer was almost too good to pass up. Besides, I'm ready for a change."

"That's so amazing. I'm happy for you, Enzo." She leans in for a hug and I can't let her go without a kiss. I could kiss this woman for days on end and never tire of her. Of course, I remember we're at her place of business in the parking lot, so I don't let things get too carried away.

We decide on a little café a few miles away to have lunch. I've never been there before, but then again, I'm not picky. I eat anything. Samantha tells me about her day and I mention that at some point I'll need to log onto a computer and check my emails from Riggs. I usually use my phone for everything, but when reading fine-print documents, I'd rather do it on my laptop, which is at my parents' house.

"Why don't you just use the conference room at my office?" She casually suggests. "Lexi is out of the office for the rest of the afternoon. I don't have any client meetings, and no one will be using it."

"Are you sure? I don't want to bother you while you're working. I need to print everything out so I can sign them." I have no idea how much paperwork I'm going to receive. I'd rather read them on hard copy so I can make note of any changes I might want to suggest.

She sighs. "Enzo, I wouldn't have offered if I'd thought you'd bother me." She has a flicker of something I can't quite read spread across her face before she adds, "Besides, I don't have to be anywhere until I pick up Maddie from practice this evening. Maybe if we're really good and get our work done, we could skip out early." She waggles her eyebrows and I can't help but fall even more for her.

"A woman after my own heart," I say as a smile spreads across my face.

After lunch, we spend the next few hours back at her office. She shows me the conference room and sets me up in there while she retreats to her office. I'd be lying if the thought of following her to her office to have my way with her doesn't cross my mind once or a hundred times. But I manage to keep my focus. We both have a job to do. I am thirty-seven, for Christ sake. Get it together, man. Stop with the one-track mind already.

Once I'm buried deep in my contract, I curb my thoughts of Samantha to a certain degree. Riggs has everything laid out for me. I'm surprised by the benefits being offered. It's a larger pay grade and a lot more options as an employee. Don't get me wrong, I've enjoyed serving my time in the Air Force, but the private sector will absolutely have its advantages.

When I get to the section about benefactors, I involuntarily think of Samantha, which is ridiculous. We've only known each other a week. But if I have any say in it, we will know each other a lot more when I'm stateside. Instead, I put my usual response, my parents. Should anything happen, I can always change it later.

By the time I have read and filled out the last form, I realize I have been working for over two hours on this. I had to leave my official start date blank, but since I've already discussed this with Riggs, it shouldn't be a problem. I get up and stretch. I'm used to sitting in a cockpit for hours on end but staring at a stack of papers is different. I gather my things and place them in the envelope Samantha left for me. To make sure I don't leave them behind, I take them out to my car.

When I return, I realize that Brenda, their receptionist, is about to leave. She asks if I can tell Samantha she has to leave for her class this evening. Of course, I have no problem doing this. I notice that she locks the door upon her exit. She quickly explains this is their standard protocol so that customers won't enter after hours when it's just Samantha or Lexi in the building. I thank her and say goodbye.

I walk to Samantha's office and lean on the doorjamb. She doesn't notice me. I take a moment to just admire her. She has that delicious lip tucked under her teeth and is completely engaged in reading the stack of papers before her. A pencil plays in her hand and her hair is now in a messy topknot. This is her in her element, and she couldn't be sexier if she tried. I'm not sure how much longer I just stare at her, but eventually, I must move or make a noise, which draws her attention to my presence.

She finally looks up and pierces me with the most beautiful smile before saying, "You gonna just stand over there, handsome?"

I cock an eyebrow, not sure I heard her correctly. Damn, I love her lack of filter when it comes to me. From what I can tell, she never has the problem with anyone else, so it's flattering that I get her unfiltered side. Sometimes it's downright hysterical, the thoughts that come out of her head. The woman has a way of keeping me on my toes.

After just a few moments of staring at one another, I ask, "And just what are you going to do with me over there?"

Yep, as I suspected. She didn't intend for me to hear that because a warm blush creeps up her face. But I love how she suddenly steels her spine and owns it. "Well, get over here and you'll find out." Her eyes dance playfully.

I walk into her office and shut the door behind me. I stalk slowly over to her as if I'm a hunter and she's my prey. "I might not let you go once I get you," I warn playfully.

The look on her face is a cross between pure pleasure and complete mischief. I can't wait to see what she comes up with next. I love that I'm finding this woman is more adventurous than I could ever imagine. *How in the world did I get so lucky finding a woman like her?*

The minute I get to her, she stands to greet me. Her arms drape around my neck and I pull her in for a passionate kiss now that we're behind closed doors. What starts out as a slow burn quickly ignites into fiery flames.

"Did Brenda leave?" she pants out.

"Yes," kiss, "right before," kiss, "I came in here," kiss. My breathing is quickly becoming just as erratic as hers as I kiss my way down her neck.

"Good," she says, the word coming out as a moan as I get to the place between her shoulders and neck that I have quickly learned is a trigger spot for her.

The next thing I know, she's reaching for the buckle on my belt and popping the fly of my jeans. "What are you doing, beautiful?" I growl into her ear as my zipper retracts at a slow pace.

"Makin' my fantasy a reality." She grabs for the hem of my shirt. *What kind of gentleman would I be if I didn't help her?* Within seconds, I'm shirtless and my hard length is being pulled out to greet one of her hands while the other pushes me back toward her chair.

"Um... Samantha?" I ask, wanting her intentions known.

Between planting kisses down my chest, she pants out, "Sit down."

"Of course," I comply. I'm usually the one to take charge, but when Samantha takes control, it drives me wild. She manages to pull my pants down further as I sit while she kisses down my torso. The sensation she's stirring through me makes going Mach 3 feel like just a walk in the park. The minute her lips connect with my cock, it's all I can do to keep my hips planted in the seat and not take control. *Fuck, this woman will be the death of me.*

When I realize I'm almost to the point of no return, I pull her off me with a loud pop from her mouth that can be heard throughout the room. *There is no way I'm going to be the one to come first.* The look of disappointment is almost priceless on Samantha's face. But I have other things in mind. I push the papers she's working on to the side, hike up her skirt like I did this morning, and shred her underwear. Taking them off would just be too much time.

I reach into my jeans for a condom and suit up before she even has a chance to contemplate what is happening. I kiss her deeply as I reach my hand between her legs and feel that she is already drenched and ready for me. I swipe my fingers from her center to her clit and spend a few moments making sure she is just as ready as I am.

"Now, Enzo," comes out on a hitchy breath. "Please."

Wanting to give her what she needs, I reply with, "Sure thing, beautiful."

Within seconds, I line the head of my cock to her entrance. She arches her hips just as I push toward her, making me slide my entire length with one thrust. *OH. MY. FUCKING. GOD! This feels incredible.*

"Again!" she nearly screams. Her reaction alone has me wanting to come on the spot. Obviously, she loves that move as much as I do, so I try to match it again and again. Pulling out to the tip, then sliding back to the hilt in one fell swoop. My pelvic bone bumps her clit each time I'm fully seated within her. She writhes beneath me and I can feel her clench tighter and tighter with every thrust. When she spasms around me, I can't help but let loose. I pump into her with all my might and give myself entirely to her until we both reach our climax.

Holy fucking hell! That might have just been the best damn orgasm of my entire life. I'm entirely wrecked. As I steady myself, I realize I have lost all feeling in my toes and outer limbs. My breath is harsh, as if I just ran a five-mile sprint. I fucking love the way her entire body is clinging to me for life. It's as if her legs are now permanently locked around my waist and I'm the only one who will help her survive.

All too soon for my liking, her legs loosen their grip on my waist. Her body relaxes as she releases her hold on my shoulders and I feel her breath steady. She finally opens her beautiful mahogany eyes, which remain sexily hooded as she seeks out mine. For a long while, we simply stare at one another before she whispers, "That. Was incredible, Enzo. Life-altering. Holy shit, I don't think it'll ever be better than that."

I can't hide the grin that forms on my face. Because let's face it, I did that to her. I put that entirely blissed-out look on her face. And what she said was the fucking truth. That *was* incredible. *But to say it could never be better than that?* I don't even think when I throw down the challenge. "Don't be so sure. I'd sure love to try to top that, beautiful. We're just gettin' started."

The look on her face shows she completely agrees. Then that sexy sassy woman I'm growing to love appears, having heard my challenge. "Enzo... if it gets better than that, you just might break me."

"I doubt it. But it'd be fun trying, beautiful. It'd be fucking fantastic to try to top that." I bend down and kiss her once more. My cock makes his presence known, and she clenches me tight with a huge grin forming on her face. "Damn, you're beautiful, Samantha," I growl.

Knowing I need to take care of the condom, I pull out. As I remove the condom, I notice I'm wetter than usual. Maybe it's just from her arousal? But it feels too slick to just be from her. I tense as I make the realization. "Fuck, beautiful, the condom broke."

I pull out all the way and reach for the tissues on her desk to help clean up the mess. "I swear on my mother's life, I'm clean. You have nothing to worry about. I have ALWAYS, and

I mean always used a condom," I say, hoping she knows how sincere I'm being. "Shit, I've never had anything happen like this before."

Samantha shudders. At first, I'm afraid she's crying or something, but when I finally look her in the eye, I realize she's shaking with laughter. *What the fuck?*

She takes a deep breath and continues to laugh. "It's okay, Enzo. Really. I'm clean, too. There's no need to worry so much. I was tested after Devin let his indiscretions be known and I haven't been with anyone else since. I get tested at each of my yearly visits. You have nothing to worry about either."

I bend down to kiss her, feeling the relief she isn't upset over this. But then another thought hits. "What about getting pregnant?"

She kisses me once again before she responds with, "Why don't we clean up and get dressed, then we can talk about it more? You shouldn't have anything to worry about."

We take the next few minutes to clean ourselves up with the tissue she has on her desk. We right our clothes and I can't help but cringe and apologize for her lack of underwear.

She laughs it off, saying, "That's an amazing first for me. So is going commando for the rest of the afternoon."

Thank God, her sexy skirt goes past her knees. It's hard enough to control my erection, just knowing she's bare under that dress. But I do the best I can to control that urge. I'm only a man.

By the time we're both back to being presentable, she takes my hand and leads me to the couch across from her desk on the opposite wall. We both sit, and she keeps my hand in hers. She looks a little nervous, so I bend down and kiss her once more on the lips.

"Go ahead, beautiful. Tell me what's on your mind."

"Well, you asked about getting pregnant..." she starts but appears as if she doesn't know what to say.

"Are you on birth control?" I ask, trying to make things easier for her.

She shakes her beautiful brown hair and her rich mahogany eyes bore deeply into mine. "No, I'm not." She holds up a hand to stop me from saying more. "Let me explain why I don't think you should be worried."

"Okay," I slowly state. *Where's she going with this?*

"Well, the thing is, Devin and I tried for years to get pregnant after Frankie. Right up until I found out he was cheating on me, in fact." She shakes her head as if she's trying to rid herself of a terrible thought. Then she resumes with, "The point I'm trying to make is if I tried for over five years to get pregnant, I likely would have, don't you think?"

"I guess," I reply. I think I'm more concerned about the fact that she tried for five years to have another child, than the possibility of getting her pregnant now. *How devastating that must have been for her.*

"You see, with each of my other children, the moment we tried to have a child, I was pregnant within the first month or so. If I were going to get pregnant again, I think it would've happened." She takes in a deep breath, and now she looks as if she has the weight of the world on her shoulders. She looks away from my eyes, not wanting to see my reaction.

"Samantha," I say but she doesn't look in my direction. I

reach out to put my hand under her chin to guide her eyes back to me. "Samantha, beautiful. I'm not worried. I'm sorry if I overreacted just then, but in the twenty plus years of using condoms, I've never had one break. I just didn't want to let you down. Or upset you."

Her deep mahogany eyes shine as a smile forms across her face. "I'm not upset."

"Are we good?" I ask, hoping she will release the stress that she has been holding onto.

She finally exhales, and I can visibly see her relax. "Yeah, we're good." She glances across the room and scares me when she yells, "Oh, shit!"

"What?" I grasp her shoulders to get her to look at me. "What's wrong?"

"I have to pick up Maddie in less than thirty minutes!" She runs her hands through her tousled hair and pats it down frantically. Then she takes it out of her topknot and goes through the process of brushing out her hair with her hands to position it again into another messy bun-like thing. This time it doesn't look as if she's just been thoroughly ravished, but still sexy as hell. Relief washes over me that the time is the only real concern she has. I can deal with that. She looks stunning with her afterglow from the best sex we've ever experienced.

"What can I do to help you?" I ask, wanting to be of some use to her.

"You must think I'm the shittiest of girlfriends. Leaving you behind after that out of this world experience." She suddenly stops and stares at me, as if she didn't want me to hear that comment. Panic covers her features.

"What's wrong?" I ask, suddenly concerned that she's becoming upset.

I barely hear it when she whispers, "I said girlfriend." She closes her eyes as if she doesn't want to see my response.

This woman is fucking adorable. I can't help it. I laugh. "Samantha, beautiful. Look at me." I wait a few seconds for her to comply. "You *are* my girlfriend in every sense of the word." I kiss her lightly on the lips, making her facial expression turn into a smile. "I'll admit I haven't had one in years. But I'm pretty sure that's what you are... that's if you want to be?"

Her nod is emphatic. "Yes. I want to."

"Okay then. You'd better get out of here if you're going to get Maddie on time. I want my *girlfriend*," I emphasize the word to make my point clear, "to drive safe and call me later this evening." I kiss her once more on the lips, then turn her in the direction of the door and swat her on the ass. "Go. You're going to be late."

She chuckles as she gathers the things on her desk and slips them into an envelope. She finds her purse in her desk drawer and is ready to head out the door within minutes. We walk hand in hand out her office door to the reception area. Since the door is already locked, all she does is set the alarm and walk out the door. I walk her to her SUV and kiss her once more.

"I really wish I didn't have to go," she pleads. "But Maddie's waiting. I have to meet her date for Friday and take her dress shopping." She kisses me once more. Then she whispers, "Apparently, I'm doing all this without any underwear." She smirks at me, then shakes her head and gets into her car. I swear I hear her say, "There's a first time for everything," before I shut the door and wave her off.

I can't help it. I burst into laughter. A deep belly laugh rolls through me as I watch her drive out of the parking lot. *This woman may be the death of me, but, man, I'm going to enjoy the ride.*

22

SAMANTHA

I CAN'T BELIEVE I'm going to pick up my daughter and meet her first date with no underwear. Really? Is this my life now? Not that I have a problem with it after the mind-blowing sex Enzo and I just had. How can I discreetly buy underwear without her knowing and slip them on?!?!?

When I think about how sexy it was when Enzo ripped them off me, I can't lie. I'd do it again in a New-York minute. He's every wild fantasy come true. Our chemistry is so combustible, I'm surprised I haven't burst into flames. It doesn't hurt that he's H-O-T either! Between his deep, gravelly voice, amazing good looks, and his huge heart, I don't think I could ever ask for more.

Though I'm glad we were alone at my office this afternoon, I don't think anyone could have stopped me from what I started with him, either. It was pure torture having to get my work done while he was just a wall away. I did eventually read through most of a manuscript before I noticed him standing at my door. Just thinking of the things we did in my office has me starting to clench all over again. That man is sexy, that's for sure.

I manage to maneuver my way down side streets to get to Maddie's school with time to spare. When I pull into the parking lot, I take out my phone to see if she's texted me. There's one notification, but it's not from her. Butterflies flip in my stomach just looking at the name that flashes on the screen.

Enzo: Hey, beautiful, your boyfriend is thinking about you.

A smile spreads across my face as I realize he's referring to me calling myself his girlfriend. Before I can respond, another text comes through from Enzo.

Enzo: Okay. That sounded much better in my head. I'm really not a loser. Please disregard that last text.

Me: I thought it was sweet.

Enzo: Aren't you driving?

Me: Just arrived at the school. Waiting for Maddie to get out of practice.

Enzo: So, my girlfriend is also a speed demon. Good to know.

The thought of him referring to me as his girlfriend sends butterflies to my heart. This man is more than I could ever ask for. But I can't let him get away with thinking I'm a speed demon.

Me: Just know good shortcuts. ;-)

Enzo: Good to know. Just arrived at my parents' a few minutes ago myself. I, too, may know a shortcut.

Another notification comes through but this time it's Maddie.

Maddie: I just got done with practice. Grabbing my things now. Want to meet me by the gym doors?

Me: See you in a few.

I return to my messages from Enzo. I love the way he makes me feel. I really wish I didn't have to wait until tomorrow to see him again. Since Devin usually takes the kids on Wednesdays, I'm looking forward to spending more time with Enzo then. *I just hope he doesn't have other plans.* I get out of the car and walk toward the gym as I type a new message to Enzo.

Me: Sorry, Maddie is ready for me. Do you have plans tomorrow evening?

Immediately, he responds, and I let out a breath I didn't know I was holding.

Enzo: Only if they involve you, beautiful.

Me: Sounds good. Gotta run. Meeting Mads. TTYL

Enzo: Call me when you make it home.

Me: Will do. <3

I love the fact he wants to know if I've made it home safely. It warms the corners of my heart to know he cares as much as he does. I can still feel occasional tremors passing through my body. I'm so looking forward to tomorrow night. I can only imagine what'll happen once we have an entire evening to ourselves again.

By the time I make it to the gym, Maddie is waiting on the steps with a boy who looks as if he could perform with a boyband. His curly brown hair is short on the back and sides, while longer on the top. It covers his face on one side. He's wearing athletic gear, in the sense; he has on fitted cuffed black sweats and a black hoodie over a white t-shirt. He's holding a large athletic bag with what must be his lacrosse gear. He's looking at Maddie with respect and admiration as she explains something to him. *Point one for him.*

When I reach the top of the steps near the door, Maddie greets me. "Hey, Mom. This is Soren." She points to Soren, then back to me. "This is my mom."

Soren looks me in the eye and holds out his hand. Impressed with this boy's manners, I shake it as he says, "Nice to meet you, Mrs. O'Reilly. Maddie's told me a lot about you." *Okay, the kid knows how to show respect. Another point in his favor.*

"Likewise," I reply. "So, what are your plans for Friday evening?" I ask, trying to remember all the things my parents asked my dates when I was Maddie's age. *Damn. Life really does bring things full circle. I've turned into my dreaded parents.*

Soren explains how he has had his license for over a year. If I'm okay with it, he'll pick Maddie up and they'll go to a local Italian restaurant. Then he'll take her to the dance and bring her straight home when it's over. He even makes a point to tell me he has an early lacrosse match the next day, so he won't be able to stay out too late. I must hand it to him. He seems like a decent kid.

"I'll even come over early enough for you to take pictures since this is a semi-formal dance. *Whatever that means.*" He smiles at his assessment.

"That sounds wonderful." I can't help but agree with his

plan. "I will give you a heads up. Maddie's dad will be there to meet you as well when you pick her up since he couldn't be here this evening."

"Mom..." Maddie scolds, but Soren interrupts her.

"That won't be a problem, Mrs. O'Reilly. I have an older sister. I know how important it was for my parents to meet her dates as well." At first, I think he's pulling one over on me, but upon further inspection, I realize he seems genuine.

"So, what are you doing now?" Maddie asks Soren.

"Uh..." He looks from me to her before he answers. "I was actually going to head to the mall to pick out a new shirt for Friday." He seems a little nervous to admit he isn't prepared.

Maddie looks at me as if she's asking if she can invite him to come along. I nod in agreement. It will give me a chance to get to know him better. Though there will be fewer chances for me to slip away and purchase some underwear... *Geesh... the things I do for my kids.*

"We're heading to the mall now. Do you want to ride with us?" I offer.

"Are you sure?" he asks. "I don't want to impose. What about my car? It's parked here."

He looks to Maddie and me for confirmation.

"I can always drop you back here to get it, or you can drive yourself and meet us at the mall," I offer.

I see the hopeful look in Maddie's eyes, knowing she wants him to ride with us. Soren picks up on it, too. He suddenly says, "I guess I'll ride with you."

The ride to the mall is interesting to say the least. We all walk up to my car and Soren automatically goes to the back seat. Upon seeing that, Maddie walks around to the other side. *I guess I'm playing the role of chauffeur.*

As I drive, I learn a few more things about Soren. He's worked at a local restaurant as a busboy since he was fifteen, and now he's a waiter. He bought his own car and is hoping to get a scholarship to college with lacrosse. He's already talking with some coaches from universities across the country.

Since both Maddie and Soren just got out of practice, I offer to buy them both dinner in the food court. They both eagerly accept, and we head there first. We all decide to get Thai food and grab a spot to eat next to the restaurant. Our conversation flows, and I can tell Maddie really likes Soren, if the permanent smile stretched across her face is any indication. I'm impressed with him so far. He seems like a nice kid with a good head on his shoulders. He also has manners, which in this day and age is something to cherish.

When we finish eating, we make our way through the mall looking in every dress section. Maddie tries on a few, but she just keeps moving right along. She's a lot like me. She knows what she's looking for and seems to be on a mission.

Soren, bless his heart, is a champ. He doesn't look bored and takes interest in what choices Maddie makes. He even chats with me while we wait for her to come out to model some of her choices.

I soon learn he's a character, too. While we're waiting for Maddie to try on another dress, he picks up the ugliest dress I've ever seen. It's burnt orange with white polka-dots. It has huge ruffles on the arms, but the body of the dress itself looks as if it should be fitted. It's as if the 70s were on a bad acid trip and mated with the late 80s. It's a total retro-fail. He holds it up across his body and somehow manages a straight face when he asks, "Do you think this would look good on me? Maybe they have it in my size."

I lose it. I double over in laughter, tears are streaming down my face. Especially after he breaks his composure and does the same. Maddie comes out of the dressing room with a look of pure horror on her face when she sees what he's holding, and both Soren and I lose it again. Soren is a riot to shop with, I'll give him that.

Finally, after it feels as if we've scoured through every department store, leaving no dress unturned, Maddie finds the one she wants. It's stunning on her. The winner of our endless dress search is a royal blue short evening dress that has beaded lace over a sheer illusion bodice. It has a modest neckline, which her dad will approve of. There is plenty of coverage in all the right places, making it appropriate for her age as well. It has a gemstone band that breaks the dress apart, like a belt at her natural waist, and the skirt of the dress is multi-layered tulle and reaches the top of her knees. Maddie takes in our expressions and a smile spreads across her face. She does a little spin and the dress flares.

Soren speaks before I can, "Wow, Maddie. I think this is the dress. You look beautiful!" The blush that creeps up her face and the knowing look in her eyes tells me she's flattered by his compliment.

"Yeah, honey. You look spectacular. This is the dress," I tell her.

I'm not sure I like the fact Soren is looking at my daughter the way Enzo looked at me last week in my new dress, but I can't fault him. This is *the* dress. It looks as if it were made for her and fits her perfectly. It's dressy but still fun and appropriate for her age.

"Why don't you change and we can check out the shoe department, then we will look for shirts with Soren." She nods and returns to the dressing room.

"Okay, Mom, but I'm getting flats. You can't pay me enough to wear the deathtraps you love to walk around in." Maddie snickers as her back disappears into the dressing room entirely, so I can't reply. I can't help but laugh. If she has her way, I'm sure she'll be wearing a pair of Chuck Taylors.

Soren has looked at shirts in each of the stores we've shopped, but I have my suspicions he's been waiting for her to pick out the color of her dress first. He mentioned at dinner he has a black suit, but just wanted a new shirt and tie for the dance. Maddie could have done a lot worse than Soren Silva as her first date. Just with my interactions with him tonight, I know she'll have a great time and I have little to worry about.

When we get to the shoe department, I shit you not, there is a pair of royal blue Chuck Taylors out front on display. Maddie's inner tomboy is still in there because her eyes dance with absolute joy as she screeches, "OH MY GOD! These would be perfect!" She looks to Soren and asks, "You wouldn't mind if I wore these, would you?"

Soren's smile is wide on his face. "Only if I get to have a pair, too. We can wear matching shoes for our photos. It'll be savage!"

Savage? What the fuck does that mean? I look to Maddie as

she beams. "It will be total badass!" *Okay, I learn something new every day.*

A salesman comes over and gets them fitted for their matching shoes. *Who knew wearing matching shoes to a dance would be a popular thing to do?* But with the excitement and chatter that continues about how amazing this will be, it must be a thing to do.

Unlike Maddie, Soren doesn't take long picking out a shirt and tie. The department store we're currently in has a great men's section. He finds the perfect blue shirt that matches the color of Maddie's dress within moments, then tries it on to make sure it fits. Then he selects a silver and blue tie to match the shirt. Soon, with two pairs of Chuck Taylors in tow, we all make our way to the register and walk back to where my car is parked.

After dropping Soren off back at the school, Maddie and I head over to Devin's to pick up Dec and Frankie. It's later than I realize because when we pull into Devin's driveway, I glance at the clock and see that it's after eight thirty p.m. already. Maddie and I both go to the door to get them, but she rushes ahead of me and just lets herself in the door after telling me she needs to use the bathroom. I, on the other hand, wait at the doorway until Devin greets me and invites me in.

"Woah, Mads, what's the rush?" he hollers at her back as she climbs the stairs two at a time.

"Sorry, gotta pee, Dad!" she shouts in return.

We're both left shaking our heads. "Poor girl, she probably held it the entire time we were shopping," I suggest as an explanation.

"So, did you find a dress?"

I nod my head. "Yes. It's perfect. You'll even approve."

Devin sighs in relief. "That's good. So how was meeting this Soren guy? What did you think of him?"

"He's a pretty good kid. He seems like a hard worker with a good head on his shoulders," I honestly state. "Don't give him too hard of a time when you come over on Friday. He ended up going to the mall with us and I'm really impressed by him."

"I'm not making any promises." Devin laughs. "He's still a guy wanting to date my daughter."

"*Our* daughter... and I think you may actually like him," I counter.

"Hey, Sam?" Devin rubs a hand behind his neck, appearing as if he's going to give me disappointing news.

"Yes?" I prompt.

"Frankie went upstairs to read and fell asleep about a half hour ago. I didn't know how long you'd be and she was cranky this evening. Do you want to wake her or let her stay here? Dec's almost out, too."

Just then, Maddie comes back downstairs. "Where is everyone?" She looks around for her siblings.

"In bed, kiddo," Devin explains, then to me he adds, "I don't care either way, Sam. Maddie can stay, too. I can make breakfast and get them off to school."

I look to Maddie to see what she says. "That's great, Dad. I'll just grab my bag from the car so I can do my homework. Also, can I wash my practice gear tonight?"

"I guess that's settled," I say. "No sense in waking them. Do you still want to take them tomorrow night, too?"

"It isn't a problem. Besides, with your kitchen remodel, this will be easier for you. If you don't mind, they can stay until Friday with me. I'm going to leave for Seattle after I meet Maddie's date on Friday evening, and I like having the extra time with them."

"Okay." *This will certainly have its advantages for me and Enzo, too.* "Do you mind if I go kiss them goodnight, then I'll be on my way?" I know it won't be a problem, but I don't want to traipse through his house without asking first.

"Sure thing. You know the way." He gestures up the stairs to their bedrooms.

After going upstairs and kissing a sleeping Frankie goodnight, I knock lightly on Declan's room. He's awake and about ready for bed. I ask him about his day and tell him what his dad and I decided. He seems fine with it as well. I hug him once more before telling him I'll see him Friday after school, then I leave his room to say goodnight to Maddie downstairs.

As soon as I get out to my car, it dawns on me I'm going to be alone both tonight and tomorrow night. A tingling sensation spreads through my body, and I know just who to contact. I pull up his number and quickly type out a message.

Me: So... my kids are staying at their dad's for the next three nights. What will I do alone in that big house all to myself?!?!?! Hmmm...

Not even a minute goes by and I see an incoming message.

Enzo: Up for some company?

Me: I thought you'd never ask. I'm on my way home now.

Enzo: Be there in 30.

Me: I'm still not wearing any underwear.

Enzo: Make that 20.

23
___

ENZO

WAKING up with Samantha in my arms is something I would love to get used to. The past three mornings have absolutely been the highlight of my week. Not only do I get to have my wicked way with her, but I'm getting to know her on a much deeper level. I can't imagine how I've missed out on this experience all this time. But no one else is the beautiful woman beside me, Samantha O'Reilly. She has everything to do with the way I'm feeling right now.

Spending our evenings together, sleeping in her bed, and waking up beside her has all been incredible. Samantha's even managed to make it to work on time each day, despite the fact I may be keeping her up late, as well as making it more difficult for her to get ready to go in the mornings. She's just so irresistible I can't help it, and she can't seem to keep her hands off me either.

We went to my parents' house for dinner again last night, so I'm still spending time with my family while on leave, too.

That was my original intent when I came to Portland. While Samantha's busy at work during the day, I make the most of my days by seeing other family members. Today, I'm going hiking with my brother Zane.

Zane is my younger brother, who recently turned thirty-five. He's an architect here in Portland and has done quite well for himself. He and his wife Ann live in a suburb, not too far from my parents. We used to be really close and I'm really looking forward to spending the day with him. When he called and said he had the day off, we immediately made plans to go hiking at Mount Tabor, an extinct volcano right in the middle of Portland. Our favorite trail is the Blue Trail Loop, which is by far the most challenging trail. The best part is the view from the top as you pass by the water reservoirs, which used to be Portland's main water supply, but now they're for aesthetic purposes only.

Wanting to spend as much time with Samantha as I could before her meeting this morning, I dropped her off after having breakfast at another local diner.

It's just before ten o'clock when I knock on Zane's door. I'm not surprised to find he's already in his workout gear. He greets me with a brotherly hug. There's plenty of back-slapping before we quickly release. "Good to see you, Zo," he says as he pulls away.

"You, too, Zane." I see him grab a bag by the door and head to the driveway.

"In a hurry?" I ask, wondering why we're leaving right away.

"Only to kick your ass, old man," he taunts.

I scoff at him. "I'd like to see you try. You spend your time these days behind a desk." *Yep. I went there. It's my duty to give him a hard time. It's what we do.*

Our thirty-minute car ride is filled with light conversation. He fills me in on how his kids are doing. He and Ann must stay busy raising three kids under the age of six. He tells me how thankful he is now that his oldest, Riley, is in first grade and no longer requires all-day childcare. Brandon, his four-year-old will be in pre-school full time this year and Zoey, his two-year-old, is still in daycare. I just about shit my pants when he tells me how much daycare is for a toddler. Holy crap. No wonder he's excited his kids will be in school.

The premise of the word "hike" is loose when it comes to my brother and me. I know we'll be running at top speeds up the trail in no time. We each get out of the car and stretch. He carries a light backpack that allows him to run and still carry water. Zane tells me the has water for me, should I need it.

Like I presumed, we have no time to talk during our run up the trail. At first, we jog next to one another, but when we get near other people, we're forced to run single file. Of course, Zane takes this opportunity to sprint ahead. I let him go, but keep close on his tail while we pass others to our right. When there is room for us to run side by side, I kick up my pace and pass him at the last minute before we take a sharp corner. I maneuver my way to the top with ease, with him lagging the entire way. *I may be almost thirty-eight, but I still take him every time.*

When we make it to the summit, I can't help but tease, "Who's the old man now?"

"Ha! You've still got it in you." He takes a moment to unscrew a water bottle and take a long swig. "Glad to see you haven't gone soft yet, big brother."

Chugging my own bottle, I shrug my response as if to say, *'I've still got it.'* We find a bench to sit on and take in the view. Neither one of us says much while our heart rates return to normal.

Zane breaks the silence with, "So, you and Samantha..."

The smile that spreads across my face is involuntary. "Yep. Me and Samantha." Not sure where he's going with this line of thought.

"So, you're pretty serious?" Zane openly asks.

I nod my response. "Yeah, we are."

"She the reason you're retiring?" He takes another drink of water as he waits for my response.

"Not really. I've been wanting out for a while. I love the adventure, but I want to have a permanent address. When Riggs offered me the job, I just felt the timing was right. She's a huge benefit to choosing to stay in Portland, I'll give you that."

"She has kids, right? Have you met them?" He places his elbows on his knees and leans forward, keeping his water bottle in one hand.

"Yeah, I've met them. I went over for the Seahawks game on Monday. You should've seen their enthusiasm for the game. It was unreal. Samantha and the girls were screaming their heads off at the TV as if they were in the stadium itself. It was a riot to watch. Declan came in a while later and watched the end of the game. I think we hit it off okay. But it was Frankie who stole my heart that evening." I continue to tell him about how she insisted I read her a story and tuck her into bed.

Zane lets out a low whistle. "I never thought I'd see the day you'd be serious about anyone." He seems to think for a while, then adds, "Has there been anyone serious since Vanessa?"

I shake my head. "No one worth mentioning."

"So now that you're moving back to Portland, what are your plans? Are you going to get a place of your own, stay with Ma and Pops, or what?"

I take a deep breath, mulling over what he just said. I haven't even thought about any of this. I know I still have time, but it's something I should be thinking about sooner than later. I decide to just be honest when I answer Zane's question. "I have no idea, Zane. All of this is pretty new."

"Do you see yourself settling down with Samantha?" Zane raises an eyebrow waiting for my response.

Do I see myself settling down? Yes. No. I don't know. I'm going back to Germany in just over a month. The thought of even going away for the remaining months of my contract has me on edge. After the last three mornings, I know that's how I'd prefer the rest of my mornings to go. "Fuck, man, I don't even want to go back to Germany to finish my contract. I just want to get it over with, so I can come back and see where this goes."

"You don't know where it's going?" Zane asks a little shocked.

I might as well lay it all out for him. This is new for me, both in opening up about relationships as well as how I feel toward Samantha. "I know I absolutely adore her. She's smart, funny, adventurous, and always keeps me on my toes. I enjoy being with her." Zane gives me a look that insinuates I'm all about the sex. "Fuck, man, everything about her is incredible. But she means more to me than just inside the bedroom. I find I like being with her out and about, running errands, and just having lazy moments, too. Isn't it too soon to be feeling this way? I just met her a little over a week ago."

"When it's the right person, you know. It's as simple as that. I honestly knew within the first month or so that Ann would be the one."

"Didn't you date for a couple of years before you got married?"

"Yes, but that's only because we were still in college. We each wanted to start our careers before getting married. It's different for you though. You're at a different stage in life. And let's face it, you're not getting any younger." He holds up a hand and stops me from interrupting. "Hear me out. What I'm trying to say is perhaps you've already been with as many 'wrong' women as you needed to be with to prove she's the right one for you. Sure, you need to juggle what's right with her kids and all, but I think you'll find a way to make it work. If it's meant to be, you'll make it happen. Why don't you just enjoy her company until you go back to Germany? If it's still going strong, you can decide from there."

"All I know is that I think about her all the time. Thoughts of her consume me when I'm not around her, and the thought of leaving makes me cringe. I don't even think I felt this way about Vanessa and we dated for years."

"That's the difference between your first love and your forever love," Zane points out.

"Forever love?" *What the fuck is he mentioning love for?*

Zane gives me a knowing look, then I think a flash of pity? *Why would he pity me?* "Enzo, if you're not already in love with this woman, you're at least halfway there."

I just stare at him dumbfounded. *Love. Hmmm... is it love that I'm feeling?*

"Dude, even I could see the way you were looking at her this week at dinner and Ann tells me I'm obtuse when it comes to noticing details. You act as if she has hung the stars and moon. You might not have noticed, but you even seemed to intrinsically know where she was, no matter if you're in the same room with her or not."

He must see an even more confused look on my face because he continues, "Okay. Answer me this. What's your first instinct when you think of her moving on without you, should you decide long distance isn't for you while you're in Germany?"

"I'd want to throat-punch any fucker who even thinks of touching her," comes out of my mouth before I have a chance to censor my thoughts. *Since when did I get so possessive?* I've always dated casually, and it's never bothered me before when someone was ready to move on. *Holy fuck. Maybe I'm already in love with her?*

Zane gives me a knowing look as if he knows I'm not telling him everything on my mind. "So... what aren't you telling me?" he finally says after I remain silent for a while longer.

I let out a deep breath and quietly say, "I think I'm already in love with her."

"No shit, Sherlock," Zane teases, but then his tone is serious. "So, what's holding you back?"

I shake my head. "Shit, I don't even know where to begin." Zane lets me mull it over in silence while he takes another long pull from his water bottle and enjoys the view before us. When I think I finally get my head wrapped around the thousand stampeding thoughts charging through my mind, I break the silence once again by putting words to my swirling thoughts. "How have I fallen for her in such a short time? What the fuck is going to happen when I return to Germany? Will we survive it? Will I get another fuckin' 'Dear John' letter? What about her kids? How do I navigate a relationship with them? How do I..."

"Enzo, Stop," Zane encourages. "You're freaking out over things that don't have to be decided today. In fact, I think time will be your best friend in this situation. You can't rush things because you know you're going to have time apart. I think that's the best way to go about it with her kids as well. Let them get to know you while you get to know them. They already have a dad; you need to find your own relationship with them. Talk with Samantha. Tell her how you're feeling, then she won't be left in the dark either."

The mention of Samantha brings a smile on my face. *Fuck, I'm so lost to her. Just mentioning her name has my stomach doing Mach 3 maneuvers and I'm standing firmly on the ground. If I feel this strongly for her after just a week, how the hell am I going to get through the rest of my time in Germany?*

"What about when…" I can't even bring myself to say anything about a 'Dear John' letter.

"Enzo, you're in a different place than you were with Vanessa," he states matter-of-factly. It's both a blessing and a curse at times that Zane knows me so well. *Today it's a blessing.* "Zo, you're not twenty-two anymore. It's not like you're going to be deployed for a year at a time or anything. You're only talking a few months tops. If Samantha's the woman I think she is, I don't think you'll have to worry about her straying."

I nod my head in agreement. After her ex cheated on her, it took her three years to even kiss another man. "You're right, man, she'd never cheat." I fill Zane in on the details pertaining to her and Devin's breakup, though I keep the intimate details to myself. *There are just some things I don't tell about my personal life. No matter who I'm talking to.* I give him the bare facts about Devin's cheating was so devastating to Samantha, and Zane comes to the same conclusion as me. *Samantha isn't a cheater.*

"Have her come to Germany for your birthday. Then you can break up the time being apart. It will also give you a chance to get to know her better when she doesn't have the responsibilities of having her kids," Zane suggests.

"That's a promising idea. I should look into flights to see if I can get her to come the week of my birthday. I actually still have a bit of leave I need to use or lose, so I can request some time off then, too." *How does he make this seem so simple?*

By getting my thoughts out with Zane, I feel much better about the situation. I've never been one to hash out my relationship troubles, but it feels good to put things into perspective. Besides, it also gets me thinking about a surprise I can give Samantha before I leave, should things continue to go in the direction they're heading.

Eventually, Zane and I make our way back down the trail to my car. We go out to lunch together after returning to his house to clean up first. He invites me to spend the rest of the afternoon hanging out at his place once we've picked up his kids early from daycare, so I can spend time with them, too. I shoot off a few texts to Samantha when I think I can get away with it and not be harassed too much for being distracted.

Me: How is your day going, beautiful?

Samantha: Good. I'm about to head out to pick up Frankie from school.

Before I can respond to her text, another one arrives.

Samantha: Would you be up to keeping me company while I wait up for Maddie to come home from her date?

Me: I'd be honored. What time would you like me to come over?

Samantha: How about 7? No need to overwhelm the poor boy with two men to meet when he picks her up.

I wouldn't want to step on Devin's toes. I may not like the guy, but he's Maddie's father so I can't begrudge him for wanting to meet her date. I have no idea how I'd feel about a daughter of mine going on a first date. I also don't want to press my luck with Maddie.

Me: I'll be there at 7.

Samantha: I can't wait to see you. - XO

Me: Me, too. See you then.

To my surprise, an attachment comes through and the next thing I see is her beautiful face radiating through the screen. There's also a message attached to it.

Samantha: Here's something to make the time go by.

I wish it was seven o'clock already. This is sure to be a long afternoon. I decide to do something totally uncharacteristic of me. I reach my arm out and take a selfie. The smile she's put there is evident. I attach a message of my gratitude and send it to her.

24

SAMANTHA

I RUSH HOME after picking up Maddie from practice. Thankfully, they got out a little early today since the dance is tonight. I have Frankie with me and Devin is picking up Declan. I thought ahead and ordered take-out. Maddie seems a little nervous about going on her date; she is talking a mile a minute.

"Hey, Mom?" she asks from the passenger seat of my SUV.

"Yes?" I reply, knowing she's about to ask me for something.

"Do you think you could help me with my hair?"

"What do you have in mind?" Though I'm honored she's asked, I hope she doesn't want anything too intricate. I may not be able to pull it off.

"I was thinking about leaving the back of my hair down, but French-braiding a section across the front, like a crown and tucking it behind my hair on the other side. You know, like you used to do for me?" The last part comes out as a question. As if I wouldn't remember how to do that. Frankie asks for that style all the time.

"Sure, no problem," I tell her.

"I'm thinking I could leave the back down and curl it." She pulls her bottom lip under her top teeth before adding, "Do you think you can help me so it'll go faster?"

"Of course. You'll look beautiful."

"Thanks." She's quiet for a moment, then blurts out, "Mom, should I offer to pay for dinner?"

"I've picked up some cash you can have just in case, but I'm pretty sure Soren will pay for dinner. He's the one who asked you out, right?" I ask, wondering why she's suddenly bringing this up.

"Yes, he asked me. But what should I order?"

"Maddie, just be yourself, relax, and have fun. The restaurant he's taking you to is affordable. Pick something from the menu that you'll enjoy and have a wonderful time."

"My friends say to pick a salad, but do I have to?" She seems so worried, I feel for her. I remember being just as nervous on my first date.

I place an arm on her leg and pat it reassuringly. "Mads, no man, who is worth anything, will want to be with someone who only eats lettuce. Most guys truly just want to get to know the real you, not a version of who you *think* they would like. Anyone who doesn't like you for who you are is a fool."

"Are you just saying that because you're my mom?"

"No, I'm sure anyone would give that advice."

Frankie, who I thought was engrossed in the book she was reading, pipes in, "Ask Dad or Enzo what they think. They're guys. They've gone out with girls before. They'd know what Soren is thinking."

Catching both Maddie and me off guard by her profound response, we just gape at each other for a moment while at a red light. I know Devin would be Frankie's first choice to ask, but I'm surprised to hear Enzo's name added to this conversation.

Frankie takes in our expression and asks, "What? It's not like I can't hear everything you're saying? We *are* in the same car." The way she states it so matter-of-factly makes me laugh. *When did she become so grown up? She's supposed to be my baby.*

Maddie shakes her head at me. "Ut... Uh. No way am I asking Dad." Then she practically makes my jaw drop when she whispers, "Do you think you could ask Enzo, without it coming from me? He's taken you out on dates, right?"

I laugh. I can't help it. "Yes, we've gone on some dates. I'm sure I could call and ask him if you'd like." *Great, now I feel like I'm the teenager calling to get advice from a guy without telling him the reason why. What am I, fifteen? Nope. But I have a fourteen-year-old daughter who's looking as if she'd give her first born to have the answer. The things I do for my children.*

At the next light, I pull up Enzo's number on my phone. I'm connected through my car's speakers via Bluetooth, so I press send and whisper to myself, "Here goes nothing."

Enzo answers before the second ring. "Hey, beautiful,

how's your day?" I can't help the blush that crosses my features. *This man has quite the effect on me.*

"Hey, Enzo, you're on speaker. I have a question for you and need your advice," I state calmly, not wanting to give Maddie away.

"Okkaaayy," he draws out, evident that he's wondering where I'm going with this.

"Hi, Enzo!" Frankie shouts out before I can reply.

"Hi, Frankie," he says back to her. "How was school today?"

"It was good," she replies.

I smile at their kind exchange before continuing, "Actually, there might be more than one question," I hedge when I realize how I'm about to word it.

"Shoot," his husky voice booms through the car.

"Okay, my first question to you is if you're going on a date, what do you think of a girl just ordering a salad?"

He chuckles, then replies, "I'd hate it!" His voice crackles through the speaker. "Unless it's a part of the meal as an appetizer, I find it annoying to go out with people who only order that. Who wants to sit and have someone watch you eat a full meal when they stopped at the appetizer?" He laughs a little at the end to show how ridiculous the thought is. "Besides, who can live off rabbit food alone? Unless it's filled with protein, that salad isn't going to fulfill its purpose of feeding you. Most women who only eat that are hungry and crabby later because they haven't eaten. No offense," he adds on the last part as almost an afterthought.

"Okay, thanks for the honesty. I have one more question

for you. What kinds of things should a girl order while they're out on a date?"

"Um, whatever they're in the mood for?" I can hear the questions running through his mind, evident in his voice.

"I was thinking the same thing," I add. But then I want to answer Maddie's unasked question. "I was also thinking maybe not the most expensive thing on the menu, unless your date orders that, but not the cheapest thing either, right?"

"Sam, I would want my date to eat what she's hungry for. I don't want her to try to please me based on what she orders. I wouldn't have taken them to the restaurant if I couldn't afford it. As men, we research these things, if we're making the effort of taking someone out to dinner. Does that answer your question?"

I look to Maddie and she nods her head. The relief on her face is evident. "Yes, it does. Thank you, Enzo. I'd better get going. I'll see you later."

"Bye, Enzo," Frankie calls from the back of the car.

"Bye, sweetheart. You, too, beautiful. I'll be there at seven," Enzo's sexy voice draws out before disconnecting the call.

When I'm sure the call has ended, I ask Maddie, "So do you see that you should just be yourself and not worry so much? Honey, if Soren doesn't like you for who you are, he's not worth dating."

"Okay, Mom, I know. Thanks for doing that. Enzo seemed like he knew what he was talking about."

I don't even want to think about Enzo dating, but he did give good advice. "I'm sure he does, Honey."

Maddie's quiet for a while. Then she whispers, "Mom, what if he wants to kiss me?"

And... my heart falls out of my chest. Okay. I'm the mom. We've talked about this before, but now it could become a reality. I try to keep my features as calm as possible, though I'm feeling anything but calm. As much as I'm excited for her to experience this, she's still my baby.

I take a deep breath and blow it out slowly, not trying to draw attention to myself before I attempt to casually say, "Sweetie, you just have to do what feels comfortable to you. If you want to kiss him at some point throughout the evening, that's up to you. Just remember, it's your decision and your body. Make good choices for yourself. Don't feel pressured to do anything you don't want to do. If he wants more than you're willing to give, he's not worth it."

"Thanks, Mom." She lets out a giggle before whispering, "I wonder what kissing him will be like?"

I decide her question is rhetorical, and not answer it. *Oh, God, this is so much harder than I ever thought.* Is this what my parents felt like? At least she feels comfortable enough to talk to me about it. I must be doing something right.

DEVIN AND DECLAN arrive at the house a little before six. Declan runs up the stairs to put his things in his room while Devin joins Maddie, Frankie, and me in the living room. Soren told Maddie he would be here by six-fifteen, so we're all anxiously awaiting his arrival.

Maddie looks stunning tonight. With my help, it took hardly any time at all to get her hair done. I love the hint of the tomboy left inside her with the Chuck Taylors. The look on Devin's face is priceless. He doesn't say anything, but when he walked in and saw her standing there, he froze, eyes wide as he took in a deep breath to steady himself. Maddie had her back to him at first, so she didn't see. But when she turned around, she ran to hug him. Before she reached him, he slowly said, "Wow, Mads, you look beautiful."

"Thanks, Dad," she says as they hug tightly. She stands back and takes a spin to show him her entire look. Watching Devin's eye scrutinize everything is almost hysterical. As his eyes roam down her body to her toes, he seems to relax a little when he notices her shoes. He doesn't get a chance to say anything because the doorbell rings.

"I'll get it," Declan calls, heading down the stairs, almost to the door.

"Hey, man." Declan gives a fist bump to Soren as he steps through the door. "Mads is in the living room." He gestures for Soren to come in and join us.

Soren steps into the room. He looks handsome in his black suit. It looks as if it were made personally for him. The blue shirt and matching silver and blue tie he bought while shopping with us make his outfit. The matching blue Chuck Taylors are a unique feature, but when he comes to stand next to Maddie, they look like the perfect couple. In his hand is a wrist corsage with a white rose surrounded by blue carnations. The ribbon that's intricately placed around the flowers matches her dress perfectly.

"Wow, Maddie. You look great." Soren just stops and stares for a moment with a huge grin on his face, as if he has lost all train of thought. "Is this for me?" She points to the clear plastic box he's carrying.

"Yes, would you like me to help you put it on?" Soren asks as he opens the package. Within moments, he has it on her wrist and her face lights up from the kind gesture.

"I have a boutonniere for you as well." She turns toward me, looking for where it is.

"I'll get it," Frankie announces as she jets out of the living room to the garage where we kept it in the fridge.

Within seconds, Frankie bolts back into the room and hands it to Soren. "Here. This is for you." She shoves it at his chest and chuckles can be heard around the room as we take in the surprised look on his face.

"Be careful not to squish it," I warn as Maddie takes the boutonniere out of the box for him.

Soren is a saint as he patiently waits for Maddie to pin it on. She can't get it to sit straight on the black lapel of his jacket. Not wanting blood to be drawn, I volunteer to help her.

While I'm doing this, Devin continues his inquisition with Soren. He asks where they're going, who will be with them, what time they will be home. I can hear Maddie huff a few times, but overall, she's getting off easy considering this is her first date. When the basics are out of the way, he asks Soren which sports he plays and other 'get to know you' questions. Soren takes it all in stride and I can feel him relax as the questions continue.

When I'm done, Maddie walks over and stands next to

Soren. She grabs her silver wristlet purse. It's tiny, but it holds her phone, lip gloss, and money. She looks at him and asks, "Do you mind taking pictures?"

"Not at all," Soren replies then looks to Devin and me. "Where would you like us?"

Maddie pulls out her phone and hands it to me. Soren hands his phone to Devin as he asks, "Would you mind taking a few pictures of us? My mom wants me to send her some."

"We should have invited them over," I state, feeling like a schmuck for being so thoughtless.

"It's okay," Soren states. "They're going out to dinner tonight with some friends."

We spend the next twenty minutes or so taking photos. I think Soren wins Devin over a little when he offers to take pictures of Maddie and her dad. Maddie asks to take a photo of her and me together, then Soren graciously steps into the photo as well. Frankie is eager to get her turn next to the happy couple while we force Declan into a couple photos. At least he manages a smile.

Enzo arrives just as we're finishing up. I thought it might be awkward, but oddly enough it isn't too bad. After the initial shock on Devin's face, he manages to school his features and is cordial. Frankie greets him with a hug, taking Enzo by surprise. Since we're trying to finish up the group poses, Enzo offers to take one of all of us, which is gracious of him.

The next thing I know, Maddie is off on her date. Devin says goodbye, reminding me he will be out of town until next Wednesday, so I'll have to get Declan to his practices. *Thank goodness for other team parents who are willing to help.* I tell him I'll manage and he's out the door. The delivery for our food arrives just as Devin leaves. *Whew! What a whirlwind.*

"Who's ready to eat?" I ask as Declan and Frankie settle in around the coffee table and eat the Chinese take-out I had ordered earlier. I didn't know what to order for Enzo, so I ordered a few extra of my favorites to make sure there is enough food for all of us.

Enzo comes up beside me and leans in to whisper in my ear, "Hey, beautiful, you doin' okay?" He plants a kiss on my cheek before pulling away, leaving a wake of tingles sprawling across my body.

I sigh. "Yeah, I'm fine. It's just a little surreal having her go out on her first date."

He raises his shoulders in a shrug. "I can only imagine. It all seemed to be going well when I got here. Did I miss anything?"

"Only Dad giving Soren the third degree," Declan chortles. "That poor guy must have been asked a hundred questions before he was able to leave."

"Watch it, buddy," I tease. "You'll be going on dates before you know it and you'll be the one in the hot seat."

"If that's what I'll have to go through, I think I'll pass," Declan says with a mouth full of fried rice.

"You might change your mind someday," Enzo adds to the conversation. "I know I used to feel the same as you, but I soon changed my tune. Besides..." Enzo sits down on the couch next to me as he dishes himself up some food. "When it's the right girl, you won't have any troubles answering those questions." Enzo winks at me and I sigh.

Then I turn to look at Declan. I can't help but laugh at the look he has on his face. It's a cross between being forced to eat a lemon and complete astonishment. "Yeah, Dec, you'll feel differently in a few years. Trust me."

"Whatever you say, Mom." He shakes his head and focuses his entire attention on his heaping plate of food.

While we eat, we each talk about our day. Declan seems interested in the hike Enzo took earlier with his brother. They even talk for some time about other places they would like to hike locally. It pleases me to no end to see them getting along. Frankie, being Frankie, tries to contribute and invites herself to join them. When Enzo asks if we would all like to go hiking this weekend, both kids light up like the Fourth of July. They beg me to go Sunday morning since Declan has soccer tomorrow. Of course, I say yes. *Like I'm going to turn down more time with Enzo anytime soon.*

As we finish with dinner, I ask Frankie if she has any homework. Knowing I'd rather her spend tonight working on it than Sunday, I encourage her to get it. She reluctantly admits she has some math and of course, reading. Enzo offers to help her, and she immediately changes her tune. I ask Declan if he has any work to do. To my surprise, Declan goes upstairs and grabs his bag and returns to do it in the living room with us. *Who are these people and what did they do with my children?* Maybe it has to do with the fact Enzo is here. Who knows, but I'm not going to complain.

It's almost eight when all homework for the weekend is complete. Frankie still has reading to do, but I know we will get that done over the weekend. She never lets me send her to bed without a story first, so I have no worries about it not getting done. All we have is a soccer game at nine tomorrow, and now apparently, hiking this weekend. *I'm so looking forward to a low-key weekend. Especially, if it involves Enzo.*

I'm learning many new things about Enzo tonight as well. I haven't missed his subtle closeness. From the casual brushing of his fingers across my skin, his patting my leg to make a point, or the way he brushes my loose hair from my face. All are signs he's thinking of me as much as I'm thinking about him.

My heart melts the way Frankie insists that Enzo sit between her and me on the couch when we settle in to watch a show before bed. Meanwhile, Declan stretches out on the other couch next to us. Enzo lifts his arm, resting it behind me, and I can't help it when I lean in a little closer and sniff the amazing scent that's all him. He puts his arm around me, then looks into my eyes to ask the silent question of, '*Are you okay with this?*' I don't say anything, but I lean in and put my head against his chest.

Declan has control of the remote. He's chosen something on the Disney Channel. It appears to be the kids of supervillains coming to live with the families of the heroes in fairy tales. All the major characters from the movies I've watched growing up now have kids and they're going to school together. It's a cute concept and I find myself being sucked into the plot. We're all sucked in because the next thing I know, the ending credits are rolling. Declan is almost asleep, and Frankie has conked out against Enzo's side.

"So, what did you think?" I ask Enzo as I stretch and ready myself to stand.

"It was surprisingly good. I don't think I've watched a Disney movie in its entirety for years."

"Mom, I'm going to head up to bed." Declan walks over and gives me a kiss goodnight. He may be getting older, but these are one of the few things I still cherish. "Night, Enzo."

He turns to walk out of the living room but stops. "Hey, Enzo?"

"Yeah, buddy?" Enzo responds.

"If you're not doing anything tomorrow morning, I'd love it if you came to my game."

Enzo turns to me with a brief look of awe crossing his features, but he quickly tamps it down. "Let me know the time and I'll be there."

"It's at nine. We'll leave here around eight." Declan looks to me. "You don't mind if he rides with us, do you?"

"Not at all, Dec. See you in the morning. Love you." I snuggle Enzo further after Declan leaves the room.

"What shall we do about her?" Enzo points to Frankie, who is now deadweight against his arm.

A light laugh escapes my lips. "I'll carry her upstairs." I get up to move, but Enzo stops me.

"No, I've got her. I just didn't know if you wanted to wake her," he says as he extracts himself from her. Within seconds, he has her scooped up in his arms and is carrying her up the stairs. Now that she's eight, it's a lot harder for me to carry her. He makes it look as if she's an infant.

"She sleeps like the dead. I'm afraid if we wake her, she might be up for hours," I tease as I follow him up the stairs. Once we reach her room, I pull back her blankets and he lays her down on the bed. I tuck her in and kiss her goodnight.

Once we leave Frankie's room, we walk down to Declan's. I notice the light is still on and the door is open. I knock lightly, and he tells us to come in.

"Hey, Dec, are you about ready for bed?" I ask him.

"Yeah. I'm just getting my gear ready for my game. Are we going to breakfast tomorrow? Or are we having cereal here?" he asks, knowing I had bought disposable dishes and silverware just for that reason.

"It depends on when you get up. If all else fails, I can get you a breakfast sandwich on the road to the game," I state as he zips up his bag of gear for tomorrow. "Want me to turn off the light?"

"Thanks, Mom. Love you."

"Love you, too," I say as I turn off the light and shut the door.

Enzo and I walk downstairs together. Once we're in the living room, he says, "Thanks for having me over. I had fun tonight."

I don't respond with words. I show him just how much tonight meant to me by kissing him for all I'm worth. The moment my lips touch his, the chemistry between us ignites fast and fiery. I can't control myself. *God, I've been waiting for this all night. I thought my kids would never go to bed. Being so close but so far away all evening has taken its toll on me.* I fist his hair in my hands and pull him closer to me. Instinctively, as he tightens his grip on my back, I wrap my legs around his waist and he walks toward the couch.

He lays me down on the couch and climbs up my body. "We can't do much, Samantha," he whispers, "But, God, how I want you."

"Me, too," comes out in a moan as I pull him closer to me so I can make contact with those delicious lips of his.

I'm not sure how long we kiss. Could be minutes or hours, but it isn't long enough. I have been craving Enzo since he walked in the door this evening. It took everything in my power to keep my desire for him to a minimum amount of PDA in front of my children. I'm a mom, but, God, when this man is around me, I want to be the randy teenager without a care in the world.

Suddenly, we're interrupted by my phone ringing. Enzo reluctantly pulls himself off me, but nuzzles me close, kissing my neck and collar line of my V-neck shirt. When I reach for my phone on the second ring, I realize it's Maddie. Panic replaces desire in an instant. Enzo pulls back when he sees me go rigid. "It's Maddie," I announce before answering the phone. Enzo is suddenly ramrod-straight on high alert. "Maddie? Are you okay?" I ask when I answer.

Through the phone, I hear, "Yeah, Mom, I'm okay. But there's been a bit of a problem."

I look at the time on my phone and the dance should have gotten over only a few minutes ago. "What kind of problem?" I ask hesitantly.

"Well, Soren and I were on our way home since the dance just ended. We got about halfway there and he got a flat tire."

"Are you guys safe?" I notice Enzo gather his jacket and pace the room.

"Yeah, we're pulled off into a parking lot. Soren's tried to change the tire, but his jack is missing. He's called for roadside assistance, but they told him it would be about three hours before anyone could get to us."

"I'll come and get you," I state. "Just tell me where you are."

I start to gather my things when Enzo interrupts my thoughts and our conversation, "Samantha?"

"Just a second, Maddie," I tell her to wait while I hear what he has to say.

"She has a flat tire?" he asks for clarification.

"Yeah, I'm going to get them. They don't have a jack and the roadside assistance will be a couple of hours."

Enzo looks at me pointedly. "I have no doubt you can get them home safely, but what about the kids asleep upstairs? I'd be more than happy to go. Besides, I have a jack in my rental and I can change the tire quicker than waiting for someone else."

"Are you sure? You don't have to," I hedge, not wanting him to feel obligated.

He gives me a '*Did you really just ask that*' look and I immediately see my answer.

To Maddie, I say, "Hey, honey, Enzo is here and he's going to get you."

"That's great, Mom. Soren's worried he won't make it home by his curfew and he can't get a hold of his parents. He also has an early game he needs to sleep for."

"Tell her to text me the address," Enzo states. "I'll be there as soon as I can."

I relay the message and Maddie and I get off the phone. A moment later, a text chimes on my phone. I immediately forward the address to Enzo.

"Thank you, Enzo. I appreciate it," I sigh and pull him in for a quick hug. *He really is a modern-day hero.*

"Not a hero, beautiful. Just someone who knows how to use a jack." He smiles, making that damn dimple pop and me at a loss for words.

25

———

ENZO

THE RIDE TO pick up Maddie is quick. I easily spot the black Jeep Soren had in the driveway at Samantha's house. The boy has a sweet ride, but I'll bet changing that tire is going to be a bitch. One of my buddies has one and it's one sick SOB to change. Oh, well. It can't be worse than a Humvee in hostile territory.

When I arrive, Soren and Maddie are safely locked inside the Jeep. I can see which tire is flat from across the parking lot. I angle my SUV so that my lights will assist in changing the tire. I put my vehicle in park and head to the back to get the jack out of the cargo space. By the time I approach the Jeep, Soren is out of the driver's side and Maddie hops out, too.

Soren shakes my hand as he greets me, "Thanks, man. I appreciate the help." He points to the back of his car. "I can't believe I didn't make sure there was a jack in here. I just assumed when I bought my Jeep a few months back, that it had one with the spare. I guess I know what I will be buying tomorrow."

"Not a problem. I'm just glad I could help." Soren walks back to the driver's side and takes off his jacket. He comes around to the back passenger side to where the jack is and is about to crawl under to place the jack I brought.

As much as I'd like to let him show he can take care of things, I feel guilty for letting him get his suit potentially ruined. "Hey, Soren, wait up," I say as I step around to block him off.

He looks at me hesitantly. "What?"

"I'm sure you're perfectly capable of changing your own tire, but you've got a suit on. I don't want you to ruin it."

He looks a little hesitant. I can't say I blame him. Most men wouldn't sit back and let someone else do the dirty work for them. Then he looks down at his shirt and the wet pavement from the rain earlier this evening. "Are you sure?"

"Yeah. My mom would've killed me if I came home with my suit all muddy. You can assist me when you can but stay off the ground."

I look to Maddie, who is slightly shivering now that she's standing outside. Doesn't she have a coat? "Maddie, would you like to wait in my vehicle while we do this? I can start it for you so you can stay warm."

"Or you can wear my jacket if you'd like," Soren states as he opens the door to the passenger side and leans across to get it. *The guy's smooth, I'll give him that.*

"I'll take the jacket, thanks. I'll need to know how to change a tire when I get my license, so if you don't mind, I'll watch." *Strong and independent.* She sure is Samantha's daughter.

Before I place the jack, I loosen all the lug nuts. Then, I hand Soren the wrench to loosen the lug nuts on his spare tire, which is attached to the back of his Jeep. The tire is covered, so it shouldn't be too dirty once he gets that off. Within minutes, the spare is off the back of the Jeep. I have the jack securely placed, and the vehicle is lifted high enough to pull off the flattened tire. As I inspect it further, I see a piece of metal that is the culprit. I point it out to Soren so he can show the repair shop. "It looks like you ran over something."

"Yeah, it does." Soren runs his fingers over the two-inch piece impaled in the tire.

I switch tires with his spare. Thank God, it's full-sized because if he just had a donut, I would worry about him making it home. I'll still follow him, just to make sure there are no more problems. But at least I won't worry as much.

Soon, I finish and the tire is changed. I make a point of explaining each step as I complete it since Maddie's genuinely interested in learning how to do it on her own. When I finish, I notice Maddie is sheepishly rocking back and forth on her toes. Knowing this is her first date, I'm sure this isn't how she wanted it to end.

"Thanks again, sir, for your help. I'm going to call the car service and cancel it." Soren pulls out his phone and frustration fills his face. "Crap. It's later than I thought. I really do need to get home. I have to be at school by seven to get to our game on time." He then looks to Maddie with the utmost sincerity. "I've never skipped out on bringing my date home, but do you mind riding with him?" He gestures to me. "I'd rather you not ride in my Jeep until I can inspect the rest of the tires in the daylight. Can I make it up to you another time?" he asks hopefully.

"Of course, Soren," Maddie states, but continues to rock back and forth nervously as if she's unsure of what to do next. *And that's my cue to give them some privacy.*

"Why don't I wait for you in the car, Maddie. I'm going to move it so I'm parked legally. Take your time saying goodbye." I shake hands with Soren and state, "It was nice meeting you."

"You, too, sir. Thanks again for the help."

"No problem. Anytime," I state before walking to my vehicle.

Okay, so I *try* to give them some privacy. I really do. I move my SUV so that I'm no longer putting a spotlight on them with my headlights. I'm not facing them, but I can't help but see them both standing there awkwardly for a moment from my rearview mirror. I'll try to look away if anything should happen, but I want to make sure Maddie's all right. I know she's not my kid, but right now I feel responsible for her. I don't want that boy to take advantage of her. I didn't get any vibes that he would, but he's still a guy, not to be trusted with a young impressionable girl.

They seem to be talking about something important. The way she's looking at him shows me she's hanging on his every word. She nods her head yes. He says something, then she nods again with a huge smile on her face. The boy must finally feel like it's time to make a move. He places one hand on her hip and she takes a step closer to him. He brings the other to the nape of her neck and she steadies herself by placing her hands on his chest. He leans in and kisses her.

This is when I truly do look away. I'm not into voyeurism. I pull up my phone and text Samantha, letting her know I have changed the tire and will be following him home first to make sure he arrives safely. She thanks me again and I tell her it really isn't a problem. I'm happy to do this for her and Maddie.

I glance back at my mirror, thinking they might be done. They seem to have stopped for a moment but start once again. I've gotta hand it to him, Soren must have balls the size of Texas if he's giving her a kiss like that in front of me. I'm not her dad but being a good half foot taller than him, plus fifty pounds heavier, I'm not one to be messed with. I notice he tries to pull away and she kisses him once more. I can't blame the guy. If a woman kissed me like that, I wouldn't be wanting to stop any time soon either.

Finally, when I've looked in every direction I can but at them, I hear him holler, "Thanks again for a great night. Sorry, it had to end this way."

Maddie is almost at my door when she states, "No problem. You'll make it up to me." She laughs and slides into the seat next to me.

Maddie turns to me, cheeks flushed, eyes glimmering with emotion. "Thanks again for coming to help us. It's really nice of you."

"No problem at all. I'll be here any time you need me," I say as I pull out behind Soren and follow him home.

For the entire ride to Soren's house, Maddie appears lost in thought. She has a grin that says she's just been thoroughly kissed and her eyes are slightly glazed over. I can also tell what she's thinking by the fact she keeps running her fingers over her swollen lips. She seems to come out of this haze she's in when she waves to Soren before we pull away, but the rest of the way to Samantha's, she falls back into this trance.

When we're only a few blocks away, I decide I should ask, "Are you okay, Maddie?"

Her grin becomes wider, if that's even possible. "I've never been better."

"Just making sure," I add, not knowing what else to say.

She's quiet for some time, and then I hear her whisper, "So, this is what it feels like to have been kissed."

"Only when you're with the right person," comes out before I can even think to censor my thoughts.

"Are you going to tell my mom?" She looks a little hesitant.

"Not my story to tell, Maddie," I say honestly.

"You sure you won't tell her?"

"Did he hurt you? Or put you in harm's way? Did he take advantage of you?" I ask, trying to make a point.

"Not at all. It felt wonderful," she says dreamily.

"Well, then it's your business to tell your mom."

We pull into the driveway and get out of the car. I wait for her to walk around to the front of the vehicle so I can follow her in, but Maddie surprises me with a hug. "Thanks so much, Enzo. I appreciate your help tonight."

"You're welcome, Maddie."

We go inside and Samantha greets us. Maddie gushes about everything that happened, and we get a count-by-count replay of her evening. When she gets to the end, she can't hold it in any longer. "Guess what, Mom?" Samantha doesn't even get a chance to respond when she states, "He kissed me. Like, *really* kissed me, and it was wonderful." She lets out a big yawn. "I'm beat. I'm going to go to bed."

"Goodnight, honey. I'll see you in the morning." Samantha gives Maddie a huge hug, then kisses her on the forehead. "I love you."

"Love you, too, Mom," Maddie says.

Then she turns to me. "Thanks again, Enzo." She takes a few steps up the stairs then turns around. "Enzo?"

"Yes?" I ask, wondering what she's going to say.

"It's really late. Are you going to be able to drive safely?" The sincerity in her face pierces my heart.

"I'll be fine," I offer reassurance.

"We do have a guest room. I'm sure Mom would be fine if you use it." She turns and says nothing more.

Did she really just say that?!?!? I'd like nothing more than to stay over since our time is so limited, but we have been doing our best to stay respectful for the kids' sake. Hell, I don't even know what to say to that.

"She's right, you know. It's late. You said you'd be here in less than six hours. You might as well stay the night," Samantha says as she traces the collar of my button-down shirt and undoes the first button.

"Are you sure, Samantha? I don't want to give your kids the wrong impression of us."

"Maddie will set Declan and Frankie straight. Besides, the guest room is right next to mine. If they see you go in there and come out in the morning, it won't be a problem."

"Samantha," I growl. "Are you going to take advantage of me this evening?" I say with a hint of teasing among the seriousness of my gravelly voice.

"Only in the best way," she whispers to me as she places a quick kiss on my lips. "Come on, let me show you where you will be sleeping."

LAST NIGHT WAS AMAZING. Fuck, I honestly don't think it could get any better. When I think of every lick, suck, and kiss, I want to live it all over again. Jesus, I'm getting hard just thinking about it.

I'm at a friggin' soccer game. These aren't appropriate thoughts to have on the sidelines. But the beautiful woman standing beside me evokes something in me I can't get out of my head.

I wouldn't say we got much sleep last night, but what a night we had. She showed me to my room and had her wicked and glorious way with me. I can't even count the number of orgasms we shared. Trying to be quiet brought things to an entirely new level of intimacy. We eventually wore ourselves out and fell asleep. I had to wake her this morning at five to go back to her own bed since I didn't know when her kids start moving around the house. After the sensual wake-up call I gave her just before five, she stumbled back to her own room and got ready for the day. If the smile on her face every time she looks my way is any indication, I would say she's just as satisfied with our sleepover as I am.

By the time we get everyone up and ready, we're running late due to our extracurricular activities this morning. We rush through a drive-thru to order breakfast burritos at one of the kids' favorite 24-hour Mexican restaurants. Being a part of Samantha and her family's routine this morning makes me realize I've been missing out on a lot. *God, how I loved waking up and being able to have my way with Samantha this morning. I'll gladly take the chaos of her family if it means getting to experience this.*

A whistle pulls me from my real-life fantasy into the present. FUUUCCKKK! I need to get a grip and get my mind off Samantha. Trying to get my head in the game, I watch Declan as he sprints down the field and takes control of the ball at the last moment before it goes out of bounds. He makes a swift bank to the left and shoots for the goal. The sound of everyone sucking in air as they hold their breath is audible around the sideline. The ball sails high into the air, misses the goalie's fingers by a fraction of an inch, and sinks into the goal in the top right corner of the net. The crowd suddenly goes wild. *Damn, that boy is good.*

The action on the field helps keep my focus on the game. Being a forward, Declan has several more attempts at scoring, but ends up with just two of the four scored this game. His team is ecstatic when they pull off a win. If I thought Samantha and her girls were avid Seahawks fans, that's nothing compared to their enthusiasm watching Declan play. Their pride shines throughout the entire game.

After the game, we all head back to Samantha's house. We pick up sandwiches on the way home for when we're hungry for lunch. Declan surprises me by asking if I'd like to go to a park and play frisbee golf when his sisters each beg Samantha to take them to the mall. The look on Samantha's face shows me she wasn't expecting this either, but I gladly accept. The next thing I know, I'm changed into workout gear and driving to the park.

Declan and I seem to be getting along well. We have a lot in common with us both being athletic and competitive. He's asked me about my time in the Air Force and seems genuinely impressed with the fact I'm a pilot. I tell him if it's okay with his mom, I'll take him out flying sometime. I don't have a plane of my own, but I know enough people that I can make that happen. Working with Riggs will certainly have some benefits, too.

Declan and I arrive at the park and start on the course with ease. Since it's late fall, not too many people are out and about this morning. We go through the course, laughing and joking the entire time, especially if a throw goes awry. Somehow, I manage to get one way off target. A huge gust of wind picks up just as I release, taking my disc about thirty-five yards off my course, nearly hitting a flock of geese roaming the grass. They scatter like crazy, making sounds of their displeasure known. Declan and I burst into laughter at the sight. *That didn't go as planned.*

It takes us a few holes to settle down, but then I notice Declan is unusually quiet suddenly. I figure I can let this go two ways, wait it out or ask him directly what's on his mind. Not being one to shy away, I decide to break the silence with, "What's on your mind, Declan?"

He stops and stares at me for a moment. I notice him straighten his spine like his mother does when she's about to confront something head on. This tells me something serious is on his mind, but it still shocks me when he blatantly asks, "So, what are your intentions with my mom?"

Nope. Didn't see that coming. "Well, I like her very much and we're dating." With eyes much older than a boy his age, he just stares at me as if that isn't a good enough answer.

"What do you want to know?" I ask, looking him directly in the eye. With the look he's returning, I feel like a teenager asking to date a man's daughter. But in a sense, this is like that. If he doesn't think I'm worthy, it will be a no-go with Samantha.

"You're still in the Air Force."

"Yes?" It comes out like a question because I'm not sure where he's heading with his statement.

"You're stationed in Germany. You go back soon, don't you?" He makes his questions sound like he's prompting me to say more. But for the life of me, I'm not following his line of thought.

"Yes," I say again. Still not sure what else he wants me to say.

He shakes his head in disgust. Then he strikes me through the heart. "So, are you just going to dump my mom when you leave?"

What. The. Fuck? I shake my head adamantly and quickly dispel his line of thought. "Not a chance!" *So, this is where he was going with this. Shit. I guess we haven't told him I'm retiring, have we?*

Now Declan seems confused. "What do you mean?"

I let out a low chuckle. "I guess you haven't been told," I say more to myself than him. "Yes, I'm going back. But only until the end of my service contract in February. Then I'm coming back to Portland to work for a private security firm. I'll be doing the same thing as I was in the Air Force, but in the private sector."

A huge relief washes over him. "Really?"

"Yeah, really."

"So, you're not just a fling for her?" Declan puts his hands in his pockets and rocks back and forth from his heels to his toes, no longer making eye contact.

Holy Shit! This is what he's thinking?!?!

"No!" I shout, then I get a little calmer with my explanation. "Your mom is special, Declan. She's the first woman in a very long time, if not ever, to make me feel the way I do. She's smart, funny, and beautiful. She's certainly not a fling and I'm not going to break up with her. I respect her a lot and I hope to continue to be with her when I'm stateside again."

"Are you going to marry her?" *If I thought I was shocked by his last question, I'm flabbergasted by this. Apparently, I'm unprepared for this conversation.*

Without a thought, I state, "It's a little early to know right now, but I'd be honored if it goes that way. You and your sisters are amazing, and I really care about your mom." *Holy shit. I just admitted to Samantha's son, I'd like to marry her. Did this just happen? Who knew this is what I was in store for when I said I'd play frisbee golf?*

"Okay." He turns toward the next target. "You ready for me to whip you at this?"

And just like that, we're back to frisbee golf. I would love to understand the inner workings of a ten-year-old mind. The kid keeps me on my toes, that's for sure.

THE NEXT MORNING, I arrive at Samantha's house a little after eight o'clock. When Samantha greets me at the door, I'm still stunned this gorgeous woman wants to spend time with me. I had the most amazing day with her and her family yesterday and it was a test of my will to drive home last night. I stayed late enough to have Frankie insist I read her a bedtime story, but since the other two kids were still up and watching a movie downstairs, I decided to make a respectable departure time. Man, did it suck sleeping alone.

"Good morning, beautiful," I draw out as I pull back from a passionate kiss. "How was your night?"

"Lonely." She pretends to pout.

I can't help but laugh at her put-out expression. "I'd have rather been here," I whisper in her ear as I continue to keep her embraced in my arms. Finally, after a few more moments of taking in her delicious scent and feeling her body against mine, I reluctantly pull back. This isn't the time to let things get out of control. "You guys ready to go hiking?"

She cringes slightly, making me wonder if something's wrong.

"What?" I ask, hoping it's nothing serious.

"Um, we kind of slept in. I woke up with just enough time to sprint through a shower and pull on clothes. I haven't gotten around to waking them yet."

"You didn't need to get dressed on my account," I whisper in her ear and I can feel her shiver.

"Well, Mr. Punctual, I didn't want to come downstairs looking like Medusa and scare you to death."

"I've seen you in the morning, beautiful. It's quite a sight to be seen. Nothing Medusa-ish about it." We step through the doorway and shut it behind us.

"Why don't I go upstairs and wake the kids? Then we can get going." She turns to walk back up the stairs.

"Or... if you're not in a hurry, we can just hang out and go when they wake. I'm in no rush and I'm sure we can think of something to occupy our time together," I tease, loving the way the subtle blush creeps over her body.

"I don't think that will be a problem." Samantha smiles, taking my hand and leading me to the living room.

SAMANTHA

I LOVE MY KIDS. Don't get me wrong. But having Enzo to myself for an hour and a half is fantastic. We talk, we snuggle on the couch, and of course, enjoy some scorching kisses that send me upstairs to change my underwear before getting the kids ready for our hike.

Thank goodness, I had stocked up on snack foods. I was able to load a backpack for us to take hiking. We're heading up the Gorge on the Washington side to go to Beacon Rock. It's an easy hike with a beautiful view of the Gorge, Mt. Hood, and the Columbia River. We laugh and joke the entire way. Enzo drives my SUV because it has a DVD player in the back and Frankie is excited to watch a show.

When we arrive, we take our time getting to the top. We stop to take lots of selfies of us as a group along the way. *I can't help but feel like we're a family, although I don't want to get ahead of myself here.* At one point, someone offers to take our picture. After looking at it through my phone, I know this is one I will be framing. Enzo has his arm around me and the kids are standing in front of us. Everyone's genuinely smiling at something funny that Frankie just said. The kicker is that we all are looking at the camera at the same time, which is a miracle. Pictures like this never happen with multiple children.

As we reach the top, we get a call from Sara, Enzo's mother, inviting us to come for dinner this afternoon. When Enzo emphasizes the fact that my kids are with us, I hear her tell him 'the more the merrier.' I nod that it's okay, so we finish our hike and head over to his parents' house.

By the time we get there, his brother and sister's families have arrived, too. *Apparently, Sunday dinners are something they partake in each week. I should've figured this out by now. Silly me.* Thankfully, they welcome my kids and me with open arms. It doesn't take long before we're all sitting down to dinner. My kids are a lot older than Enzo's nieces and nephews, but everyone includes them the best they can.

Frankie and the rest of the grandkids that can eat on their own sit at a children's picnic table set up in a corner while Declan and Maddie join us at the table. As I look around the room, I realize it's filled with love, laughter, and lots of happiness. It gives me another glimpse of the life Enzo grew up in. Not that mine was much different, but we see each other less frequently now that everyone's older and has lives of their own.

"So... Pops, when do you think Samantha's remodel will be done?" Enzo's brother Zane asks after finishing a bite of food.

"Well," Lorenzo looks to me before turning to Zane, "I

should be done with the cabinets, floor, and counters this week. All that we're waiting on is Samantha's appliances. Hopefully, they will arrive around the same time."

"When it's all done, I'll have you all over for dinner," I announce to the room. "It will be beautiful. I can't wait to show it off."

"We'll take you up on that," Sara says with a smile on her face. "Be warned though, this lot can get a little wild," she teases, making the room roar with laughter.

"I might even cook," Enzo adds. When jaws drop all around the table, including mine, I'm afraid, Enzo rebuts. "What? I can cook! You just wait. I'll prove it to you."

"I'll hold you to it," Sara teases.

The rest of the meal is filled with easy conversations and laughter. As we're about to leave, Sara reminds us that we're welcome to come next week as well. I mention that the kids will be with their dad, but I'll gladly be here. She also offers to have us over another night this week, with my kitchen in disarray, but once I tell her our weekly schedule with volleyball, soccer, and ballet, she understands completely why I must decline.

Later that night after Enzo leaves, my phone rings. He told me he would call when he got to his parents' place. Without looking, I automatically say, "Miss me already?"

"Uh... Hey, Sam. How's it going?" Devin's deep voice comes through the phone. Mortification creeps through me.

"Oh... Devin... hi," I reply, wondering why he's calling out of the blue. I haven't spoken with Devin on the phone in a while. His voice sounds so different compared to Enzo's. I remember a time when the voice on the other end of this phone meant everything me. *Boy, how times have changed.*

"Hey... ah... listen... I just found out I have to meet with a client in Denmark next week. They're going to pull their campaign if I don't go personally. Ugh... one of my employees really fucked things over and I need to smooth things out or it's going to be costly."

"Okay?" I draw out as a question. *What does this have to do with me?*

"Would you be willing to take the kids next weekend? I won't be back until Tuesday night..." He pauses like he's about to say more but doesn't.

"Sure. Just let me know when you get back into town and we can play Wednesday by ear." This is usually something we handle through texts. Why does he feel he needs to call me? He's so quiet, I wonder if he's still on the line. "Devin?"

"Yeah, Sam. I'm here... So..." he trails off again. He's usually quick and to the point. He sounds tired, but there's something else on his mind.

"So..." I prompt.

"So, the kids say things are getting serious with you and this Enzo guy."

Hmmm... Interesting. "Yep. I'd say they are." *Not that it's any business of yours.*

"But he's going back to Germany," he says as a statement, not a question.

"Yes, he's going back. He *is* in the Air Force and has obligations," comes out a bit snarky at the end.

"I know, but..." He trails off again.

Geesh, get to the point already. "But what?" comes out sharper than I intend. Before he can say anything, I remind him, "Devin, this really isn't any of your business. I've watched you move on and have said nothing. Not a word. Not a snarky remark. Nothing. What is it you have to say?"

"Aren't you afraid you're going to get hurt? Getting so close to him then having him leave. How is that good for you... or the kids? I'm okay with you making your choices, but I'm worried about the kids. They're getting pretty attached to him. Well, at least, Frankie is. He's all she talks about when she comes over."

I see, he's worried more about Frankie at this point. Okay. I get it. Taking a deep breath, I slowly release it before responding. "Once again, not that it's any of your business, but he's only going to be in Germany a few months. Then his plan is to return to Portland *permanently*." I stress the last word to make my point. Hopefully, he gets it.

"So, this is really serious." He seems more confident now.

"Yeah, I'd say it is," I sigh, and thoughts of Enzo flood my mind.

"Are you happy?" Devin asks, sounding sincere. *This is the Devin I remember.*

A smile forms on my face when I realize just how happy I am. "Yeah, Devin, I am. He totally caught me by surprise, but I don't expect him to go away anytime soon."

"Okay." He remains quiet for a moment before adding, "Samantha, I'm happy for you." Devin takes a deep breath and continues before I can say anything else. "Look, I know I've said it before, but I'm sorry for all the shit I've put you through.

I never knew what it was like to be on the other side in this situation, until I saw him with you. I have to say it kind of sucks." He chuckles at the end. "But you seem happy and that's what matters here."

"I am," I almost whisper, still reeling from his revelation. But somehow, I find my voice again, "I know it's new, but he and I are going to see where this goes. I'm not going to do anything to jeopardize the kids. You'll just have to trust me, okay?"

"I do, Sam. You're a great mom. I just didn't know he was coming back. I don't want the kids, well, Frankie getting her mind set on him being around when there is a time limit, that's all." *Is he really saying this?*

"Well, I can't predict the future, but I don't see him leaving anytime soon, Devin. There's no need to worry."

"Okay, Sam. I'll leave you to your night."

As I hang up the phone, I can't help but do a little fist pump. I'm proud of myself for completely holding my own and not letting him interfere with my business. I finally told him my thoughts on his dating, too. Go me. I could care less what he thinks about Enzo and me, but I'm glad he cares enough about our kids to confront me about it. I know I'd want to do the same if I were in his shoes.

The phone rings again. This time I check the caller ID, and the smile that spreads across my face is infectious as I greet him. When I hear "Hey, beautiful," my heart melts even more.

IT'S BEEN three weeks since dinner with Enzo's parents and my conversation with Devin. Enzo and I have somehow managed to see one another every day. When the kids are at Devin's, he stays the entire time with me. *Which is magnificent, by the way. I don't think I will ever tire of him.* When they're home with me, we still spend time together, but with much more focus on my family and, unfortunately, he goes home at night to his parents.

He's been a godsend to my family. Devin had to be out of town a couple of times and Enzo stepped in to help with carpool since I haven't figured out how to be in two places at once yet. Enzo tries to be at every soccer game or volleyball match that he's invited to. My kids seem to get along with him, which is a huge relief to me. I can't imagine how these past few weeks would have gone if they'd hated him.

Knowing he's leaving within the week, we're trying to squeeze as much time together as possible. Today, he told me to wear the green dress he bought me on our first date. He won't tell me where we're going, but he said to make sure I bring a coat since it's the middle of October and fall is in full swing. Living in the Pacific Northwest is unpredictable this time of year.

He showers in the guest bathroom while I put on the finishing touches to my outfit. We both know we would never leave my house if he was in here "helping" me get ready. *We've learned that lesson.* I'm thankful I'm my own boss because I've been late to work plenty of times in the past three weeks. The man is insatiable and turns me on like no other.

Once I'm ready, I meet Enzo downstairs in my

beautifully remodeled kitchen. I can't be prouder of what Lorenzo Harper and his team did in here. We still haven't had the chance to have everyone over, due to crazy schedules, but Enzo assures them I will once he returns from Germany.

Enzo looks stunning in his suit. I'm breathless as I take him in. I honestly think he looks even better than the last time I saw him this dressed up. It might have something to do with the fact my feelings have exploded for him since then as well.

"God, you look beautiful," Enzo murmurs as he pulls me in for a kiss.

"So do you, handsome," I reply.

"Are you ready?" he asks with a gleam of excitement shining in his glorious green eyes. My stomach still flips and flops when I see that dimple pop.

He leads me to his rental SUV and we're on our way. I'm surprised when we don't go downtown, but to an industrial area. There's nothing but brick buildings around us, and I can't for the life of me think of where we might be going, especially dressed up the way we are. He's unusually quiet on our ride, making my senses heighten.

He pulls up to a high, chain-link fence with razor wire spiraling on the top and it opens without any indication of him doing something to move it. I quizzically look in his direction, but he just smirks a knowing look, telling me to be patient. *He should know by now I'm not a patient person. I'm a planner; I like to know what's happening. He's taking me out to Timbuktu, for all I know.*

"Not Timbuktu, Samantha. I'll keep you stateside for

tonight." He chuckles at my remark. *Damn, my lack of filter around him.*

Once we drive around the building, I see a small plane with a private airfield behind it. I raise an eyebrow and ask, "Going somewhere?"

"Yep."

That's all I get. One word. He's grinning like the Cheshire cat, but nothing comes out of his mouth.

He parks his SUV and I notice a man standing outside the plane with a clipboard in his hand.

Enzo gets out and rounds to my door. He assists me in getting out and walks me over to the plane to where he holds out his hand to shake. "Good to see you, Boone. Thanks so much for helping me set this up."

"No problem, Harps. Glad to help." Harps. *Okay, so this has something to do with the military or with his new security team. At least I have some idea now. Sort of.*

"Boone, this is Samantha O'Reilly. Samantha, this is Nathan Boone. He works for Riggs." *Yep, I at least guessed part of this.*

I hold out my hand to shake. "Nice to meet you."

"Likewise," Boone says, smiling at me kindly before turning to Enzo. "Harps, I've pre-checked the plane myself. I have your flight logged and you're ready for takeoff. Need anything else?"

"Nope, that about covers it. Thanks again for all your help. I'll see you in a few months, if you're not here when we return."

With that, Boone leaves and Enzo walks me over to where

a plane is waiting for us. I've flown on plenty of planes, but nothing small and private like this. "So, I guess we're flying the rest of the way?" I tease.

"Yep." There's that word again and that's all I get.

He assists me into the plane. Apparently, I'm sitting in the co-pilot seat. *God help us if Enzo needs any assistance.* There's a small cabin where I could have been comfortably seated, but all I get from Enzo is, "I want you to have the best view."

He goes through the process of checking the instruments on the monstrosity of a board in front and around us. He puts on a headset and talks with someone in aeronautical gibberish I don't understand. But when the plane moves, I take it he's said the right things. We taxi down the runway, and soon, we're high in the sky above the beautiful city of Portland. I can't believe the view from the cockpit.

"Wow! This is incredible," I whisper as I take in all I see. I can see all the mountains in our vicinity: Mt. Hood, Adams, St. Helens, Rainier, and Jefferson. Sure, I've seen them from the small window of a plane, but this view is phenomenal. We turn south once we get to the elevation and I give a look to Enzo asking, "Where are we going?"

"Have patience, beautiful." He fiddles with a control then continues, "I have a weekend planned for us."

"What?" I exclaim, yet question at the same time. "What do you mean a weekend?" Suddenly, I'm beyond excited. I can't believe Enzo planned all of this.

"Well, since Devin has the kids, I packed us a bag of clothes. We'll be back tomorrow evening. Don't worry, I spoke with him about our plans and he knows you're out of town until tomorrow evening."

"So, Devin knows where I'm going, but I don't have a clue?" I pretend to pout.

"Relax, Samantha. You'll know soon enough. It's only a two-hour flight."

Where the hell will we be in two hours? I rack my brain and try to think of flights I've taken.

I must pull my lower lip between my teeth because Enzo suddenly growls, "Samantha, if you don't remove that lip, I can't promise what I'll do to you when we land."

As tempting as that sounds, I decide to play along. "Okay... Okay. Calm down, Rockstar. I was just thinking about where we could be in two hours."

The flight to wherever we're going seems to go by fast. Enzo and I talk about many things. Eventually, there is a lull in the conversation as I take in the forests below us. I can see the ocean in the distance and I can't for the life of me figure out where we're going.

Enzo breaks the silence with, "So what do you think of flying?"

"It's pretty impressive. I'll never forget this experience, that's for sure."

"What do you think of longer flights?" I look at him, wondering where he's going with this.

"They're okay. But nothing will top this. Thank you for planning this trip, to god only knows where you're taking me." I can't help but add that last bit on. I still haven't figured out where the heck our destination is, and it's driving me crazy.

"You're welcome," he says, glancing at me with a smile. "What do you think about hanging out with me for my birthday?"

"Isn't your birthday December sixth?" I ask, thinking about the fact he will be in Germany at that time. The thought alone makes me a little sad.

"Yeah, it is. But I have big plans for my birthday."

"What do you mean?" I'm confused, and my interest is piqued. He has plans, but he wants me to hang out with him? How will that be possible?

"I want you to visit me in Germany. I still have some vacation time left, so I'll be off for a long weekend. I'd love to have you come visit me."

Me, go to Germany? Not only would I get to spend more time with Enzo, but I'd get to go on an incredible vacation. This is a huge step in seeing where things will go between us. But uninterrupted time with Enzo? Only a crazy person would turn that down. "I'll have to look into tickets," I say, thinking I might be able to afford them by using my air miles or something.

"Well, what would you say if I already bought the tickets?" He waggles an eyebrow in my direction.

"Are you serious?" I ask, my excitement filling the cockpit.

"Yep. I'd love for you to visit. I've gotten used to seeing you every day and it's going to be hell being apart from you. My birthday is right about the midpoint for my time left in the Air Force. If you come to Germany, we won't have to be apart from each other much longer than a month before and after."

"How long will I be there?" I ask excitedly, but also to know so I can make arrangements for the kids.

"About ten days. With it being a long flight, I want you to enjoy our time together and not be exhausted from travel."

Wow! Ten days without my kids? Sure, I'll miss the heck out of them, but ten days of uninterrupted time with Enzo sounds incredible. There's no way I can pass this up. "I'm sure I can arrange something for the kids. Devin goes out of town frequently, so we swap our time with the kids when necessary. My parents could even come into town if I need them."

"Lexi said she would help out with them as well," Enzo casually mentions.

"You've told Lexi?" *What else does this man have planned?*

"Yes. I wanted to make sure you could take the time off. She helped me plan this weekend as well." He shrugs as if it's no big deal.

"I'm going to kill her," I mumble. She has some major explaining to do when I get home.

"Are you mad?" he asks with genuine concern.

I shake my head. "No, I'm just frustrated she's been keeping secrets and I'm the last to know. We don't usually keep secrets, but I can't wait to see Germany." I look at Enzo and smile. I feel so fortunate that he took the time to plan all of this for me.

"I can't wait to show you, beautiful. Besides, I don't think I can go months without seeing you. I can't come here in that time, so I figured you can travel."

We settle into an easy silence, but my mind is anything but quiet. It keeps racing back and forth between all the surprises he has in store for me. I can't believe he and Lexi pulled this off. I'm beyond ecstatic! Lexi and I talked about Enzo going away. She knew my worries about him going away for so long and forgetting about me. Not that he'd forget, but from my experience, distance makes dicks wander. Enzo's a man. He has a dick... I don't think he'd cheat on me, but we haven't been dating for very long. He could meet someone else.

"What's on your mind, Samantha? You're about to chew through that delicious lip of yours. Spill it."

Where do I begin? "Well..." I let out a sigh. I might as well lay it all out on the table for him. "I'm so excited to be going on this trip. I was kind of afraid you'd go back to Germany and forget about me."

"Are you serious, Samantha?" Enzo asks in a shocked tone. "I don't think I'll ever have you far from my mind. I love you, and it's going to be pure hell being away from you for any amount of time, let alone for a couple of months on the other side of the world."

I'm not sure he realizes what he just said, but all I can focus on is the fact he said he loves me. *He loves me!* "You love me?" I ask him, my heart about to jump out of my chest.

Enzo looks over at me, and sincerity is clear in his eyes. "Hell yes, I love you, Samantha. I have for some time now. I hate the fact I must go away from you. I've grown to love both you and your kids in the time I've been home." He stops and shakes his head with a light laugh escaping. "I honestly don't think I've loved anyone more." He reaches out and takes my hand, giving it a hard squeeze for reassurance. *It's amazing how just a single touch from him can center me.*

"I love you, too, Enzo. I was afraid you'd find someone else once you got back to Germany."

"Samantha Elizabeth O'Reilly. You get one thing straight in that beautiful mind of yours. I. Will. Not. Cheat. *Ever!* I've been on the other side of that act and I'd never put anyone through that pain."

"Okay," I say quietly. "I believe you."

"I don't think I've told you about Vanessa, my ex. Well, at least not to the full extent. We were high school sweethearts. We started dating at the end of our junior year and it lasted until I was in the Air Force. We were young and in love, or at least I thought we were. I'd known for a while my plan was to go into the Air Force. She told me she was completely on board with it. I went through BASIC and was stationed at McChord Air Force Base near Tacoma, WA. We got a place together and lived off base in a small apartment. Within a year or so, I was ready to propose, but I got deployed overseas. She was going to school and wanted to get her degree before we got married, so we decided to wait until I got back." Enzo stops for a moment and seems to gather his thoughts. I don't want to interrupt, so I wait in silence.

"About three months into my year-long deployment, I got an infamous 'Dear John' letter. To say I was devastated would be an understatement. She told me she didn't think she loved me because she'd met someone else. He was in one of her classes and he was there for her in ways I wasn't."

"Oh my God. That's awful," I whisper and place my hand on his lap to give him reassurance.

"Right then and there, I vowed as long as I'm in the Air Force, I'd never be serious with anyone. I'd never commit to anything long-term because I just wasn't cut out for it."

"What changed?" *I need to ask, but do I want to know the answer?*

"You," he simply states. "I walked into your home, fell into your heart, and don't ever want to let you go." My heart skips a beat at his sweet confession. "I'm older now. I know not everyone cheats. I'm sure you understand. You waited three years to kiss anyone after your husband cheated on you. I highly doubt you're the type of person to cheat either."

He's right. I'd never cheat on anyone. "You're right. I won't. What Devin did, shattered me. It wasn't even just once. He cheated on me multiple times before we finally called it quits. I'd never do that to anyone."

"I'm sorry you had to go through that, Samantha. He was a fool. But..." He leaves off, making me wonder what he's about to say.

"But what?"

"But if he hadn't done that to you, I wouldn't be with you now. So, things do have a way of working themselves out, don't they?" The smile on his face is wide and I can see the love he has for me pouring through.

"They sure do, Enzo. They sure do."

"I love you, Samantha." Enzo's deep voice sends shivers up my spine.

"I love you, too," I tell him with my entire being.

Suddenly, I'm distracted by the sight below me. I notice we're approaching a larger city in the distance. Before long, I see the Golden Gate Bridge. "We're in San Francisco?" I say gleefully.

"Yep. We're going to lunch by the Fisherman's Warf and spending the day sightseeing."

"Wow, you are a rock star. This is an incredible trip you've planned."

Enzo is suddenly busy radioing the tower to land properly. All I can do is look out the window in awe. I can't help to steal another glance at the sexy man who's completely in his element for the moment. As he radios back and forth and adjusts the gadgets in front of us to make a smooth landing, I'm even more in awe of him. I can't wait to show him my gratitude for everything.

From the small airfield, we take an Uber to the Fisherman's Wharf. We walk along shops and go to a fantastic seafood restaurant. Then we take a trolley car up and down the expansive hills of San Francisco. I've been to the airport before, but I've never explored the city. Being with Enzo just makes it that much better.

I should be tired when we reach the hotel. But I only have one thing on my mind when we step behind those doors. I want to show him my deep appreciation for everything he has done for me. He's carrying a small overnight bag with him, which I hope has a change of clothes for me. If not, I really don't want to wear anything for the remainder of our trip anyway.

I immediately strip out of my clothes the minute I hear the door click closed. I kick off my shoes, unzip my dress, and turn to face the gorgeous man beside me.

"In a hurry?" He laughs, his eyes roaming up and down my body.

I nod as the dress slips to my ankles and I step out of it. I'm only wearing a lacy green underwear and bra set I bought to match the magnificent dress Enzo bought me. Enzo's eyes darken to a deep green as they take in what I'm wearing. He's already removed his jacket and is unbuttoning his shirt, but I stop him. I want that glorious task. I close the distance between us, reaching my hands to his chest.

I slowly make my way down his shirt, placing a kiss under each button I open. I enjoy the flex of each muscle as his scent envelops me and slight moans escape his lips. When I finally reach the last button, I push the shirt off his broad shoulders, running my tongue along his collarbone as I trace my hands over his strong shoulders and sculpted arms. I can't help but stare at his chest, filled with the perfect combination of tattoos and muscle, making him the sexiest man I've ever seen. I don't think I'll ever get over how much he turns me on. My body is on fire as my need takes over.

He kicks out of his shoes as I reach for his belt, undoing it so I can get to the fly of his trousers. I can see his cock vying for my attention, but I ignore it for a moment as I slide his pants and underwear over his thick-muscled thighs to the floor in one motion. I quickly make work of his socks. I want to see this man in all his glory.

Finally, the only thing Enzo is wearing is the sexy smile, which makes his dimple pop. *God, I could stare at him all day.*

"I hope you do more than stare, beautiful." His sexy voice makes my panties want to spontaneously combust.

"Oh, I'm sure I'll think of something to do," I tease, my

voice sounding gravelly. I lead him to an oversized chair next to us and force him to sit down.

Feeling sexier than ever, I slowly dance in front of Enzo. Though his thick, beautiful cock bobs for my attention, I focus on his green eyes, turning darker with need, as I do a strip tease, removing my bra. I sway to a rhythm in my head and soon my panties are on the floor as well. I dance for a while longer until Enzo shows he can't take it anymore and gives me a firm warning, "Samantha." His voice is barely controlled, and with his hands bunched into fists, resting on the arms of the chair, I can tell he's doing all he can to keep himself from reaching out to me. *I love that I have an effect on him.*

Careful not to touch anything else, I reach for his cock to take it in my hands. I slide one hand up his shaft while the other reaches for his balls. He widens his legs without any prompting and I kneel between them. I start to lick, stroke, and tug the perfect rhythm, using my hand and mouth in such a way that drives him wild. I hear his breath catch every now and again, letting me know this is what he needs.

When I can't take it anymore, I release the hand cupping his balls and slide it into my own wetness. Within moments, I find my clit and work it roughly as I continue to enjoy the taste of Enzo.

"Samantha," he growls in a low warning, letting me know he's close. He tugs my arm to get me to stop. "I want to come with you."

Without a second thought, I stand and he guides me to straddle him. I know I'm drenched, so there's no need for any preparation. I place both my thighs on the outside of his and slide home to the base of his cock. He can't stay passive. Enzo takes control from the bottom and it's all I can do to hold on for dear life. His lips lock onto mine as he thrusts into me over and over again at a relentless pace. *God! I love this man. I love this feeling.* Feeling myself build higher and higher, I need to take Enzo with me. I put every amount of effort I have into showing him how I feel and taking the pleasure he gives me.

I scream, "I love you!" as one of the best orgasms of my life rips through me. I feel Enzo thrust into me a few more times and his body stiffens. He holds onto me as if I'm his last dying breath. Then he fills me with love from the inside out.

"I love you so much, Samantha. You're so beautiful," he says as he rests his forehead against mine.

Holy Hell! It's going to take a long time to recover.

Nothing can be heard except the panting of our breaths and the beating of our hearts as we both come back to Earth from that out-of-this-world experience. *How is it that each time keeps getting better?* I think as I relax into that perfect place between his shoulder blade and chest.

After a long while, Enzo breaks the silence. "It does get better each and every time, Samantha." His voice then turns playful as he pats me on the ass to move. "Are you ready to see what we can do to top that?"

I swear to God, with his words alone, he grows once again from inside me. He doesn't even remove himself as he lifts me to a standing position and carries me to the bed across the room. He gently lays me down on the bed, careful not to slip out and proceeds to show me just how much better round two can be.

27

———

ENZO

SAYING goodbye to Samantha is one of the hardest things I've ever done. She takes me to the airport, but I won't let her walk me in since there's no point with security, so we say our goodbyes in the departure lanes at the Portland International Airport. My legs feel like lead as I walk away from her. My only saving grace is knowing our time apart will be short.

We spent the last of our time enjoying every moment with one another. Devin had the kids while we were in San Francisco, then Samantha took a few days off to spend more time with me. In the evenings, we enjoyed activities with her family. Life couldn't have been any better. Well, except for the fact I have three months left on my contract. It sucks being away from her.

As soon as I get back to Ramstein, I realize my vacation is over. I talk with Samantha whenever I can. But time differences and being on duty proves to have its challenges. I sleep near my phone so I can answer her calls. We video chat or talk every day, except when I'm required to go radio-silent for the mission I'm on.

I have literally flown all over the world for the past few weeks. I'm glad to say I safely made it in and out of various places in Sudan, Afghanistan, and Pakistan. There have been some touchy situations, but I know I had to make it out unscathed. The men and women who depend on me to be their wheels make it essential I return, not to mention I now have Samantha counting on me, too.

Thank the fucking Lord time flies when I'm busy. Knowing there's an end in sight to my misery has made it bearable. I miss Samantha like crazy. Each time I close my eyes, her rich mahogany eyes stare back at me. I can't wait until she arrives at the airport.

Knowing I can't spend another minute without her being mine, I managed one important shopping trip while I was off duty last week. I had to guess at her size, but I'm pretty sure I have it right. I just can't wait until she gets here. I never knew I could miss anyone so much.

These last two hours have been the worst. I have flowers waiting for her as I pace the lobby of the airport. The monitor keeps changing for when her flight should arrive. It appears as if they have a good tailwind, so they're making up time. I'm in civilian clothes, wearing dark jeans, t-shirt, and a thick sweater. In Germany, it's cold in the winter. I have a plan in place for tonight; I just hope she's up for it.

I paid for her to fly first class, with only one layover at JFK. I hope she was able to stretch out in a sleeper bed and rest the entire way here. It's still morning, so I'm hoping she got some sleep to help with jetlag.

When she finally approaches, I feel as if I'm dreaming. She looks even more beautiful than I remember. When she reaches me, I pull her in tight. Damn, I've missed her. I can't get enough of her. I kiss her thoroughly and completely. I don't care that we're in the middle of a crowded airport. I lift her off the floor and she squeals as I spin her around.

"God, I've missed you, beautiful," I whisper before setting her down.

"I've missed you, too," she whispers as I kiss her once more.

When I finally put her on her feet, I hand her the flowers I've been holding onto. Then, I take a good look at her. She's wearing a beautiful, dark-red, flowing top with black skinny jeans and short brown boots. She appears as if she just stepped off a runway, which brings an even bigger smile to my face because she has no idea about our plans this evening. She appears a little tired, but not dead on her feet. Her hair is flowing perfectly around her shoulders and the smile she has plastered on her face makes me feel as if I'm the luckiest guy in the world.

I take her carry-on bag and direct her to baggage claim. It doesn't take long before we're out of the airport and climbing into my silver Land Rover. She seems in awe that she's here. Her eyes take in the scenery as we drive down the highway, and the smile on her face is infectious.

"Are you hungry?" I ask, wanting to make sure she isn't starving after her long flight.

"I could eat," she says as she takes in the sites outside the Frankfurt Airport.

Knowing we'll have to go inside to dine, I take her to the place I think she'll love. It's located in a small town just outside of Frankfurt. As we pull into town, she lights up at all the beautiful Christmas decorations lining the streets. I find a place to park and we make our way to the restaurant. On our way inside, Samantha spots a shop with Christmas ornaments displayed in the window.

"Oh, can we go in there? I'd love to bring home an ornament to remember this trip."

"Let's go, beautiful." I take her hand and pull her close to me once we're on the sidewalk. Thankfully, she brought a warm jacket because it's freezing out here. I wrap my arms around her, so fucking relieved she's finally with me. When she pulls back, I reach for her face, and with a kiss, show her once again how much I've missed her.

All too soon, I remember we're in public and I need to curb my enthusiasm. Fuck, it sucks being honorable sometimes. I motion for the shop she wanted to look in. "Let's go see what's inside."

Christmas music with German voices being sung fills the shop. It smells like sugar cookies and pine trees and the blast of warm air that welcomes us is inviting. The small shop is lined with shelves. Samantha peruses them, and I follow along with her hand in mine. Even though I usually despise shopping, being with her is worth every moment of torture. Seeing her enthusiasm as she browses through the trinkets makes me feel things I've never felt before.

"Oh, Enzo! Look at this." Samantha holds up a hand carved Santa ornament. At the bottom, it has "St. Nicholas Day" and the year carved into it. "Do you realize that your birthday is on St. Nicholas Day?" she asks when she realizes in Germany, they celebrate that on the sixth of December.

"Yeah, I know." I hold out my hand, asking her for the Santa to inspect it further. "You should get this. It's beautiful."

"I think I will, but I want to look around some more." She turns to look at more decorations around her.

"Uh, Enzo?" She seems a little hesitant.

"Yeah?"

"What's up with the pickles? They seem to be everywhere." She holds one up, then looks around at the variety of choices she has before her.

"Ha! For St. Nicholas Day here in Germany, the parents decorate the tree. Then the first time the kids look at the tree, they search for the pickle. The first one to find the pickle gets an extra present under the tree," I explain.

"Well, we should get one of those, too. It'd be a fun tradition to start."

"Would you like to find *my* pickle?" *I'm a guy. I can't help it.* The burst of color that explodes across her face was so worth it. Samantha winks at me, then picks out her favorite before continuing to shop.

By the time we're finished with this shop, Samantha has quite a few new things to decorate her home with. God, I wish I could be there with her this year. It's going to suck spending the holidays alone again, especially now that I have someone I want to share them with. But I'll be home at the end of January for good.

When we finish shopping, we walk down a few doors to the restaurant. There is no wait, so Samantha and I are seated right away. Since this is a small town and the woman who greets us speaks only in German, I take the liberty of asking Samantha what she's in the mood for, then I order for both of us. *You can't live in a country and not pick up on at least the basics of the language.*

We fill our time talking about everything and nothing. She fills me in on each of the kids and I tell her what I can about my most recent missions. Granted, I can't say much, so I tell her about some of my buddies stationed here at Ramstein. She's eager to meet them. Though I'd rather keep her to myself, I realize I want to share that side of my life with her, too. I warn her that some of them are rough and rowdy, and she doesn't miss a beat by telling me those are the ones she should meet first.

There's about an hour drive to my apartment off base. To my surprise, as soon as Samantha gets settled in the car and the heater flows through the frigid space, she falls fast asleep. *She did just travel over fifteen hours to get here.* I just lay my hand on her thigh to keep a connection and make the trip with ease.

Samantha is as cute as can be when we arrive. She doesn't appear to be willingly waking up anytime soon. At one point, I reach for her hand to hold it, and it drops like a lead weight when I try to wake her. I've made plans for this evening, but I think I'll just postpone them until she can enjoy them more.

When I open her door to help her out, Samantha wakes,

seeming embarrassed to have fallen asleep. "Shit! I fell asleep. Are we already here?" She looks around in a panic.

I try not to laugh as I reply, "Relax, beautiful. You didn't miss much. I'll take you sightseeing another time."

She eagerly gets out of the car, taking my hand as she says, "Now that I've rested, what do you want to do this afternoon?" I lead her to my one-bedroom flat. "Let's get you settled, then we can decide."

Now that I'm looking at my flat from an outsider's perspective, I realize there isn't much to it. "I hope you aren't expecting anything fancy." I look at Samantha, who seems to be taking my living space in. "It's basically a basement that has been converted into an apartment. There's a three-bedroom flat above me, which is also rented out. Three guys live in it. All are stationed at Ramstein, though not in my unit. We get along okay."

"I'm sure it will be fine, Enzo. Don't worry." She leans up on her toes and kisses me quickly once more.

"I've warned you that I'm not home much, right?" I feel like shit inviting her to this place now that she's here. "I just got this place so I could come and go as I please, have some privacy, and stay out of base housing. It's nice to get away from it all, if you know what I mean." We reach the door and she puts her hands on her hips.

"Enzo, I could care less what it looks like. I didn't come here to stay at the Ritz. I came here to see you."

"If you don't like it, I can get a hotel for the week you're here," I offer, knowing it only has the bare necessities.

"Don't be ridiculous. Does it have a clean bed and shower?"

"Yes," I sigh. "It's not a dump, just tight quarters. You're used to living in a big, beautiful home. I just don't want you to go without."

She shakes her head and laughter comes out. "As long as I have you, I'm fine."

With that, I open the door and let her walk in. I give her the five-second tour because that's all it takes. My kitchen lines one wall and a living room the other. There are two doors off the back of the living room wall. One goes to a bedroom that's at least big enough to fit a king-sized bed along with my dresser, the other goes to the bathroom.

I take her things into my bedroom and place them near the dresser on the floor. "If you'd like to hang anything up, feel free to. There's plenty of room in the closet."

"Thanks. Do you mind if I take a shower?" she asks innocently.

"Sure. You can grab your things and go through that door. It also opens to the living room, so if you don't want the neighbors to see, be sure to shut the other door," I tease.

She walks in and I hear the other door shut. Wanting to give her some space, I do everything I can to force myself back to the living room. After a few minutes, I hear Samantha call, "Enzo, can you help me with something?"

Not knowing what she should need, I rush through the bedroom and stop dead in my tracks. There she is, in all her naked glory, standing before me. One arm is held high against the bathroom doorjamb, the other is casually on her hips. Her body is on full display and the look on her face lets me know the help she needs.

Trying to play coy, I ask, "Need something?"

Her rich mahogany eyes grow darker. "Only you."

It takes me less than thirty seconds to rid myself of the clothes I'm wearing. There's no way I want to have our first time after a month of being apart to be in the moderately sized shower. I bend down and swoop her up without giving her a chance to comprehend my intentions. Within two strides, I'm laying her on the freshly washed bedding. Then I pause to stare at the beauty before me.

"Took you long enough," she teases. I'm not sure that she meant to say that aloud, but I can't help but chuckle.

"I was giving you some space, beautiful. I've wanted to attack you since you stepped into my arms from the plane. I was *trying* to be a gentleman."

"Have your wicked way with me, Enzo. I can't wait any longer." The invitation couldn't be clearer if it was tattooed on her forehead. I don't wait any longer and I don't disappoint. I spend the next several hours worshiping her body the only way I know how. We do make the time to refuel with dinner, but we eat it in bed and I continue to sing my praises to her throughout the night.

The next morning, I awake to a retching sound. It makes me bolt out of bed once I realize Samantha is no longer beside me. I find her naked body hovered over the toilet, praying to the porcelain God. "You okay?" Fuck. She isn't okay. She's puking. What a stupid thing to ask, so I try again. "Anything I can get you?"

"Go away, I don't want you to catch this," Samantha croaks.

"Not happening, beautiful." I may feel helpless, but I'm not going to be a complete douche and leave her when she is sick. I walk over to her and pull back her hair. I rub her back as she seems to dry heave over the commode. I realize she's freezing, so I take a towel I set out for her to use and wrap it around her body.

"Thanks," she whispers weakly.

When she stops trying to heave, she slumps against the wall and the toilet. I realize this can't be comfortable, so I ask, "Do you think you're done puking for now?"

She nods, then rolls her head to lean it against the wall. I take this as my cue to help her move. Within moments, I have her lying back down in bed. I cover her up, then walk over to my drawer and get her a pair of boxers and a t-shirt. I'm not about to take the time to get into her suitcase. Besides, there's no reason she should ruin her clothes if she gets sick again. I slip on a pair of boxers for myself, then walk back over to the bed and pull back the covers to help dress her. At first, she protests, but then she realizes what I'm doing and eagerly accepts what I'm offering.

I walk to the kitchen and get my largest cooking pot. It isn't much, but it'll do if she needs it again. I place it on the floor next to the bed with a towel underneath. Then I attempt to crawl back into bed to hold her, but she protests.

"Enzo, I don't want to get you sick."

"Samantha, we've swapped enough DNA since last night. If I'm going to get sick, I'm already exposed," I try to tease, but then I take mercy on her. "Beautiful, I just want to hold you. Please let me do this. I feel helpless right now. Not to mention there's no way I'm going in the other room after spending the last six weeks apart."

She reluctantly agrees. The next thing I know she's snuggled into my chest, sound asleep. I hope she just ate something that didn't agree with her, or that this is just a twenty-four hour virus. I settle in and eventually fall asleep again with her by my side.

A few hours later, she wakes up. She gets up to go to the bathroom, but all she does is use the facilities. I hover around in case she gets sick, but want to give her privacy if she needs it. When she returns, I notice her hair has been brushed and she smells like mint, so she must have brushed her teeth.

"Are you feeling better?"

"So much better. I'm a little hungry. Do you have any toast?"

Thankful for something to do, I quickly get up to put some bread in the toaster. She joins me in the living room and sits on the couch. While the toast is cooking, I walk over to the closet by the door and get a blanket to place over her.

"I don't know what I did to deserve you," she whispers as I kiss her lightly on the forehead while tucking her in.

"I'm the lucky one," I whisper back, and I can tell she hadn't meant for me to hear. A beautiful blush brings color back to her cheeks.

"Damn filter," she mutters, and I can't help but laugh.

"I love you, Samantha, lack of filter and all."

She pretends to glare. "You're lucky I love you, too, Enzo."

"Damn right I am."

After fixing her toast, we lounge around for a few more hours. When it's one o'clock in the afternoon, Samantha groans. "Can we go do something? It feels like such a waste to come all this way just to sit in an apartment."

"Are you sure you're up for it?" I ask, remembering how much she heaved earlier this morning.

"Yes. I feel fine. Let's stay out of public areas, so I won't spread germs if I'm sick, but I really want to see the sights. We can drive around and see them from the car and come back to them after we know I'm better."

Of course, I honor her wish. Within the hour, we're loaded into my car and driving around. I take her to Ramstein Air Force Base and show her around. She says she's hungry again, so I run in and grab something for us to eat at a deli on base. Unfortunately, we don't even make it thirty minutes after she eats before she's begging me to pull over. She empties her stomach in some bushes and begs me to take her back to my place, claiming she has embarrassed me enough for one day. We spend the rest of the evening watching movies. She seems to do better after a few hours, so I feed her some chicken broth for dinner, not wanting to take any chances.

The next morning, I feel like I'm Bill Murray in the movie '*Groundhog Day.*' My life is stuck on repeat. Samantha's back to retching on the floor and once again, I'm feeling helpless. I help her take a shower, keeping things task oriented, then get her back into bed. I feel awful for her. She seems lethargic and

I can hardly get her to eat anything for the remainder of the day because she can't keep it down. She has me worried.

Thankfully, the next day she's better. It happens to be my birthday, so *Happy Birthday to me!* She seems vibrant and full of energy. Back to her normal self, or at least not knocking on death's door at any moment. She begs me to get dressed up and get out of the house to celebrate my birthday. *Who am I to complain?*

I'm on cloud nine because today might finally be the day I get to follow through with my original plans. While Samantha is getting ready, I make sure I have everything I need to make my dreams come true. She nearly knocks me on my ass when she greets me in the living room in that stunning dress I bought her on our first date. She looks spectacular.

Even though it's only early morning, we decide to make the most of the day and start celebrating early since she claims we have a lot of lost time to make up for. To be honest, I could care less what we do today. I just want to be with her.

"So, are you ready to finally show me around?" she saucily asks.

"You keep that look on your face and we won't ever leave this place," I tease in return. God, it feels amazing to have Samantha back in the land of the living.

From my flat, within thirty minutes, we can drive to three different castles. I start with the closest. It's the Nanstein Castle. It was built in 1162 in Landstuhl, Rhineland-Palatinate. Thankfully, Samantha brought knee-high boots, so we're able to get out and tour the grounds of the castle. It has spectacular views that overlook the city. We learn that it was built after Holy Roman Emperor Frederick I demanded its construction as an additional defense for the Palatinate. Samantha and I take several pictures of the architecture, as well as the views from the castle walls. I sneak quite a few pictures of Samantha, too, because she's absolutely glowing with excitement.

Afterward, we stop at a local café. Samantha claims her stomach isn't completely back to normal yet, so she only wants a light pastry and coffee for breakfast.

After we eat, we go to another castle, in Thallichtenberg, Germany. It's the biggest castle ruin in Germany, and it's a fantastic sight to see. Samantha is in awe of its vastness. It sits upon a large hill, overlooking the farmlands below.

Samantha can hardly control her enthusiasm for the history we're experiencing. I can't help but laugh when, "This is what fairytales are made of," comes out of her mouth. The brilliant woman before me is always referencing books.

"Does that make me your Prince Charming?" I tease.

Samantha doesn't respond, just kisses me soundly on the lips, making me wish we were back at my flat again.

UNFORTUNATELY, just as I'm about to take her to our final destination for the day where I have my big surprise planned, she begs me to pull over. Yep. She gets sick once again.

When I feel her head, it's clammy and I can't help but notice she has lost all color. Maybe we overdid it and I'm overreacting but throwing up for three days straight and not keeping anything down in all that time has me extremely worried. She just lies limp in the car as we head back home, which scares the shit out of me even more. When she moans and rubs her upper stomach, I nearly lose it.

Screw this. I'm not taking any chances. Instead of taking her back to my place, I make a rash decision. I drive straight to the on-base hospital. I know she's a civilian, but it's the closest hospital around. When Samantha figures out my plans, she throws a fit. "Enzo, I don't need to go to the hospital. I've just got the flu. There's no need to go to this much trouble."

But suddenly, she turns completely green and points to the shoulder of the road. I barely have a chance to get off safely before she's opening the door and releasing the remaining contents of her stomach.

I give her a pointed look and ask, "Will you just humor me? Let's go make sure that's all this is. I can't idly sit back and watch you suffer like this, not knowing the cause."

"Okay," she reluctantly agrees and falls asleep within moments.

Fuck! Her lethargic state is scaring the shit out of me. I step on the gas and get her there as safely as possible.

When we enter the waiting room, I explain her situation. Samantha is offered a wheelchair because she can hardly stand on her own. Thank the fucking Lord, there isn't a long wait. Most people are home celebrating St. Nicholas Day and we've beaten the evening rush, according to one of the nurses.

The entire time, I can't help but hold Samantha's hand or have some part of me touching her. I feel so fucking helpless. She moans a little more and I nearly take out my frustrations on a nurse that finally comes to get us.

The nurse asks if I'm family and I say, "I'm her fiancé," before any questions can be asked. There's no fucking way I'm going to sit out in a waiting room because I'm not family. Besides, if I had had the chance to ask her, I would be telling the truth right now anyway.

The nurse records her vitals and asks her a series of questions. What feels like eons later, a doctor comes in and does a quick exam. Samantha's sore throughout her stomach, so the doctor orders a series of tests to be done. Blood is drawn, and a nurse asks Samantha if she can give urine. She smiles weakly and the nurse assists her to the bathroom. It takes everything in my power not to insist I be the one to go with her, but Samantha gives me a knowing look, putting me at ease. A little, anyway. Who the fuck am I kidding? I'm still a nervous wreck.

The doctor has been throwing words around like appendicitis, gallbladder, kidney infection, and about four other things they will test for. In a little while, they will be taking her for an ultrasound. Samantha has been the voice of reason through it all. Just the touch of her hand on my skin is enough to calm me to the point of being reasonable to be around.

While we're waiting for her tests to be done, I realize I can't take it anymore. I'm a fucking ball of nerves and I must let her know how much she means to me. "Samantha," I almost shout.

Surprised, she looks in my direction. "Yes?"

"I need you to know how much I love you," I start, but she interrupts me.

"I love you, too," she whispers, placing a hand on my forearm and I immediately calm once again.

I clear my throat and begin again, "Samantha, I need you to know how much I love you. I've never met anyone like you. You've become the most important person in my life."

Finally, I have her full attention, as her round eyes are entirely focused on mine. I kneel on one knee and I bring both her hands in mine as I lean against her hospital bed. I hesitate for a moment until I finally get a grip on my emotions and continue, "Samantha, no matter what those test results say, I'm going to be with you in sickness and in health. I want you to know that I will always have your best interests at heart. I'm sure there'll be times you're going to have to put me in my place because I can be a little thick headed..." I can't help but laugh when she chuckles at my comment. "...but know I will always do it out of love."

I take a deep breath to collect my thoughts once again.

"These past six weeks of being apart have made me a miserable bastard. I don't want to spend another day without you being mine." I take another deep breath as I keep to my mission, getting the words I desperately need to say out, "Samantha Elizabeth O'Reilly, would you do me the honor of being my wife? Will you marry me and make me the happiest man alive?"

My heart pounds in my chest with anticipation and of course, Samantha chooses this moment to stay silent. Her face is a mask, void of emotion, and her beautiful mouth remains firmly closed.

Christ, was this the wrong place to ask her? Should I have waited until she was well again or stuck with my original plan and been more romantic? Where the fuck is her lack of filter when I need it?

To be continued...

RESOLUTION

BOOK TWO OF RESILIENCE DUET

1

———————

SAMANTHA

"LADIES AND GENTLEMEN, our final destination is approaching. We should reach Frankfurt, Germany, in thirty minutes. The local time is nine thirty-eight a.m. The weather is thirty-nine degrees Fahrenheit, which is four degrees Celsius, and clear. It's pretty but cold. Be sure to wear your coats," the captain announces. Then it's translated into German and French before the announcements are made about storing our belongings and putting our seats and trays in the upright positions. Butterflies flip in my stomach as I hear this. I've been traveling for over fifteen hours and can't wait to land.

Never in a million years did I think I'd be doing this. Here I am at age thirty-eight, on a plane to see my *boyfriend* in Germany. *Germany, as in the one on the other side of the world from Portland, Oregon.* If you'd asked me just three months ago if I'd be doing this, I would have told you, you're crazy. First, there's the fact I now have a boyfriend. Second, there's the whole issue of flying around the world. But when Enzo Harper walked into my house that fateful day to surprise his dad, we were both in for the surprise of our lives.

From the moment I saw Enzo walk into my disheveled kitchen, my life hasn't been the same. It feels like it was yesterday. I was simply sitting there, minding my own business, while a work crew remodeled my kitchen. In walks a man I didn't recognize, but was instantly attracted to. He was well over six feet tall with short, tousled, dark-blond hair. He was easily in his mid-thirties. He had an athletic build and glorious green eyes that sparkled with delight.

From the very start, I thought he was sex on a stick. I didn't think any man could ever be that good looking in real life. He's the type of man women spend billions on each year to buy as their next book boyfriend. I should know, I publish and market said books on a daily basis. I make it my business to know what sells, and the stranger before me was a mint in the making.

At the time, I could tell Enzo was up to something when he walked into my house, but I couldn't figure out what it was. When he motioned for me to "shhh" as he winked, I was locked in my spot waiting to see what would happen next. He approached Lorenzo Harper, my contractor, who had been talking on the phone to someone. The minute he hung up, Lorenzo was swept into a bear hug, which was no small feat. Lorenzo had been nearly as bulky as the mysterious man in front of me.

Of course, I was quickly introduced to Lorenzo's son,

Enzo. Then, as he showed him the progress his crew was making on my home, I felt a magnetic pull to Enzo, even after just a few short moments. It's something I'd never experienced before. Of course, after they left, I went about my business, though there were frequent thoughts about the sexy man I had met earlier in the day.

As I left my house to get dinner that evening, I was happily surprised to find him outside retrieving his car after spending the afternoon with his dad. To my utter shock, I actually asked him to join me for dinner. Yes, me, Samantha O'Reilly, the single mother of three, got up the courage to ask him out. I hadn't even kissed a man in three years. No one I dated after my divorce was even worth a second date. I felt pretty courageous asking him. There was something about that sexy man with the swoon-worthy dimple, that gave me my mojo back.

Lorenzo Harper's a pilot for pararescue in the Air Force. He can fly just about anything he's given the chance to. He was home on leave, contemplating his career decisions. Should he retire? Should he switch to Air National Guard? Or should he move to the civilian side and work with private contractors for security? Thank God, he chose option three, which keeps him in Portland, Oregon. Now, he has less than two months left in the Air Force and will be returning home, for good. Sure, he'll have to travel with work, but his home base is near me, so who am I to complain?

To say our relationship's been a whirlwind is putting it mildly. I almost blush at the heat and chemistry we instantly displayed. No, I didn't sleep with him that first night, but when we did, the intensity was beyond anything I'd ever experienced. Enzo brings out a side of me I never knew existed and I can't wait to see what the future has in store for us.

Yes, I've been married before, and I've obviously had sex before. I do have three wonderful kids with my ex, Devin. But nothing could prepare me for Enzo Harper. I'd like to say I feel ashamed I want to strip naked the moment the man enters a room, but that would be a lie. After having my heart closed off for so long, due to indiscretions in one form or another, it's a glorious feeling to have someone accept me for who I am and loves me wholeheartedly. I've never been happier.

That's Enzo in a nutshell. Since he's practically been married to the Air Force for the last twenty years, having never found someone to settle down with, I think he's just as shocked to experience this, too. Years earlier, there had been one woman, but soon after his first deployment, he received a 'Dear John' letter from her, forcing him to keep his heart closed... that is, until he met me.

Boy, did I luck out. He's thoughtful, kind, and wonderful to my three kids. My youngest, Frankie, who's eight, simply adores him. Declan, my ten-year-old, also gets along with him well. Ever since Enzo rescued Maddie while she was on her first date with a flat tire, she's befriended him, too.

When he returned to Germany six weeks ago, there was three months left on his contract with the Air Force. It's been a long six weeks, almost torturous at times. Sure, we talk as much as we can when he isn't out on a mission, but he's literally been all over the world. I don't even know about the *where* of his location until it's already happened. It sucks not knowing, but that's how he's kept safe, so I understand and force myself to accept it. We've managed countless talks over the phone, and there may have been some sexy video messaging as well, which has been kind of fun, if I'm being honest.

I bring myself back to reality as I feel our descent, and the Frankfurt Airport comes into view. These last thirty minutes have been pure torture. I can't believe I'm so close, yet so far from Enzo. *God! Can't this plane go any faster?* I don't want to be away from him any longer. My body's a bundle of nerves and I feel as if we'll never make it there.

We finally touch down with a huge bump, coming to a careening stop, before the end of a runway. Thank God, Enzo put me in a first-class sleeper. I'm well rested and eager to see him.

It takes FOREVER for the cabin doors to open and the crew to let us off the plane. I make my way through customs and into the airport. Suddenly, the sexy man I have been dreaming about night and day, for the last six weeks, stands in front of me. He's still just as tall and handsome as ever. Being six-foot-six, he stands out among the crowd. His blond hair's shorter than before. High and tight, like a military cut, but upon further inspection, there should still be just enough to get my hands into. The thought alone makes my mouth water. Enzo's in civilian clothes, wearing dark jeans, dark sweater, and I can tell there's a collared shirt underneath. The moment he spots me, he closes the distance. A large bouquet of flowers is in his hands, but that doesn't stop him from swooping me up into his arms to kiss the life out of me.

Fuck, if we weren't in a crowded airport, I'd beg him to take me right now. But I'm an adult, so I can practice some patience. *I hope.*

"God, I've missed you, beautiful," he whispers into my ear as he sets me down.

"I've missed you, too," flutters against one last kiss.

Like the gentleman he is, he grabs my carry-on bag, leaving me only my purse to carry, leading me to the baggage claim.

After getting my luggage, we walk hand in hand to the parking garage. His large hand warms mine, making me feel secure and safe with him.

"Are you hungry?" he asks as we get into his silver Land Rover.

Taking in the sights around me, I finally answer, "I could eat." I've been a ball of nerves and haven't eaten since last night. My stomach feels a little off, but flying will do that to me from time to time.

We get on a highway and drive for a while. I'm in awe of actually being here, in Germany. With Enzo. This is so far from my life in Portland, Oregon. I've traveled abroad a little, but never to Germany. Enzo keeps his hand on my thigh and I hold it, keeping me grounded in reality, even though it's still hard to process I'm really here. My mind reels with possibilities. I'm relieved to find the electric pulses that flow between us haven't eased in our absence. If anything, they're stronger. *How's that even possible?*

Eventually, Enzo pulls off the highway into a little town I didn't catch the name of. It's lined with what I would imagine most German towns are like. The houses and buildings are a

Bavarian design, like rustic chalets. My only experience with Germany before this was going to Leavenworth, Washington; a town that mimics Germany in its architecture and tourism, but that hardly does this beautiful town justice.

Enzo pulls into a parking spot in front of some shops. There's one in particular that draws my attention, so I ask, "Oh, can we go in there? I'd love to bring home an ornament to remember this trip."

"Let's go, beautiful." He takes my hand, and before we can make it to the storefront, he pulls me in for a kiss that could lead to so much more, if we weren't in public. This man makes me weak at the knees. Every nerve ending comes alive and I'm completely caught up in the moment. Eventually, all good things must come to an end, and he reminds me when he says, "Let's see what's inside," before giving me one last, chaste kiss.

I'm in Christmas Heaven. Christmas, hands down, is my favorite holiday. I love decorating and making memories with my family. I peruse up and down the aisles, peering at everything on the shelves. This place is amazing. I could spend an eternity here and never get bored. Enzo's a champ, taking it all in with me.

When I finally see a hand-carved Santa ornament with St. Nicholas Day and this year's date, I hold it up for Enzo to see. "Oh, Enzo! Look at this. Do you realize that your birthday is on St. Nicholas Day?" His birthday is December sixth. This ornament would be a perfect way to remember not only his birthday, but this incredible experience.

"Yeah, I know," he says modestly, as he holds out his hand to further inspect it. "You should get this. It's beautiful."

The next shelf catches me a bit off guard, I can't help but notice there's lots of pickles. And I mean *a lot*. It's stacked higher than me, full of pickles in varying sizes, made with different materials. *What in the world do pickles have to do with Christmas?* "Uh, Enzo?"

"Yeah?"

"What's up with the pickles? They seem to be everywhere." I hold one up for him to see.

His eyes light up with delight. "Ha! For St. Nicholas Day, here in Germany, the parents decorate the tree. Then the first time the kids look at it, they search for the pickle. The first one to find the pickle gets an extra present under the tree."

"Well, we should get one of those, too. It'd be a fun tradition to start." I wink at him to show just how much he means to me.

He winks back at me as he whispers, "Would you like to find *my* pickle?" I can't help the blush that creeps over me. God, I love him, horniness and all.

The thought of starting new traditions with Enzo is exciting. I spend some time picking one out for our tree at home. Enzo gives me his input, and before we know it, we're moving on to the next shelves. Unfortunately, Enzo won't be home this Christmas. *But there's always next year.* Besides, St. Nicholas Day is only a few days away.

We finish with our purchases, then head to a restaurant nearby. I'm slightly impressed when Enzo speaks in German to our waitress. He's kind enough to ask me what I'd prefer, and since I'm still a little queasy from the flight, I order something light, with a large coffee. He orders it effortlessly, then we slip into an easy conversation.

I tell him about the events of the last few days, getting my three kids ready to go to their dad's this week. I'm sure my kids will miss me like crazy, just like I'll miss them, but they're excited that I'm visiting Enzo. They know it's been hard for us to be apart. They didn't even complain about spending the ten days with their dad.

Devin and I have officially been divorced for the past year, but separated for much longer than that. We agreed to joint custody, so every other weekend, as well as Wednesday nights, the kids are with him. He lives relatively close, so the kids can still ride the bus to school from either house.

Personally, I've made every effort I can to get along with Devin. We may no longer be marriage material, but we chose to have three kids together. They are what's important, and we try to put them first. Though it's definitely easier said than done, sometimes. But I love my kids and will do just about anything for their happiness.

While I update him on the kids, Enzo suggests I call them before it gets too late. He offers his phone since it has international rates and it won't cost me a fortune. We video conference from the table, while we wait for the food. Frankie's eager to see us and chats a mile a minute about her day. I think she mentions wanting a souvenir at least three times in our short conversation. Declan is growing up before my eyes. I can tell he's happy to see me. He's doing homework, so he doesn't talk long. Maddie, my fourteen-year-old, tells me about going on another date with Soren Silva, the same young man who Enzo had helped change his tire a few months ago.

It melts my heart when Enzo pipes in and asks, "He has a jack now, right?" referring to their incident.

Maddie grins with delight. "Yep, though I hope he won't need it anytime soon."

We try to get off the video call as soon as our food arrives. Frankie insists on seeing around the restaurant as well as what our food looks like before she will let us go.

To ensure we're both on the screen, Enzo scoots to my side of the table to drape an arm around me. I love the fact that he stays that way throughout the rest of our meal. Being apart from him has been hard, and I don't want to let him go anytime soon either. Unfortunately, I know my time here will fly by and I will have to leave all too soon. Then we will have about seven weeks before he returns home for good.

As soon as we get back in the car, the heat stirs around me and fatigue sets in. I'm not sure if it's my travels, my full stomach, or being close to Enzo, but I completely relax. The next thing I know, Enzo's outside my door and we're at a small house. "Shit, I fell asleep. Are we here?" My arms and legs feel like dead weights, so I must have been knocked out.

"Relax, beautiful. You didn't miss much. I'll take you sightseeing another time."

I let out a deep yawn. "Now that I've rested, what do you want to do this afternoon?" I get out of the car and take his hand.

He leads me to the ground-level apartment. "Let's get you

settled, then we can decide." He looks in the direction of where we're going and pauses. "I hope you aren't expecting anything fancy. It's basically a basement that has been converted into an apartment. There's a three-bedroom flat above me, which is also rented out. Three guys live in it. All are stationed at Ramstein, though not in my unit. We get along okay."

He looks a little nervous to show me. His eyes dart around and he looks anywhere but at me. "I'm sure it will be fine, Enzo. Don't worry." To reassure him, I lean up to quickly kiss him.

He rubs the back of his neck nervously when I pull away. "I've warned you that I'm not home much, right? I just got this place so I could come and go as I please, have some privacy, and stay out of base housing. It's nice to get away from it all, if you know what I mean."

I stop outside the door and put my hands on my hips, to make a point before entering his home. "Enzo, I couldn't care less what it looks like. I didn't come here to stay at the Ritz. I came here to see you."

"If you don't like it, I can get a hotel for the week you're here," he offers.

What a crazy idea. Why would we waste money like that? He just bought first-class tickets for me, and that was more than generous. His apartment can't be that bad. "Don't be ridiculous. Does it have a clean bed and a shower?"

"Yes," he sighs. "It's not a dump, just tight quarters. You're used to living in a big, beautiful home. I don't want you to go without."

I laugh. I can't help it. *What does he think I am, a pampered princess?* "As long as I have you, I'm fine."

With that, he opens the door and lets me in. I see a modest living room with an open floor plan and a kitchen along one wall. He quickly shows me that one door leads to the bathroom, while another one leads to his bedroom. He takes my things into the bedroom and says, "If you'd like to hang anything up, feel free. There's plenty of room in the closet."

"Thanks. Do you mind if I take a shower?" I ask, realizing I must have grime on me from traveling.

"Sure. You can grab your things through that door. There's another door which opens to the living room, so if you don't want the neighbors to see, be sure to shut it," he ends teasingly.

I quickly use the facilities and do my business. After inspecting the shower to see if there's room for two, a plan forms quickly and a smile spreads across my face. I undress in record time and as casually as I can manage, I call out, "Enzo, can you help me with something?"

Within moments, he's at the door asking, "What do you need?" He peers around the room, looking eager to be of assistance.

God, I want this man right now. Why the hell is he waiting? "Only you," I say, making my intentions clear. His eyes lock onto mine before sweeping up and down the full length of my body.

Thank the fucking Lord, he takes my hint. He's undressed in record time, clothes flying everywhere. Before I know it, he bends down and swoops me into his arms. Seconds later, I'm being placed on the bed.

"Took you long enough," I pant. *God. I've been wanting him to do this since I laid eyes on him at the airport.*

"I was giving you some space, beautiful. I've wanted to attack you since you stepped into my arms from the plane. I'm *trying* to be a gentleman." The way he emphasizes that last statement has my insides doing flips off a mountain.

Not wanting there to be any misinterpretation, I tell him, "Have your wicked way with me, Enzo. I can't wait any longer." The beautiful man before me reads my signals loud and clear and spends the next few hours worshiping my entire body, the only way he knows how. His delicious mouth nips, sucks, and licks his way across my body, getting fully reacquainted. I don't think I have ever been this insatiable, but he gives me everything he has and then some.

Hours later, when his stomach rumbles, we force ourselves to the kitchen to make dinner. But our break doesn't last long. Let's just say, naked picnics have their advantages. We pass out from exhaustion, wrapped in each other's arms, from pure orgasmic bliss.

I'm not sure what time it is when I wake, but it's still dark outside. Nature calls my name with urgency. As much as I want to stay entwined with Enzo, there's no way I can ignore it much longer. I untangle myself from Enzo and sit up slowly. The minute my feet hit the floor, a wave of nausea hits and it's all I can do to run to the bathroom to make it to the toilet in time.

Yep. That's where the sex god himself, finds me. Praying to the porcelain throne, giving her all I've got. He's all sexy with rumpled hair and still entirely naked. Meanwhile, I'm lying on the floor, camped out between the wall and toilet, trying to keep my head in the vicinity of the bowl, so I don't make an even bigger mess.

"You okay?" he anxiously asks, worry etched in his voice. "Anything I can get you?"

"Go away, I don't want you to catch this," I croak in humility.

"Not happening, beautiful," is, of course, his perfect response.

He gets a wet washcloth and places it on my forehead. He also grabs a towel from the counter and wraps me in it. I think I thank him, but all I can do is lay my head against the rim of the, *thankfully clean*, toilet seat once I stop dry heaving.

"Do you think you're done puking now?" *God, just let me die.* Why does he have to witness my humility? This is awful. No one should witness this, let alone the sexy man of my dreams.

All I can manage is a nod. I don't have the energy to do much else. Strong arms suddenly envelop me and I find myself airborne. Enzo walks me over to the bed, then covers me with the blankets.

I must drift off for a moment; the next thing I know, he's there standing in his boxers, offering me a t-shirt and boxers to wear. When I don't do anything but stare at him, he dresses me like an infant. I'd like to say I try to protest, but I just don't have the energy to give a fuck. I'm miserable. I can't believe he even brings me a large pot to puke in. I don't remember the last time anyone helped me when I was sick. The thought alone has my heartstrings being plucked rapidly. Emotion overwhelms me. But all that ends abruptly, when he crawls into bed with me. I protest with a croak, "Enzo, I don't want to get you sick."

"Samantha, we've swapped enough DNA since last night. If I'm going to get sick, I'm already exposed." He laughs a little at the end, but then his tone changes. "Beautiful, I just want to hold you. Please let me do this. I feel helpless right now. Not to mention, there's no way I'm going in the other room after spending the last six weeks apart." Who am I to resist the face he gives me?

A few hours later, I wake again. This time, feeling much better. I make it to the bathroom, brush my hair and nasty teeth, as well as use the facilities, without any further sickness. *Thank goodness for small miracles*

I hear, "Are you feeling better?" through the door.

I take pity on him and don't make him wait for my answer. "So much better. I'm a little hungry. Do you have any toast?"

I walk out into the living room to find Enzo making toast, as well as getting a blanket for me to snuggle with on the couch.

"I don't know what I did to deserve you," I whisper as he tucks me in.

"I'm the lucky one," he says as he brushes a kiss on my forehead.

Then I realize I've said my thoughts aloud again and mutter, "Damn filter."

"I love you, Samantha, lack of filter and all."

I try to be angry that he finds my lack of filter endearing. "You're lucky I love you, too, Enzo."

"Damn right, I am." The smile on his face nearly melts my heart entirely. This man's so loving. I wouldn't want to be anywhere else right now. I'm in heaven when he sits beside me and wraps me in his arms to snuggle.

We rest for a while, but eventually, I get restless. I feel so much better and I'm in a foreign country after all. Why would I want my only view to be from this couch?

Though when I look at Enzo, I realize it is quite a view. But still. I don't want to be sick and helpless on the couch all day.

A little while later, I convince Enzo I'm well enough to see some sights. He reluctantly agrees to drive me around Ramstein Air Force Base. He shows me where he works, where he likes to shop, and where he works out. We do this all from the car so I don't expose anyone to my germs, in case I'm contagious.

After a while, we pick up something to eat from a deli. Unfortunately, I quickly find that I can't hold anything down. I find myself begging Enzo to pull over so I can relieve myself in the bushes. Like a perfect gentleman, he doesn't complain once. He simply takes me back to his apartment and we spend the rest of the evening resting on the couch, watching movies and snuggling. I'm thankful to keep some chicken broth down before going to bed for the night.

FUCK! The next morning's a repeat of the day before. Like the movie 'Groundhog Day,' it totally sucks. To make matters worse, I'm so weak Enzo has to help me shower. I spend the entire day in bed sleeping and just trying to be in the land of the living. I must say, the man's a saint. There's not a wish I have that he doesn't answer. If I actually had the ability to care, I'd be mortified for being such an invalid.

Thank the Lord, I feel alive again the next morning. Not feeling like death warmed over is almost like a miracle. I'm eager to make the most of our limited time together. Today's Enzo's birthday and I can tell he's relieved that I'm on the mend. We get dressed and I decide to wear the green dress he bought me, but this time I wear knee-high boots and tights to keep my legs warm. My jacket's thick, so I have no worries about being chilly.

Within a few minutes of being in the car, Enzo takes me to the Nanstein Castle. It was built in 1162. I'm eager to get out and walk around the grounds of the castle itself. After being stuck in bed, it's a relief to walk about and enjoy the culture and history. I soon learn this castle was built after the Holy Roman Empire. Fredrick demanded its construction as an additional defense for the Palatinate, which is the area we are in. I dig out my camera and take as many pictures as I can of the architecture and view of the city below us. I also insist Enzo and I take a few selfies together, since it's his birthday after all. You don't turn thirty-eight every day. He teases me the entire time about being a cougar trying to steal his virtue. Yes, I'm nearly a year older than him, but it's not that big of a deal. Age is just a number anyway, not something that defines you.

We stop at a café for a late breakfast. Still scared of being sick again, I only get a light pastry and coffee. Then we make our way to another beautiful castle in Thallichtenberg, Germany. This one is the biggest castle ruins in all of Germany. It overlooks the outskirts of town and looks much more rustic than the previous one we toured.

As we walk the grounds, I'm in complete awe. It feels like something fairytales are made of. I can't believe I get to experience this. You don't see something this old in the United States. Not only do I get to share this magnificent experience with an amazing man, I get to learn more about the history of Germany as well. I'll never forget this trip with Enzo. I take it all in, trying to engrain this experience in my memory.

Enzo whispers in my ear while I'm lost in thought, "Does this make me Prince Charming?" My only response is to kiss him senseless and make this a dream come true.

On our way to the third castle for the day, my stomach starts to quiver. *Fuck! I know I'm going to be sick again.* I beg Enzo to pull over, and I relieve myself on the side of the road. This time, after he's assured that I'm done puking, he insists on taking me to the hospital. I'm feeling so fucking weak again, I can hardly protest. *This isn't how I wanted to spend my fucking vacation. I'm a single mother of three, can't I catch a break? I just want to spend time with the man I love, explore a new country, and enjoy this once in a lifetime opportunity. What the hell is wrong with the universe? I should not be sick right now.*

In sheer exhaustion, I fall asleep cursing the universe, only to be woken when we arrive at a hospital. Since all my energy has been zapped out of me and I can barely stand, the nurse insists on me being in a wheelchair. *Great. Now I'm an invalid as well as a puking monster. What must Enzo think? I sure know how to live it up while I'm with him. Geesh!*

When the nurse asks if Enzo is family, he says, "I'm her fiancé." I don't give it much thought. There's no way I want to go through those doors alone. I'm sicker than I've ever been, and I'm beginning to worry about the possibilities of what might be wrong as well.

A nurse comes in to take my vitals. She draws some blood and asks a series of questions. After a while, the doctor comes in and does a quick exam. Well, *quick* may be an oxymoron. *Nothing* seems quick when I'm feeling this miserable. He throws around words like appendicitis, gallbladder, kidney infection, sending Enzo and me into heightened tension, as we await the results. Neither of us says much, but I can tell we're both more anxious as time slowly passes. A nurse comes back in and asks if I can give a urine sample and thank God, she offers to help me. *Enzo has been a godsend, but that might be pushing our love too far.*

As soon as I get settled in the hospital bed, Enzo takes my hands. He kneels beside me on the bed and he almost shouts, "Samantha!"

Surprised by his sudden enthusiasm, I ask, "Yes?" wondering what has him so worked up.

In a much calmer tone and demeanor, he states, "I need you to know how much I love you."

I'm not dying. Just really sick. He doesn't need to get so worked up over this. "I love you, too," I soothingly say as I place my hand on his forearm to calm him.

He clears his throat and begins again, this time his words coming out as a caress. "Samantha, I need you to know how much I love you. I've never met anyone like you. You've become the most important person in my life."

Okay, now he has my attention. Where's he going with this? I don't respond to let him continue.

"Samantha, no matter what those test results say, I will be with you in sickness and in health. I want you to know that I will always have your best interests at heart. I'm sure there will be times you're going to have to put me in my place. I can be a little thick headed."

Gee... you think? I still don't know where he's going with this, but I can't help but laugh at the last statement. Thankfully, he joins me as well.

Once we stop, he continues, "But know that I will always do it out of love."

He takes a deep breath to collect his thoughts. I nod at him to continue. Something about the way he just said, 'in sickness and in health' and he's professing his love for me, has piqued my curiosity.

Oh My God! Could he be...???

"These past six weeks of being apart has made me a miserable bastard. I don't want to spend another day without you being mine."

Oh My God, he is...

I can't help it, I'm a nervous laugher. I pull him to me and give him a quick kiss, not caring that I have vomit breath. I'm too caught up in the moment.

He pulls away and continues, this time capturing my

entire heart, "Samantha Elizabeth O'Reilly, would you do me the honor of being my wife? Will you marry me and make me the happiest man alive?"

He reaches into his pocket and pulls out an exquisite white-gold diamond ring. It's a three-diamond setting that represents the past, present, and future, the largest being in the middle. I'm nearly in tears. This is the last thing I expected.

When he looks me in the eye, I know without a doubt what my answer will be. He's everything I could ever dream of. Although I'm sick as a dog, he loves me. He loves me no matter what.

I nod profusely because I can't talk. Tears stream down my cheeks and I'm certain I've terrified him.

He eyes me warily to get my full reaction. *Why can't this be one of the times my filter doesn't work? I need to tell him yes, but I can't even speak. Emotion consumes me.*

"Is that a yes, Samantha?"

"Yes!" I gasp through tears. "Yes, I'll marry you!"

He stands to lean over me in the bed, embracing me with everything he has and nearly squeezes the life out of me. "Samantha, you just made me the happiest man on earth. I love you so much!"

"I love you, Enzo," I say as he pulls back to look me in the eye.

He takes a look around the room, then he lets out a laugh. "I know this isn't the most romantic place, but I've been wanting to ask you to marry me since you stepped off that plane."

He did? "You did?" I practically stutter. I'm shocked.

"Yes, being apart from you put things into perspective. I've never let myself get close to anyone, but our time apart has made me realize you're it for me. I'll move heaven and earth to make things work with you."

"Wow," is all I can whisper. I know we have a lot to work out, like how to tell the kids, when we'll tell them, and most importantly, how will they react?

Enzo continues, "What do you say we get you better first, then we call the kids and tell them the news?"

It's as if he's reading my mind.

A few minutes later, the doctor comes back in.

He looks at each of us, then takes a deep breath. "It looks like we can't do the CT scans at this time."

Oh. My. God! What's wrong with me?

Enzo barks, "Why the fuck not? She's been sick for days."

"Well..." The man before us doesn't cower in Enzo's sudden anger. The doctor stands a good six inches under Enzo and calmly says, "I already know the reason for her sickness."

Enzo's vein on his neck pops and he's enraged, barely holding it together. "Are you a New Age doctor who has premonitions? Why aren't you giving her the tests?" I almost feel sorry for the man in white.

Once again, calm as can be, "Sir, I have. Calm down and I'll explain."

Tension rolls off Enzo in waves. I feel it as it stretches across the room. I reach for his hand and he immediately calms. *I love knowing that I have that effect on him.*

I squeeze his hand, causing him to look at me. "I love you," I whisper.

"I love you, too." He bends down to kiss me on the forehead, then we look to the doctor for further explanation.

"Go ahead," I say.

The doctor looks sheepishly for a moment, which seems a bit out of place, then steels his features and simply states, "You're pregnant."

What. The. Fuck.

I can't get pregnant!

"Excuse me? I tried for years. Nothing happened. I thought I couldn't get pregnant."

"Well, you apparently can." The doctor smiles. "I'll have an ultrasound brought in. From your hormone levels, you appear to be pretty far along."

I gasp and count back the weeks from my last period. "But, I've had my period not that long ago."

"We'll find out more with an ultrasound, Mrs. O'Reilly."

I finally turn to Enzo, who has been unusually quiet this entire time. When his eyes lock with mine, the expression on his face is complete and utter shock. *Oh my God, he's going to think I've trapped him.*

What the fuck am I going to do? I'm thirty-eight years old, for crying out loud. I already have three kids, and Maddie's almost fifteen. People are going to think *she's* the mother, not me. I'm going to be asked if I'm this child's grandma. I'm going to be a laughingstock.

How the hell am I even pregnant? *Well, I know how.* But Devin and I tried for years. *Years!* I remember month after month hoping for it to happen, getting to the point where I utterly hated my period. How did I not get pregnant then? What's different now?

Enzo. That's what. I turn to look at the man next to me. His beautiful features are like stone. For once, I can't read his expression. It scares the shit out of me.

Enzo's kind, loving, and has spent his entire life being single. He's never settled down or been with anyone serious. Being with my family and me is one thing. Adding a baby to the mix? He's going to run for the hills the first chance he gets.

2

———

ENZO

YES, I'm scared shitless. Yes, this is completely unexpected. But when I look at the woman before me who looks utterly freaked out, I'm at a loss for what to do. I love her no matter what, but what if she doesn't want this? What if she doesn't want any more kids? Would I be okay with letting her make that decision for us? I wish I could find a way to take the look of terror off her face. It's my fault we never use condoms. It's my fault she's going through this now.

The doctor and nurse return, wheeling in a large machine. It has a wand-like thing and a monitor. There's also a long stick thingy on the side, next to where the wand for the ultrasound is.

The doctor presses his hands across Samantha's belly. It's light, but it makes me nervous. *What if he hurts the baby?* Samantha's already in a hospital gown since she was expecting to take a series of other tests, not an ultrasound for pregnancy.

The doctor adjusts the sheet so she's covered and opens up

her gown to expose her stomach. He squirts some gel onto the wand, then moves it around. For a few minutes, there's nothing.

"I was afraid of this," he says ominously. *What. The. Fuck. Is. Wrong? We just found out she's pregnant.*

"What?" Samantha squeaks.

"I'm afraid I'm going to have to use the vaginal wand," the doctor says as an explanation.

Samantha lets out a sigh and I still don't have a fucking clue as to what's going on. I finally ask, since no one says anything else, "What does that mean, Doc?" I feel the muscles in my jaw clench.

The doctor looks at me with kind eyes, and I relax a little. "It means she's likely not that far along and I'll have to do a vaginal ultrasound since it's too small to see at this point."

Samantha reaches for my hand. "Don't worry, Enzo. I did this with my other pregnancies. All turned out fine."

Her touch soothes me, along with her words. I feel myself relax.

The doctor wipes the gel off her stomach. "Would you like me to step out of the room while you remove your underwear?"

Samantha sighs and shakes her head. "What's the point? You're going to see it all anyway. There's no modesty in pregnancy, right?"

Meanwhile, I'm over here thinking, *What the fuck is she talking about? I don't want any man looking at her vagina, but me.*

Before I can say anything, Samantha shimmies out of her underwear and hands them to me. She manages to stay covered, but *what am I supposed to do with them? Shit.* I don't want to look like a fool, so I stuff them in my pocket. That takes care of one problem.

The doctor picks up this long-handled thing and squirts gel onto the end. *He's going to stick that... where?* Then it dawns on me and I can't help that I'm suddenly thinking of dildos. *Jesus Christ, I'm about to see my child for the first time and I'm thinking about dildos. Great! What a great dad I'll be. Thank God, she can't hear what I'm thinking. This woman's carrying my baby and here I am acting like a randy teenager. What the fuck is wrong with me?*

"Oh, that's cold." Samantha gasps, breaking me out of my revelry.

On the monitor, there's a blur of motion. Suddenly, I hear a birdlike drumbeat. It's soft and fast.

"There's the heartbeat," the doctor announces to the room.

I. Am. In. Awe. I can hear my child's heartbeat. I look to Samantha, who has tears welling in her eyes. She's the most gorgeous woman in the world, and she's carrying my baby. I'm a lucky bastard.

"I love you, Samantha," I whisper to her. If I speak any louder, my voice will break.

When the doctor moves the wand around, I hear something different. This time it's louder and slower.

"What's that?" I ask.

"That's Samantha's heartbeat."

"Here." The doctor points to a place on the screen. "You can see the heartbeat on the screen. See the flitter? There it is."

But I see more than one flitter.

"Um, Doc?" I'm about to ask more when Samantha beats me to it.

"Do I see two heartbeats on that screen?" Her voice is high at the end.

The doctor beams with excitement and his nurse says, "Congratulations!"

"Yes," the doctor confirms. "You're having twins!"

"Holy shit!" Samantha exclaims. She looks to me and adds, "You not only knocked me up, but you gave me twins?" She seems a little bewildered at the end.

I'm pretty sure her filter has left the building. I laugh aloud.

I look at her with shock written all over my face, I'm sure. "Twins, beautiful. We're having twins."

The most beautiful smile spreads across her face, and I nearly melt.

3

SAMANTHA

THE MOMENT I hear my unborn child's heartbeat I'm already in love. Tears roll down my face as I'm overwhelmed with joy. I realize, no matter what fears I've had before, I can get past them. I have a baby to care for. The light strum of the heartbeat brings a calming sensation over me. Though, that calmness is short lived. When I see there are two heartbeats, I go into utter shock. *What. The. Ever. Loving. Fuckity. Fuck!!! This can't be happening!*

Enzo's face is almost humorous as it's the perfect mixture of shock and awe. I can't help but smile when his dimple pops. The damn thing gets me every time.

The two of us remain silent as we stare at one another. Soon, the nurse and doctor excuse themselves and it's just us. They mention something about bringing a prescription for anti-nausea medicine and prenatal vitamins, but I can only focus on the man before me. *I wish he would tell me what he's thinking.*

He places his hand on mine and the inevitable pull we seem to share is back in full force. It calms me, even though there's a storm inside my head at the moment. Like a cyclone, I have ten thousand thoughts swirling through my mind. I wish I could catch one and voice it aloud. I wish I had the words to put his worried look at ease.

Just as I'm about to say something, a nurse comes in and gives me instructions for the medication. She takes the IV out of my arm that they had put in for dehydration when I first arrived. I laugh and shake my head at the thought of worrying about a gallbladder, kidney, or my appendix. Instead, the news I received today has totally knocked my world off its axis.

Soon, we'll be released from the hospital, though our lives will never be the same. We came in as Enzo and Samantha. We're leaving as Enzo, Samantha, plus two.

I continue to be lost in my head during the short car ride to Enzo's apartment. Not surprisingly, he's a gentleman through and through. He's held my hand through it all and not gone running for the hills, yet. Though, I wouldn't blame him if he did, with my freak out at the hospital. I'm dying to ask him if we're okay, but I'm mortified of what his answer will be. What if he doesn't really want kids of his own? We've never talked about this before. Now that I think about it, there's still so much about him I don't know.

We go inside, and Enzo remains unusually silent as he makes dinner. Making sure I eat properly was one of the doctor's suggestions. I can't help but find it endearing that Enzo still wants to take care of me.

I make a quick trip to the bathroom, then curl up on the

couch, and snuggle under the blanket. I'm exhausted from all the puking, as well as the emotional whirlwind of the day, but a part of me can't help but be a little excited. The initial shock is wearing off and the thought of having another baby—correction—*babies*, makes me a little giddy.

Holy crap, I'm going to be the mother of twins. I know that having one baby is a rollercoaster ride of its own, but I can't imagine what it will be like with two. I really hope I haven't scared Enzo off. I don't want to do this alone. I know I can, but God, I hope his silence is just him processing this information, not him trying to find the words to let me down easy.

Apparently, I'm lost in thought. The next thing I know, he's bringing me dinner and it smells delicious. Thank God, the doctor gave me anti-nausea medicine. I still have about a week left in Germany and I want to see more than the inside of a toilet. I almost feel human again.

Once I've eaten, I set my plate down on the coffee table. I notice Enzo hasn't eaten a bite. The man always eats, so something must be wrong. *Fuck, how did I miss this?*

"Are you okay?" I ask hesitantly.

"The more important question is, are you?" Enzo locks eyes with me and it's as if he's peering deep into my soul.

"I'm okay. I'm apparently pregnant, but okay," I whisper as I cradle my belly in my hands. "I can't believe this happened. With twins. It's a lot to take in." I inhale a deep breath and release it slowly.

"Yeah, it is," he whispers, still holding my gaze. I can't get a read on him, and the unknown is enough to do me in for good.

I take a deep breath and steel myself for what I need to tell him. This uncertainty has gone on long enough. It's time I let him off the hook and deal with whatever reality may bring. Tears prick my eyes as I start, "Enzo, I understand if you… I mean, I really didn't think I could get pregnant…" I stammer.

Before I can say anything more, his deep voice fills the room, "I meant what I said. I want to marry you. Now, we'll just do it sooner. I can't wait to have these babies with you." The pensive look on his face still has me completely unsettled.

I let out a shaky breath. "Are you sure? Babies change a lot," I say, giving him an out. I don't want him to feel trapped. He didn't sign up for this.

Enzo looks at me with kind eyes and says, "Samantha Elizabeth O'Reilly-soon-to-be-Harper." *Oh, I like the sound of that.* "Get this through your head. I. Love. You. I want to be with you. Having children with you is a dream I didn't know could exist, but now, I'm ecstatic to have it become a reality." The sincerity on his face gives me hope. He cocks a light smile and that damn dimple pops, making me swoon.

His words calm me, but only for a moment, before another thought pops in my head. "What about my other children?" I ask, panicking. Crap, how could I forget about Maddie, Dec, and Frankie? I didn't forget. No, I just hadn't considered he was already taking them on. These twins are certainly throwing me off. Can pregnancy brain be blamed, this early in the game?

Enzo releases a deep belly laugh, letting that delicious dimple pop once again. It stops me in my tracks, keeping my panic at bay.

"Samantha, beautiful. I already love your children.

Otherwise, I wouldn't have asked you to marry me. Don't think for one second that I will love them any less. I have room in my heart for all of you."

"You do?" I stupidly ask, not knowing what else to say.

He takes my hands in his. "I didn't know what I'd been missing until I met you. You've made my meager existence thrive. I can't imagine my life without you and your kids now. Correction—*our* kids. Now we'll just have more to love."

Relief washes over me to know that he thinks of my kids as his own. "You're right," I sigh. "I love you for pointing that out."

"Anytime, beautiful, anytime."

"What if people call us grandparents?" Another worry wiggles its way out of my mouth.

Enzo chuckles. "No one's going to call you a grandma anytime soon. You're far too sexy for that. Besides, people have babies in their forties all the time. You'll only be thirty-nine; it's not like it's *that* unusual."

"Great, now people are going to be calling me the cradle-robbing grandma. Just what I need." I pretend to pout.

"Samantha, I just turned thirty-eight today. You're still thirty-eight for another six months. You're not that much older than I." His laughter does wonderful things to my insides.

"Happy Birthday, Enzo!" I exclaim in pure joy, then tease, "I guess I don't have to give you a birthday present now, do I?"

Enzo's smile spreads even wider across his face. "Happy Birthday to me, indeed. Thank you for the most wonderful gift." He kisses me on the lips.

"*Gifts,*" I remind. "Although, you might not be thanking

me at this time next year when neither of us is getting any sleep."

"Best birthday, EVER!" he emphasizes by rearranging us on the couch, so that we're both able to fit and bends down to kiss me again. Maybe it's the extra hormones I have flowing through me, maybe it's just Enzo, but suddenly, I only want to focus on him.

4

———

ENZO

SAMANTHA FEELS MUCH BETTER NOW that the anti-nausea medicine has kicked in. A look mixed of hunger and lust suddenly fills her face and I couldn't care less that I've yet to eat the dinner on the table in front of me. I'm just so fucking happy that she's healthy and not upset about being pregnant.

The car ride home was brutal. For once, her filter stayed intact and I had no clue what was going through her mind. Of course, I was silent as well, but it's not every day I find out I'm going to be a father. I also wanted to give her some time to process this new information. I know I needed it.

Twins. That's a hell of a lot to take in. Samantha already has three wonderful children, but now she's going to be a mother of five. *Fuck! Talk about an instant family.* I already love her children as much as I love her, and I hope they at least like me a little. It's all pretty new, but I have never felt as close to anyone as the way I feel about Samantha. And those babies inside her, I'm already in love with them, too.

I honestly never thought I'd be a father. I love kids, but with my age and the fact that I've never settled down, I just didn't think kids would be in the cards for me. Hell, I'm thirty-eight years old. Haven't been in a serious relationship in nearly twenty years. *What makes me qualified to be a dad?* Give me something to fly out of any type of danger zone imaginable, I'm your man. But toting tiny tots that are mine?

Samantha distracts my hurricane of thoughts and suddenly has my sole focus, when she straddles my lap. The second her hands run through what little hair I have on my head, thanks to my high and tight haircut from being back on duty, my senses are on overload. When her lips graze mine, I can barely contain myself. I force myself to let her take the lead. It takes every bit of effort I have to sit back and enjoy her every move. My instinct is to stand and take her to the bedroom, but for now, I'll just see what she has in mind.

"I love you, Enzo," she whispers as she kisses across my jawline and down my neck. Her hand roams down my chest and pulls at the hem of my shirt. I lean forward and quickly remove it with one hand, barely breaking our contact.

"I love you more than ever, beautiful," comes out huskier than expected.

She resumes kissing down my jawline to my neck, then chest, sending my body on fire. My hands seem to have minds of their own as I reach under her shirt, connecting with her silky-smooth skin. Electricity zings through me, making my nerve endings come to life. One hand reaches around her back to pull her closer while the other caresses her breast through her bra. *This just won't do.* With a practiced move, I release her bra with one hand and cup her full, smooth breast, causing her to make the most beautiful moan I've ever heard.

"That's right, beautiful. Tell me what you want." Fuck, I just want to lay her on this couch and completely have my way with her.

"You," she says in a groan as she goes for the fly of my jeans. "I just want you."

I can't take it anymore. I stand and she wraps those sexy as fuck legs around my waist. I walk to the bedroom and set her down in front of the bed. The minute her feet hit the floor, she's undoing her pants and sliding them down. I take her lead and shed myself from my own clothing briskly. I can't even assist her in removing her shirt because as I take a step toward her, she rips it over her head, sending it flying through the air, across the room.

Now that we're both naked as the day we were born, I close the gap between us, kissing her with everything I have. I grip her ass firmly in both hands and lift her gently onto the bed, as my mouth devours hers. She tastes slightly of marinara sauce and something that is entirely Samantha. I break our kiss, making my way down her body, making sure I pay close attention to all the places that I've learned drive her wild. I kiss that spot behind her ear, which sends her toes and fists grasping the sheets. I trail down her neck and worship each breast the best way I know how. Her body writhes as if it's ready for release. I reach with one hand between her legs and find she's exactly as I thought. Wet and ready for me. I barely press my thumb against her clit, slip a finger inside of her, and she detonates. Her core clamps around my finger and pulsates fervently as I pull on one nipple with my teeth, playing with her other taut nipple with my free hand. I continue to assault her senses as she rides her high to completion.

The moment her body's calm and sated, I remove my fingers and kiss down to her belly. It's still flat and sexy as hell. I can see faint stretch marks from previous pregnancies, and I can't help but wonder what she will look like, round with my children inside her. I can't help but whisper to Samantha's belly button, "I love you already, little ones. Be good to your ma and let her stay healthy for you. We're going to do everything we can to give you the best future we can."

I look up at Samantha, who has tears threatening to fall, as they pool at her lashes. "Oh, Enzo." Her voice cracks at the end of my name. "You'll be the most amazing dad."

Pride soars through my heart, feeling as if it could burst out of my chest. I don't know shit about being a dad, but that look of confidence Samantha has on her face, makes me feel as if I can conquer anything. "I sure hope so, Sam. You're already a pro and I'm just a rookie. I'm sure I'll make lots of mistakes." Honesty pours from my soul as her tears release and a smile takes over her face.

"Enzo, honey," she sighs and a light laugh escapes as she rubs her hand through my hair. "No one is perfect. We all make mistakes. Trust me. I'm nowhere near perfect. The key is to make the best decision for the situation and hope like hell it all turns out in the end."

"You make it sound so easy," I say as she pulls me to her for a quick kiss. My treacherous dick makes its presence known. I groan and pull back, not wanting to make her feel any pressure. She has been sick for days and I want this to be about her. *Yeah, I want her just like a dying man wants his next breath, but I can show some restraint.*

Apparently, she doesn't want me to pull away as she reaches out and strokes me. I'm still hesitant. I know what I want, but, *what if I hurt her or our children? Is it even safe to have sex?!?!?*

She sees my hesitation and a flash of concern crosses her face. "What's wrong, Enzo?"

How should I say this? I don't want her to think I don't want her. I obviously do, but now's not the time to be thinking with *that* head. He's what got us into this situation, to begin with. "Um..." Fuck. I'm a grown man. Why can't I ask this simple question? "Are you sure you want this?"

"Enzo..." She looks between our naked bodies and gives my cock another tug toward her. "I want this." Her desire is evident and makes my hesitation even more unbearable.

"Are you... Are you sure I won't hurt you or the babies?" I watch her closely to see if there's anything left unsaid.

She laughs. Not just a little chuckle or a smirk, but full-on belly laughs. She shakes her head, showing no empathy as she takes my hand and pulls me closer to her. Why is she laughing?

"Enzo, sweetheart." She takes in a deep breath before continuing, "There's nothing you can do to me that will harm me or the babies."

"Are you sure? There are two living beings in your belly. I don't want to do anything that could harm either of them. Or you for that matter." I look away, feeling slightly ashamed for jumping to this conclusion. I've never been with a pregnant woman before. I don't know the protocol for this. I just want to do right by her.

"Enzo... Sweetheart. Look at me." My eyes immediately lock with hers as her voice is suddenly urgent. "I'm safe and the kids are safe. Pregnant women have sex all the time. It's perfectly safe and acceptable. In fact, if my memory serves correctly, in just a few short weeks, I'm going to be demanding it on a regular basis. Once I hit the second trimester with all my kids, I practically craved it." A devilish grin appears on her face before she continues, "With you... Since I even want you when I don't feel at my best..." A loud groan escapes her, "Heaven help you if I want to jump you from the moment we wake up, until the moment I pass out at night..." She pulls me closer to make her point and kisses me like she's never kissed me before. I could fuckin' die, right here, right now, and I could say I've lived a blissful existence.

After all too short of time, I pull back, "Well, if you insist... who am I to resist?" I quickly resume kissing her and work my way to completely making love to her until we both pass out from pure exhaustion.

THE NEXT MORNING, Samantha wakes with energy, thanks to the anti-nausea medicine the doctor gave her. She actually beats me out of bed and is in the kitchen making an enormous breakfast wearing nothing but my Air Force t-shirt. Her dark mahogany hair's in a messy bun, and she's swaying to the music playing from her phone. Her back is to me as I enter the room and I can't help but just stop and watch her enjoy herself. I recognize the song as Justin Timberlake's "SexyBack." *Yeah, she has no problem bringing sexy back. It never left her.* I know I should let her know I'm here—*it'd be the polite thing to do*—but I'm simply too mesmerized. Samantha's the sexiest woman I've ever met, and when she lets loose and enjoys the world, nothing's better than the sight before me.

The song ends and Ed Sheeran's "Shape of You" begins and I can't help but grin. To me, this has been 'Our' song, since our first dance together. Every time it plays on the radio, flashbacks of that night come to mind. There's no way I'm letting her dance alone with those words filling the room. I walk up to hold her from behind and dance with her like our night at Allure, the club my friend Rowan owns in Portland. She continues flipping pancakes, even as our bodies sway together. Once they're done, she turns to finish the song by dancing in my arms.

"I could get used to waking up like this," I say as she finally faces me.

"Good morning, Enzo."

She places her arms around my neck and kisses me.

"Mornin', beautiful."

She pulls back to look me in the eyes. "After breakfast, let's go to Frankfurt and see the sights. I want to make the most of my time here, now that I'm not puking my guts out. That medicine is a lifesaver, really. I can't wait to see more of Germany."

"Your wish is my command," I tease as I kiss her lightly on the lips.

"Don't get carried away," Samantha warns with a tease. "I love your place, but I want to see more of Germany."

Although I'd rather get carried away with her, I release Samantha to get the plates from the cupboard. "Let's eat then."

We spend the day being tourists. I drive her through Frankfurt, and she loves the skyscrapers and the buzz of the busy city. She recognizes the Euro symbol as we pass the European Central Bank and asks to stop to take photos there. It's right next to the S-Bahn Station, so we decide if we're going to be tourists, we might as well ride the street cars.

Another of Samantha's favorite places is Eiserner Steg. It's an older iron pedestrian bridge across the River Main, which connects the center of Frankfurt to the district of Sachsenhausen. It was originally built in 1868, bombed in World War II, by Hitler's troops near the end of the war, and rebuilt for pedestrians afterward. We arrive there right as the sun is setting. I manage to get some spectacular shots of Samantha. We also capture some of my favorite pictures of us on the bridge, thanks to a couple who offers to take our photos.

By the time we get back to my place, Samantha looks dead on her feet. We'd eaten out at one of the local restaurants, and I'm so relieved Samantha has her energy back, as well as her appetite.

5

———————

SAMANTHA

THANK GOD, *I'm feeling better.* I'm fully convinced the doctors gave me miracle medicine. Sure, I'm tired but that is to be expected with any pregnancy. I have to say, now that I'm not nauseous, I love the local foods, such as the fresh bread rolls with fruit marmalade. Give me that with some eggs for breakfast, and I'm set for the day. I also love schnitzel, spätzle, and bratwurst with local vegetables. Now that I can eat, I seem to be devouring everything in sight. *God, I hope I don't gain a hundred pounds in this pregnancy. But, I'm eating for three, right?!?!*

Enzo, unfortunately, has to return to work for a couple of days during the last week of my visit. He manages to stay on base, so he's home at night. I spend my days either reading or touring locally. Enzo lets me drive his Land Rover, which makes it so I can go to the City Museum in Ramstein. It's interesting to learn about the local history. I also venture to Trier, Germany, which is one of the oldest cities in the country. It's heavily influenced by the Romans. If Enzo and I have time before I leave, I'd like to return here to visit one of the Roman bathhouses with him.

The best part about my time with Enzo is the evenings. I just love being with him, in his element. I'm getting used to making love through the night and waking up in his arms. I can't wait until we can do this every day.

It's going to suck when I have to leave on Monday, and he has to stay for two more months. I do my best not to think about it now; long-distance relationships have taken their toll on my life. When these horrific thoughts make their way into my mind, I try to squash them like a bug. Enzo isn't Devin, plain and simple. He knows firsthand how devastating it was to have someone move on while he was away. There's no doubt in my mind that he won't stray in the slightest. He's head over heels for me and these babies growing inside me. I know from the bottom of my heart he feels the same way I do, though it doesn't hurt that he makes the time to assure me of this each and every day I've been here. I think I love this man more than I've ever loved anyone. There's just no comparison.

Yes, of course, I miss my kids at home like crazy. I video-chat with them daily. Seeing them on the screen makes me miss them more. I don't remember the last time I've been away from them this long. After a lengthy conversation, Enzo and I decided not to tell them about my pregnancy until I'm through my first trimester, which is after he returns from Germany. We want to tell them together, in person. I just hope these babies will let me keep this secret until he gets home. Between morning sickness and the fact I'll likely start showing sooner with twins, I'm keeping my fingers crossed.

Today's Friday and Enzo's expected home in the early afternoon. He's off for the weekend, so I stayed in for the day and let him take his car. I've finished reading a manuscript I brought with me and spent the day responding to emails from work. With the time difference, it's easier to keep in contact with clients via email.

I'm deep in concentration when I hear the door handle rattle with the sound of keys. I look up to find Enzo walking through the door. He's dressed in his uniform, which consists of a dark green jumpsuit and combat boots. Holy Hell, is he hot. In a well-practiced move, he removes his cap and stuffs it into his pocket on his pants leg. The smile that lights up his face has me melting in seconds. That damn dimple will have me spontaneously combusting on the spot if he continues to use it at full force. His deep timbre greets me, "Hey, beautiful. How was your day?"

I try my best to clear my laptop and the mound of papers around me so I can get up to greet him. He laughs at my distress and closes the distance between us within seconds. He reaches for my computer and sets it beside me on the coffee table. I reach my hand out to him and he effortlessly assists me into a standing position. I manage to get, "Great, how was yours?" out before my lips are crushed by his.

Damn! He tastes delicious. I don't think I will ever get used to the backflips the butterflies in my stomach like to perform when he appears. I wrap my hands around his neck and pull back to look into his glorious, green eyes. For a few moments, I'm mesmerized by the look of pure pleasure reflected in them.

"I've never been more thankful l get to spend the weekend with you. Since I wasn't off base, my day was a shitstorm of prepping for our mission next week." He pulls me in for another kiss, then bends down to kiss my belly over my clothes and talks to our babies, like he does every day. "Have you been good to your ma today?"

I can't help the giggle that escapes when he nuzzles his slightly scruffy cheek against my abdomen. "That miracle medicine seems to have done the trick. I've been a little tired, but no nausea to speak of," I sigh in relief.

Enzo stands and wraps his arms around me in a hug once again. "Good to hear. I have no fucking clue how I'm going to survive being apart from you when you leave Monday." The tone of his voice by the end nearly slays me. There's a desperate need and desire that nearly rips me to the core.

I take in a deep breath and steel my spine, knowing this is hard on both of us. There's no need for me to make it more difficult for him than I need to. "I know. I feel the same."

"Will you do me a favor?" Enzo asks as he pulls away from our embrace to look me in the eye.

"Anything," I say without hesitation because there's nothing I won't do for the man.

"Will you send me a belly shot each day?"

Belly Shot? I cock my head to the side and look at him, wanting to make sure I understand him correctly.

Before I can respond, he says, "Send me a picture of a side

profile, so I can see them grow and not miss any of the changes that happen during your pregnancy."

Understanding washes over me and I smile. "Of course, I'll do that. Though, the changes will be very subtle every day. You know that, right?"

"Sam, I don't want to miss anything. I hate that I'm not going to be there with you. There'll also be times when I'm out in the field, and I won't get to contact you each day. The photos will be something I cherish." Enzo seems to be in deep thought for a moment, then all of a sudden, he chuckles. "I used to harass the guys who lived for their daily photos from home. Now, I'm going crazy just thinking about you leaving." He strokes his hands down my back as he pulls me in for a tight embrace.

"If I didn't have kids to attend to, you know I'd rather be here so you wouldn't miss anything, right?" I try to assure him. "Besides, you'll be home in less than two months. We won't be apart for that long." I'm not sure if I'm trying to convince him or myself that this won't be too difficult.

"How do you think we should tell your kids we're engaged, let alone having twins?" Enzo sighs, catching me off guard.

"I've been wondering the same thing." I haven't come up with a good plan yet, but maybe we can come up with one together.

"What if we video-call them tonight and let them know I proposed to you? Then, when I come home for good, we can tell them about their new brothers or sisters."

"What if we have one of each?" I ask in wonder. This still doesn't seem real and I've known for almost a week.

"As long as you're *all* healthy, I don't care what we have. I just want you all to be safe." He pulls me toward his bedroom. "I need to change. Come with me, so we can continue to talk."

He turns and walks to his bedroom and I follow. "So, how do you think we should tell them?" Though the minute I see him shed his clothes, I'm no longer focused on the kids.

Enzo completely catches me off guard when he nonchalantly says, "I've already told Declan and Maddie my intentions to ask you to marry me."

What?!?!?

"You have?" I ask, my words almost coming out as a shriek. Enzo gives me a dubious grin while that fucking dimple pops out, making me weak in the knees.

"Um, Sam." He suddenly looks sheepishly at me. "I spoke to each of them separately before I left for Germany."

"You did?" *When could he have done that?!?! How could they have kept it a secret for so long??? God, I wonder what their reaction was? Oh, to be a fly on the wall.*

The laugh that escapes Enzo lets me know my filter has gone amuck again. *Great.* "Samantha, I wouldn't have asked you if they weren't on board with it. They kept the secret because they wanted this to be a surprise for you. We all agreed that Frankie wouldn't keep it, though, so she, unfortunately, isn't in the know."

"Are they really okay with this? With you and me getting married? Us living together?" *I'm on sensory overload. There's no way this could go so easily.* I've been fretting about how to tell them, but I wanted to stay in this blissful bubble for as long as I could.

Enzo goes into specific details about each of his conversations with Maddie and Declan. I can tell he doesn't leave anything out because he cringes, as well as laughs, throughout his explanation. He admits they were both hesitant and maybe even shocked by their conversations. But once he had explained that he'd never felt this way about anyone before, they seemed to be more open to the idea.

I think the clincher for both Declan and Maddie was the fact Enzo readily admitted his ultimate goal is to make me happy and be a part of our lives. He wants to spend as much time with us as possible when he returns to the States, and for the first time in his life, he wants a family of his own.

Having the twins will likely cause shock to my entire family, but I can't worry about that now. It's a bridge we'll have to cross later.

Enzo has me in stitches when he explains how serious Declan was in their conversation. Apparently, Dec alluded to the possibility of injuring Enzo, if he ever hurts me. I absolutely love that Enzo's response to Declan's attempt at a threat was, "I'll happily help you, should that ever happen. I never want to see your mom hurt." This, evidently, defused Declan's worries.

After I settle down from envisioning my ten-year-old puffing out his chest, posing a serious threat to the glorious man before me, Enzo continues to tell me how he promised them he wasn't trying to replace their father. He assures me that he let both Maddie and Dec know that he thinks Devin has always been a great dad to them, but he wants to find his place in their lives as well. This got both kids on board, which is a huge relief. I can't imagine telling our news to them without any forewarning. I guess I've been so wrapped up in our blissful bubble, I hadn't thought about the aftereffects.

Maddie was more resistant to the idea of us getting married at first, bringing up the fact it was too soon. In typical teenage fashion, she seemed standoffish and told him she didn't need another dad. Enzo further explains how he wore her down by telling her all the things he loves about me. This part makes me swoon, if I'm being honest. His charms seemed to work on her as well. Eventually, she told him she noticed how happy I'd been since he came into our lives, and she hoped he would keep the smile on my face.

When he's done with his explanation, Enzo lets out a huge breath. "So, what do you think about calling them later this evening? I know Maddie's dying to hear your response." He waggles his eyebrows and makes me fall in love with him even more.

"That sounds like a plan," I say as I wrap my arms around his neck, pulling him in for a hug. With Enzo being the sexy man that he is, it doesn't take long before I'm desperately wanting more.

6

ENZO

THE MINUTE SAMANTHA SAYS, "Guess what, kids?" to all three faces on the screen of our video chat, Maddie immediately screams with excitement.

"You said YES!" Maddie enthusiastically concludes.

"Yep," I say before Samantha can respond. I couldn't be happier to share this news. I glance at Samantha and the excitement's evident on her face as well.

"I knew it." Maddie's smile is wider than I could have imagined. "When will it happen?"

"What happen?" Frankie asks everyone on her end of the screen.

"Congrats," quietly comes from Declan, ignoring Frankie's question. His arms are crossed against his chest and his face looks as if he's bored with this conversation. Not exactly how I pictured this moment, but he's not looking upset, so I'll take it.

"Thanks, Dec. Well, Frankie." Samantha takes a deep

breath and squeezes my hand out of sight of the camera for support. "Enzo asked me to marry him."

The look of pure astonishment has me wondering if I should have included her in my conversation with Maddie and Declan. I know she's only eight, but she seems a little put out by the fact her brother and sister were *'in the know'* and she was not. *Fuck. Did I mess up here?*

"Really?!?!" Frankie still seems dumbfounded. Her eyes are wide and her mouth hangs open until she asks, "You're getting married?"

I look to Samantha to see how we should proceed, but she just gives me a slight shrug and lifts her eyebrows. *Why couldn't her filter be broken at this moment?* I'm dying here. Fuck, I have no clue if Frankie's excited or pissed! Jesus. What should I do? How can I fix this?

I glance over at Samantha once again and she's scrutinizing the screen to gauge Frankie's reaction as well. I can't take the silence any longer, so I break in by saying, "Yeah, sweetheart, we are."

Frankie looks far too serious for an eight-year-old. Damn, she could put my CO to shame for her pensiveness. The mask she wears on her unresponsive face has my stomach dropping to my feet. *Shit. Damn. Fuck. I screwed up.* I love Samantha more than anything, but not knowing if her kids will accept me is worse than the thought of being captured by insurgents. There's no way I want to live without any of them in my life. But I can't marry her if her family isn't on board.

"Frankie?" Samantha quietly says as she reaches for the screen. Her desire to comfort her child is evident.

"What's wrong, Franks?" Maddie asks as she puts her arm around her little sister. I can tell by the look on Samantha's face it's killing her not to be there comforting Frankie herself. Hell, *I'd* give anything to be there to comfort her, if I could.

"I..." Frankie gasps, taking in a big breath of air. My blood turns to ice as I await her response. "I..."

"What is it, Frankie? You can tell us anything," Samantha coaxes as she reaches out and places a vise grip on my leg beside her.

Through the screen, I can see tears well up at the corners of Frankie's eyes. I might as well be sliced through the heart with a dull tablespoon, this pain caused by her reaction is immeasurable.

"I... missed it?" Frankie asks in disbelief, causing more confusion than anguish to wash over me.

"Missed what, Sweetheart?" I attempt to get her to clarify.

"I—" *gasp*—"missed—" *sniffle*—"the...wedding?"

Relief washes through both Samantha and me immediately. I can physically feel each of us relax, as we realize her misconception. "No, Frankie. You haven't missed anything." Samantha lets out a low laugh. "Enzo only has *asked* me to marry him. We will include all of you in the ceremony!"

Suddenly, Frankie beams with delight. It's as if she hadn't been about to fall apart just moments ago. "Really, I get to be in it?"

With tears filling her eyes, Samantha nods. She attempts to say something, but it gets stuck in her throat. I break the silence by saying, "Frankie, we couldn't get married without you."

"Wheeeee!" Frankie shouts, "Do I get a fancy dress and everything?"

"Goofball," Maddie chides as she rumples her sister's hair.

"Does this mean we *all* have to dress up?" Declan asks as if he seems really put out by the idea. The look of pure disgust is almost comical. I can't say I wouldn't have said the same thing at his age.

I glance to Samantha since we haven't discussed any of the details yet. I would marry her today if we were all in one place. I have no idea what kind of wedding she wants. If I'm being honest, I couldn't care less. I just want to spend the rest of my life by her side.

"Of course, we're going to dress up, dork," Maddie says in disbelief as she gives her brother the stink-eye, as only a big sister can. "This is Mom's wedding. It's a special occasion."

I hear Declan groan quietly and can't help the grin that forms on my face.

"We won't torture you too much," I assure him.

When Samantha asks what's new with everyone, the subject naturally changes. We chat for a while longer, with each of them telling us what they have been doing for the past day or so. Of course, we don't tell them Samantha's been in the hospital, or that they are about to have two new siblings. That's something that needs to be done in person. This has already been more of a roller coaster ride than I could have ever imagined. One thing's for sure, I'll never underestimate Frankie's need to feel included again. Just the thought of her feeling completely left out and rejected sends shivers down my spine. Lesson learned.

UNFORTUNATELY, the rest of our weekend passes much too quickly. Samantha and I spend every moment possible wrapped in each other's arms. We manage to tour more around Frankfurt and the surrounding areas. She even convinces me to spend an afternoon at a Roman bathhouse. It was a relaxing and unique experience. I would certainly never have done anything like that without Samantha's encouragement. She makes being a tourist an art form. I'll never forget this experience with her. It's as if her mere presence brings vibrant colors to my life, that had once been only contrasting shades of gray.

I know she's exhausted with the pregnancy, but Samantha has more than enough energy to show her true feelings toward me. Of course, the highlights for me include making love to her until we both fall asleep from pure bliss and utter exhaustion. I have no fucking clue as to how I'm going to spend a day apart from her, let alone six weeks.

Thankfully, I know I'll be busy after she leaves. Not only do I have to work, but I have to pack my apartment and ship things back to the States within the next few weeks. I've scheduled the movers to be here in two weeks. Then I'll live in the barracks on post until I complete my contract, since I'm shipping my car home as well.

Since Samantha packed only one bag to travel, I've

decided to send another bag with her when she returns. That way I'll have some of my civilian things with me when I return as well as some of the photo albums and a few mementos I've collected over the years. Who knows how long it'll be until I get the remainder of my things. Sometimes it's taken weeks or even a month or more for things to get reunited with me when I've been relocated. Yeah, I don't need more than my "Go" bag, but the comforts of home are nice once I get settled in a new place and are a luxury to have.

AS MUCH AS I love spending the weekend with Samantha, the dreaded day has arrived. Samantha's set to leave tomorrow morning. My gut twists and turns at the thought of letting her go. I can't believe how, in such a short time, she has become everything my world is tethered to.

Samantha and I talked earlier this morning, and contrary to her typical behavior, she insists, just for today, she simply wants to live in the moment. She can't focus on leaving tomorrow, or she won't enjoy the rest of our time. She knows it's going to be extremely difficult for her to leave. I'm doing my best to make that happen. Fuck, it's hard not to speak of the inevitable. I plan to keep her "in the moment," while making memories that'll last a lifetime.

After giving it some considerable thought, I decide to take her to Metz, France. Not only will it put another stamp on her passport, but it'll give us a memorable destination for her last full day with me. I pack some snacks and encourage her to get ready after agonizingly removing her beautiful body from my comfortable bed. I'd much rather spend the day in bed with her, but I force myself to remember that we'll have a lifetime ahead of us.

It doesn't take long to cross the border into France. Within a few hours, we arrive at our destination. Samantha loves the view from the passenger seat as we drive. Once in Metz, I park near the train station. Though we won't be traveling by train, the architecture inside Cara de Metz is beyond impressive and I can't wait to show it to her.

As I suspect, Samantha falls in love with the building as soon as it comes into view. There's a gigantic Christmas tree decorated with lights as we approach the massive building, as well as impressive, lifelike statues that seem to come off the wall. This building's designed by Jurgen Kroger in 1905 and he did a magnificent job.

"Enzo, this town is what fairytales are made of." Samantha gasps as she spins in a slow circle to take in the town. Her eyes shine bright, filled with wonder. *God, can she get any more beautiful?* "I love the narrow cobblestone streets and the massive buildings around it. Thank you so much for bringing me here." She nibbles on her lower lip as if she's still processing everything around her.

"Let's go inside for a better view," I suggest.

The moment we pass through the entryway, her eyes are drawn toward the vastness of the large room. "This might be bigger than Grand Central Station! I love the dark beams that inlay the ceiling and all the unique, almost lifelike sculptures."

"Come here." I motion for her to go down one of my

favorite walkways. I was blown away by my first impression, I can't wait to share it with her. "I want to show you something." I lead her down a hallway that's substantially brighter than the areas around us. The ceiling's made of stained-glass squares, illuminating in the sunlight. It's a magnificent view and I'm dying to show Samantha.

I fell in love with this the first time I went through this station as a passenger.

"Oh, wow!" Samantha gasps as she appreciates the new view. She pulls out her phone and snaps picture after picture. "This is so amazing." She seems lost in thought as she takes everything in.

"Here, why don't you stand over there." I point to a lifelike statue coming out of the wall. "I'll take your picture so you can remember it."

Samantha absolutely glows in this light. Her smile's infectious and I can't help but enjoy this moment. I honestly don't think I could love her any more than I do right now. She's not only captured my heart but will be the mother of my children. My wife. How the hell am I going to watch her get on a plane tomorrow? As much as I want to say something, I choose not to. I promised her fun and adventure today. I hope I've shown her just how much she means to me.

After I've taken quite a few pictures of Samantha, I feel a tap on my shoulder. I turn to see an older woman greeting me with a smile, motioning to my phone and then to Samantha. "Puis-je prendre votre photo?"

"Oui, merci." I nod. "Appuyez simplement sur cette, Madame."

I walk over to Samantha and place an arm around her. I can't help myself as I graze my lips along her cheek and tuck her in front of me. Samantha melts into me, and I grip her even tighter. I could hold this woman for the rest of my life, and it will never be enough.

After the woman takes our photo, she walks over to hand my phone back to me. "Merci beaucoup," I thank her.

She pats me on the arm, nodding her head with a smile shining across her wrinkled face. She brushes her short, graying hair and says, "Je vous en prie. Prenez soin de cette femme. Soyez bénis."

I nod, indicating I'll take care of Samantha before she walks away. Her blessing was kind.

Samantha whispers, "Just how many languages do you speak?" The look on her face is priceless. It's a mix between wanting to kick my ass for showing off and astonishment. I'm not sure which one will win out in the end, and that in and of itself is the beauty of Samantha O'Reilly.

"A few." I shrug in an attempt to be humble. I only speak English, French, Spanish, and a bit of Russian, as well as German. Mostly enough to get by in public.

She rolls her eyes and elbows me in the side as I attempt to back away from her, but I was too late in realizing her intent. She gets me firm in the ribs and a huff as what's left of my breath escapes me in a rush as she says, "Sure, just a few... And I'm only a *little* pregnant."

Samantha cocks her chin to the side and raises an eyebrow in my direction. "Are you going to fill me in on the conversation you just had?"

I chuckle. "Um, she said to take good care of you."

Samantha's eyes shine with delight as she grins. We spend more time walking around the train station. When we're done, we walk around the town of Metz. Samantha and I enjoy the narrow, cobblestone streets and looking in the various shops. We make our way over to the well-known cathedral in town. It's another phenomenal structure that's completely awe-worthy.

By the time we arrive back at my apartment, it's nearly eight p.m. Samantha fell asleep on the way home, so hopefully she'll be well rested. I know the long flight tomorrow will wear her out.

As soon as we enter my apartment, I'm surprised when Samantha wraps her arms around my shoulders. Her fingers lace behind my head as she leans up on her tiptoes. "In case I've forgotten to tell you, I've had the most wonderful time here, Enzo." Her voice comes out like a purr, setting my senses on fire.

"Me, too, beautiful. I'm so glad you came." God, I wish she wasn't leaving. I have the morning off so I can take her to the airport, but it will suck ass, having her away from me. The weeks before she arrived were practically unbearable. I can't imagine how it will be now, knowing I'm half of a world away from the woman I love and our children growing inside of her.

She pulls my neck toward her and I kiss her sensually. Samantha boldly quickens our pace when she reaches between us to undo my belt. It's like she has hands with lightning speed. My pants drop down my thighs at a moment's notice.

I don't get a chance to respond before she drops to her

knees and her mouth's on me. "Fuck," I growl. "You're going to be the death of me, beautiful." In tandem movements, her hand fists my shaft, as her mouth applies the perfect amount of pressure. When she reaches up with her other hand to find that sensitive spot behind my balls, *fuck!* I. See. Stars. My spine tingles and I can't help the roar that escapes from the unexpected orgasm that rips through me. Holy fucking shit. What the hell was that?

As I open my eyes to refocus on her, there's a look of pure contentment with a mix of pride filling her features as she milks every last drop out of me. *Fuck, this woman knows just how to do me in.*

Though I nearly die on the spot, *and God, what a way to go,* I somehow muster up the energy to haul Samantha into my arms and crush my lips to hers. I can't get close enough. When my brain registers my desperate need, I toe off my shoes and kick my jeans off as they fall to my feet. I somehow manage to do this all while kissing the living hell out of Samantha. I lift her, and her legs curl around my hips as if she were made for me. I intend on finishing this in my bed.

After a few steps, I realize the bedroom is just too far away. I set her feet down on the floor, and in one fell swoop, I have removed her jeans and underwear before hoisting her again. I take the two necessary steps to place her on the small island in my kitchen.

I continue to pepper her with kisses as my greedy fingers make their way down her body to find that magical place that has her writhing in seconds. First, I slide my fingers along her folds, teasing... testing... to see what she needs. Her deep pants and subtle moans tell me everything. I insert two fingers to really work the woman before me.

My kisses pepper her jaw, behind her ear, along her lobe, where I nibble before I whisper, "I love you, Samantha," as I make my way down her body. I break apart for a moment to literally tear her thin t-shirt from her body. I'm not sure who's more shocked, her or me, when the fabric's torn. There's a moment of laughter, but it's soon replaced with deep desire. Our mouths fuse together again, and my fingers intimately inspect the inner workings of Samantha's body. Like a road I could navigate with my eyes closed, I know exactly what Samantha needs. I instinctively do what it takes to make her pleasure mine. Within seconds, I feel her inner walls tighten. The moment my thumb brushes her clit, she detonates and the pure bliss that crosses her face is the most beautiful fucking thing I've ever seen. *God, I love this woman and her responsiveness.*

Of course, I'm a greedy bastard, and I want to see just how many times I can make this happen. I drop my lips to her inner thighs, teasing and tasting with the perfect combination of fingers and tongue. As soon as she has ridden her high to completion again, I feast on her desire to see if I can bring her there once more.

Just as she's about to light off like the Fourth of July, I reach down and stroke my dick. I give my balls a tug, so they won't crawl up my throat before she's finished. The second she quakes, I quickly stand and thrust deep inside her. I feel myself bottom out with ease from the slickness of her desire. I pull out and urgently thrust deep within her, setting a pace I know she enjoys. She comes gloriously around my cock and with a few more thrusts, I follow her right over the edge into heaven. I lean over her body, completely spread out on the counter before me. Her dark, mahogany hair is fanned around her face, her pants eventually slowing, as her breathing returns to normal. I kiss her jaw, neck, and make my way to her breasts, still covered by her bra.

She pulls at my shirt and I break our contact to haul it over my head in a mere instant, our bodies still connected. The next thing I know, there's a clamping sensation around my cock. The moment I look into Samantha's eyes, I realize she's laughing.

"You're really going to start laughing with me still inside you?" I growl.

She looks around us and her mouth quivers more. "I definitely would say we got a bit carried away." She reaches out and touches a scrap of the t-shirt I ripped off her.

Fuck. Did I really just do that?

"Oh my God, Samantha." I pull her into an embrace and oddly enough, my dick chooses that moment to surge again inside her. "I'm so sorry about your shirt." I kiss her cheek, her eyelids, and place a tender kiss on her mouth, to show her how much I love her.

She pulls me down into a deep kiss that somehow reignites my desire. I've never been able to recover as fast as I do with her. And somehow, I think she feels the same way.

SOMEWHERE IN THE middle of the night, as we cuddle in bed, reality seeps in. "Enzo, how the hell am I going to live without you for the next six weeks?"

"Beautiful, I feel the same way," I whisper, cherishing this moment. "We've been apart a long time already. We can do this. I love you and I will do everything in my power to contact you when I'm able. This sucks for all of us, but just think, it's only temporary."

We talk about how we will call, text, and video chat. Of course, me being a guy and all, this leads to me prompting about how much I'm looking forward to sexy video chats. Being apart has its disadvantages, but even from thousands of miles away, there's nothing I like more than to watch her come apart, thinking of me. The thought of Samantha pleasuring herself has me hard in an instant, but I do my best to dismiss it, so we can continue our playful banter and conversation. Samantha's mouth nearly hits the floor when I ask, "So, do you have a vibrator?"

Eventually, she closes her mouth. Opens it to say something, but then closes it again. After a few moments, she asks somewhat hesitantly, "W... W... Why would I need one of those?" *Obviously, she doesn't have one. If she did, I'm sure she would have used it in our earlier conversations.*

Since our bodies are entwined, I snuggle her close and nip at her neck. "I'm just curious. We've never talked about it, so I thought I'd ask." I'm a bit surprised about the blush that crosses her features. After spending as much time with her as I have, I wouldn't think much would embarrass her anymore.

"I... uh... have one, but never use it," she stammers, then looks away.

"Why not?" I ask intrigued.

"Well... The battery's never charged and doesn't last," she rushes out in a blur.

She's adorable. "Beautiful, there's no need to be embarrassed." I chuckle lightly as I snuggle closer. "I thought it would be fun to watch you get off, that's all. You mentioned before you have needs while you're pregnant." I waggle my eyebrows at her and she giggles before I add, "Since I won't be there to help you, I want to make sure you're not left hanging..."

She gasps and shakes her head. "Enzo. I've gone years without so much as a kiss. I'm sure I can manage a few weeks without you... even with pregnancy hormones."

Suddenly, a flash of something unreadable crosses her features. It's something like desire and intrigue, but it's gone in an instant. If I hadn't been paying attention, I might have missed it. *Hmmm... I might have to remedy this.* Obviously, this is something she has an interest in. Her expression drastically changes, catching me off guard.

"Where will you live when you return?" she suddenly blurts out, catching me off guard. We haven't talked about the details, but I assume since we're getting married, moving in together is something we would eventually do. I know I certainly don't want to be away from her, and with the babies coming, I have no intention of being far from her for long.

"Where do you want me to?" I say in a teasing tone, but in my mind, there's only one place I want to be.

I'm met with silence, which is unusual for Samantha. She seems lost in thought and I can't read her expression to save my damn life. There's no way I'm letting her clam up like she did in the hospital. "Beautiful, talk to me," I almost plead. "I'll be wherever you want me."

"But where do *you* want to live, Enzo?"

"Um, with my wife and kids." I raise an eyebrow to get my point across.

"Do you think we should live together before getting married? What about my kids? Would that be setting a good example to them?"

Christ. I hadn't thought about that. "Samantha, I plan on marrying you the minute you're ready. I would've taken you to a chapel this week, but that wouldn't have been fair to your kids. Unless you change your mind, my vote is to get married as soon as possible, when I return to Portland."

Samantha's dark eyebrows shoot up and her mouth forms an 'O.' She squeaks out, "Are you serious?"

"As a heart attack. I've gone a lifetime without you and the past six weeks have been hell being away from you. I want nothing more than to have you as my wife and start a life together. I'll wait until you're ready, but you're it for me, Samantha. Why wait any longer?"

"Okay... But what should we do until we get married?"

"I can stay with my parents or get a place of my own until you're ready to get married. Then, as long as I'm with you, I couldn't care less where we live."

"Enzo, renting a place is just plain silly. I meant, would

you like to move in with me? Or would you prefer to get a new place together?"

I smile at Samantha, loving the fact she's putting so much thought into our future together. "Beautiful, I will move to Timbuktu if that's where you want to live. Seriously. I. Don't. Care. A house is just a house. I want to be with you and our children, and that's about it."

"I did just remodel my house to make it into my dream home, and the kids would have one less adjustment if we stay put." Samantha bites on her lower lip and it takes all my restraint not to remove it and kiss her senseless.

"Then it's decided. I'll move in with you. Now, for the bigger decision. When will I get to officially call you my wife?" I bring my thumb to her mouth and release her lower lip. I can't help but outline her features with my thumb as she contemplates.

"What kind of wedding did you envision for yourself?" she asks.

"Uh..." I've never actually thought about it. "Well...I guess the kind where we simply say I do and be married."

"Enzo, I'm being serious. You've never been married before and I want you to have your dream wedding," Samantha pleads.

My heart melts at her thoughtfulness. "Beautiful, so long as you're there, it is my dream wedding."

"But what about our friends and family? Do you want a big or small wedding?"

I can see where she's going with this. I should have known

better. I remember the infinite details of my sister's wedding. I'd better stop this freight train before it gets rolling out of control. "Samantha... How about this... We can have a small ceremony with our family and close friends. Besides you, your kids, and your family, I just want my family there. That's all I need. Nothing big."

A look of relief washes over Samantha's face, telling me she's content with a small wedding as well. "You say you want to get married right away. Are we talking weeks, months, this summer?"

"There's no fucking way I'm waiting until summer," I practically growl. "Honestly, even waiting until I get stateside is a lot to ask. Why don't we plan something for the week or so after I get back? I don't want you to worry about that much. Just give me a date and what you want, and I'll hire someone to take care of the details." There. That should do it.

Samantha shakes her head and rolls her eyes. "Enzo, you know nothing about weddings and brides."

"All I care about is *this* bride and making her *mine*." I pull her close to me and plant a chaste kiss on her lips. "Please tell me we can do it ASAP?"

"Enzo, weddings take time..." she pleads for my understanding.

"What do we need besides you, me, and our families?" I shrug as if it's not a big deal.

She lets out a deep breath, shaking her head. She ticks things off on her fingers as she says, "Well... There's a dress, a venue, food, and guest lists. Not to mention a photographer, cake, flowers, and music."

Geesh, that list's fucking huge. "That's for a small

wedding?" I ask in assurance. Of course, she nods and I cut her off before she can say anything else. "How about this… You take care of your dress and clothes for the kids, and I will take care of the rest. I promise to run things by you before I make a final decision, but this has to be possible, right? I don't want you to stress out about anything. Your focus needs to be on staying healthy, nothing else."

"But, Enzo…" she starts, but I stop her with a finger over her beautiful pouty lips.

"Samantha, all I care about is being married to you. Give me a week or so and I'll have some ideas to run by you. My sister's friend is a wedding planner and I'm sure if I ask her, she would be willing to help us. Or at the very least, point us in the right direction."

"Okay, Enzo." Samantha slowly exhales. "I trust you. I've already done the big wedding before, and the thought of something like that again has me breaking out in hives. I just need you. It doesn't have to be elaborate, but it does have to be what you want. This is your first wedding and I don't want you to miss out on anything, just to do it quickly."

"Oh, beautiful. It will be epic. Simple, but epic. I will be marrying the woman of my dreams. I couldn't give two shits about the specific details, but I will do this right by you. I love you and want to start our life together right." I kiss her deeply to show just how much she means to me, which ends most of our conversation for the rest of the night. I spend the remaining hours we have left together memorizing her body, cherishing it and making sure she doesn't forget me while we are apart.

7

———

SAMANTHA

GETTING on that plane is probably one of the hardest things I have ever done. Though my life and family are in Portland, there's no way I wanted to leave Enzo. My body aches in glorious ways, and I can't help but smile when I think about the love and attention Enzo showed me. It is agonizing to actually say the words, "goodbye." Though I'm proud of myself for not breaking into tears until I actually have to say it.

Enzo's just as wrecked as I am. He takes the time to walk me into the airport and help me get my luggage settled. Since I'm taking his extra bag back, he claims he needs to ensure I don't have any problems or have to lift anything unnecessarily. I keep reminding him I'm pregnant, not an invalid. But if I'm being honest, it's really sweet of him to care so much.

He was stoic the entire trip to the airport. But when I begin sobbing as I embrace him one last time, he breaks down, too. His eyes well up with tears as he whispers, "Beautiful, I'll be home before you know it. I love you so much and I can't wait to meet these beautiful babies growing inside of you."

Then he takes me completely off guard, kneeling down on one knee in front of me to softly say, "You take care of your ma until I can get to you all. I love you all so much. I'll be there as soon as I can." He kisses my belly and holds me close before standing to kiss me senseless once again. I don't care that we're in a crowded airport, in front of everyone to see. I love this man, and though a part of my heart is being left with him, his love for me is what gets me on that plane and sends me home.

As I take my seat and make myself comfortable for the nine-hour flight to New York, I glance down at the beautiful ring on my finger and shake my head at the thought of how he insists on taking over the wedding plans. Devin never had any interest in planning our wedding, so to have Enzo say he only wants me to worry about my dress and clothes for the kids, seems unbelievable. I hope he knows what he's getting into. He's set the bar pretty high for himself.

I've never been more thankful for first class than I am right now. I'm not sure if it's the pregnancy or my lack of sleep from last night, but I feel as if I'm about to drop at any moment. Thank God for the anti-nausea medicine. I haven't been sick since I was in the hospital earlier this week. I watch out the window as the plane taxis away from the terminal, and I feel my eyes getting heavier as we make our ascent into the sky. I take one last glance out the window at Frankfurt and can't believe how much my life has changed in less than two short weeks. Drifting off to sleep, I know I'll never forget this experience for as long as I live. All of it was incredible. Thanks to Enzo.

AS I FINALLY TOUCH DOWN IN Portland, Oregon, I'm relieved to feel refreshed after traveling for nearly twenty hours. My layover in New York went off without a hitch and I managed to get plenty of rest on my two flights. Thanks to being in first class, I didn't have a single whim that went unnoticed. It helps I was able to walk around the cabin when I got stiff, have quick access to the bathroom, and I stayed well hydrated and fed during the trip. I've been wide awake for most of this last leg of my journey, having slept nearly the entire flight from Frankfurt to New York.

I've never been more relieved to see Mount Hood as I am now. Eager to see my kids, I'm practically bouncing in my seat when I hear the final call for landing. I haven't been away from Maddie, Frankie, or Declan like this in ages. I miss them more than ever. I'm dying to tell them everything, and I have no idea how I'm going to keep this pregnancy a secret for the next six weeks.

Since the kids are still in school, Lexi, my best friend, and co-owner of our company, insists on picking me up from the airport. Normally, I catch a cab or Uber it home, but after finding out I was engaged, she cleared her schedule, determined to meet me in person. Knowing Lexi, she just wants the juicy details about Enzo, and I have to say, I'm excited to share them with her. *After all, what are best friends for?*

I don't even make it through security at PDX before I hear her scream of excitement. She pounces on me like paparazzi looking for their next big break. I whirl to the sound of her voice and make my way over to her. Her brown, curly hair and dark-rimmed glasses make her appear to have a bigger personality than ever. As she weaves through the crowd, her hair bobs and springs into action, taking on a life of its own as she hightails it directly toward me. I don't even get a word of greeting out before I'm being squeezed like a vise.

"Sam, I'm so excited for you!" Lexi exclaims. "I've missed you so much."

I manage to say, "You, too," before she pulls back and studies me further.

"Love looks great on you. You're simply glowing." She eyes me up and down and stops on my left hand, a telling smile pulls at her lips. I know what's coming next. "Okay, show me the ring!"

I can't contain my excitement. I eagerly show off the perfect ring Enzo picked out. I love how our past, present, and future is symbolized. I gush over the details as I tell Lexi as much. Once she's done ogling my ring, we make our way to baggage claim.

Lexi and I spend the time catching up as we wait for the luggage to funnel onto the conveyer belt. She tells me about some of our clients' needs, and I tell her more about Germany. She insists we take the afternoon off and go to lunch before my kids get home.

Once we settle into a booth at our favorite Mexican restaurant, Lexi orders her usual margarita. Her jaw nearly drops to the floor when I don't follow suit, sticking with water. She doesn't say anything, but I can tell her wheels are spinning. *Maybe she will buy my jet lag excuse? Highly doubtful.*

Just as I take a huge bite of my chicken enchilada, her silence breaks. "Okay, so what's the plan for when Enzo returns?"

"What do you mean?" I play being obtuse for a moment, trying to see where she's going with this.

"Where's he going to live? When will you get married?" Lexi eyes me dubiously in that knowing look, only a best friend can give. "You know... all the deets!"

"Well..." I swallow, then rush to say, "We're getting married, he's moving in, and we're having babies." Once I finish, I take another bite of the mouthwatering food before me. For some reason, I'm starving. The fact that it keeps me occupied while I wait for her reaction to the bombs I've just delivered, doesn't hurt either.

"When's the wedding?" she asks, but then gasps as if she has just inhaled all of the air from the room. "Baby... did you say, baby?"

Hmmm... Is it getting hot in here? I squirm a little as I slowly finish chewing and take a long drink of water.

"You misheard me," I say with as little emotion as I can muster. I love catching Lexi off guard, and this will be priceless. "We're getting married soon after he returns."

"Um, I swear I heard you say *baby*..." she trails off,

appearing as if she's replaying the scene in her head over and over again.

"Well, I didn't," I calmly state. I wait until she's looking at me directly in the eyes and her curly hair has stopped bobbing with excitement. "I said *babies*," I whisper.

Her jaw drops almost to the table. She starts to talk, gets out a muffled sound, then clamps her mouth shut again. *God, it's taking all my inner strength not to laugh at her reaction.* Like a fish out of water, a rattled Lexi's something to be seen.

"I'm pregnant with twins. Apparently, I got pregnant before he left, and he has super sperm." Her eyes nearly bug out and I lose my composure by bursting into laughter. "Oh My God, Lex, I'm going to be a mother at thirty-nine years old! Can you believe it?"

"But you tried for years with Devin! I thought you couldn't get pregnant?"

"Me, too," I sigh. "Like I said, super sperm."

"Have you told the kids?"

"No, we're waiting until Enzo comes home to do it in person. They apparently knew he was going to propose before he left for Germany, so we thought one change, for now, is good enough. He proposed before we even knew what was wrong with me."

"Wrong with you, what do you mean?" she asks with confusion.

I launch into the story about being sick for days and not being able to hold anything down. She soon becomes just as smitten with Enzo as I am when I tell her how amazing he was at taking care of me. She can't believe he proposed in the hospital and that he had been carrying the ring around the entire time I'd been there. We both agree Enzo's amazing. Soon, we are talking about wedding plans, and the best friend that she is, insists on helping with anything I need. I'm so lucky to have a friend like her.

WHEN THE ALARM goes off the next morning, I have to drag myself out of bed. The kids all have school, so I know I have to get up to help them. *Those are the perks of being a mom.* I have no idea if it's the jet lag or the pregnancy, but I certainly don't want to get up, and I'm clearly dragging this morning.

I reach out to check my phone. Sure enough, there's a text from Enzo. A smile immediately forms on my face, as my day just got better. We had spoken last night, but he's heading out on a mission at some point today.

> **Enzo: Morning, beautiful. I'm heading out. Will call or text when I can. I'll have to be radio silent for a while though, so don't worry. Take pictures of the babies and know that I love you all. Counting the days until I see you again! (Kiss emoji)**

My heart swoons at how thoughtful he is. I can't help but

squeeze the phone to my chest tightly and wish it were him in person. I take a moment to look through some of our photos together from my trip. I select one, making it the background for my phone.

As soon as I'm dressed, I pull out my phone again. I lift up my shirt and snap a side profile of my belly in the mirror. I'm not one to take selfies like this, or at all for that matter, but for Enzo, I'll do just about anything. I text the picture to him.

Me: I miss you like crazy. One day closer. Be safe. Love, us

I rush downstairs to find Frankie eating cereal in the kitchen.

"Hey, Squirt." I give her a quick squeeze and kiss the top of her head. "Did you sleep well?"

"Yeah, I've been up forever."

I glance at the clock. It's barely past seven. She still has nearly forty minutes before she has to leave.

"Have you seen your brother or sister yet this morning?" I ask, wanting to know if I should go up to check on them.

"Yeah." Frankie rolls her eyes before continuing, "Maddie's in her room texting Soren, and Dec's in the shower, I think."

"Good to know you're keeping tabs on them," I tease, then pull out food to make the kids' lunches.

"Mom?" Frankie sounds rather reluctant, so I turn my attention to her.

"Yeah, Franks?"

"If you get married to Enzo, does that mean he's gonna live

here?" she asks so innocently, and I can't help but smile. But, if I know my daughter, there's more on her mind.

"Are you okay with that?" I ask, rather than just telling her that he will be.

"Um, yeah." She seems shy all of a sudden and ducks her head to the side as she whispers, "I just miss him and can't wait to see him again."

My heart melts. Right there. "Oh, honey. He misses you, too." I pull out my phone and open a text message. "Here, why don't you tell him. It'll make his day."

"Okay." She smiles as she types. The complete concentration she uses is almost comical. When she's done, she hands me the phone. I can't help but tear up a little as I read her message. She's so sweet. *God, I love this girl!*

> **Me: Hi Enzo. This is Frankie. How are you? I miss you. I can't wait till you're here. Can you take me ice skating? Also, I want your chocolate chip pancakes. You make them better than Mom-but don't tell her. Write me back soon. Love Frankie**

Declan and Maddie barrel into the kitchen on a mission to grab some breakfast before I can say anything more to Frankie. Maddie gets cereal from the pantry while Dec grabs the milk from the fridge. I step out of their way to let them pass and can't help but think how much I missed the simple things like this when I was away.

They hastily eat their meal in silence before Maddie asks, "Hey, Mom, can Soren come over after practice tonight? Neither of us have games and we want to study together."

"Is that what you're calling it these days?" I tease. Soren's been nothing but respectful to me and I have no problem with him being here. They respect our house rule of 'no boys' upstairs. But I love to make Maddie squirm when I can. Parents have rights.

"Mom…" she huffs out in irritation. "I can go to his house instead, if you'd prefer…"

"Relax, Mads, it's fine. I'll plan dinner so we can eat here. How does honey chicken and rice sound to you?"

She exhales and I see her visibly relax. "It's fine." She scarfs down her cereal and rushes out the door. Now that they have been dating for a while, he picks her up for school from time to time, and I have a feeling it hasn't happened much when they were at Devin's house. Maddie was unusually chipper about this as she made arrangements with him last night. *I might need to have "the talk" with her once again to make sure she's being careful.*

As soon as I drop off Declan and Frankie at school, I head to my office. I have a meeting with a client at ten. I want to make sure Lexi and I get back on track for what I need to do, now that I've returned. It's nice to be in business for myself; it gives me flexibility, but I feel out of it after taking the last few weeks off.

As the end of the day approaches, I'm ravenous.

Thankfully, while I was in Germany, I kept up with most of my work while Enzo was working, so I'm fairly caught up with everything by the time I'm ready for dinner. Just as I pack up my purse to head out to grab some groceries and the kids, my phone rings. Enzo's beautiful face flashes across the screen.

I quickly sit back down at my desk as I swipe across the screen. I'm greeted with the sexiest voice I never knew I could miss so much. "Hey, beautiful."

I sigh in relief to hear Enzo's safe and sound. "Better now that I'm talking with you."

"Are you settling in okay? How are you feeling? I actually have good WIFI, would you want to video chat?"

"Absolutely," I gush. "Your sexy voice isn't enough. I need to see the real thing!"

Enzo chuckles. "Good to know. I'll call you right back." He ends the call and immediately, there's an incoming call to video chat.

I feel my face flush with heat as my eyes land on the rugged Enzo. His deep, green eyes pierce me on the spot. His eyes crinkle in the corners as a beautiful smile spreads across that chiseled jaw, that's now sporting a few days' growth of dark-blond beard. That damn dimple pops and I still feel my knees go weak. It happens every. Single. Time. *Will I ever get used to his absolute handsomeness? God, I hope not.*

Amusement fills his features. "God, I hope you don't either."

Crap. My filter's been misplaced again.

"Samantha, you are a sight for sore eyes. I've missed you

like crazy since you left." The longing in Enzo's eyes is undeniable.

"Me, too. I thought you were going radio silent for a bit. Everything okay?" I knew they were expected to be traveling for most of today and into tomorrow. *Wonder what happened?*

"Well, the men who are supposed to go out on this mission just got called out on something else. While they are prepping for the new orders, I'm here twiddling my thumbs."

I know better than to ask where *here* is. He told me he can't tell me any specifics, so as much as I'm dying to know, I refrain from asking. "I'm so glad to get to talk to you now," I sigh as I touch the side of his face on the screen.

"I'll text you something for Frankie in a bit. Her message was so sweet this morning. I've never wanted to get stateside more than I do right at this moment. Speaking of stateside, I used some of my downtime and talked to my sister about using her friend as a wedding coordinator. Erin says Melanie Hill's amazing. When I spoke to her, she said it was perfect timing since she just had a cancellation, and it'll work out perfectly for our timeframe."

Holy crap, this man's amazing. "You already spoke with her?" I ask in disbelief.

"If you don't like her, we can go with someone else," Enzo assures me. The look on his face is actually a bit hesitant for once.

"No, I'm sure it will be fine. I'm just surprised you've moved so quickly into the planning."

"Samantha..." Enzo chides. "I've waited my whole life for you. I have no need to wait any longer. Besides, with the babies coming and the fact you also have kids, I want to do this right. I want to be married to the woman I love before I live with her officially."

"Enzo..." I start, but he interrupts, with a gorgeous smile on his face.

"Samantha, I'm a selfish bastard. I want to be with you every chance I can get. There's no way I'm waiting to be with you when I'm finally in close enough proximity to touch you every day." Enzo's eyes are almost emerald green as they darken with obvious desire.

I can't help but shake my head and laugh. "You are too much, Enzo Dean Harper. But I love you all the same."

We spend the next few minutes talking over the plans. Melanie will contact me later today or tomorrow to discuss my thoughts and feelings about the wedding and reception. Enzo assures me that it won't be a problem financially when I offer to help pay. He claims he's had years of overseas missions, and nothing to spend it on.

Right before we get off the video chat, Enzo asks me to show him my belly, which still feels a bit weird. But the man's thousands of miles away serving our country, the least I can do is feel awkward for a few minutes. He asks me to place my phone next to my belly. Thankfully, he can't see when I tear up as I hear him say, "Hey, babies, I'm your daddy. I can't wait to see you. I love you so much. Be good to your ma and I'll be home before you know it."

There's a moment of silence, so I pull the phone up and look him in the eyes. I know he can see the tears, even though

I've done my best to wipe them away as he spoke. "Beautiful?" Enzo's voice nearly breaks, "Are you okay?"

"Just pregnancy hormones." I try to laugh it off. "I miss you and that was the sweetest thing ever. I love you so much."

"I love you, more," he says into the phone. He kisses his fingertips and places them on the screen. I can't help but do the same. "I've gotta get going, Sam. Are you sure you're okay?" His face is filled with compassion and concern. I couldn't love him more at this moment if I tried.

"Absolutely. Hurry home, I love you." I whisper, though he's able to hear.

"I'll call when I can. I'll also send a text to Frankie. Tell everyone I miss them, too. Love you, beautiful. Take care of our family for me." His deep, sexy tone completely does me in.

"Will do," I manage to say, then he ends the call.

I sit at my desk as the tears freely flow. I absolutely loved talking with him, but it makes me miss him even more. I'm so thankful for everything I have and can't wait to start my life with him. I sit at my desk in awe.

Of course, this is how Brenda, our receptionist, finds me when she knocks on the door. I'm staring out into space with tears running down my cheeks. She gasps in surprise when she finds me in such distress.

"Oh my God, Sam, are you okay?" She rushes over to a box of tissues I have on my conference table and swoops the entire box up to hand them to me.

"Yeah." I take the tissue and blot at my eyes. "I'm fine."

Brenda raises an eyebrow and eyes me speculatively. "You

don't look fine. If you were fine, you wouldn't be crying. This isn't like you. What's going on?"

She's right. I hardly ever cry. "Well, this is the new hormonal me," I suggest as an explanation.

"Hormonal you?" Confusion is clear on her face. "Are you on your period or something?" she suggests as an explanation.

"No," I mutter. "This is apparently, the new pregnant me." I blow my nose and look her in the eyes as I await her response.

Like Lexi, Brenda doesn't disappoint. Her jaw drops and her eyes round to look like saucers. "Excuse me?" she asks as if she couldn't have possibly heard me right. After all, I'm an old lady who already has plenty of kids. Why would she think I'm pregnant?

"You heard me. I'm pregnant. With twins, no less." There's no sense in keeping this a secret. She sees me every day, and if crying jags are something she's going to experience, I might as well prepare her. I don't recall being this emotional with my other kids, but with Enzo being gone and his super sperm giving me twins, I just might be in for a rude awakening.

"Wow." Brenda gasps as she rounds the corner of my desk. I stand and she embraces me in the biggest hug we have ever experienced together. "Congratulations?" she questions to make sure I'm on board with celebrating.

"Enzo and I couldn't be happier," I tell her. "With him being gone, I think I just miss him, too much. Hopefully, I'll have my emotions in check when he comes home."

"Congratulations on your engagement as well. You guys sure know how to move fast," Brenda teases.

I can't help but roll my eyes. "That's an understatement,

but with Enzo, I wouldn't have it any other way." I glance at the clock on my wall. "Crap. I need to get moving if I'm going to get to the grocery store and pick up the kids on time. Was there something you needed?" I say when I realize I never did find out what she came in here for.

She looks a bit perplexed for a minute and shakes her head. "I can't remember. Apparently, it isn't that important. You should get going and when I remember, I'll message you." She hugs me once more, then walks to the door. I grab my purse and jacket and follow right behind her. We walk out to the main office together and say our goodbyes.

I quickly make my way to the grocery store to pick up everything I need for dinner. Since Soren's coming over, I stop by the bakery section and pick up a cheesecake for dessert. I haven't been major grocery shopping since I've returned from Germany, so when I realize I have plenty of time, I get a few more things than I had originally come for.

As I load the conveyer belt, I realize one thing. *I should never shop while I'm hungry or pregnant, apparently.* Ice cream, cheesecake, pretzels, pickles, tortilla chips, cheese, avocados, and sour cream are just the first items I unload from my cart. Of course, I've got everything I need for dinner, but when I look at the combination of items placed on the conveyer belt, I wonder if anyone will wonder if I'm pregnant or just think I'm weird.

By the time I pick up everyone from school and drop them off at practice, I have a little less than an hour to make dinner. Thankfully, Maddie's catching a ride with Soren, and Devin brings Declan from practice, so there'll be no interruptions.

Frankie's upstairs doing her reading homework. I make my way to the kitchen and start the rice for later. I chop up some vegetables and set them in a pot to steam. Just as I begin cutting the chicken, a wave of unexpected nausea comes over me. *Oh, shit. Not again.*

It seems different from before. I don't think I will get sick, but I sit and rest my head in my arms on the counter, anyway. I slowly take deep breaths and soon the wave passes. When I feel like it has passed, I force myself to get up and attempt to make dinner a second time. I manage to cut all of the chicken and am just about to start cooking it when another round of nausea hits.

This cannot be happening. I don't have time for this shit. I glance at the clock and realize I have another twenty minutes or so before the kids will be home. After a few minutes, I realize I might need to eat something to calm my stomach. I walk to the pantry and pull out some crackers and 7-UP I keep on hand for when the kids are sick. I snack on them as I make my way to the couch in the family room, just off the kitchen. After a few more bites and a small sip of soda, I lay myself down, covering my eyes with one arm. *Much better. The world has stopped spinning for a moment and I can finally relax.*

The next thing I know, I hear the front door opening and voices coming from the hall. *Crap. I must have fallen asleep.* I soon realize the voices are coming from Declan and Devin. I make it as far as a sitting position before they stop talking and notice me.

Declan greets me with, "Hi, Mom. What's for dinner?"

I stand and stretch off the sleep that just consumed me. I

can't believe I took a nap in the middle of the afternoon. "Honey chicken," comes out in a yawn.

A grin lights up Declan's face. It's his favorite. "Awesome. I'm going to shower. Soccer was muddy." For the first time, I notice that he's indeed covered from head to toe in undeniable dirt. Well, his feet are clean since he obviously changed his shoes before getting into the car.

"Sure thing, Dec. See you in a few," I offer to his backside as he darts out of the room.

Devin looks around the room and eyes the crackers and 7-UP. He doesn't say anything but asks, "So, how was Germany? I hear you had an exciting trip."

"It was wonderful." I turn to start the chicken again. *Thank goodness, no nausea. Must remember to eat and be well rested before cooking again.*

"The kids said you got engaged. Congratulations," Devin offers as he sits at one of the barstools at the island next to me. "When's the big day?"

"Well, we're actually going to be married shortly after Enzo returns from Germany." I might as well lay it out on the table. He has every right to know since it'll affect the kids as well.

Devin takes in a big breath and slowly releases it. Evidence of shock flashes across his face, but he recovers. "Wow... That's soon."

I shrug. Not that it's any of his business. "Well, there's no reason to prolong an engagement. We think it is important to be married before living together." I make eye contact with Devin to ensure he gets that I'm doing it to set an example for our kids as well. *Though, if I'm being honest, I just want Enzo and I could care less if there was an official paper stating we were together. But with the babies coming...* "It makes sense to do it right away. There's no use in him getting his own place and just have to move a few months later."

He takes a moment to process what I said. In the short time Enzo was here, Devin and he actually spent a bit of time together. With Devin and I wanting to be an active part of our kids' lives, we're usually both at their activities. Devin knows Enzo's a decent guy who cares about our kids. I don't think they'll ever be best friends, but they tolerate each other the best they can.

I can tell the moment it clicks into place. He shrugs and says, "It makes sense. I guess... If you're happy, I'm happy for you."

"Thanks. I appreciate it." I go back to adding spices and honey, as I turn up the heat to caramelize the chicken.

Devin's quiet for a moment. Long enough for me to look his way to see what he's thinking. When I glance over, he's looking at the sleeve of saltine crackers and 7-Up. Knowing Devin like I do, he appears as if he's going to say something else but closes his mouth before anything comes out. His expression changes as if he changes his mind and instead says, "Well, I'd better get going. Let me know if you need help picking up the kids this week."

We say our goodbyes, and just as dinner is ready, the door opens again. This time it's Maddie and Soren. I'm still not used to seeing them holding hands as they enter, but I guess there could be far worse things for them to be doing. It's weird watching my baby grow up. It feels like it was yesterday when she came into the house with pigtails and dirt on her face, claiming boys were disgusting and there's no way she would ever have a boyfriend. Times sure have changed.

"Hey, Mom." She beams as she enters the kitchen. "Smells great. I'm starving." She sets her bag on the floor near the island and takes a seat on the barstool next to it.

"Me, too," Soren says as he rubs his stomach. "Coach had us run lines forever when we kept missing our shots this afternoon."

"Well, if Jack hadn't been mouthing off, I'm sure that would have helped," Maddie snarks out, which is out of character for her. Especially around Soren. "You said he's the one that brags about staying out all night with Anna and kept missing his shots today, right?"

I can't deny my eyebrows aren't shooting through my hairline with this line of talk. *Do kids really stay out all night with one another?* The mom in me acts before I think it all the way through. "By staying out all night... You mean..."

"Mom!" Maddie's cheeks turn pink. "You know what I mean." She shakes her head. "Don't make me say it..."

Soren uses this exact moment to take a long drink from the water bottle he has in his hands and seems rather uncomfortable.

I look back and forth between the two of them. Neither of them will make eye contact with me, but when I scrutinize Maddie, I can tell she's hiding something. *Fuuuck, I don't want to broach this subject. Sometimes it sucks being the responsible adult.* But when neither says more, I guess it's time to put on my big girl britches and face this head on. *Here goes nothing.* "Is this something the two of you intend on doing in the near future?"

Water bursts from Soren's mouth and spews all over the counter. He immediately sucks in a deep breath and begins to cough, as Maddie shouts, "MOOOMMM!" *Well, that was priceless. It takes all I can to keep a straight face.*

I cock a hip against the counter and raise an eyebrow. "What?" I say defensively. "You obviously talk openly about this, so why can't I do the same?"

Not a peep comes from either one of them, but I'm in for a penny, might as well go in for a pound. "Not that I condone the two of you having sex. AT ALL. Only the two of you can decide IF the time is right for you." I glance at Maddie, who's wishing she could vanish into the floor, she's staring at it so intently. *Mission accomplished.*

Soren, on the other hand, takes me seriously, wondering where I'm going with this. I gotta respect the guy for not squirming away from our conversation. Sort of, this is my baby he's dating... so my point needs to be clear here. Time to hike these britches higher and get this show on the road.

I clear my throat and continue with a shrug. "I won't always be there all the time to stop you." I pause for effect. "But just know this... there are steep consequences for your actions. Sure, there's STDs and side effects of having sex. Some can be cured. Some can't." I stop to look directly at both of them before continuing, "Everything is a risk... Then there's the possibility of a baby. Now, as a teenager, I'm not going to say your life will be over because that's a lie. I will say this though…" I take great care to look each one of them in the eye, to drive my point home. "Your life will change. It will no longer be your own. Dreams and goals you have are still achievable, but it'll take a hell of a lot longer to accomplish them. Your life's no longer your own and your child becomes the top priority. Do you understand what I'm trying to say?"

"Yes, ma'am," comes quietly out of Soren's mouth, whereas Maddie's still frozen in shock from my speech. Her mouth hangs on the floor.

To save us all from any more of this conversation I turn to Maddie. "Get your brother and sister. Dinner's ready."

IT ISN'T until bedtime that I finally get a chance to be alone with Maddie. She'd been pretty quiet through dinner and that isn't usual for her, especially with Soren here. I'm pretty sure my little speech had something to do with it. I had just gotten Frankie to bed and Declan upstairs when she approaches me in the kitchen.

"Hey, Mom?" comes quietly from across the room.

"Yeah, Mads?" It feels like this might be a conversation worth sitting for, so I gesture to the couch in the family room and bring the glass of water I had just filled myself over to get comfortable.

She takes a seat in the corner of the couch, propping her legs under her, but she remains facing me. Maddie's usually my most direct child, so I'm a bit surprised she hesitates. I decide to wait her out. It feels like forever. Just when I'm about to ask what's up, she says, "We're not. You know."

Um, what the hell is she talking about? "Not???" I draw out as an attempt to get her to share her thoughts.

"We're not having sex," she says as her cheeks paint a rosy color and she looks away from me.

Well, that's a fucking relief. I hadn't really suspected they were, since we've been pretty open about it. But I wasn't certain when I launched into my tirade this evening. "Okay," I manage to calmly say.

She stays silent. I wonder if there's more she wants to tell me, but I'm charting new waters here. Before when we've talked about the prospect of having sex, it was always about hypothetical people. Soren is about as real as they get.

"I just wanted you to know. I'm... Well, I'm still... a virgin," she sputters as she picks at some invisible lint on the couch.

Okay, still relieved. I take in a deep breath and let it out slowly. Suddenly, there's something I have to know. But, help me God, I don't want to ask it. "Are you wanting to have sex with Soren?" Somehow, this comes out naturally and not at all exposing how I feel about this conversation.

This shocks Maddie. "Oh." She lets out the deep breath she had apparently been holding and shakes her head vehemently. "No. I'm not ready."

"Is Soren pressuring you?" I ask, biting my lower lip. He doesn't seem to be the type, but then again, I'm not the one dating him.

"Oh, no." Maddie smiles. "Not at all. He actually was really impressed with you today. His older sister had a pregnancy scare in college and he wished his parents had been as open about this as you are."

Okay, wow! "Really?" is about all I can manage at this point. I wasn't expecting this conversation.

Maddie sighs and runs a hand through her thick, brown hair. "Yeah, they were pretty pissed. But the funny thing is, they had never even had 'The Talk' with any of their kids. They just assumed they would abstain or it wouldn't be a problem, I guess."

"Well..." *What can I say to that?* "At least in terms of communication, talking can help. It doesn't mean there won't be pregnancy scares or anything." I shrug, wishing there was a manual to help with situations like these. "There's only one way to prevent that." I look pointedly at her to make sure she comprehends my meaning.

"Yeah," Maddie sighs. "I know."

"You know you can talk to me about anything, right?" I reach out a hand and she grabs it. I give her a squeeze and thankfully, a smile spreads across her face.

"Yeah, I know," she repeats once again, but with a more promising tone.

"Love you, kiddo."

"Love you, too, Mom." She stands and walks to me. Before I know it, she has her arms wrapped around me in a hug. "Thanks, Mom. I'd better get to bed."

"Anytime, sweetheart," I offer to her as she turns to leave the room.

Well, that went better than expected. Where's a manual when you need one?

8

ENZO

FUCK. I'm tired. I've been working nonstop since Samantha left. I've literally flown across two continents and won't be back to Ramstein for another week or so. I'm not sure if it has to do with these being my last weeks in the Air Force and I'm ready to retire, or I'm dying to see Samantha again, but it feels as if time's standing still. The next six weeks are never going to get here.

I've been able to keep minimal contact with Sam, but nothing compares to the real thing. I'm one moody SOB and my buddies have been letting me know it. Gunderson, my life-long friend since Basic has been riding my ass about me actually dating someone seriously. Hell, if our roles were reversed, I'd be doing the same thing.

We're on call, waiting for orders to extract Team 6. Gunderson and I catch up to pass the time. He's recently been on leave and I can't get over the stories he's telling about his trip to London. It seems he had more than one woman catch his attention. Now, I'm not saying he's a man-whore, but the dude likes to have his fun. Ever since his divorce ten years ago, he's sworn off commitment and takes being single to a new level.

"You should've been there, Harps. The club was fantastic. I had to swat women away like flies. It was an epic vacation. I don't think I've ever enjoyed myself more. What did you do on your leave?" Gunderson asks. He takes a long pull on the water bottle he's holding while he waits for my answer.

Christ, I'm not passing judgment, but after being with Samantha, I'm so fucking happy those days are over for me. There's something to be said about spending time with the one you love. Gunderson has no idea I actually proposed to Sam. He's heard the guys razzing me about dating one woman seriously and this is the first time we've been alone or had the time to say anything.

"Samantha came for my birthday and we had quite the celebration." *Boy, did we ever.*

"Really?" he asks in disbelief. "I'll bet it's nowhere near as epic as London."

I attempt to catch him off guard, by understating, "Well, it was epic for me." This catches his attention.

"What happened?" Gunderson asks with more interest.

"Well, for starters, I'm engaged…" I get interrupted before I can say more.

"No. Shit?" Gunderson's frozen in place, awaiting my response. His eyes bulge in disbelief.

"When have you known me to lie?" I raise an eyebrow to prove a point.

"Wow!" He actually seems a bit shocked. "Not to be rude, but isn't it a little soon? Didn't you just meet this woman a few months ago?"

"When you know, you know." I feel a huge grin spread across my face at the thought of Samantha. "I already had the ring picked out before she got here. I just didn't get around to asking her for a few days since she got sick."

"Oh, man, that sucks. Was she okay?"

I can't help but laugh at the situation now. I was such a wreck not knowing what was wrong with her. That poor doctor. I was such a dick. "Yeah, she's okay. She's pregnant, but okay. Thank God for anti-nausea medicine."

"Oh, shit!" He brings his fist to his face and looks as if he's going to take a bite out of his knuckles. Then Gunderson's quiet for a moment as he studies me. "Fuck, you're serious."

"Dude, you haven't heard the best part yet."

"What's that?" He looks as if I can't say anything else to shock him.

"We're having twins! I'm going to be a fucking father of twins. After Vanessa, I was sure that ship had sailed for me. But not only do I get to be a part of Maddie, Frankie, and Declan's life, but we're having twins. Isn't this fucking fantastic!" I can't control my excitement by the end. I'm going to be a father. I waggle my brows to emphasize my point. *Fuck yeah, I'm excited.*

"Holy shit! You went from being single and carefree to a family with five children in two seconds flat. Aren't you freaking out?" The sincerity on his face shines through.

Gunderson's one of my best friends. He genuinely wants to know how I feel about this, all BS aside.

"Not gonna lie. I freaked the fuck out at the hospital. Samantha had been so sick and the doctor wouldn't tell us what was wrong." Shaking my head at the memory, I continue, "Then, when I saw two flutters as heartbeats across the screen..."

"Fuck, that had to be a sight to see." Gunderson's face could've mirrored mine when I witnessed it firsthand. It's filled with a mixture of shock, awe, and disbelief.

"Aside from Samantha saying yes, it's the best fucking thing I've ever seen in my life, man." Words don't exist for my emotions. Hell, I've known for weeks and I still feel as if I'm on a rollercoaster. But one thing's for sure. I can't wait to be a dad.

"Wow," Gunderson whispers in disbelief as he shakes his head. Then he finds his voice, "Congratulations, man. I'm happy for you. So... When's the big day?"

"As soon as possible. If I had it my way, we'd already be married. But, we want her kids involved."

"So, we're talking later this year sometime?"

"No, man. We're talking as soon as I can get stateside. I don't want to wait another minute not being married to her."

"Uh, Harps, correct me if I'm wrong, but I recall weddings being a big event, which involves lots of planning. That means you're eloping?"

"Nope, we'll have a family affair. My sister's best friend is a wedding coordinator and she just had a cancellation, so if all goes well, we should be married within weeks of me being home."

"Damn, man, your life's changing so fast I can hardly catch up," Gunderson teases, but the pat on my shoulder tells me he's happy for me.

Before I can say anything else, our orders come through. We need to be wheels up in fifteen minutes to extract the guys in the field. Gunderson and I've already done our preflight check, so within minutes, we're in the cockpit of the helo, ready to move.

WHEN I FINALLY GET BACK TO my apartment, I barely have a week to pack and get things ready for the movers. It's hard to believe this is going to be my last move. I'm so fucking ecstatic to be this much closer to being with Samantha and her kids.

I've just spent the last hour going over wedding plans with my sister's friend Melanie. I still can't believe all the shit that goes into planning a wedding, even a relatively simple one like ours. But, I know she's worth every penny it's going to cost me to have our wedding go smooth. I know Sam has a lot on her plate, so I want to lift the burden as much as possible.

When I look at the clock, I realize there's another hour or so until Samantha even wakes up for the day. With it being Saturday and the kids at their dad's, I want to let her sleep in as much as possible. I hop on my computer and pull up a website one of my buddies told me about. I love surprising her, and what I have in mind will definitely be a surprise. After a few clicks, it's being sent. I can't wait to see the look on Samantha's face when she receives it.

Since that took all of ten minutes, I'm left with the dreaded chore of packing. How the hell did I get so much shit after just being here four years? Last night, Samantha and I discussed what I should bring to her house. Since my living room furniture's only a year old and Samantha's furniture in her family room is much older, I'm bringing this along with my bed and dresser. As I look around my kitchen, most of this crap will be donated to a local charity or to one of the guys on base. There's no way we'll need all of this. Samantha's kitchen is already full. But while she was here, she mentioned how much she liked my coffeemaker, electric skillet, and a new set of knives. Knowing she doesn't have a waffle maker, I place that in the box as well as a few kitchen gadgets I can't live without. The rest is put aside to donate.

Just as I'm finishing up the cupboard under the sink, my phone alerts me to a text.

Samantha: Hey, handsome. How was your day?

Me: Good morning, beautiful. Packing kitchen now. Video chat?

Within seconds, Samantha's beautiful face appears on my screen. Her smile drives me wild and she has no idea the effect she has on me. She's still in bed and I can see she has just awoken by the rumpled way her hair lays behind her and the slight haziness of her eyes. She has never looked more beautiful. God, I wish I were there to wake with her each morning. Being apart from her is harder than I ever imagined. Her voice is huskier than normal as she says, "Morning, handsome."

"Good morning, beautiful. How'd you sleep?" I notice her eyes are slightly puffier than normal. I hope she hasn't been sick again.

"Fine. I'm sleepy today. These kiddos sure know how to kick my ass. I fell asleep watching a movie last night before eight."

"You're kidding me?"

"Nope, I awoke at two a.m. and found myself alone in the dark family room, freezing because my blanket had fallen on the floor." Samantha shakes her head and rolls her eyes. She couldn't look more adorable. I long to reach out and just run my fingers through her hair.

"You've had a long week. You must have been tired," I offer as encouragement.

She heavily sighs and I see her shoulders hunch through the screen. "I'm not sure how much longer I can keep this pregnancy a secret, Enzo. Frankie and Maddie both have asked if I feel all right. I'm already resorting to wearing my 'fat pants' and I won't be able to keep this under wraps if I suddenly decide to pop."

"What the hell are 'fat pants,' Sam? You're nowhere near fat," I ask, confused. She's been wearing her regular clothes in all the pictures she sends to me each day.

I can hear her eyes roll from across the screen. "Uh... Fat

pants are clothes you wear when you're feeling fat. You know, when you feel bloated?"

Uh. No. I don't know. But from the look on her face, it's best I don't mention that. "Do you need to go shopping to get a bigger size?" I offer, thinking this is something I can help her with. I've got the one-click shopping thing down to a tee. We can fix this.

"Ugg... With the others, I didn't have to wear maternity clothes until I was nearly twenty weeks. But since there's two in there... I'm guessing it'll be sooner than that." She bites on her lower lip and even from across the world, she still drives me wild.

"Why don't you and Lexi go shopping sometime this week?"

"No. I'm fine for now. I just don't like tight things around my waist. I'll just pull out my baggier clothes and that should do the trick." She then gives me a conspiratorial grin as she says, "Our secrets are safe for now." Her arm vanishes from the screen and I can imagine she's patting her belly.

"So how are the babies today?" I ask, hoping she will show them to me on the screen. Her stomach is a little fuller now, but she barely has a bump. If you didn't know she was pregnant, you could assume she'd just put on some weight in her mid-section. *There's no way in hell I'm mentioning that either.*

"They're doing great." Then in a cooing voice, she says, "They let their mama sleep in today and I haven't felt nauseous in a while. Life is good!" She moves her shirt up over her belly, then says, "Here. Have a look for yourself."

"Mornin', kiddos. Be good to your ma. I love you so much," comes out naturally as if it's not at all crazy to be talking from thousands of miles away to a beautiful belly. I can't help myself, I want my kids to know me. "I can't wait to..." Samantha interrupts me with a loud, uncomfortable groan and suddenly, I'm on instant alert. "What's wrong? Are you okay?"

"Yeah. Relax. I just moved and now I feel like the weight of the world is pressing on my bladder." Her face is now a slight shade of pink as embarrassment spreads across her features. Suddenly, the phone is a blur as she bolts out of bed. "I'll call you right back," is heard with sudden urgency in the distance and the screen goes black.

Oh, fuck. Is she sick again? Please God, let her be okay. Being halfway around the world has never sucked harder than it does at this instant. I hate not being there for Samantha.

Thankfully, my thoughts don't get too far out of control before my phone notifies me of a video call coming through. I'm greeted with a guilt-ridden face. Samantha shrugs as "Sorry," becomes the first thing I hear.

What's she sorry for? "Are you okay?" My mind nearly spins out of control wondering what could have happened to make her end the call so abruptly.

Her face turns a brighter shade of red. Her shoulders are nearly attached to her ears as she states, "Had to pee."

Seriously? I got worked up over that? I burst out with laughter. "Christ, Sam. You had me thinking you were sick again or something was seriously wrong." I laugh some more at my ridiculousness. "Had to pee? Really?"

"Well, yeah... It felt like I wasn't going to make it. I didn't want you hearing me pee." Her face suddenly screws up with a look of disgust. "Or worse, watch me pee."

"Fuck," comes out in another spout of laughter, but I somehow manage to get it under control. Somewhat. "Beautiful, I know I've never been married, so this is new territory for me, but don't you think this is something we ought to get used to?"

"Enzo," comes out almost like a curse.

"Seriously, Sam. Chances are, at some point, I'm going to see or hear you do your business. It's not a big deal."

"Maybe for you it isn't," she pouts defensively. "Nearly peeing my pants just because I rolled over is embarrassing enough, I think... I'm not even that far along. Wait until I sneeze or cough when I'm *really* pregnant... Besides, I didn't need you to experience it firsthand."

I can't win this argument, so I simply admit, "Even if you did, beautiful, I'd love you anyway. You've got nothing to be embarrassed about."

She's quiet for a moment. Her features have returned to normal and she sighs. "I know."

To change the subject, I state, "You should receive some packages in the next day or so. I bought the kids some presents to put under the tree from me, and there's one being sent to your office. I'd advise you not to open that one until you're home alone." A conspiratorial grin spreads across my face. There's no way I'm giving away her surprise. But I'll give her a warning.

"Enzo. What did you do?" She attempts to use her mom voice with me. But it won't work today.

"Some things are just better left alone," I tease. Dropping the subject, I switch to one she's sure to latch onto, and hopefully forget about her surprise until it arrives. "So, I talked with Melanie today. We hashed out a lot of the details for the wedding. She'll be contacting you today to verify things."

"Oh, really?" She glances at her bedside clock and blanches. "Did you wake her at the ass-crack of dawn or something? Geesh, Enzo. Not everyone likes to know there's two five o'clocks in a day."

I lightly laugh at her reference to my inability to sleep in. "Actually, she called me knowing I'd have time to talk."

We spend the next twenty minutes going over the details for the wedding. Before long, she has to get off the phone to make it to her hair appointment on time. As I disconnect the call, I can't believe how much I love Samantha and our newly forming family. I'm one lucky SOB to get to have her in my life. Sometimes, I shake my head in disbelief that she actually said yes. I just hope she appreciates me after the gift I'm sending her.

9

———————

SAMANTHA

WITH CHRISTMAS BEING LESS than a week away, I make the most of my time to finish last-minute details, while the kids are in school or at Devin's. While I was in Germany, I picked up a few things for Enzo and left them at the top of his closet. They're small and won't take up much space.

I know he's about done packing his apartment, but he'll still be there through Christmas. After that, he'll either bunk with a buddy in a guest room or stay on base in temporary housing, depending how often he's actually at Ramstein. He's been radio silent for a few days, since our last video call. I miss him like crazy, and though he told me to expect this to happen, it doesn't make the distance any easier. He can't tell me where he is, so for now, no news is good news. He seemed to think he'd be back on base by Christmas, so hopefully we will at least talk to one another then.

With Christmas vacation for the kids starting tomorrow, I've arranged my schedule so I won't meet with clients until the New Year. I want to relax and spend time with my family. Though various projects need my attention, I'm relieved not to have work commitments for the next two weeks.

Just as I'm about to leave the office for lunch, I get an unexpected phone call from Sara, Enzo's mother. She greets me warmly, "Hello, dear. Am I catching you at a bad time?"

"Not at all, Sara. How are you?" I ask as I sit back in my chair and stretch my legs out under my desk. For some reason, just the sound of her voice puts me at ease.

"Oh, I can't complain. I've spent the morning with Zoey and she's napping now." Sara lets out a low sigh, then laughs. "Boy, keeping up with a two-year-old is a sure way to stay young at heart. But honestly, I'm not sure who's more ready for a nap, her or me."

I chuckle right along with her at the thought. "I remember those days. Frankie always kept me on my toes..." I almost add, *just wait until we're chasing twins.* But thankfully I catch myself beforehand. *I wonder what she'll think about being a grandma again.* I can't wait until we're past our first trimester and we can tell people. I hate keeping secrets.

"So... Enzo mentioned you're going to be alone on Christmas Day," Sara states as she jumps to the point of her call. I guess Enzo was right when he said his mother never minces words.

"The kids are with me until Christmas morning. Devin's going to pick them up around ten to visit his parents in Seattle for a few days. With this being my niece's first Christmas, my parents are spending this year with my brother Blake in Montana... So yeah, I guess I'll be alone most of the day." This is the first time I haven't spent the holiday with my kids and the thought alone has my heart clenching.

"Well, we'd love to have you come spend the day with us. Everyone does their own thing on Christmas morning, but they all end up here around noon. You're welcome anytime."

Truth be told, I've been dreading spending Christmas alone this year. My plan was to do something to keep my mind off the fact my kids are so far away. Don't even get me started on Enzo. Who knew I could miss someone so much in such a short time? "That's really sweet of you to offer. Is there anything I can bring? I'm used to doing all the cooking, so I'd been wondering how I was going to fill my day since there's no use cooking for just me."

"Oh, you can just bring yourself. Relax and enjoy the holiday for once. Unless there's something you can't live without?" A holiday to sit and relax, what kind of alternate universe have I landed myself in? But I can't show up empty handed.

"I do make a great seven-layer dip I can bring as an appetizer," I offer. "Are there any food allergies I should be aware of?"

"None that we know of." Sara chuckles. "Whatever you like is fine. There will be enough to feed an army, so it's your own fault if you go away hungry."

"I'll keep that in mind." I laugh in return.

"Well, I'd better rest while the wild child does, or I'll be paying for it later. I'll let you get back to work. I'm looking forward to seeing you on Christmas Day, Samantha," Sara kindly states before we say our goodbyes.

Just as I'm leaving for lunch, the package Enzo mentioned arrives. As much as I want to rip it open now, I know I should do what he said and wait until I'm home alone. Lexi and Brenda have been in and out of my office helping me with all the last-minute things that need to be done before we take our holiday vacations. Who knows what he has up his sleeve. I place it in my bag to take out to the car later.

I spend the rest of the afternoon wrapping up things with clients before rushing out to pick up the kids from school. I've never been more thankful to have an entire unplanned evening ahead of me. I'm dead on my feet, and as soon as dinner is dealt with, I have a date with my couch. A jammies and movie night sounds amazing.

Apparently, word gets out about movie night. The next thing I know, Maddie has Soren over and Dec has invited his friend Jacob for a sleepover. I make things easier on myself and order pizza. I also pull out the air popper to make popcorn. Once the pizza arrives and we have our food and drinks, we all get settled to watch *Guardians of the Galaxy II*.

The atmosphere in the room hums with excitement. Maddie and Soren are on the opposite end of the couch as Frankie. They are close enough to hold hands, but still have enough distance between them to not cause me to worry. I'm sitting in my favorite recliner, and Dec and his friend lounge across the other couch in the room. I'm apparently the only one in the room who has yet to see the movie already, but we're all looking forward to it. I let them turn the lights down and the volume up as the movie begins, and I snuggle into my blanket.

That might as well be my demise.

The next thing I know, the lights are being flicked on and the kids are all raving about how great the movie was and what their favorite parts are. I didn't even watch any of the credits, the beginning or the end. I glance at the clock and realize nearly two and a half hours have passed. Holy crap! How could I have slept that long?

Soren stands and stretches. "Well, I'd better get going if I'm going to make my curfew on time."

"Okay." Maddie reaches out her hand to have him assist her in standing. "I'll walk you out."

I extract myself from the comforts of my recliner, placing my blanket to the side, as Maddie makes it to her feet. Then Soren turns to me. "So, what did you think of the movie?"

"Uhhh..." What am I supposed to say? I feel embarrassment spread through me as my ears heat.

Maddie lets out a sound that is a cross between a cough and a snort. "Uh, I guess you didn't see her sawing logs... I'm not sure she saw much of the movie." Maddie rolls her eyes as she shakes her head in my direction.

I inwardly cringe, feeling worse that she noticed my unplanned nap. So much for family night. I try to pull it off with a light laugh. "Uh... she's right. I don't think I saw that much of it."

Soren grins wide. "Well, you missed a great movie. You should watch it sometime when you're not so tired. Are you feeling all right?"

Maddie suddenly looks very concerned in my direction.

"Yeah, Mom, are you feeling all right? You've seemed really wiped out lately."

Not wanting to give anything away, I brush my hand in the air with denial. "No. I'm fine. Just had a long couple of weeks."

"Are you sure?" Dec chimes in. "You never fall asleep before us."

Great, now they're choosing to be extra observant?

"Guys, what's with the Spanish Inquisition? I was tired and fell asleep. No big deal." *Yeah, I'll keep feeding them that lie and watch it bite me in the ass.*

Thankfully, they let it go when I look over to see Frankie's reaction and realize she's zonked on the couch. She's at that awkward age where if I wake her, she might be up all night. I opt for just covering her with the blanket I'd been using as she stretches and takes up most of the couch. Dec and Jacob say goodnight to Soren and make their way upstairs. Maddie walks Soren to the door, then heads upstairs herself. I'm left with locking up and turning off the lights. I'm still exhausted and ready for more sleep. I drag myself up the stairs and get ready for bed.

Just as I'm about to fall asleep, I hear my text notification. I reach out for my phone on my nightstand and can't help the smile that spreads across my face.

> **Enzo: Night, beautiful. I can't talk but want you to know I am thinking about you. Love you all.**

I tap out a quick response, not knowing if he will receive it.

Me: Love you, too. Night.

With a full heart, I drift off to sleep with thoughts about the man of my dreams.

THE NEXT MORNING is a bit of a blur. I wake up and make pancakes, eggs, and bacon for everyone. I take Maddie and Frankie to the outlet mall to complete our Christmas shopping lists, while Declan spends the day with Jacob and his family. Maddie takes forever to pick out a gift for Soren, while Frankie's eager to be done shortly after arriving. Thankfully, we reach a compromise and split up to complete everything we need within a few hours.

By mid-afternoon, I'm dead on my feet. It's all I can do to make it back to the house and pull a lasagna out of the freezer to cook for dinner. Maddie offers to make no-bake cookies with Frankie and I take this opportunity to go upstairs and catch up on some reading.

As I look in the bag I brought home from work, I'm reminded of my surprise from Enzo. I love the giddy sensation that warms my body when I think of how thoughtful he is. God, I miss him so much. I can't wait until these next few weeks pass and he's here permanently. As I look at the medium-sized, non-descript box, my interest is piqued. He'd specifically told me I should open this alone. *What the hell is he up to now? Why be so secretive?* Before opening the package, I shut my bedroom door to give myself some privacy.

Of course, inside the plain cardboard box is another box. This time it's white with gold-embossed lettering in a language I can't read. I pull off the end since it slides open, but all that comes out is a charging cord, leaving the rest still in the box. *He bought me something electronic and I had to open it in private? My kids will likely know how to use it better than me.* As I pull out the plastic remains of the packaging, I find a pink object with controls and a gold-plated end. I gasp.

Oh, shit. This isn't for my kids. Holy hell, he bought me a vibrator.

Twin emotions course through me. On one hand, I'm mortified. On the other, I'm intrigued and slightly aroused. I'm so relieved I listened and opened this in the privacy of my own room. I can't imagine what would have happened if my kids had seen this.

I pull it out to inspect it further. I feel my body heat and tingle in places I haven't thought about since being with Enzo. I press one of the buttons and it comes to life. A low hum of vibration fills the room. Not knowing what all the buttons do, I press the arrow button again and the pulsation changes to a higher pitch. *Hmmmm... this has possibilities.* A vision of showing Enzo just how much I like this takes hold of my mind as I grasp one end to imagine what it would feel like inside me. I press the arrow again, and I feel simultaneously a new pattern of vibration form, and the wider end warms. *Holy crap. This sucker's heat sensitive. What else can it do?* I press the button again and the vibration speeds to a higher pitch and faster pulse.

Suddenly, I hear running up the stairs and, "Moommm," being called.

I press the down button to turn it off, but the sucker keeps vibrating. No fucking way! "Turn off. Turn off. Turn off." I will the damn thing to oblige. But no such luck. FUCK!

I hear the footsteps getting closer. Another holler of my name. *Where the hell is the off switch?* I rush to my bathroom, slam the door shut, and turn on the fan to mask the noise as I frantically keep pushing that damn arrow button to get it back to the start of the cycle. Holy fucking shit! This thing has no off switch. The sound it makes gets higher and higher, louder and louder.

When I hear Frankie enter my bedroom, I know she's only seconds away from knocking on my bathroom door. I give up. I send the vibrating, traitorous bitch into the linen closet with a hard toss and slam the door. I quickly march to the bathroom door to cut Frankie off at the pass. There's no way I can let her in here. I open the door, nearly out of breath, and shut it as quickly as possible behind me as I enter my bedroom.

"Mom?" Frankie asks with concern etched across her face.

I slowly inhale and release it, trying to steady my breathing and appear less guilty. "What's up?"

"Are you okay? Your face is really red." Frankie eyes me skeptically.

Fuck. This is so wrong. I can still hear the faint hum of the friggin vibrator mixed in with the bathroom fan, and my entire body feels as if it might burst into flames. I have to get her out of here.

Thankfully, I'm able to get my wits about me and say, "Oh,

I'm fine, I was just in the bathroom and accidentally turned on the heat lamp instead of the fan when I rushed in." God, I hope she buys it.

"Oookkay," Frankie draws out, but doesn't look as if she's convinced.

"What do you need?" I ask, trying to get the subject off me, and I'm relieved when it works. Her expression changes instantly.

"Oh, Ava just came over and asked if I can play. Can I go?" Frankie asks enthusiastically, seeming to be happily distracted.

"Sure. Be home by six for dinner."

As Frankie rushes out of the room, I sigh heavily. I fall back onto my bed from pure exhaustion and shake my head from embarrassment. I pick up my phone and dial Enzo. It goes straight to voice mail. "A vibrator. Really? Ohmigod!"

As I hang up, I see the directions have fallen to the floor. I pick them up and look for the English explanation of how to turn the fucker off. *Hold any button down for three seconds. Really?!??!?* It could've been that fucking simple?

10

———

ENZO

IT'S BEEN WAY TOO FUCKING long since I've been able
to talk with Samantha. I've been working non-stop since I last
spoke to her. Team 4 almost got their asses handed to them,
but I managed to get them to safety. I glance at the clock and
curse it again. I've already missed Christmas here, but back in
the States, it's still early evening.

I power up my phone after days of no use, and
immediately, my text notifications chime. As I look through my
voice mails, I see there's only one I want to hear. Samantha's
sexy voice is what I've been craving for days. But the minute it
comes through, I instantly cringe and my blood chills. "A
vibrator. Really? Ohmigod!"

If spoken in a different tone, those words could've been a
good thing. But there was zero excitement in her voice. Zero
room for interpretation. Unlike my expectation or intent when
I purchased her gift, she sounds like she's anything but smiling.
Fuck! How could I get things so wrong? I'd been sure she'd at

least be intrigued and hopefully aroused like me at the thought of using that badass toy together. Damn, I'm a dick.

I glance at the date on the phone for when I received the call and it's been a nearly a week since she'd left it. "FUUUUUCCCCKKKK!" I growl into my nearly empty living room. I'm so fucking screwed. She hasn't called since. There're multiple text messages, but those will have to wait. I need to talk with her now.

Waiting for our call to connect is almost unbearable. I pace between my couch and bed as I wait. Three, four, five rings later. It goes to voice mail. Fucking voice mail. Her unbelievable sexy voice pulls at my heart, making it both speed up and drop through my stomach as she tells me to leave a message. When the beep finally comes, I want to beg, borrow, and plead for forgiveness. God, what have I done?

"Samantha, beautiful. I'm so sorry. I WILL make this up to you. I love you so much. Please forgive me. Please call me no matter how late you get this message. We need to talk. Give me that chance..." Her voice mail cuts me off. It asks if I want to re-record the message or leave it as is.

Feeling completely defeated, I end the call and sink onto my bed. I cradle my head in my hands as my elbows dig into my knees. I'm exhausted and need a shower. I need to call my family. But that can wait. I have no idea how to reach Samantha if she's not answering her phone. I might as well hop in the shower while I figure out what the fuck I should do to make this right with her. I grab my phone and bring it to the bathroom in hopes I will hear from her soon.

Showers usually relieve my tension. This one, not so much. I need to hear Samantha's voice. To know we're okay and that we can work past this. I've never seen her pissed and have no fucking clue as to how to make this up to her. If it wasn't Christmas, I think I'd send her flowers or something, but everything is closed at this hour. Being so far away has never sucked so much in my life.

By the time I get out of the shower and get dressed in my favorite pair of sweats, I'm still no better off. I glance at the clock again. It's only been thirty minutes, but it feels like a lifetime. Not wanting to miss my family as they are sure to be eating Christmas dinner about now, I decide to call.

"Hello," Pops' deep voice answers.

"Hey, Pops. Merry Christmas!"

"Merry Christmas to you, too, son! It's good to hear from you. You've caught us at a great time. We've just finished dinner and are all dying to talk with you. I'll pass you to your ma, as she's already chomping at the bit. I'll catch you later as you make your rounds." Pops chuckles, knowing I'll be on the phone for a while with everyone.

"Sounds great, Pops." I settle back onto my bed, getting comfortable.

"Enzo, are you there?"

"It's me, Ma. Merry Christmas."

"I love you, Enzo. I'm so sorry you couldn't be here. But next year, you and Samantha had better plan on being here to share it with us!"

I cringe at the thought of Samantha, and my heart sinks even further. I miss my family, but for some reason, I miss

Samantha more. I need her like I've never needed anyone. Why the fuck isn't she returning my call?

"Enzo? Are you there?"

Fuck, I need to get it together. Trying to recall what she said, I stay noncommittal. "We'll see, Ma. It's not up to me to decide."

This makes Mom laugh. "Oh, spoken like a true husband. You always were quick on the uptake. Samantha's going to be one lucky girl."

I sigh heavily. "I don't know, Ma. I'm the lucky one." If she'll ever speak to me again. Christ. She's never gone so long without contacting me. Where the fuck is she?

"She's absolutely beautiful inside and out, Enzo. You sure are lucky. And she makes one hell of a pie."

Wait. Pie? "What do you mean?"

"Well, we're all eating her delicious grasshopper pie and cheesecake she brought over for dessert. I can't believe she made them from scratch. You're going to have to keep working out if you eat this delicious food of hers."

"She's there?" I ask in disbelief.

"Well, of course! We weren't going to let our future daughter-in-law stay home alone for Christmas. What kind of family would that make us?"

A mixture of relief and anxiety flow through me. I'm so fucking thankful to know where she is. She can't be too mad if she's at my parents' for Christmas dinner, but how can I be sure?

"Hey, Ma, can I speak with her?" God, I hope she'll take my call.

"From the look in her eyes, I think she's dying to."

No better words could be heard. My body instantly relaxes and I eagerly anticipate Samantha's beautiful voice. A shuffle can be heard through the phone and I'm almost at a loss for words when her voice reaches my ears.

"Merry Christmas, Enzo," comes out nearly breathless and those three simple words are all I need. The dread I'd been feeling drifts away. Even though she may be mad, I know I've worried for nothing.

"Merry Christmas, beautiful. This will be the only Christmas we're apart," I vow. There's no fucking way I'll be apart from her like this again.

Her beautiful laughter flows through the phone and warms my body from the inside out. "I'll hold you to that." Her saucy voice lingers and clutches my heart further.

"So... You're not mad at me?" I hesitantly ask, not wanting to ruin the moment, but having to know at the same time.

There's a long pause, causing my heart to plunge as I await her response. "No, why would you ask that?"

"Your voice mail. You sounded pissed."

"Voice mail?"

I cringe. Not wanting to bring it up unnecessarily, but having to make sure she isn't mad at me. "You know, about buying you a vibrator?"

Samantha almost snorts as laughter spills from her. "Ohmigod. You're never going to believe the story about that." She takes a deep breath, trying to control her laughter. "I can't tell you about it now. I'm having dinner with your family, but no, I'm not mad. Trust me, I'm anything but mad." More laughter spews out of her and I'm left a little confused.

"Are you sure?" I can't help but clarify. She sounded pissed on the phone earlier, so why the hell is she laughing so hard about it now?

"Yeah. I am." Then she changes the subject. "Are you almost done packing?"

Looking around my nearly empty room, I tell her I am.

"Did you pack those presents I left for you on the top shelf of your closet?"

"No, I left them out, so I could open them on Christmas, like you asked. But I didn't get back until today, so I've missed it."

"Well, it's still Christmas here. Go get them."

Within seconds, I have the presents she'd left in my hands and am eager to rip them open. "Which one first?"

"The square box."

Paper is ripped and the box is open within seconds. Inside is not only a watch, but a special ops watch called the Silencer. It is capable of holding a charge for months, has a compass, a strobe light for emergency signals, and a ton of other features if the box is any indication. "Wow, Sam, this is an amazing gift. A buddy of mine has one of these and they're great watches."

"I'm glad you like it. So..." She hesitates for a moment. "Have you read the inscription?"

I take it out of its box and my heart stutters. She couldn't have known just how much I needed this right now.

No measure of time with you will be enough,

but let's start with forever.
XOXO Sam

"Forever sounds great, beautiful." My throat clogs as I'm filled with emotion. Christ, this woman can bring me to my knees in an instant.

"Open the next one," she eagerly states. "That's from the kids."

I pick up the shoe-sized box and open it. It's filled with an assortment of things. Cards, notes, and a few other items all stuffed inside. What draws my attention is a silver 4X6 frame with the word family written on the bottom. This slays me. Samantha, her kids, and I are hiking at Beacon Rock. Just looking at the photo floods me with emotion, making me want to be in Portland as soon as possible.

"Wow, this is amazing," I say in awe of the love that is given.

I pull out a folded piece of paper and see that it's from Frankie. It's a drawing of a man flying a plane in the sky. Underneath are the words, 'Fly home soon. We miss you. Love, Frankie.' My heart soars.

There's also a card from both Maddie and Declan wishing me both Happy Birthday and Merry Christmas. At the bottom is a multi-color, hand-beaded bracelet with the letters *Love You, Enzo,* spelled out. "Is the bracelet from Frankie?" I ask to clarify my assumption. I can't imagine this being from Dec or Maddie.

"Yeah, it is. Will it even fit you?"

I place it around my wrist and I can't quite tie it together.

Damn. "Not really. But it's the thought that counts. I'll be sure to thank her when I talk with her next."

"She can't wait to hear from you. She's at Devin's parents, but will be home in a few days."

"I'll call her when she's home then. So, what have you been up to? Did the kids like the gifts I sent?"

"Yes. Funny you should mention that," she says in her best mom voice, letting me know I'm about to get a lecture. "You need to know what the word *control* means. You have none. If you buy gifts like this at every occasion, we'll be *broke*, and they'll be *spoiled*. Just because they are the latest and greatest gifts doesn't mean you need to buy them. You don't need to be so excessive."

"Oh." What can I say? I wanted to make sure I didn't fail at picking out their gifts.

She goes into great detail about how even though I went extremely overboard, I hit a home run with each of them. I sent Frankie the latest American Girl doll with all the necessary accessories. I got Declan a helmet with a Go Pro attached so he can record videos when he skateboards or plays soccer. For Maddie, I bought a MacBook Pro, to replace her laptop that died earlier in the month. I thought these were all things they needed. Or so they claimed when I asked for their Christmas wish lists. How was I to know this was too much? It's not like I've had kids before.

"So, does this mean you're mad about the gifts, too?" I wince as I wait for her response.

"Enzo..." she huffs. "If I'm mad at you, you'll know. There won't even be a need to ask. Trust me."

11

SAMANTHA

"LEXI, it's been eighteen days. Eighteen days! No text messages. No voice mails. Nothing. He's supposed to be back on base doing only God knows what to officially retire. He mentioned going on one last mission a few days after Christmas, but I haven't heard from him since!" I pace my office as my best friend listens to my rant from the sheer panic attack I'm about to endure.

It had started with a simple question. "How's Enzo?" from Lexi. She meant well, and I'm sure she had no idea I've been barely holding it together, let alone the can of worms she was about to open. I haven't told anyone my worries. With the firm belief in *don't borrow trouble*, I know worrying is just like praying for bad things to happen. Nothing bad can happen to Enzo. It can't. I've done my best to stay positive. I figure no news is good news, but with that simple question, I feel like I'm on the verge of losing my fucking mind.

"Sam." I hear Lexi try to rein me in as only a best friend

can. She walks over and places a hand on my shoulder, in hopes to calm me, I'm sure. But nothing she says or does will pull me back from the frenzy I'm feeling. I attempt to pull away, but she grips my wrist to make me stop pacing.

"Sam, you've got to calm down. This isn't good for you or the babies."

"I know," I moan and do my best to stop fretting for their sake. "Why haven't I heard from him, Lex? Why?"

"I'm sure there's a good explanation for this, Sam. He wouldn't do this to you on purpose."

Letting my worst fears come out, I whisper, "What if something's happened to him?" God. Please don't let anything happen to him. I almost feel guilty for voicing this aloud, but Lexi, of all people, won't judge. "We're not married, so I have no way of knowing. I'm not his next of kin." Fuck. Nothing can happen to him. *Goddammit, Enzo, where the hell are you? Why haven't you contacted me?*

"Sam, if something's happened, his family will let you know," she says, trying to be the voice of reason. "They love you nearly as much as Enzo. They wouldn't keep you in the dark."

"I know," I whisper as I let out a long, slow breath, in an attempt to calm my nerves. It works, a little. I may not be ready to jump off the deep end, but I'm not calm by any means. I'm not a crier, but I feel the prickly sensation begin around the edges of my eyes and I curse. "What the fuck's wrong with me? I can't get my shit together today and I feel like I'm going crazy."

I expect her to say something, but Lexi's silent for a

moment, which catches me off guard. When I finally stop my pacing and look her in the eye, I see her head is cocked to the side, her lips are slightly turned up in an almost smile, and she shakes her head slightly. Making me feel even more crazy.

"What?" I almost shout. *How can she be smiling at a time like this?*

"Oh." She chuckles. "That wasn't a rhetorical question?"

"Uh, no."

"Well... Let's see. One, you love him. Two, you haven't heard from him in what seems like forever, and he could possibly be in a dangerous, hostile area..."

I interrupt before she can say more, "Lex! You're not helping!"

"Hear me out, Sam." She comes over and squeezes me with one of her bigger than life hugs, which somehow creates a sense of calm over me.

"Sam, all those are reasons to be losing your shit. Add a baby or two..." She winks and I can't help but smile. "That could push anyone right over the edge."

"I know," I sigh as I wipe a stray tear that has escaped. "But what should I do?"

"Live."

What the fuck? Why would she say that? I am living!

"Sam, calm down. I'm just saying live your life the way you have been. Assume no news is good news. Calm down. Relax and try to get your mind off Enzo being gone. You can only control so many things, and some things are just beyond your control. You're going to worry yourself sick." She's quiet for a moment, then gasps. "I know... let's take the afternoon off and get our nails done."

"But I have work to do, Lex," I protest.

An eyebrow quirks, and her curly hair shakes as she cocks her head to the side to peer at me from behind her dark-rimmed glasses. "Really?" She looks around my office and at my empty desk. "You think you're going to get much done freaking out like this?"

She's got me there. There's no way I'll concentrate on anything important in this frame of mind, so I concede. "Okay, you win."

She claps her hands in triumph and hops in my direction to hug me once more, taking my breath away. "Umph... Lex. Careful, I'm carrying precious cargo here."

She pats my belly and singsongs like she's actually talking with the babies growing inside of me, "See, I know how to get your mama to calm down."

"OH MY GOD, THIS FEELS AMAZING," I nearly moan as the technician massages my feet and rubs my lower legs with hot stones. Between that and the massaging chair I'm sitting in, I feel myself completely relax. My muscles were much tenser than I'd realized.

"I hate to say I told you so, but..." Lexi trails off as she laughs.

I ignore her comment, but admit, "We need to do this more often."

"Next we're going shopping to get you some new clothes. There's no need for you to look frumpy just because you're preggers."

"Uh... how am I supposed to take that?" I feel my mouth still hanging open.

"Oh, come on, Sam. You're wearing all the clothes you usually wear when you're feeling less than the beautiful woman you are. I know you're trying to hide a baby bump until Enzo returns, but with this being your fourth pregnancy, not to mention the fact you're carrying twins, I'm not sure how much longer you can hide this."

"Lexi..."

She puts her hands up to surrender. "Hey, I was surprised to feel the bump when I teased you earlier. You have to be uncomfortable in tight clothes. I know I always was."

She's got me there. I can only wear so many leggings and sweaters. Thank goodness it's winter, but she's right. I don't think I will last much longer in these clothes. Besides, I'm down to only two skirts and a few pairs of leggings that fit anyway.

"Okay, but nothing that makes me look too pregnant."

"Define *too* pregnant. You've got two babies inside you and they want to be seen by the world. You're absolutely stunning now that you're no longer sick every morning. Why not flaunt it?"

"Lex, I hope I can hold off until Enzo returns. We want to tell the kids together. I have no idea how they're going to react. It's already going to be a big adjustment that I'm getting married in a few weeks, add twins to the mix and they might disown me," I tease.

"They will not," Lexi huffs. Then to change the subject, she asks, "So do you need any help with the wedding?"

I sigh. "No, I've just got to get fitted for my dress the week before and that's about it. Enzo and Melanie have taken care of everything."

"You sure are lucky. What bride only has to show up for her wedding?" she teases. "I'm jealous. Enzo sure is a keeper," Lexi sighs and has a dreamy look on her face.

I'm so fortunate Enzo's taken care of everything. My heart melted when he told me he wanted to get married at the Multnomah Falls Lodge, in memory of our first date. I can't wait to have him here and make this dream become a reality for both of us.

Melanie's been a godsend. She's made all the arrangements, and except for actually trying on dresses, I haven't had to do much. Sure, I've had my opinions and she has helped make those happen in every way possible. I'm sure it helps we're having a small, intimate wedding. Enzo only wanted to invite our families and a few close friends. By the time we sorted the guest list, we have about fifty to seventy-five people invited, but who knows who will actually make it, with our winter weather in the Pacific Northwest.

After our pedicures, Lexi takes me shopping for maternity clothes. Thank God, times have changed and you don't have to look like a tent when you're pregnant. I managed to get some things for work and to relax in at home. They just look a little baggy at the moment, but there's room for growth. I didn't get too many winter things, since spring will be here before we know it.

By the time I get home, I'm exhausted. Even though we got pedicures today, my feet feel tired and swollen from walking around the mall. I somehow manage to get everything unloaded from the car and put away. With the kids at their dad's house this evening, I stealthily hide the clothes from the maternity stores. No need to have snoopy eyes find my secrets.

It's only a little after seven, but my eyes feel like lead bricks, and my body is sluggish. There's nothing to describe this depth of exhaustion. I decide to give into it by going to bed early. It's not often I can do this, so I might as well take advantage. I put on my pajamas and sink into the comforts of my bed. My sheets have never felt more inviting. Within seconds of my head hitting the pillow, I feel myself fall to unconsciousness.

I'm woken by the sound of my favorite ringtone. At first, I think I'm dreaming, but when it continues, I throw myself out of bed and race for my phone I'd left in the bathroom. By the time I get to it, I'm out of breath. "Enzo..." I nearly pant. "Is that really you?"

I hear the most beautiful and sexy laugh come from the other end of the line. "It sure is, beautiful. Did I catch you at a bad time?"

I walk back to my bed and snuggle under the covers, wanting to be as comfortable as I can for any length of time he can give me. "Not at all. I fell asleep and left my phone in the bathroom."

"It's only a little after nine, are you okay?" Enzo's concern is evident in his tone. *But, God, his voice sounds amazing to my ears.*

I fluff my pillow to get more comfortable and chuckle. "Well, Lexi took me shopping and we walked all over the mall. The kids are at Devin's and I'm tired. I took advantage of a night without commitments." But this isn't what I want to talk about. "Enough about me. How are you? Where have you been? Are you okay?" I rush out in a blur.

Another chortle comes out, then I hear, "Slow down, speedy. I've been doing my damnedest to tie up loose ends and have done a bit of traveling."

"Really? Are you able to tell me where?"

Suddenly my doorbell rings.

"Hold on, Enzo, there's someone at the door." *Who the hell would be here at this time of night?*

"Sure." I hear another muffled sound of laughter.

When I get to the bottom of the stairs, I peek out the window near the door and see a large figure on the porch, which makes me cautious.

When I flip on the light, I scream at the top of my lungs as I drop my phone. My pulse hammers, my adrenaline spikes, and suddenly, any bit of exhaustion I've had today disappears.

"Ohmigod! Ohmigod!"

The fucking door won't open.

"Oh, my fucking God! This isn't happening!"

Once I finally get the deadbolt to disengage and fling myself into the strong arms of the handsome man before me, I squeeze him for all he's worth. "Where the hell have you been?"

12

———

ENZO

I HEAR a scream from the other side of the door. She's realized I'm here. The light flips on and there's a rustle at the door. I hear, "Ohmigod! Ohmigod!"

Then the knob continues to be fiddled with. But the door doesn't open.

I know I shouldn't laugh, but her excitement to get to me sounds so fucking good. I'm just as eager to break through the door to get to her. Just knowing she's on the other side of the door sets a wave of emotions through me. I can't wait to set eyes on her.

Finally, the door flings open and a blur of excitement attacks me. She hugs me for all she's worth, climbing me in the process. As her legs wrap around me, I take in the delicious scent that is entirely Samantha. I have never been more relieved to see her.

These past few weeks have been hell. Not only did I have to fly one last mission, which was a shitstorm that took longer than necessary to right itself, I had to complete all my paperwork to separate and retire from the Air Force. I had started filling them out the minute I made my decision to retire, but there was still some last-minute paperwork, inventory, and things to take care of before I could leave.

My parents will probably have my ass that I didn't invite anyone to my official retirement ceremony, but I just wanted to get stateside. Having everyone travel to Germany would have postponed my departure date. When my CO told me I was free to leave, I got my ass on the next civilian plane out of Germany. It took a lot longer flying stand-by, but I'm so fucking relieved to be here. The sight of Samantha has made it worth every bit of hassle it caused.

Samantha takes me by surprise when she says, "Where the hell have you been?"

"Doing all I could to get to you, beautiful." I nuzzle her neck and pull her tighter.

"You couldn't have called or let me know you were okay?" She pulls back and levels me with a look I hope not to see often in our future.

Fuck. I was so set on getting home to surprise her, I just spent the last two days traveling. I hadn't considered she might be worried. I'm such an ass. How could I do this to her? "I... uh..." Fuck. I don't even know what to say. Nothing will be good enough.

Samantha pulls me close again. "It doesn't matter. You're here now. We can discuss where you've been for the last eighteen days later. Let's get inside so I can greet you properly."

Fuck, this woman's amazing. I pull her in tight and kiss her one last time before saying, "I think I can get on board with that."

She still has my hand as she gestures to the bag near our feet. "Is this all you have?" She looks around for a vehicle and a brow raises skeptically and the unasked question of '*how did you get here?*' crosses her features.

"I took an Uber," I state to get the questioning look off her face. "This is all I have until the rest of my things arrive in the next few weeks." I shoulder my bag on my right while tucking Samantha in on my left. We've been apart for far too long, there's no way I'm going to let her go anytime soon.

We walk through the door and I drop my bag and jacket in the living room, then turn to face her once more. "God, you're so fucking beautiful, Samantha." Now that she's in the light, I can see sleep lines from her pillow and her hair's a rumpled mess, but she has never been more exquisite to me.

"Are you hungry?" she asks.

"Only for you," I growl as I place my hands on her hips and pull her even closer.

"I can work with that," she breathily states, making her intentions clear as her hands find their way under my shirt and slowly move up my back. When it's clear she wants my shirt off, I step back and jerk my Henley over my head.

Samantha's eyes follow my shirt over my body. A low, "You are so freaking sexy," comes out of her mouth and I can't help but laugh. She's absolutely adorable when her filter's missing.

"Not as much as you, beautiful," I say as I step toward her and close the gap between us. I reach out and kiss her soundly as my hands become reacquainted with her body. There's no fucking way I will ever get enough of her. "Let's go upstairs."

I reach out to pick her up, but she shifts out of the way, and with a mischievous look in her eyes, she taunts, "Race you."

Before I can even register her intent, she's sprinting in the direction of the bedroom. I'm right on her trail, but instead of going to her bed as I expect, she races to the bathroom. "Give me a second."

"Oookkkaay," I draw out, wondering why she's going to the bathroom alone and not inviting me in, since she was nearly climbing me downstairs. A few seconds later, my question is answered when I hear the toilet flush, water turn on, then a cupboard door or two be thrown open and slammed shut. "Uh... Sam, everything okay in there?"

"Yep, be right out. Just want to get something."

Within another moment, Samantha walks out and completely leaves me breathless as she stands there in nothing but her naked glory. My eyes slowly roam up and down her body as I take her in, noticing some distinct changes due to pregnancy. Beautiful can no longer be a word that can adequately describe her. I suck in a deep breath before I pass out and continue to take in her features.

Her breasts immediately have my attention as they appear to have grown since last time I saw her. Her areolas have darkened, and her arousal is evident as her nipples pebble in my presence. They're pressed out further than normal because her hands are behind her back, apparently holding something. As I look further, I can see the beautiful swell of a very defined baby bump that I can't wait to cradle and put my hands on. I want to kiss every square inch of her body, devour her in ways I never thought were possible, and never let her go. I lick my lips in anticipation.

She clears her throat. Her face is an unusual shade of pink, as a sly grin forms. "Eyes up here, mister."

Damn, she caught me, but I have no shame. "I know, Sam, but how do you expect me not to take inventory since it's on display?"

"Um...." She appears shy for an instant. *What's she so hesitant about?*

"This is me, Samantha." I try to assure her she has nothing to worry about. "What's going on?"

"I... Uh... Thought we might try something."

Well, this has my attention. What could she possibly want to do that we haven't done?

"What do you have in mind?" I ask, my interest entirely piqued.

"You know that *gift* you bought me?"

From the way she says *gift*, my mind immediately goes to the vibrator, but I don't want to be a complete horndog. "By gift, you mean..."

From behind her back comes the vibrator in question. She hands it to me and lowers her lashes in a sultry way that would make me do just about anything for her. "Wanna play?"

Holy fuck! I was expecting a good old-fashioned ravishing, but she's up to bringing toys into the bedroom. I'd bought it to help get her off while I was gone, but if I'm being honest, I've often fantasized about using it with her as well. I've been dying to bring her to the edge so many times, she begs me to finish.

Before I can utter a word, my body kicks into overdrive and I find myself frantically kicking off my shoes and ridding myself of the rest of my clothes. "You can bet your sweet ass I'm interested in playing, beautiful," I growl when I reach out and pull her mouth to mine. I'm not sure how long we stand here kissing one another, but when she pushes me toward the bed, I take the hint.

Once there, we trade positions so that she's with her back on the bed. She quickly scoots up to lay her head on the pillow and I can't help but climb up after her. I nip and suck at each and every part of her body as I make my way up each sensual curve. My lips trace her inner thighs and she squirms in anticipation. I purposely skip over her center and make my way up to her belly bump. It's small, but it's extremely evident and couldn't be sexier. This woman's pregnant with my children and I'm the lucky bastard she's agreed to marry.

"Hello," I whisper as I get to her belly button. "Daddy's home and he's going to get to see you grow every day now."

"Enzo," Samantha groans. "I know you love our kids. But their mama has needs."

I know she's joking, but I can't help but laugh at the pure desperation in her voice. "Okay, beautiful. I won't keep you waiting."

I trace the frame of her body with my lips as I place an arm above her to brace myself and not put weight on her. Once I reach her neck, I go to the place that drives her wild behind her ear. She squirms, and I know I've met my mark.

With my free hand, I reach over and grope around the spot where I saw Samantha set the vibrator down. I continue to assault her with my lips and drive her wild in the best way I can. It feels like fucking forever, but finally, I find it and bring it to my face so I can peer at the buttons and switch it on. When she hears the vibrator come to life, her entire body jolts and I feel her body arch to reach mine, making me nearly want to forget about the toy in my hand.

"If you press the buttons again, it changes modes," she desperately pants.

What Samantha wants, Samantha gets. I'm just as desperate to fuck her like a wild animal, but if she wants to play first, I'll play with her until her heart's content. I press the button a few times and finally, I hear her breathless declaration. "There. That one. Gets me off like a rocket every time."

Holy fucking shit! Her words alone have me nearly coming undone. The thought of her actually using this to get herself off is a turn-on like no other. I bring it to her clit and gently massage it. I swipe it to her center and bring her wetness up to act as a natural lubricant. The way she simultaneously moans, arches her back, and claws at my biceps lets me know I'm doing something right. I reach down and grab a nipple with my mouth and tug ever so slightly.

"Oh... Enzo. Right. There," is one of the sexiest things I have heard.

I continue this until my need becomes too great. I have to taste her. I pull back on my haunches and press the wand inside of her as I take her clit in my mouth. I don't think she lasts longer than seconds before she detonates around me. Her body thrashes and screams fall from her lips.

"Holy. Fucking. Hell. Are you trying to kill me?" she pants as she pulls my hair to get me to back off. "I can't take any more. Ohmigod. I feel too much. It's sooo fucking good. I never thought I'd say this, but you have to turn it off."

Instantly, I pull the wand out her and leave it still vibrating on the bed. I reach down and press my hand to her slit and I feel the most indescribable tremors racking her body.

"Keep that up, Enzo. Ohmigod. It feels amazing." She places her hand over mine and presses harder, sending wave after wave of aftershocks going through her body. I've never seen anything so erotic in my life. The look of pure bliss that spreads across her face would keep me here for days.

I lie down beside her, keeping my hand in place as I prop my head up with my other one. I reach over and kiss her neck and she turns her face to kiss me. I lose track of time as I get swept up in a kiss. Her body eventually stops shaking and she shifts positions to reach my raging erection. God, if I let her touch me much longer, I will explode.

"Beautiful," I give out a warning and the next thing I know, she's straddling my lower legs as my erection bobs between us. She fists it and strokes me up and down. Her delicate fingers are firm and knowing their effect. A wide grin spreads across her face and I know she's up to something.

"I read about something online." *God, what could she possibly do now?* I'm seconds away from busting a nut and she acts like she wants to go all night long torturing me.

She lifts up to climb on top of me and I hold her hips to keep her steady. *She slides down my shaft until I'm balls deep in her and slowly works her way up.* She feels amazing. *Slow and steady will be the death of me, but what a way to go.*

"Christ, Sam," I growl. "You're killing me."

If I thought slow and steady was going to do me in, I was wrong. She steadies her hand on my chest and reaches over to grab the vibrator. Realizing her intentions, I eye her quizzically. *What's she up to now?*

She switches the speed, causing the pulse to make slow then fast movements and places it on the base of my shaft. Fuuuccckkk, that's the strangest and most amazing sensation I've ever felt. I've never used toys for myself, but holy hell, this takes things to an entirely new level. Each time she bottoms out, she grinds her clit onto it, sending me into the most epic orgasm I've never known to exist. Her breasts bounce in the best way, being etched into my mind forever. I do my damnedest to hold on until I feel her break apart.

I know she's there when she screams, "Enzo, omigod! I'm... I'm..." A large breath of air releases and as soon as she feels me emptying into her, she pulls the vibrator away and collapses onto my chest, panting hard and out of breath.

I lace my arms around her as we come down from whatever universe we'd just entered. I flip us to our sides, still completely seated in her, so she doesn't put any weight on our babies. I rub her back and hear her breathing settle to normal.

Before I know it, her breath is so deep I'm sure she's fallen asleep. The fact I'm still in her twitching like crazy has no effect on her. I pull back slightly and brush her hair from her face. Crap. She's asleep. *What the hell am I supposed to do now?* I can't say this has ever happened before. Talk about a hit to the ego. But I've never orgasmed like that either. I have two options: disentangle and clean us up or deal with the mess later. Her pussy feels like magic and I don't want to let her go for a second. Samantha in my arms is the absolute best fucking feeling in the world. After days of traveling, I'm exhausted, too. I reach over and cover us up with the blankets and drift off to sleep.

13

____

SAMANTHA

I'M HAVING the most erotic dream of my life. I know it's a dream but it feels so amazing and real. I miss Enzo so much, I may never want to wake up. Enzo's finally here and we're snuggled in bed. I have my back to him and he's rubbing my clit in slow, lazy circles. I feel him lift my leg over his outer thigh and he thrusts inside of me. He's buried to the hilt inside of me and kisses my neck as his fingers work their magic. His soft whispers feel phenomenal against my neck as he does his best to make love to me.

His, "I love you so much, Samantha," sounds too real to be just a dream and the hairs on my neck tickle as I feel a warm breath flow over them.

"Oh, Enzo. God. Enzo. Don't stop," I moan and bring my own hand down to touch myself. But instead of feeling myself, I'm met with strong hands.

My eyes bolt open. *Holy crap. This is really happening. Enzo's really here. Last night wasn't just a dream. God, Sam, your imagination runs wild.* I reach up and pull his face closer to mine and turn my head to kiss him for all I'm worth. Reality is so much better than a dream.

By the time we actually surface from the bedroom later that morning, it's nearly eleven. I'd only gotten up once to call Lexi and let her know I wouldn't be in today. Thankfully, I didn't have any meetings with clients, so I'm able to take the day off without any repercussions. I would've taken it off even if I had to reschedule an entire day of meetings. There's no way I'm letting Enzo out of my sight anytime soon. That man has been away from me long enough.

We're settling down for breakfast, well, lunch really, when I ask, "So, what are your plans today?"

"Um..." He smiles around a bite a food and his freaking dimple pops. It gets me every time. I'm glad I'm sitting as I feel myself go weak in the knees. I've spent an entire night with him and I still can't get enough.

"Well..." Enzo wipes his face with a napkin then continues, "I will need to pick up a rental car at some point."

"How long will it be until your things arrive?" I know he said a couple of weeks, but maybe he knows something specific.

"If it goes like it usually has, it could still be a few weeks, possibly a month. My things have to arrive, then they have to clear customs before they're released to me."

"That seems like a long time. Are you sure you want to waste the money on a rental car? I'm sure we can work things out, and you could use mine."

"Samantha," Enzo chastises. "We need two cars. I've seen

your crazy schedule and I want to lighten the load. Not add to it."

"Or... Since Maddie's starting driver's ed and my car won't be big enough for the new additions to our family." I involuntarily pat my stomach as I mention the reminder, then continue, "I was considering getting myself another car. We're going to need three within the next year."

"Well, that has possibilities. When does she start driver's ed?"

I laugh as I remember the argument she finally won. "Well, her fifteenth birthday's next week, on the sixth of February. She's miraculously convinced her father she should be enrolled as soon as she is legally allowed, to get as much experience as possible."

"Her birthday's next week, and you've never mentioned it?" He drops his fork to his plate and stares in disbelief.

"In my defense, I didn't think you'd be home. I would have told you, but it's never come up."

Enzo places his hand over his left brow and shakes his head as he looks at the table. I think I hear him mutter, "I'm an ass." But I'm not sure.

"What's wrong, Enzo?" I ask, wondering what he's calling himself an ass for.

"We'll be married in a few weeks, Sam. Don't you think I should know your kids' birthdays? I knew Maddie's was in February, but not the exact date."

I reach my arm out to comfort him. "Enzo. Honey. It's okay. I don't know your family's birthdays either. We have time to learn that." I get up from the table and walk to him and place my arms around his neck.

I kiss him once as his arms snake around my waist. "For the record, Declan's birthday is April fifteenth, and you already know Frankie's is November eighteenth." I kiss him on the nose before adding with a tease, "And so you never get into trouble, mine's June eleventh."

"Okay, smartass. I know that one." He swats me on the ass and pulls me close for a quick kiss. "I guess I just forgot Maddie's. I knew the rest. I've just been busy lately."

"Uh, you could say that again." Just thinking about what he's done in the last few weeks alone has given me hives. I'm glad it was him and not me moving to another continent.

"So what kind of car are you thinking?" His eyebrows waggle, letting me know he's no longer upset.

"Well, we need something that seats at least seven if we're all together."

"Holy shit, our family is huge," he says in disbelief.

"Well, you and your super sperm have seen that we're growing by two, in just a mere matter of months," I tease. "And —Just to be clear, there's no freaking way I'm driving a minivan. You can do it all you want, but I refuse. Even with our ginormous family, I refuse to stoop to that level."

"Um, not that I ever pictured myself rolling up in a minivan, but what do you have against them? Aren't they what all the hip parents are driving these days?"

"Ugh! Not on your life. You just watch when we go to pick up the kids from school today. Everyone has one... It's like they multiply like bunnies. They're everywhere. Nope. No way.

Not for me. I like driving on the beach and not worrying about bad weather."

Enzo's expression turns surprised. "Okay. No minivans."

We spend more time talking about the possibility of different vehicles to drive, but never come to a consensus. He agrees that until we find the right vehicle for us, we'll just use my car to get us around. He doesn't have to report for work with Riggs until after our wedding, so it shouldn't be a problem.

Since Enzo's the epitome of punctual, we get out of the car and walk to meet Frankie and Dec at the front of the school, instead of pulling through the drive-thru parking routine, or the DNR as I refer to it each morning when the kids are running late and I have to push them out the door to arrive on time. He hoots with laughter when I inform him DNR refers to Dump-N-Run.

Students file out of the school as Enzo and I take notice of just how many minivans fill the parking lot. He had no idea they even made that many different models of the same car.

A high-pitched scream interrupts our conversation. Before either of us can register who made the noise, Frankie launches herself at Enzo. Thank God, his reflexes are phenomenal. He manages to catch her as she jumps into his arms and squeezes him with all she's got. I've never seen her so excited to see anyone, and her reaction instantly melts my heart. Apparently, I wasn't the only one to miss him so much.

"Enzo!" She pulls back to look him in the eye but doesn't let go. "You're here," comes out in almost a whisper in comparison to the scream she released just seconds ago.

The look of pure joy that spreads across his features makes my ovaries burst. There's nothing better than seeing the man you love, loving your children as much as you do. Holy hell. The burst of emotion that flows through me nearly has my eyes springing a leak. As I wipe at my lashes, I shake my head and curse. *These damn hormones.*

"I'm here, sugar." Enzo squeezes her once more before placing her on the ground and ruffling her hair. "How was your day at school?"

"It was good. I was on the school news for the Joke of the Day."

"Really? What's the joke?" Enzo asks like he's waiting on pins and needles.

"A farmer had one hundred ninety-six cows in a field. But when he rounded them up, he had two hundred." Frankie laughs so hard at her own joke, we can't help but join her.

When Declan spots us, his pace picks up. "Hey, Enzo, when did you get back?" He, too, surprises me when he hugs Enzo in front of everyone. Enzo should cherish it. I don't even rate like that these days.

"Last night. What do you say to picking up your sister from school and going out to dinner to celebrate?" Enzo eagerly suggests.

As Frankie shouts, "Yes!" Dec has a defeated look cross his face and mumbles, "Can't."

Before I can interject, Enzo notices immediately. "What's wrong, bud?"

Declan kicks a rock on the pavement as he states, "I have soccer tryouts this week. I won't be done until seven."

Enzo nudges his shoulder to gain his attention as they walk side by side. "Dec, we have no problem waiting for you."

"Really? Mom always feeds Frankie while I'm at practice." He looks to Enzo for assurance.

"We can grab you both a snack on the way to practice," I offer, knowing how crushed Declan would be if we celebrated without him.

Relief washes over Enzo's features as he adds, "It wouldn't be a celebration without you, Dec."

When Maddie rushes to the car in the high school parking lot and automatically opens the passenger door to jump in, she's surprised to find me sitting here. She'd been oblivious with her face glued to her phone as she shot off another text to one of her friends. When she sees our driver, she screams, "Oh. My. God! Enzo, you're back!"

His deep chuckle fills the car as he points with his thumb behind him to the one and only empty seat left in the car. "I sure am. Hop in."

Since all three kids rarely sit in the back seat together, I notice what a tight fit it's becoming. Frankie sits in the middle and she bobs up and down with excitement when she fills Maddie in on our plans for the evening. I can't help but feel content when I see how effortless it is to have Enzo as a part of our daily routine.

While we wait for Declan to finish practice, Enzo asks if I'd mind driving by a few car lots to pass the time. He insists we won't buy one, but wants to get an idea of what I am looking for. It gets a little dicey when we let it be known to the sales woman we're looking for vehicles that seat seven or eight.

Frankie shouts out, "Why do we need something so big? Is it because Enzo's so tall? He needs more leg room?"

Like a fish, Enzo's mouth opens. He attempts to say something, then closes it again. He's got to have an answer for everything if he's going to keep up with her.

I burst out laughing and tears threaten to flow as well as some other bodily functions, forcing me to cross my legs as I bend with laughter. *The joys of being pregnant, for the fourth time.* I manage to mutter when I catch my breath, "Enzo... This is all on you." Though I'm referring to his super sperm and cock an eyebrow in his direction, the girls look to him for an answer.

Enzo finds his voice and without skipping a beat, asks, "Don't you like having friends come with you?" *Damn, the man's smooth.*

The girls seem to take it in stride and we move on to look around the lot. Even though we're both perfectly content to purchase a used vehicle with low mileage, Enzo insists on looking at the new vehicles because they have better safety ratings and warranty options. Though we find a few vehicles that would fit our needs, we tell the saleswoman we need more time when we realize it's time to pick up Declan and make our way back to the soccer fields.

As soon as Dec enters the car, he nearly shouts with excitement, "You'll never guess what happened tonight at practice. I made the team!" He bounces in his seat as he fumbles with his seat belt.

I knew he'd make the team. There are three in his age

group and plenty of positions to go around. "That's great, Dec!" I encourage.

"No, Mom. You don't get it. I made the top team."

"Wow, Dec. That's awesome." Maddie fist bumps him as Frankie lets out a squeal of excitement.

"I knew you could do it," I state proudly.

Enzo chimes in with, "Now we have something to really celebrate! Why don't you pick where you want to go for dinner?"

Without a second of hesitation, Declan exclaims, "John's Incredible Pizza!"

"Pizza it is." Enzo's smile is infectious as he puts the car in drive.

14

SAMANTHA

ENZO BEING home is better than I could have imagined. Waking up in his arms and falling asleep in them every night is more than a dream come true. Between being pregnant and making up for lost time with Enzo, I may be tired but I've never been happier. With Maddie's birthday tomorrow evening and our wedding next weekend, Enzo and I have been in pure planning mode.

Thank God for our wedding coordinator. All I need to do this week for the wedding is try on my dress. I hope like hell it still fits. My boobs are getting out of control and the baby bump is evident, especially if I wear anything remotely fitted. Being in my second trimester usually does this to me, but these twins want their presence known. I can't wait for the wedding to be over with, so everything will be official, and we can tell the kids about the new additions to our family.

As I drive to meet Lexi at the mall to do some last-minute shopping, I can't help but smile when I think of how sweet

Enzo is with our children. He not only continues to go out of his way to get to know Maddie, Dec, and Frankie better, but he has daily conversations with the babies growing inside me. Sure, there's been some stumbling blocks along the way, like Frankie trying to play both of us to get extra dessert before bed, but there hasn't been anything we can't handle.

Lexi meets me outside of our favorite department store and gives me a low whistle.

"What was that for?" I ask, looking around to find what I'm missing out on.

"Your girls." She looks pointedly at my boobs and smirks. "Have they grown overnight? I swear, you wore that shirt last week and looked nothing like you do today."

I feel my eyes roll at her dramatic statement. Sure, they've grown, but I don't think it's too noticeable. Dripping with sarcasm, I reply, "I give new meaning for needing an over-the-shoulder boulder holder, don't I?"

"You've got that right. I'm sure you don't have any complaints from that sexy man of yours, though. You look hot!" She waggles her eyebrows to emphasize her point and I can't help but laugh.

"Enzo certainly has taken a liking to them." I shake my head and look down at my chest. Crap. I can't see my toes since my chest is in the way. "But seriously, I think we need to add shopping for bras to our list today."

"As long as we pick up something sexy for your honeymoon, too."

"Lex, Enzo's seen the goods." I point to my belly and laugh. "He's sampled them, too, obviously. I'm not even sure something will be considered sexy in the size I'm going to need."

"Now you're being ridiculous, Sam. This is his first night as a married man. You need something sexy as sin that will have his heart beating out of his chest."

The thought alone has me picking up my pace to the boutique. I can't wait to find something that will blow Enzo's mind.

Unfortunately, as soon as I'm back in the dressing room with a bra I thought would be my size, I realize I need to be fitted. These suckers have taken on a life of their own and I have no idea what will contain them. The sales associate comes to fit me, and my jaw drops when she reveals my size. When Lexi hears it, she laughs hysterically.

"What the fuck is E?" I mutter after the saleswoman goes to get some choices in my size.

"E is for enormous," Lexi boldly states, like this is a normal occurrence.

"I didn't even know they went past size D," I complain. Holy Hell, I'm huge. I've always been a C-cup. How the hell did I get this big? "Being a woman, sucks."

"No kidding," Lexi commiserates with me, then adds with a straight face, "No man ever has to measure their parts to get something to fit. Heck, no one even thinks man parts should be supported, except for direct-contact sports."

So many images flash through my mind at her comment. The thought alone of how they would even measure it has me in stitches, making me lean against the wall for support. "Only you would think of that, Lex. Thanks for the mental image I now need to burn from my mind."

Once we contain our laughter, Lexi gets back to business. "Now that we know your size, let's get you something sexy to wear."

By the time I arrive home, I'm dead on my feet. Lexi's a born shopper. She managed to help me find something I can't wait to wear on my honeymoon and finish picking out Maddie's birthday gift. The woman's a shopping queen. I even picked up my ring for Enzo from the jewelers, now that I know his ring size.

The next morning, after getting the kids off to school, Enzo and I do some last-minute preparations for Maddie's birthday party this evening. For some reason, Maddie convinced us having a birthday party on a Friday night would be a good idea, but this means I had to take the day off for preparation. Enzo volunteered to run errands this morning, while I cook some of Maddie's favorite foods. Maddie thinks a taco bar will be a hit. Everyone gets what they want, and I can do a lot of the prep work earlier in the day.

At first, Maddie wanted a sleepover with a few of her closest friends. Then she wanted to invite Soren, a few of his friends, as well as some other guys. Needless to say, nearly thirty teenagers will arrive around seven.

Devin and his girlfriend Aubrey are coming over to help celebrate, as well as be adult reinforcements. This should make Maddie's first boy-girl party interesting. Devin promises to behave, but keeps teasing her about walking around with a ruler when people dance, making sure we have every light on in the house, and that Frankie and Dec will be on patrol. *Heaven help him if he actually follows through with any of this.*

Just as I bend over to reach the pan of seven-layer dip at the bottom of the fridge, I feel two strong arms snake around my waist, making me yelp in surprise. *How the hell can Enzo be so stealthy? Was he a ninja in another life?*

"Hey, beautiful," he whispers into my ear.

"How do you always manage to sneak up on me?" I forget about the food and twist in his arms to face him. His smile makes his dimple pop and my knees go weak. *How can I still feel this way after all this time? Won't I build up an immunity at some point?*

"I simply walked in the room, Sam. Nothing to get worked up about." He nestles into my neck and kisses up to my earlobe. "God, I hope you never get immune to me. I love how responsive you are."

There's a carnal need to be closer to him, but the doorbell rings and we hear feet coming down the stairs, forcing Enzo to pull away. Frankie's the one person who will never sneak up on you in this house. I turn to hide in the fridge for a moment, regaining control of myself. Remembering why I was in here to begin with, I grab the seven-layer dip to place on the center island where I have the rest of the food laid out, ready for the party.

Enzo greets Devin and Aubrey, "Glad you could make it. Come on in. You can put the presents in the family room on the table set up, and I'll put this beer and bottle of wine in the fridge."

Devin reaches out his hand to shake in greeting before he

walks to put the gift out of the way. Aubrey follows Enzo into the kitchen.

"Wow, Sam. You've outdone yourself." She looks around hesitantly. "Is there anything I can do to help you get ready?"

"I've about got it covered. But if you want, you can put some serving spoons in these dishes. The kids should arrive shortly, and we told everyone to bring their appetite." I laugh as I point to the drawer beside her to find the spoons.

Devin walks into the room and looks around. "Looks good, Sam. When will everyone arrive?"

"They'll be here at seven," Frankie pipes in as she picks up a chip to snack on.

Devin looks at his watch. "So, how many boys?"

Of course, he goes there. This is Devin. I shouldn't be surprised. Maddie comes barreling into the kitchen. "Daaad, you promised," she pleads, then looks to me for help. "Mom, you won't let him be mean to my friends, will you?"

Before I say anything, Devin adds, "Don't worry, Mads. I'm teasing." He walks to her and gives her a hug. "A dad has some duties in life. Scaring boys is just part of the fun."

It's hard to contain our laughter but I manage to keep a straight face at least for a few seconds until Maddie turns away. Poor girl. She's been stressed about her dad all afternoon. Hopefully, her friends will arrive soon, so she can get out of the hotspot.

"So, Maddie, did you pass your test to get your learner's permit?" Aubrey changes the subject gracefully and Maddie changes her mood drastically.

If the grin on Maddie's face was any bigger, it would split in half. "Yep!" she draws out, popping the end.

"That's great, sweetheart. I'm happy for you."

"Now, I just need people who are willing to ride with me," Maddie teases as she looks pointedly around the room at each of the adults.

"I'll take you later this week when you come to visit," Devin offers as he attempts to rustle her hair but she dodges his hand.

"Can I stay home?" Frankie pleads. "I'm too young to die," she dramatically adds, making us laugh.

"Cut it out, Frankie." Maddie glowers in her sister's direction. Then points her focus on me, raising a knowing eyebrow.

"Of course, Mads," I offer, but before I can say more, Enzo interrupts.

"Add me to the list. I know the perfect place to practice and no one will be in any danger." He winks at Frankie.

"Wow. It looks like I'll be getting lots of experience."

The doorbell rings and Maddie's friends soon fill our home. Soren's the first to arrive, and more guests immediately follow after him. He greets Maddie with a kiss on the cheek. That's bold with both Devin and Enzo in the room, but he's been doing this for some time. Maybe they're immune? I glance to Devin who narrows his eyes in Maddie's direction. Not everyone is immune to this, apparently. Dads will be dads. He can deal with this. I need to show our guests where the food is and keep the kitchen stocked.

The party's in full swing by the time I take my first break.

Presents have been opened, cake has been served, and everyone's eaten. Well, they've been through the kitchen multiple times. If they go hungry, that's on them. I'm not sure the total headcount, but if I had to guess, I'd say there were more than thirty teenagers here. Aubrey, Enzo, and I sit at the island in our kitchen while Devin plays a video game with Declan and Frankie in his room. Enzo sits beside me, stroking my leg absentmindedly as he takes a drink from the beer in his other hand.

Aubrey stands and walks to the fridge. "Want some wine?" she offers as she pulls it out.

"No, thanks," I sigh regretfully when I see the bottle again. I love Latah Creek's huckleberry wine.

She looks at the bottle, and then at me. "Did I get the wrong kind? I swear Devin said this is your favorite."

"No," I exhale, remembering the taste of the Riesling she holds in my direction. The thought alone makes my mouth water. It'll be months before I can relax with that deliciousness again. "He's right. It's my favorite." I stare at the bottle, wishing I could have a taste. It's not like I drink it often, but knowing I can't have it makes me suddenly want it.

"You sure? I feel bad drinking it without you. I can save it for you and drink something else, if you don't want to open it," she offers sincerely. As I've gotten to know Aubrey more this evening, I really do think we could be friends in the future. We seem to have much more in common than I imagined.

My hand instinctively rubs along my growing belly, under the countertop. "No, go ahead and enjoy it. There's no sense in letting it just sit there."

"Really?" Her head tilts to the side, gauging my response.

"Absolutely."

"Here." Enzo reaches for the bottle. "Let me open it for you."

He walks to a drawer on the far side of the kitchen and pulls out the corkscrew to open it for her. I can't help but be mesmerized by his muscular back as he removes the cork from its bottle. Is there anything he does that isn't sexy? Before returning to Aubrey, he pulls out a wine glass from the cabinet and pours it for her.

"Thank you, Enzo," she says, then takes a sip and quietly moans. "Wow. This is so good. I've never had it before."

She brought it just for me? How sweet of her. "It's fantastic," I offer.

Aubrey returns to her chair on our side of the island and glances at my hand rubbing along my stomach and quirks an eyebrow in my direction. "You sure you don't want any?"

"Really, I'm fine. Just relax and enjoy yourself. We'll have to make the rounds soon enough to check on everyone."

Her face fills with a knowing expression and I realize she's staring at my hand caressing my stomach. Crap. There's no denying my actions. I hear Enzo let out a quiet chuckle as he realizes the cat's out of the bag.

Aubrey whispers in our direction, "Are congratulations in order?"

"We want to wait until after the wedding before saying anything," I whisper in return, so that it won't become a rumor spreading throughout the party and the kids find out.

"Wow." Aubrey's eyes turn wistful. "That's amazing. I've

always wanted to have kids of my own someday. But that's not in the cards for me."

How sad. Aubrey would make a great mom. The kids seem to love her. "I'm sorry."

"Oh, don't be. It's not like I can't get artificially inseminated, should I choose to."

What the hell is she talking about? Why would she need to do that? Better yet, why is she telling us this?

The puzzled look on my face must make her want to explain further. "Well. You know..." She looks in the direction that Devin left to play with the kids. "With Devin's vasectomy and all. If he and I stay together, I'll have to either accept that I won't have kids of my own, adopt, or since Devin refuses to get it reversed, I could always go to a sperm bank." She giggles a little at the end. *Just how much has she had to drink?*

I feel Enzo tense beside me. I can't look in his direction. I'm shocked by the news of Devin's vasectomy. I try to respond, but my thoughts get stuck in my head. When did he do this?

Without any prompting, Aubrey continues, not realizing she's just dropped a bomb on me. "I can't see him wanting any more than three kids, since that's the reason he got the vasectomy in the first place. Right after Frankie was born."

What. The. Fuck. "Devin's had a vasectomy?" I mumble to myself.

Enzo must hear. He suddenly stands from the stool he was perched on and holds out his hand to me. He glances at Aubrey. "Would you excuse us for a second?"

Aubrey says something, but I have no idea what it is. I feel myself being tugged up the stairs to my bedroom. My mind keeps replaying the last few moments on a loop. I can't even think of how to respond. I'm so stunned Devin's had a vasectomy. *Wait. Right after Frankie was born?* Holy fucking shit! All those months of us trying to get pregnant. Month after month of having my period. Those tears I shed when I started my cycle each month.

As we reach the top of the stairs, I feel like it's getting harder to breathe. My chest tightens and my eyes sting from the prick of tears attempting to fall. What the actual fuck? Devin had a fucking vasectomy years ago and didn't bother to tell me? My vision blurs completely and suddenly, all I see is red.

15

ENZO

I DIDN'T HEAR that correctly. There's no fucking way the
fucker got a vasectomy years ago and didn't tell Sam. Who the
fuck does that shit to his wife? Or at least, let her be a part of
the decision. I can't help but think of when the condom broke
in her office. She heartbreakingly explained why she thought
she couldn't have kids. It's evident she'd been devastated each
and every fucking month. Hell, I'd been decimated for the
sheer thought of her loss.

What a cock-sucking bastard. I knew he was selfish. Who
the fuck cheats on a woman as amazing as Samantha? Since
I've met him, I can't say Devin and I have been close or
anything, but we seem to have a mutual respect for one
another. We get along for the sake of the kids. Now, I just want
to punch his fucking throat out.

The look on her face when the realization hit. I'd murder
him right now and spread his body across the continents, if I

knew it wouldn't hurt the kids or Samantha even more. I had to get her out of that fucking kitchen as fast as possible. There's no way I would let her implode, or worse, explode in front of Maddie and her friends.

Christ. What the fuck do I say to her? I can tell she's working herself up. I've never seen her mad, but if I were in her shoes, I'd blow a gasket. I'm not even the one who had to deal with having a period month after month, thinking something was wrong with me. Fucking bastard isn't even a strong enough word to describe my loathing for Devin at this moment.

As soon as we're in the privacy of our bedroom, I shut the door, quickly pull her to me, and kiss the top of her head. "It's okay, beautiful. I'm right here. There's nothing you can say that will make me love you any less. Get it off your chest and let's deal with this together." I wrap my arms around her tightly and feel her body taking large breaths, as if to calm herself.

"I... I... I can't even..." she mumbles as she pulls me tighter.

"Shhh, beautiful. It's all right. I'm right here. Just say what's on your mind and let's get it out there."

Her voice is calm, but there's an eeriness when it's barely heard above a whisper. "Enzo. He kept this from me, for years. He mentioned wanting to get one, once. But he never told me he went through with it. I'd told him I wasn't sure if I wanted more kids. I wanted to wait and see how things went with Frankie before any final decisions were made. When she was about a year old, I realized I wanted a little brother or sister for her. Maddie's so much older than Dec, it's like she was an only child. There's always an odd man out."

I don't say anything but hold her closer.

"Devin started working more trips out of town to help cover the costs of the new baby. Holy shit!" she suddenly exclaims, as if she has had a new thought. "You don't think he started having affairs around that time, do you?" Samantha's fists ball up and I can tell she's getting angrier by the second.

"I have no idea. But anyone who'd cheat on you is a fool, Samantha. You're the most amazing woman in this world. I'd be so lost without you," I offer as I pull her close once again.

Samantha holds me for a long while. Eventually, her breathing calms, her body loosens, and her mold to me intensifies somehow. Thousands of thoughts run through my mind. None of which are worth repeating, as they would only fuel the fire of discontent.

"Was I a fool for not knowing?" Samantha's voice is weak and breaks at the end, causing my heart to constrict. I fucking hate seeing her in pain. Devin's lucky she's my priority right now. Her self-doubt rips me apart and who the hell knows what I'd do if he and I were alone right now.

"This is on him, Samantha," I grit out as I pull her closer. What a bastard. Now she's doubting herself.

"Why wouldn't he tell me?" she asks, but I'm sure it's for her benefit, not mine. I sure as hell don't have the answer. How the hell is this her fault?

"We'll get to the bottom of this once Maddie's friends leave," I suggest, not wanting her to cause a scene.

I seriously can't wait to hear what Devin's fucking excuse will be when he's confronted. I hope she finds the anger she started with, rather than this self-deprecation. *Seriously, who the fuck gets a vasectomy and doesn't tell his wife?* Maybe he had something to hide or didn't want to risk anyone else getting pregnant. Fuck, Devin is such a douche. After a long moment, she takes in a deep breath. I feel her pull back to look me in the eye. Her expression surprises me as she says, "No, I don't think that's necessary."

"Why the fuck not?" I ask in disbelief. I would want fucking answers. He lied to her and should be fucking called on his shit.

"Some things are just better off not knowing. I don't want to know when he started cheating on me. Finding out about the affairs I do know about was hard enough to go through. It won't change anything, and I've spent years dealing with the hurt he put me through. I refuse to hang on to anger. It consumed me for so long." She pats her belly and stares at me lovingly. "I have too many other things that take priority."

I have no words. This woman continues to amaze me at every turn. I'd go fucking ballistic. Not only would I rip him a new asshole, but I'd tell him where to go and how to get there. There'd be no doubt about my feelings over this. But I can see where she's coming from. A little.

"I wouldn't hold it against you, if you told him off." I tip her chin so I can look directly in her eyes and she can't hide her feelings about this.

"I'm serious, Enzo. It won't do me any good to say anything."

"He deserves to know how you feel, Sam. It was shitty of him to not tell you about this. Not only did you experience month after month of misery, hoping your period would never come, but the fact that you longed for a baby for years is beyond words to me."

"Ha, I guess the joke's on him," she mutters.

What the fuck is she talking about? What joke? She reaches for my hands to place them on her growing belly. "What do you mean, beautiful?" I whisper, trying to calm myself.

"I mean, if he hadn't cheated on me, I wouldn't have been content with my life. I would never have experienced this." She motions between the two of us to prove her point. "If he hadn't gotten a vasectomy, I'd have never thought the problem was with me."

"That's fucking bullshit," I seethe. "You never should have felt like something was wrong with you, Samantha."

Somehow, Samantha smiles. Her knowing look and the coy smile that follows almost knocks me on my ass. "If I hadn't thought there was something wrong with me, I would have never had unprotected sex with you, silly." She pokes me in the belly and almost makes me crack a smile. "I would have been on some form of birth control. That's the kind of responsible person I am. I'm a planner." She's quiet for a moment then adds, "Holy hell, I never saw you coming. Everything about you sets my world on fire and makes me feel things I never imagined."

I chuckle, but before I can respond, she continues, "With you, Enzo, I'm reaching dreams I never thought were possible.

I never knew how much I wanted more kids until I saw those two blips on the screen."

"Me, too, beautiful," I whisper, suddenly choked with emotion.

"Of course, you and your super sperm had to do the job extra well." She shakes her head and laughs at the absurdity. "Just wait until Devin finds out we're not only pregnant, but having twins. He'll never experience this." She wraps her arms around my neck and pulls me closer. "He'll never experience the kind of love we share with one another and for our growing family."

When she reaches up on her toes, I lean down to close the gap, pressing my lips to hers. The warmth of her body as it presses against mine is something I never want to live without. I place my arms around her waist and revel in the moment. My hands roam her back and we stand here for a long moment, just enjoying one another.

Wanting her closer, I reach under her ass, lifting her to my height and kiss her for all I'm worth. Her baby bump rests against my stomach as her legs naturally wrap around my waist. Before getting too carried away, I suddenly feel something strange move across my stomach, causing me to instantly still. *What the fuck was that?*

I pull back from the kiss and stare into her eyes, hoping she will answer my unasked question. There's a slight movement again, as if something is slowly moving across her stomach.

I set her down and eye her suspiciously. "Did you feel that?" I ask in wonder.

"The better question is, did you?" She quirks an eyebrow. "I think these little monsters heard us talking about them."

"That's what they feel like when they kick?" I ask in disbelief.

She lets out a little chuckle. "That's not how it usually feels. I started feeling them flutter from time to time, but that was the first real kick." She places her hand on her belly to feel them again.

When I see movement, I quickly reach out to her and place my hand right along with hers. Holy hell. It's like there's an alien inside her. There's a thump, thump, thump against my hand. It's not hard, but definitely movement. I'm in complete awe of this woman. She's had five humans grow inside of her. "How often do they move?" I whisper, not wanting to accidentally stop the action.

"It depends. I've never had multiples before. Usually I don't feel much movement this early, but maybe there's less space in there." She shrugs as if she's speculating at the end. Samantha couldn't be any cuter if she tried.

After a moment, the babies still. She presses on her belly, but no further movement happens. "I think they're done for now," she sighs wistfully.

A thud from downstairs interrupts our moment, and reality comes crashing back. As much as I don't want to leave this room, I suggest, "We'd better get back downstairs. We left a house full of teenagers on the loose, and Aubrey and Devin are alone."

"Yeah," is all I get in response.

"You sure you're okay?" I pull her close to me for a hug.

"I'm not pleased he kept it from me, but I'm not willing to let this ruin Maddie's party, or our happiness."

The woman is a fucking saint. I'm still pissed at the asshole. But if she's taking the high road, I'll follow her lead. *Even if I want to sucker punch him in the nuts.*

16

SAMANTHA

SOMEHOW, Enzo and I manage to make it through the party without any further drama. Even though I'm incredibly irritated with Devin, having the two of them here was handy. By the time Enzo and I come downstairs, most of the kitchen's clean and leftover food has been put into tubs and placed in my fridge. Aubrey even took the liberty of doing the few dishes in the sink. Devin realizes something's wrong but is smart enough not to bring it up. Maybe Aubrey let the cat out of the bag to spare us from having to fill him in. When they leave, they graciously offer to take Declan and Frankie for the night. They know how loud slumber parties can be.

The next morning, as Enzo piles on pancakes to everyone's plates, I add sausage and eggs. Each girl's melancholy compared to last night and eats in silence. Occasionally, conversations continue about what had happened at the party, but for the most part, they keep to themselves.

As soon as they finish eating, the majority of the girls go

home, leaving only Nicole and Maddie visiting in the family room. Enzo's doing dishes and I'm sitting to eat while Maddie and Nicole curl up on the couch, deep in conversation, which is typical for them. I'm surprised when I hear Nicole mention, "Hey, Maddie, is your mom feeling all right?"

Maddie glances in my direction and I shrug, wondering where Nicole is going with this. "Yeah, I think so."

When Nicole realizes I'm paying attention, she directs her comment to me, "Sorry, Mrs. O'Reilly. No offense."

"None taken." I shrug, wondering why she thinks I'm sick.

"Well, it's just that." Nicole blushes and appears embarrassed, but I eye her skeptically to continue and she does without any further prompting. "Well... you seem to be really exhausted and there's something about you that's different. I don't know. I... I mean, you look great. Glowing even, but you're dressing differently and..." she trails off.

Holy fuck. She knows I'm pregnant. How the fuck can she know this? I take in a deep breath and slowly release it, trying like hell not to let my sudden tension show. I turn my attention to Maddie and see the wheels turning in her head. She boldly eyes me up and down. When she reaches my mid-section, she stops and stares. Maddie's expression morphs from confusion, to shock, to what I can only describe as denial.

"Oh. My. God. You're not... Are you? There's no way you can be..." Suddenly, she grits out in a hiss, "You're such a hypocrite."

Wondering where the anger is coming from, I ask, "What do you mean?"

"You sat Soren and me down in this very room and lit into

us. You had the 'sex talk,' right here in front of him. It was beyond embarrassing."

Without thinking, I burst out a response to her, "Well, the timing was right. You came in here talking about one of your friends staying out all night with a girl. You and Soren have been together awhile. The odds are you were either A... Already having sex or B... At least thinking about it. I thought I would hedge my bets and take the side of safety."

"But you know we're not having sex," Maddie retorts.

"I know that, now. I would have had that talk with you no matter what. I've always been frank with you, Mads. You know that."

"But... But..." she mutters and I see the wheels still turning in her head.

I feel Enzo come to my side as I wait out Maddie, to find where she's going with this. He places a hand on my back, showing moral support.

After a long while, I quietly state, "I'm not a hypocrite, Maddie. You know that."

"But are you..." She looks between Enzo and me, then back to my belly. If I wasn't in the midst of having to defend myself, I'd almost think her ogling was comical. Unfortunately, this means I have a lot more explaining to do than I ever intended.

"But what?" Enzo finally breaks his silence.

"Are you guys... Um... Pregnant?" Maddie finally whispers, her eyes still wide in disbelief.

"Yes," Enzo's deep voice rings out. "But I want you to be clear on a few things before you jump to any more conclusions." His tone is one I've never heard before. It's commanding, and not to be messed with.

Maddie takes the hint and waits for him to continue.

Enzo reaches for my trembling hand. I'd been worried as to how to tell the kids, and didn't think we'd have to say anything until after the wedding. A pin drop can be heard throughout the house as we all wait for him to continue.

"First," Enzo's deep voice breaks the silence. "Like I told you when I asked if I could marry your mother, I love her more than life itself. Second, I love you kids, too. I never knew what I'd been missing until I met your mom and you kids. Did we expect to add more kids to the family? No. But are we ecstatic about it? Hell yes. I'm so happy I get to be a part of five kids' lives. I'm freaking scared to death I won't know what to do, but I'm hoping with all of your help, I'll be a great dad to all of you. Don't get me wrong. I'm not trying to replace your dad, but I want to be there for you, too."

He takes a big breath, then continues before anyone can say anything. "Your mom loves you. She does everything in her power to protect you, even if it means causing embarrassment to set things right. You need to get a few things straight. She's not a hypocrite and this isn't her fault." Enzo takes another settling breath and I swear, the tips of his ears turn a few shades darker, but only if you know him like I do. He continues with, "It... Uh... Takes two to tango. I'm just as at fault as she is for this unexpected pregnancy. Not that it's any of your business, but we were careful, and it still happened."

Maddie's mouth hangs open and my heart squeezes as tears prick my eyes. His words have my emotions reeling. I don't think I could love this man any more than I do right at this moment.

The torch of anger Maddie's been carrying is quickly put out. She looks from me to him, then back to me. She approaches me with tears in her eyes. "I'm sorry, Mom." She reaches out for a hug and I squeeze her tight.

"It's okay, honey."

Maddie pulls back and looks me in the eye. "I'm really going to be a big sister again?"

"Yep." I smile widely with tears still blurring my vision. "You most certainly are."

She then turns to Enzo and holds out her arms to him. She hugs him as well. "I guess congratulations are in order."

"Thank you, Mads. It means the world that you're happy for us." Enzo's voice is thick with emotion at the end.

"When are you due?" Maddie asks enthusiastically.

"July," I state, not knowing how long I'll be able to last with two kiddos. Each of my other kids came a week early, so who knows with twins.

"Wow. That's just... Wow." Maddie eyes me over. She places her hands on my belly and I'm sure she can feel the bump that I've been trying to hide.

When she releases me with wonderment in her eyes, I look between her and Nicole. "Hey... Uh... If you don't mind, can we wait until after next week to tell everyone? I'd really like to keep the focus on our wedding."

"No problem," Nicole speaks as Maddie nods in agreement.

Nicole's face suddenly fills with confusion. "Wait... Enzo,

you do know you're only going to be a father to four kids, right? You said five kids."

Enzo's eyes shine with delight. This eagerness rolls off him and his smile's infectious. "Nope." He pops the p at the end. "I meant five. Sam's having twins, can you believe it?"

Both Maddie and Nicole's jaws drop nearly to the floor. Maddie is the first to recover. "Wow. There's two growing inside you? That's. Just... Wow..."

Enzo wraps his arms from behind me, his hands cradle the baby bump that's the center of attention. Though I'd rather this be under different circumstances, I'm glad everything's out in the open. I'm sure Frankie and Declan will be shocked when they learn about the twins.

"When will you know if they're a boy or girl?" Nicole asks in awe. "I've always wanted a younger brother or sister. But now that I'm in high school, I'm fine with being the only child."

"Oh my God, Mom!" Maddie gasps. "People are going to think I'm their mom if I take them in public."

"We'll make sure you set them straight." Enzo chuckles. "We can get you an 'I'm the sister' t-shirt, so you never have to explain."

"Hopefully, it'll be a long time before you have kids of your own, Mads. I'm too young to be a grandma, officially. Besides, these two are likely going to be amazing birth control for you in the future. You're in charge of late-night feedings and diaper changes." Sarcasm drips off my tongue at the end, making us burst into laughter. *God, I hope she knows I'm joking, even if it might be the most effective birth control I could ever give her.*

17

———

ENZO

WHIRLWIND DOESN'T EVEN DESCRIBE what life's been like since I've been stateside. I can't wait to be married to Samantha. Not only will we get to tell the world I'm going to be a father, but she'll be officially mine. Four more days. Just four more days and Samantha will be my wife.

I love that woman more than I ever thought was possible. She handles things with grace and dignity. Between finding out about Devin's vasectomy and Maddie finding out about the twins, these past few days have taken their emotional toll on us. Though I would've punched his fucking lights out, Samantha, as usual, took the high road.

Tonight, Lexi has asked Sam to go out to dinner. I know it's going to turn into her bachelorette party since Erin let the cat out of the bag when she called to ask me for directions earlier. With it being a Wednesday night, the girls can't get into too much trouble. I'm heading over to my parents' and have dinner with Pops and my brother, Zane. We're on kid patrol, so Erin can go out.

I'm so fucking relieved none of the guys from my former unit are around for a bachelor party. We've done some crazy shit over the years to each man who took the plunge into matrimony. Being the perpetual bachelor, I'd be in some serious trouble if they'd had time to plan anything. Thank God for small miracles.

When I get to my parents', I let myself in through the kitchen. There's noise in the living room, but it doesn't sound like kids. The hairs on the back of my neck rise when I realize there's more than the sound of three men's voices coming from the other room. Who the hell are Dad, Nate, and Zane talking to?

When I enter the family room, I'm blown away when I hear, "Here's the man," from none other than Mack Gunderson, my buddy since basic. How did he get leave so soon after his vacation to London? He must have pulled some serious strings. But then again, he probably has plenty of time to spare as he, too, is single and nearing retirement.

"Holy shit, is that really you?" I shorten the distance between us to shake his hand before pulling him into a man-hug. After a few hard slaps on the back, we let go of each other. "What the hell are you doing here?" I ask, still reeling in disbelief.

"You think I was gonna let you get married without fuckin' being here? I have to report back to command that you, the king of perpetual bachelors, has fallen from his throne."

There's laughter from around the room and for the first

time, I look to see who's here. Holy fuck. There's got to be about fifteen full-size men in Ma's family room. Where the hell did they park? Each of them has shit-eating grins plastered on their faces and I can't help but join them.

"Damn, you got me." I laugh, shaking my head. *I didn't see this coming.*

"Harps, we couldn't let you get away without a bachelor party." Nate Carson reaches out his hand and pulls me in for another back-slapping hug.

"Hell, it's great to see you, Cars." I feel like a tool to let them slip this over on me.

Before Cars can respond, Rowan interrupts, waggling his eyebrows, "I've taken the *liberty* of planning tonight's events. You can thank me later."

Oh, fuck. This could go so wrong tonight. "No fucking strippers. I've got all I need with Samantha."

"Oh, don't be such a sourpuss," Pops, of all people, chimes in. What. The. Fuck. I'd never take him for a strip-joint man.

Zane walks over to greet me with a handshake. "Hey, man. I distinctly remember, you were all about the strippers at my bachelor party. Payback's a bitch, brother." Zane's mischievous grin tells me he knows something I don't. Christ. I hope it's not what I think it is.

The next to greet me is Nate, my brother-in-law. He's flanked by my boisterous cousins. Each is about ten years younger than I, but are married nonetheless. Gabe, Mike, and Heath all have smug grins plastered on their faces. They know what's coming, but knowing these numbskulls, they won't let me in on the secret. *God, I wish I wasn't such a jackass to them at their bachelor parties. I have a feeling I'm going to pay for my sins tonight.*

Each of my cousins greets me with a handshake and slap on the back. They all have something snide to say that makes me worry my fears are coming true.

I'm pleased to see Riggs, Boone, and many of the guys from Riggs' barbeque here, too. Carson must have invited them. Sure, we've worked together before, but I guess nothing says bonding like a bachelor party. Christ, I hope I don't live to regret this night.

Holy shit, Brian Ford, my buddy from high school's even here. I haven't seen him since his wedding, about five years ago. I walk over to him and thank him for coming. He razzes me about finally taking the plunge, but before I move on to greet another guest, he sincerely states, "Congratulations, man. You're in for the ride of your life." I can't help but think of Samantha and everything that's happened since we met. It sure has been a ride, but it's one I never want to get off.

I take the time to introduce Jason Riggs and the members of the team I will soon work with to my family. I haven't worked with Trent Daniels, Drew Warren, or Ira Michaels much in the past, but from the way they're joking around, I'm sure to get along well with them.

Once I've greeted everyone, Rowan announces to the crowd, "Gentlemen..." Quickly, the crowd settles and he continues, "If you'll follow me, I've arranged for our night of festivities as we celebrate Enzo's end to being a bachelor."

Hoots and hollers erupt around the room. Comments range from, "Sorry, sucker," to "It's about time," and probably everything these bozos in front of me can think of. These guys let me know their thoughts on my impending nuptials.

We walk outside to find two large custom passenger vans, with accompanying drivers, parked in my parents' driveway. They weren't here before when I parked. We each pile into one of the vehicles. Once inside, I find they seat fifteen, but with most of us being larger than average height, I'm sure Rowan took that into consideration when he ordered the vans.

Rowan takes a seat next to me. I turn to him, shaking my head. "How the hell did you pull this off?"

"You know me and secrets, Harps. Planning this was a walk in the park." Rowan waggles his eyebrows, causing me to sigh and shake my head.

"At least tell me this," I plead. "Will Samantha be speaking to me in the morning?"

The entire van erupts with laughter. I internally cringe at all the things he could have up his sleeve. Why the fuck did I get in this car?

Gunderson doesn't make it any better when he chimes in, "Oh, Harps. You should be scared."

"I've been looking forward to this night for the past few weeks," Ira Michaels pipes in. "Tonight's going to be legendary! It's sure to keep up with the stories Carson's told me about you."

Fuck a duck! I'm utterly screwed. I look out the window and wonder if there's a way to come out of this night without smelling like cheap perfume and lipstick on my collar. I used to pay the strippers extra to do that for my buddies. We're heading downtown. It's a little-known fact that Portland's the strip capital of the world, if I recall statistics from my youth correctly. I guess I can always Uber it home if necessary before things get out of control.

It's funny. As a single guy, I was never much into strippers. I have no problem with them, but I never got my kicks going into strip clubs. I did, however, love to act like it was my thing. I always was the one who paid for the bachelor's last lap dance and did whatever necessary to make sure he went out of the single life in style. Now, the thought of anyone other than Samantha being near me is completely repulsive.

We drive down a road known for its establishments, and my palms sweat. Why the hell did I have to be so rebellious in my youth? When I see we're passing a few of the better-known places, I relax my stiff muscles, *a little*. When we pull into a parking lot, all my tension returns.

To my relief, we've stopped at some food trucks. Not a stripper joint in sight. Thank God. We all pile out and look over various carts. I make my way to a place called Chicken and Guns, where I order wood-fired chicken with a Peruvian sauce made of cilantro, jalapeños, and sour cream with a side of sea-salt fries. There're tables between the vendors and I take a seat as I wait for my meal.

"Gotta get some grub before we hit the bars," Heath, my youngest cousin, says as he rubs his belly in anticipation of the delicious-smelling food.

"Eat up, sucker," Mark McGowen, my new teammate, teases. "You'll be doing shots before the night is through."

Oh, hell no. My days of doing shots with these crazy-ass people were done, the moment they mentioned strippers. I'll gladly go out of bachelorhood as a dud, if it means I won't have a hangover and actually remember my night. I've seen *"The Hangover"* enough times, as well as experienced the real-life version of that movie, to know what I *won't* be doing tonight.

When everyone finishes their meal, we get back into the car and head to the outskirts of town. Though we approach it from a different side of town, I quickly recognize our location as Riggs' headquarters. *We'd better not be getting in a plane.*

To my surprise, we end up at an underground shooting range. *Who would have known? I* guess with all the ops that he runs, Riggs needs a place for people to keep sharp. We break out into groups, taking turns at unloading at a target for the next hour or so. Of course, there's friendly competitions and side-wagers going on. After taking a bet with Ira Michaels, I know he's a guy I want on my six. *Damn, the man has a great aim.*

When we exit the building, I realize the night's still young. We pile back into the vehicles and make our way back to the city. Once downtown, my fears from earlier return with a vengeance. Music plays in the background and people have conversations. We make a large loop and end up in front of Allure, Rowan's restaurant and club. Relief once again washes through me.

Once inside, I'm surprised to see the club has been closed for a private party. Shit. It never occurred to me. Rowan might hire strippers and bring them here. The entire ride up to the club has my nerves on edge.

I nearly sing when I see tables set up for poker. Rowan even has dealers and a waitstaff to bring us drinks. When he announces, "Hey, guys, anything you want from the kitchen, just me know." I could almost kiss him.

"Let the games begin," Pops announces. "It's twenty-five dollars to join. Winner will take three-seventy-five home at the end of the night."

Once everyone gets settled with their chips in place and a drink in hand, I really start enjoying myself. I'm at a table with Drew Warren, another new teammate, Zane, Gunderson, and Brian, my buddy from high school. Between hands, we catch up with one another and shoot the shit. I end up doing pretty well, and when the tables consolidate, I move over. Eventually, I lose and continue to drink and visit with the other guys who are out of the game.

Carson comes over with shots for everyone. "Let's toast," he announces to the crowd.

There are various cheers heard from all around.

My brother Zane's the first to stand and raise his glass. "Zo, I never thought I'd see the day when you'd rather chase kids than skirts. I'm beyond thrilled Samantha came and knocked you on your ass. You have no idea what you've been missing out on. Here's to my big brother. May he find health and happiness and never have to use a blue pill."

I nearly double over when he tacks that last bit on without any warning. Holy shit. Did he just say that?

"Here, here," can be heard and we all take a drink.

Gunderson's the next to stand. "I have to say, I'm sad you won't be able to go on any more epic single adventures with me. You've been the best wingman through it all. I can't wait to meet the woman who's made you change your ways. Congratulations, Harps."

After more cheers, Pops clears his throat. "Son, I never in a million years thought this day would come. But I've been here from the beginning. I was there the day you laid eyes on Samantha. You've grown into a man I'm proud of. My only advice for marriage is, never do something once, you don't want to do for the rest of your life. Love with all your heart, and in the middle of the night, put the toilet seat down."

The room bursts into laughter and I just shake my head. As I look at the room. I'm so thankful for those who've shown up to support me. I've been through thick and thin with most of these men, and having them here is everything.

18

SAMANTHA

SHOCKED IS an understatement to describe showing up for dinner at Lexi's, only to find a house full of women I know and love. Each of these women have been a part of my life over the years. Lexi has our dinner catered and I'm pampered beyond belief.

I have no idea how she managed to get Mom and my sister-in-law, Megan, here as a surprise, either. But I'm beyond ecstatic. I squeal with delight when I see them in the living room. They weren't due in until tomorrow, so they could be here for the rehearsal dinner.

After eating, the ten of us go to a day spa. Somehow Lexi's worked her magic and got them to stay open just for us to be pampered. When we arrive, we fill every pedicure chair available. As we chat about the details of the wedding, Lexi wanders off for a bit before returning with a huge smile on her face. She's up to something, but for the moment, she's not filling me in.

"How did Enzo propose?" my college roommate Brooke asks. Everyone in the room quiets as they await my response.

I know this question's inevitable, but I feel guilty for not being honest with everyone. There's no way I'm announcing my pregnancy, so I launch into my visit with Enzo in Germany. I tell them how he greeted me with a beautiful bouquet of flowers at the airport. Audible sighs can be heard as I describe how he swept me up into his arms, like no one was watching. I tell them about touring castles, seeing the sights, and of course, how utterly perfect he is. I omit the part about being sick or my stint in the hospital. There's a ton of laughter when I explain how I convinced Enzo to go to a bathhouse. Keeping things casual, I mention, "One day while we were out and about, he got down on one knee. And... Well... You know my answer." Everyone sighs at how romantic I made it sound.

Lexi catches my eye and winks, letting me know my secret's safe with her.

As soon as our toes are dry, most of us opt to get manicures, too. Just as I'm about to get a French manicure to match my toes, a woman comes out from another room and calls my name.

"That's me."

"Great," she says with a more than cheery smile. "Come this way and we'll get started."

Get started with what? I look to Lexi and her grin almost splits her face in half. *Christ. What has she done now?* I take a deep breath to prepare myself for the possibility of answers. "Started with what?"

"I've got you booked for a Brazilian wax. Just follow me to

our back room and we'll get you all set up." I glower in Lexi's direction but with everyone in the room looking at me, I obediently follow the all too cheerful woman in front of me.

"Just think of this as my gift to both you and Enzo," Lexi hollers out.

"Ohmigod," falls from my lips in a whisper. "I'm going to kill her."

The woman leading me away tells me her name, but I'm not paying attention. When we're out of earshot from my bachelorette party, Little Miss Sunshine leads me to a room with a table set up in the middle like I'm going to my obstetrician. At least there aren't fucking stirrups for my legs. That would just be too much. "If you'll just remove your clothing from the waist down, I'll get everything ready."

"O... Kay," I draw out slowly as I look around the room. I guess it makes no sense in her leaving. It's not like she won't be up in my business in a matter of minutes. I drop my underwear from beneath my skirt and decided to just let it gather at my waist.

"So, when's the big day?" Miss Sunshine gleefully asks as I lie on the table, keeping the back side of my skirt around my waist, and the front covering me, for now.

"Saturday." For a second, I can't help the smile that forms. I'm dying to be Enzo's wife. I can't wait to tell everyone about our growing family as well as simply be with him. I adjust the pillow behind my head and get comfortable.

"Wow, that's exciting. I got married last year. We honeymooned in Italy. It was amazing." She rolls everything necessary on a cart and comes to stand behind me. "Have you ever had this done before?"

"Nope. I've only gotten my eyebrows and lip waxed," I let out slowly. My eyebrows I can handle, the lip on the other hand, never fails to hurt like a bitch. The sheer thought of waxing my nether region has sweat beginning to form.

"Just relax. It'll all be over in about fifteen minutes."

I reach down and pull up my skirt to let it gather at my stomach and my nerves tremble. I typically stay trimmed, so I'm not worried about my personal grooming habits. After having three kids, I'm not shy about having anyone poking around there either. I've been to enough gynecologist appointments to last a lifetime. No. What scares the ever-loving shit out of me is the thought of having each hair ripped out. I don't even want to imagine the excruciating pain.

"Why don't you pull up your knees, keep your feet together, and let your legs fall to each side," Miss Sunshine suggests. As she begins to apply warm wax to the crease at my inner thigh, she asks, "So, where's your wedding taking place?"

Next comes the paper being pressed against the wax. If I'm not mistaken, there's likely a sweat ring of my ass on the tissue paper I'm lying on. This next part will be the true test of whether or not I can handle this. I grip each hand with all my might against the edge of the table I'm on. "The lodge at Multnomah Falls," I grit out. I know she's getting closer to becoming a torturing technician, rather than the sunshine, unicorns and shit she's trying to portray at the moment. I mentally prep myself, in an attempt to convince myself I can handle this, all the while having a normal conversation with her.

"That's wonderful. Now on the count of three, you're going to feel this." *No shit.* I close my eyes to prepare myself for the torture. "One..." My ass cheeks clench. "Two..." A bead of sweat trickles down my face. "Three..." I let out a strangled scream.

OH... MY... MOTHER-FUCKING... GOD. That fucking hurts like a son-of-a-bitch. How the hell am I going to be able to finish this? I look down and see one side of me is smooth, while the other's a jungle in comparison. There's no way I can go on my honeymoon looking like this.

"You okay?" Miss Sunshine sweetly asks.

No, I'm not fucking okay. I take in a deep breath and let it out slowly. *But I can't be seen like this either. Christ, what did I get myself into?* I nod my reaction, knowing that if I were to speak at this precise moment, I'd curse a sailor out of the bar, making him go crying home to Mommy.

All the while, she preps the other side. By now, I'm certain this flimsy paper beneath me will shred apart from the amount of sweat coming out of my pores. I don't even want to look at the aftermath when I'm done in this torture chamber. God, get me the hell out of here.

"Will you have a big or small wedding?" Miss Sunshine chooses the time right before she applies the paper again to ask. As she pats it down and smooths it over my skin, my entire body tenses, bracing for the impending agony. My knuckles are straining against my skin where I manage to grip the edge of the table even harder than before.

"Small," I grit out, while I do my best to keep this mantra running through my head. *You can do this. You will do this. You already know what it feels like. You will get through this.*

When she rips the paper off, it hurts even worse than before. FFFUUUCCCKKK!

I manage to keep my thoughts to myself, somehow. Goddamit, that hurts. Sweat covers my body, my breathing's short, and it takes all I can to nod in her direction, so she can finish and I can get the fuck out of here as soon as possible.

There's some relief with the gel she liberally applies afterward. It feels so good, I want to jump into a bathtub full of it. My body relaxes and after a while, she wipes me up and tells me I can sit up. I attempt to put my underwear on, but they feel itchy. When she suggests I leave them off, I gladly do so. There's no way I want to have anything rub on me in the near future. *Now I get to hang out with my friends and family commando. Just what I've always wanted.*

When I stand to put my shoes back on, the babies move like crazy. They must not like a tense Mama. When I cradle my hands around my belly, Miss Sunshine notices.

"You're pregnant?" she asks with disbelief.

"Yes," I whisper, but quickly add, "no one knows yet."

"Oh." Her mouth forms a perfect 'O' as she gasps in air.

"What? Did I harm the babies? Crap." I suddenly panic.

She shakes her head and places an arm on my shoulder. "No, not at all," she assures me. "It's perfectly safe. I just would've warned you that it is going to likely hurt worse than normal." *Well, isn't that nice.*

When I slowly walk out to the room, everyone's in various

stages of getting their nails done. I make my way over to Lexi. "You are so going to pay for this," I grit out when no one can hear.

She has some nerve using a singsong voice as she says, "You may hate me now, but you'll thank me later."

"Don't count on it," I growl, as another woman comes to show me where I'll get my fingernails done.

BY THE NEXT MORNING, I feel much better. I want to keep my waxing a surprise for Enzo. When Enzo came home late last night, I was nearly sound asleep. We managed to talk for a few minutes and I casually contemplated waiting to have sex for our wedding night. Surprisingly, he agreed. Knowing I'd been dead on my feet might have had something to do with it.

As we sit for breakfast, he tells me all about how the guys set him up. I was in on the plan, but I enjoy letting him sweat it out. Rowan informed me Enzo used to be the "wild one," and he needed payback. I tell him about my surprise, minus the waxing bit. He'll find out soon enough.

We spend the next two days preparing for our wedding, hanging out with family and other out-of-town guests. True to his word, I hardly had to lift a finger to prepare for our big day. When I went to the bridal shop to have my last fitting, I'm pleasantly surprised. It looks perfect. From most angles, you'd never know I was pregnant. The woman at the bridal shop is a miracle worker.

By Friday, everyone's eager for our rehearsal dinner. We drive out to Multnomah Falls in the afternoon, leaving plenty of time for sightseeing for those new to the area and to get to our dinner on time. The view's unbelievably gorgeous for February. It's bright, sunny, and clear in every direction for miles. Enzo insists on stopping to take photos at the Vista House, with the gorge in the background. Maddie, Frankie, and Declan ride with us, while our families and close friends travel in cars behind us. All stop to see what's wrong as we pull into a lookout.

As it turns out, Enzo couldn't have predicted a better place to take family photos. Enzo's mother insists on taking several pictures of different groupings of people once we arrive. Some of these photos will be cherished for years to come. I'm nearly brought to tears with the love Sara shares for my children and me. She insists on having the kids call her Granny or Granny Sara, just like her other grandchildren do. At the mention of how happy Sara is to include three more to the mix, Maddie gives me a conspiratorial grin. *Yeah, she'll be over the moon.*

Enzo catches our interaction and whispers in my ear as he holds me from behind during a photo. "She'll be out of her mind when she finds out she's getting more. I'm warning you, she takes being a grandma seriously."

I can't help but laugh and shake my head. "I'm sure we'll manage."

"Okay, but don't say I didn't warn you," he taunts as he kisses my cheek once more.

"Save it for your honeymoon, Harps," Gunderson hollers and the crowd laughs.

Without a moment's hesitation, Enzo replies, "You're just jealous. This fabulous life will happen to you someday, if you let it." He pecks me on the cheek once again, then steps away.

"Pops, has hell frozen over?" Zane chimes in.

Lorenzo chortles, "Just might have, Zane."

Enzo flips Zane the bird, everyone bursts into laughter. Once we've settled down, we finish taking our family photos.

By the time we get to Multnomah Falls, there's still time for people to hike and enjoy the scenery as those who are in the ceremony go to our rehearsal. Laughter comes easy with this group and I almost feel bad for Melanie who has worked so hard to pull this together. We get through the necessary obligations of the rehearsal. The guys Enzo's worked with over the years are a riot to be around. I can't remember when I've laughed so hard.

The night goes by like a blur. By the time we get to toasts at dinner, my cheeks hurt from laughing so hard. My emotions are in full swing and I can only hope people keep their speeches mild.

Lexi's the first to get everyone's attention by clinking her knife against her champagne glass. "We can't let the night go by without toasting the happy couple." Cheers erupt around the room. "I'd like to begin by saying it's an honor to be here."

Lexi looks to me and whispers, "Thank you," before turning her attention back to the crowd. "Let me start by saying I'm so thankful that Enzo swept into Sam's life and knocked her off her feet."

"Hey, now," I warn, but it's easily dismissed.

Lexi grin's infectious, even though I'm leery of what she's

about to say. "I'd always known it would take someone special to make her consider dating again. Let's face it… I mean, we all know Sam's far too stubborn to have thought about dating seriously."

More laughter erupts and I feel my face flush crimson. How can she do this to me? It's not like I never dated.

"The day she came into work starry-eyed and zoning out was the day I knew something changed. When she told me she'd met a pilot, who lived on the other side of the world, I'll admit I had my doubts." She smirks at Enzo before continuing, "But since this was the first guy she'd even considered going out on a second date with, I encouraged her to let down her guard and have some fun."

"I knew I've always liked you," Enzo interrupts.

"Well… Thanks. I like you, too, Enzo," Lexi chides. "But seriously, you brought out a part of my best friend I've never seen before. Your actions spoke louder than your words and it's evident to all in this room, that your love for her is real. I wish you both the best and can't wait to share this journey with you." She raises her glass to the crowd. "To the bride and groom."

"To the bride and groom," the room echoes.

The arm Enzo's wrapped around my shoulders pulls me closer to him. He kisses me on my temple, sending shivers down my spine. God, I love this man.

As soon as Lexi finishes, Zane stands beside her. As the only members of our wedding party, they have the crowd's full attention. Before he begins, he looks over to Enzo and me. He shakes his head as his body rocks with silent laughter. "God, where should I start?" Laughter from the crowd continues. "Zo, I never thought I'd see the day you'd settle down. Before seeing you with Sam, I would've bet my next paycheck, you'd be a bachelor the rest of your life."

Jeers from his friends and family fill the room, but when they settle, Zane pins his eyes on me. "Sam, thank you for making him see the light. I'm sure you'll have your work cut out for you, but it'll be worth it. Enzo's a force to be reckoned with."

Boldly I state, "I'm sure I can handle it." The room fills with hoots and hollers.

"Ohmigod," Lexi bellows. "See, she's a changed woman."

Zane clears his throat. "But seriously... Samantha." Zane looks me directly in the eye, then looks to each of my children. "Maddie, Declan, and Frankie. It's an honor to have you as a part of our family. Enzo never stops talking about you and I can't wait to get to know all of you better." The fact he's included my kids in his toast brings tears of joy to my eyes. He continues, "I wish you all the best. Let's hear it for the bride and groom."

I get up to hug Zane. As he pulls me close, he whispers, "Love you, Sam. Thank you for loving my brother so much. He means the world to me." *Gahh, now I'm full-on crying. Damn hormones.*

When he releases me, Enzo stands and looks me over with care. I shake my head to assure him I'm fine. Zane reaches out and pulls him into a bear hug. "Love you the most, Zo."

"Hey, now!" Erin shouts as she comes to join them. "I'm your favorite sibling." They each reach for her and pull her into a group hug. When they release her, she announces to the room, "I have a few words I'd like to say..."

"This ought to be good." Enzo chuckles as Zane adds, "You're in trouble," simultaneously.

Enzo chuckles as Erin takes the attention from the room. "As the baby of the family, I've always looked up to my big brothers." She eyes them both before continuing, "Enzo has spent the last twenty years flying all over the world, but has always made a point to make family a priority. I love the fact that rather than a video chat, you'll be just down the street. What's even better is that I get a new sister out of the deal... No offense, Ann. I love you just as much." Ann nods her head in approval and Erin continues, "I knew you were special the day Enzo brought you home, Sam. Hell, he hadn't brought a girl home in twenty years. We all knew something was up."

"Seriously?" Maddie says in wonder and the room erupts with joyful noise again.

"Seriously," Enzo assures her.

"As I was saying..." Erin does her best to get control of this boisterous crowd. "I couldn't be happier for the two of you. I wish you both the best of luck and love. So, let's raise our glass to the bride and groom. Here's to the happy couple."

IT WAS hard to sleep alone last night, but Sara insisted he sleep in her house the night before our wedding. Enzo only agreed because he knew he couldn't sleep next to me another night without making love to me.

As I lie in bed contemplating the day to come, I can't help but feel giddy. I'm getting married today. Sure, I've been here before, but this feels different. I get out bed, take a shower, and get dressed in clothes that can easily be slipped off, in place of my wedding dress later. Maddie, Frankie, and I are meeting Lexi at the hair salon to get our hair done in a couple of hours. Enzo melted my heart when he asked Declan if he would like to stay the night with him at his parents. He thought they'd hang out and get ready for the wedding together.

On the way to the salon, Frankie asks, "Mom, are you ready to get married?"

"I sure am, honey." I flip my blinker on to turn at the light.

"Well, how do you know you're ready?"

Maddie breaks in, "That's a silly question, squirt."

"No, it's really not," I defend. "I know I'm ready to marry Enzo because he loves me as well as you kids, more than life itself. He's proven through both his actions and words that he'll never do anything to intentionally hurt us and that he has all of our best interests in mind. There's also this undescribed feeling of happiness when I'm around him. It's been there from the start, and I doubt it will ever go away," I answer honestly.

"But didn't you feel that way with Daddy?" Frankie sincerely asks.

"Yes. I loved your dad." Not that I want to talk about this on my wedding day, but I have to be as honest as I can with my kids. "We loved each other for a very long time. But eventually, we wanted different things out of life and it didn't work out. If

I'm being honest, a part of me will always love him. He gave me you kids."

Maddie surprises me by joining in the conversation, "Are you ever worried that might happen with Enzo?"

Geesh... it's not even nine in the morning and they're already bringing out the big guns. I take a deep breath and think of how to explain. "It's a possibility. But if I focus on the 'what-ifs' of life, I'll never be happy. I'm older now and so is Enzo. We've both had a lifetime of experiences that have made us who we've become today. We also both know how things can go awry if you don't have open communication in a relationship... I could get hit by a bus tomorrow, you never know. You just have faith and trust that love will get you through."

"I guess that makes sense," Maddie states and Frankie agrees. "I know that Enzo makes you happier than I've ever seen you."

"Thanks, Maddie. That means more to me than you'll ever know."

19

____

ENZO

I'VE BEEN WAITING FOREVER for today. Samantha will be my wife before the night is through. *Wife.* I never thought I'd see the day. If anyone had asked me a year ago what I'd be doing after retirement, I would have bet my last dollar it wouldn't be this. That's simply because I had yet to meet Samantha.

I've been up since before dawn, waiting to get the day started. I force myself to stay in bed until at least six, to keep from disturbing Declan and my parents. I haven't slept in my childhood room much over the years, except while visiting on leave. As I look around, I realize Ma hasn't changed it much. After enlisting, I either packed or took most of my personal belongings with me. Ma's changed the bedding and added a few pictures to the walls, but for the most part, it's how I left it over twenty years ago.

There's a light knock on my door and I answer, "Come in."

A second later, Declan's bright eyes peer through a crack in the door. "Did I wake you?" he whispers.

"I've been up for about an hour. Come in." I sit up and pat the edge of my bed since there's no other place to sit in the room.

Dec looks around the room and spots a few pictures of me that Ma framed and put up over the years. "Is that you?" He stands to take a closer look.

He looks at a picture of me right before I went to the Air Force. My hair is longer, nearly to the tip of my nose in front and tapered to almost cropped in the back. I was scrawny, compared to how I look now. "Yep. It sure is. That's taken right before I graduated high school."

"Wow, you haven't changed much. Well.... You're bigger, but not in a bad way." He shakes his head as a chortle escapes and bats his hand in the air at me. "You know what I mean... No offense."

"None taken. I didn't bulk up until after basic. Why are you up so early, anyway?"

"I couldn't sleep... And I'm a little hungry. Granny Sara said she'd make breakfast and I don't want to miss it." He shrugs impishly.

"Trust me, Ma won't let anyone miss breakfast. Let's go to the kitchen and see if we can get things started." I push back my covers and grab the shirt I'd worn last night, having slept in pajama pants. Ma keeps her house too damn hot to wear a shirt to bed.

We find Ma in the kitchen with her back to us, making

coffee. I walk over and kiss her on the cheek. "Morning. Need any help?"

"Mornin', love." She turns and her smile widens as she sees Declan. "You two take a seat at the bar and visit with me while I cook. Did you sleep well, Dec?"

Declan tells her he slept well, and our casual conversation makes waiting for breakfast go by quickly. It isn't long before Pops joins us, freshly showered and ready for the day. When he enters the room, he pats me on my shoulder.

"Here's the man of the day."

"Morning, Pops."

"What time do we need to be out at the lodge?"

"The photographer wants us there at noon. Melanie claims everything's under control and the only thing we have to do is show up."

"So, what do you boys want to do to fill our morning?" Pops looks at his watch, then to Declan and me before adding, "It looks like we have at least three hours to kill."

Knowing Pops, he has something planned. "What do you have in mind?"

"I want to take you somewhere. It's a place my father took me. I took your brother before his wedding, and now I'm taking you." He looks to Declan. "Of course, you're coming along, too. Maybe you'll get to go again someday."

"You and your traditions," Ma says knowingly.

I'd never heard of Pops going somewhere on his wedding day or him taking Zane. My interest is piqued, so I nod at Declan. "Are you up for it?"

He shrugs. "Sure. Why not?"

As we pull into the parking lot, I can't help but shake my head. Pops sees my response, and a smile spreads across his face. He knows this place always has a special place in my heart.

"We're going golfing?" Declan asks when he sees the sign.

"We sure are, kiddo. Wanna hit a few buckets of balls at the range before we get this guy married?" Pops gets out of his truck and we follow him inside.

Declan's eyes light up with excitement. "I've never done it before, but it looks fun."

"Well, let's get going." Pops places an arm around his shoulder and leads him into the building.

Once we're set up, the three of us stand side by side and take turns swinging into the range. Declan's never done this before, but after a few swings, you'd never know it. Talk about a natural athlete. I look over to Pops and he nods in agreement. Our time at the range is filled with laughter and casual conversation.

This calms my nerves by keeping me occupied. I'm not having cold feet or anything. I don't have a single doubt about marrying Samantha. I never thought I'd feel this way about anyone, but I can't wait to set my eyes on her and spend the rest of our lives together.

"Did Gramps really bring you here?" I finally ask, wondering what the connection to this place and getting married is.

"Yep." Pops swings, and his ball goes sailing out over two hundred fifty yards.

"Any particular reason?"

"I think there might have been a few. First, I'd been up pacing at the crack of dawn and needed to pass the time or drive Ma crazy. The second was to give me some life lessons." Pops shrugs.

"Oh, yeah? What's that?"

"Ever notice how you can't hit the ball in the exact same place twice?" He points out toward the ball he just hit.

I'd never thought about this before. "I guess you're right."

"Even the best of them get close, but hardly ever in the same exact place."

Where is he going with this? "Okay?" I prompt to help him get to the point.

Pops sighs after he takes another swing and looks me directly in the eye. "I guess I'm just trying to tell you that no matter how hard you try, no matter how prepared you are, life is sometimes going to give you a curve ball, and you just have to make do with what you've got. You need to focus on how to go from where you are, not where you think you should've been."

I think about Samantha, her kids, and the twins coming. I couldn't agree with Pops more. "You're absolutely right. Sometimes the best things in life come out of unexpected circumstances."

"Of course I am." Pops snickers. "There's also another reason to come out here..."

"What's that?" Declan chimes in. I hadn't realized he'd been paying attention.

"If you ever get really frustrated about something, it's better to take your aggravation out on these balls than to say or do something you'll regret. Trust me. I've only *had* to come out here a few times in my life, but it's probably kept me out of more trouble than I was already in." He quirks an eyebrow at me and I can't help but laugh.

GLANCING at my watch for the hundredth time, I see there's less than thirty minutes before the ceremony begins. Samantha arrived earlier than us to take photos by herself and with the wedding party. Keeping to tradition, I haven't seen her since last night at the rehearsal dinner. It's been pure torture to know she's within a hundred yards of me and I can't see or touch her.

Zane finds me pacing in the room we used to change into our tuxes. "Want me to get the car ready? It's gassed and ready to go if you need it."

I stop pacing and glare at him. *How could he say such a thing?*

"What?" he asks defensively.

"Not funny at all, man."

He pats me on the shoulder. "Got you to stop wearing a hole in this carpet though."

"True," I admit. "Hey, will you take something to Samantha for me?"

"Like passing a note in grade school?" Zane teases.

"No, dipshit. Like deliver a gift."

He puts his finger to his chin, pretending to think about it. "I suppose I could do that."

I pull out an envelope and the long, skinny box I've had in my tux jacket. I'd picked this out when I'd bought her engagement ring. It's a charm bracelet she can add to through the years. I already picked out charms to represent each of her three kids: a soccer ball, ballet slipper, and a formal dress. I also got a heart-shaped charm with the inscription, *'You've held my heart from the moment we met.'*

Before Zane leaves, I ask him to bring Declan back when he returns so we can get this show started. Zane nods and is out the door within seconds. And... suddenly, I'm back to pacing the room.

When the door opens, I expect Zane and Dec, but instead, it's Samantha's dad Randall and her brother Blake. Once they've both entered the room, Blake shuts the door. *Hmmm... this could get interesting.*

Randall's deep voice is the first to fill the room. "Just wanted to stop in and see how you're doing." He reaches out to shake my hand.

"I'm doing great, sir," I offer.

"Ha... I remember being a nervous wreck before my wedding," Blake chimes in. "You sure you don't want to go running for the hills? You look like a nervous wreck."

I level Blake with a stare that's been known to make grown men quiver in their boots. Instantly, Blake puts his hands up in surrender. "Just joking, man. I had to be sure you weren't going to ditch my sister on her wedding day."

I shake my head but have no words to reply appropriately.

Randall reaches out an arm and pats me on the back. "It'll be here soon enough, don't you worry."

I exhale the breath I didn't know I'd been holding and shake my head. "The hardest part's the waiting. I just want to start forever with her and it can't get here soon enough."

"I know the feeling." Randall exhales a loud breath as well. "I knew you were something special when you flew out to meet us before returning to Germany. When you asked for her hand in marriage, I was shocked with the timing, but seeing you together, I know you're perfect for Sam."

"Thank you. It means a lot to have your support." I look them both in the eye to make sure they both clearly see how I feel.

"You have a long road ahead of you," Blake starts but back-peddles, "I mean... It's going to be hard adjusting to a life with three kids. But we've seen the way you interact with them and I can tell you've won over their hearts, too."

And we'll have two more on the way. That'll be one hell of an adjustment.

"Oh, I'm sure they'll have their bumps in the road, but they'll figure it out, Blake." Randall reaches in for one last handshake and clears his throat. "Well, we'd better get to our places. I hear there's a wedding happening today."

Standing at the altar in front of our closest friends and family is something I'll never forget. I've taken my place, waiting for Frankie, Lexi, and Maddie to walk down the aisle before Samantha. Zane and Declan are by my side, waiting for the girls as well.

Finally, it happens. The music changes and my heart picks up a few thousand beats. Maddie's the first to arrive in the doorway. She's wearing a sleeveless, red formal dress that flows to her knees. The part that makes it so her is the white Chuck Taylors with red stripes on her feet. She looks so happy as she enters the room, I burst with pride.

Next comes Lexi. She, too, has the same color dress, but it's a completely different style. She's also wearing red heels instead of Chuck Taylors. Frankie's right behind her. Her dress is similar to Maddie's, but it's white. She has a red sash tied around her waist, as well as red Chucks. The minute she sees me, she squeals with delight and my heart overflows with love. Her pace quickens and instead of going to her assigned spot, she comes straight to me, jumping into my arms with a hug. The room roars with laughter, but I don't hear a thing.

Now, I'm not a crier. I'm not. But I'll be damned if I can see straight for a few moments. I squeeze her tight and she whispers in my ear, "Love you, Enzo."

Before releasing her to her spot, I whisper, "Love you, too, Frankie."

When I look around the room, I'm not sure I see a dry eye in the house. Even Gunderson and Rowan's eyes shine from across the room when I spot them. *Who knew they could be sappy?*

When the music changes to the wedding march and people stand, I think my heart stops beating. Samantha steps around the corner, and it takes everything in my power not to run to her. She's the most beautiful person I've ever seen. Her dress fits her perfectly, and her beautiful mahogany eyes hold my gaze as she approaches on her father's arm. Her hair's partially down and flows with curls around her shoulder. She opted not to wear a veil, but her hair has something in it, similar to a tiara, that sparkles in the light.

I briefly remember her father shaking my hand and pulling me into a hug before handing Samantha off to me. I want to devour her on the spot. The knowing glance she gives me tells me she feels the same. Together, we walk to the altar and the minister we've hired for the ceremony begins. I can't actually tell you much beyond that. It feels as if I'm in a dream.

I'm so lost in Samantha. Her touch, her smell, everything about her pulls me into a trance. I can't wait until I actually get to kiss her.

When we get to our vows, I manage to pull myself out of the trance she has me under. When she steps back and looks me in the eye, my heart stills once again. Her eyes lock onto mine and I can't look away. The entire church could go up in flames and I wouldn't be any the wiser.

She licks her lips and clears her throat before clearly stating, "Lorenzo Dean Harper. I have loved you since the moment you walked into my kitchen that fateful day. Little did I know the surprise would be on me. I've never been bold enough to ask a man out, but here we are, mere months later. So, it proves I was right about you."

I can't help but laugh along with the crowd. When we settle down, Samantha continues, "Enzo, you have made me unbelievably happy. You not only love me, but you cherish each of my children as well. I promise to love, honor, and cherish you for the rest of our lives... So, let's face it, buddy, you're stuck with me." She wrinkles up her nose as she scrunches her eyebrows, daring me to say anything different.

I can't help but mouth, "I love you," in her direction.

"I love you, Enzo, with all of my heart."

The minster then turns to me.

Crap. Everything I had planned just went out the window. I look into Samantha's eyes and speak from the heart. "Samantha Elizabeth O'Reilly, you've come into my life like a heat-seeking missile and I'm beyond thankful you won't let go. I, too, have loved you from the start. One of the best things I've ever done was surprise Pops at your house that day. Your kids have burrowed their way into my heart, and there's no way in hell I'm letting any of you go." I stop and look at each of them before continuing, "I will be with you all, through thick and thin. I promise to love, honor, and cherish you for all the days of my life. Thank you for doing me the honor of becoming my wife and making me the happiest man alive."

The minister then proceeds with the ceremony. We repeat the magic words, and the best fucking thing of the day is when he finally says, "I pronounce you man and wife. I'm happy to introduce to you, Mr. and Mrs. Enzo Harper. You may kiss the bride." And boy, do I ever. If it wasn't for some less than subtle throat clearing from the crowd, I may have taken her right there. When I pull away, I can't help but grin at the blushing bride beside me. I swear I hear, "Thanks. Now I'm all hot and bothered," but I can't be sure. *God, I love her lack of filter.*

We're ushered out to the reception area where we receive congratulations from all of our guests. We then go outside to take pictures before the sun sets. The staff Melanie's hired for the wedding changes out the ceremony chairs for dining tables, and by the time we return to the room, it's been completely transformed.

The night passes in a blur. We eat, cut cake, and once again, people toast in honor of us. We thank the crowd for spending their Valentine's Day with us, and this gets a roar of cheers. By the time I get to have the first dance with my wife, I think I'm about to die from keeping my restraint. When *Shape of You*, by Ed Sheeran begins, I'm so relieved to have Samantha in my arms. It's not a traditional song, but it's ours. The smile that lights up her face when the opening beats begin has me willing do just about anything for this woman. We show off a bit while dancing as we enjoy each other's company. Before the song ends, I tell her we have to dance more before the night is through.

We each take time to dance with our parents, each other's parents, and of course her kids. For quite a few songs, the five of us try to top one another on the dance floor. I don't remember a time I've had more fun with them. Of course, Maddie dances with Soren for the slow songs. Everyone at our reception enjoys themselves.

The best part of the night comes when it's time for us to leave. Samantha and I have reservations at the Skamania Lodge, just on the other side of the Columbia River. Our friends and family shower us with love and handfuls of birdseed as we make our departure. God knows how I'm ever going to get all this birdseed out of Samantha's car. She shakes her head and more birdseed cascades over her body and into the seats of her SUV.

It's still relatively early by the time we make it to the

Skamania Lodge. I've booked us a romantic couples' package for the next three days. It includes a couple's massage, though when I found out they offer prenatal massages, I switched hers to that. So far, I've kept it a surprise as to what our plans are for the evening. I simply told her to pack for cold weather for three days, not that I care if she ever dresses in that time, but I'm sure we'll have to eat at some point.

Samantha eyes me skeptically when I exit the freeway a short distance later. When she realizes we are going over *The Bridge of the Gods*, I suspect she's figured it out.

As soon as we enter the Gorge Suite I booked us, Samantha sighs.

"What's wrong, beautiful?"

She shakes her head and birdseed still somehow manages to rattle to the floor. "Ugg... As much as I've been dying to attack you from the moment we've been alone, unless I want birdseed in my nether regions, I need to get out of these clothes and take a shower. Would you mind helping me get the pins out of my hair? There are at least forty of them in here, or so I've been told."

Well, this is unexpected. But as she pulls at her hair, it's obvious it hurts to do it on her own. She peers at me in desperation, so I jump in to help. "Sure, let's go into the bathroom and I'll see what I can do to help you out."

Forty minutes later, she's de-pinned and ninety-nine percent of the birdseed is out of her hair. Honeymoons in real life are hardly like TV, I'm coming to realize. But one look at the relief on Samantha's face is worth every second and more.

Finally, when the pins are free, she asks, "Mind giving me a sec to get ready for bed?"

I'm so fucking thankful I'm sitting when she walks out of the bathroom about ten minutes later. She takes my breath away in the sheer negligee she's wearing. It's a cream color and leaves little to the imagination. The sexy garters and silk stockings make me instantly hard. Holy. Fucking. Shit. This woman's going to kill me. A growl escapes, as I'm at a loss for words. My instincts are suddenly pure primal.

Her eyebrows raise, and a feign innocent look appears on her face. "You like?"

"I fucking love," I growl out as I find my body moving on its own accord in her direction.

"I may have gotten a few surprises for our honeymoon."

"I'll take you dressed or naked, or any variation in between. I fucking love you, Samantha." When my hands reach her body, I pull her close and kiss her for all I'm worth. "God, you smell amazing, Samantha. I'm completely addicted to you."

I lift her and carry her to the king-size bed. My first mission of the evening is to taste her everywhere and draw out her pleasure as long as I can. As soon as I set her in the middle of the bed, I crawl up her body. I pepper her with kisses on the way. I pull back when we're eye-to-eye and stare for an unknown time. She completely unhinges me and the sheer thought of knowing she's officially mine has me wanting to shout from the rooftops.

"Are you just going to stare at me or are you going to do something about it?" she challenges.

"Oh, I'll do something all right, beautiful," I tease as I lean in and swipe my tongue along her lower lip, getting her to open for me, while simultaneously dragging one hand up her luscious body. I tease her sensitive nipples through the sheer fabric and I swear they've grown since the last time we were intimate.

When Samantha moans and pulls at my boxer briefs, I move back down her neck, trailing kisses, until I can tease her nipples through the fabric of this sexy get up. "Enzo..." she writhes. "I need more."

I reach down and glide my hands from her knees to her inner thighs. The silk stockings feel magnificent against her skin. She must agree because she audibly sighs. When I skim past the garter belt, and onto her silky, smooth skin, I'm forced to stop playing with her breast. I need to see what my fingers have discovered. Samantha's silky, smooth, and bare? *Holy shit, there's not a stitch of hair.*

"Did you?" I tilt my head in wonder.

"You like?"

I flip the scrap of material obstructing my view out of the way. The sight alone nearly takes my breath and coherent thoughts away. There, in all its glory, is Samantha's glistening pussy fully on display. Not being able to control myself. I bend down and lick from her center to her clit. I vaguely hear Samantha stifle a deep moan when I do it again and again until I nearly have her coming in seconds.

Don't get me wrong, I love going down on Samantha, always have. But this brings things to an entirely new level of satisfaction. She seems to be hyper-sensitive and I can't get enough of her. Out of nowhere, an orgasm comes barreling through her, and I've barely begun to get my fill of playing with her. Once she's come down from her high, I start all over again, this time adding my fingers to the mix.

By the time I actually fuck her, my cock's about to explode in seconds. I do my best to make things last. This new sensation as I bottom out in her is a huge turn on for both of us. We finish together in an epic explosion, and I swear I almost black out. I don't think I've ever been so turned on. I'm not sure if it's because she's officially my wife, or she felt so unbelievable bare, but this is among the hottest nights of my life.

When I'm able to move, I flop onto my back until I can muster the energy to get up to clean us off.

I'm not quite sure what to think when Sam pants, "Lexi's right. This feels fucking fantastic." Her fingertips graze her bare mound. I cock an eyebrow at her and she smiles. "She's the one who booked the Brazilian wax. It hurt like a son-of-a-bitch, but my God, I think it was so worth it."

"Sam, you know I enjoy it either way. There's no need to hurt yourself in the process."

"So do I," she admits. "But wasn't this fantastic?"

"It's something I'll never forget, but I never want you in pain, beautiful."

"I think I just might have to try that again." She giggles. "For research purposes."

"I think I can handle that," I murmur and somehow, my cock has decided it's time to play again.

20

SAMANTHA

"HOLY CRAP! Being married to Enzo's amazing," I tell Lexi one morning over coffee when it's just the two of us at our office. "The man's insatiable, but with my pregnancy hormones in full swing, so am I." I can't help but laugh. "Our honeymoon was unbelievable. When we finally ventured out of our room, we had the most amazing couples' massage."

"I'm so happy for you, Sam," Lexi says before taking another drink from the mug she's holding.

"He's so thoughtful. He even arranged for me to get a prenatal massage, so that I could be more comfortable," I add as I take a bite of the bagel she's brought me.

"How are the kids handling the adjustment?"

"Well, it's only been about a week, but I'd say it's going well." I shrug.

Lexi nods in agreement. "Yeah, you're all in the honeymoon phase. I'm sure shit will get real soon enough." She winks.

"Bite your tongue, woman. I don't need to borrow trouble. We're going to tell Frankie and Dec tonight about the twins. We didn't want them to have too much thrown at them all at once."

"That should be interesting. But, Maddie seems to be handling it well, isn't she?"

I nod. "Thank goodness. I just about died when Nicole figured it out." I place my hands on my belly and rub lightly. Just a matter of days until everyone knows. "Frankie, on the other hand, might be realizing the honeymoon's over." I shake my head, remembering their standoff last night.

"Why is that?" Lexi asks with interest.

"Well, last night, Frankie wanted Enzo to keep reading way after bedtime. It wasn't a big deal, but he had to firmly put her in her place, to let her know it was time for bed. I almost died laughing when he came to tell me her quivering lip almost worked on him. He had stayed firm for her sake, but once we were alone in bed, he was second-guessing himself."

"Did you tell him, welcome to the joys of parenthood?"

"Something along those lines."

"Well, it'll get easier for him in time. Just wait until you have two more to tend to. You guys are gonna have your hands full... How does he like his new job? Didn't he start yesterday?"

"He said most of yesterday was just training at their headquarters. I think he likes it, but he hasn't had to fly anywhere yet. The guys he works with are pretty funny and like to give each other a hard time. Apparently, he's worked with many of them before, so he's not the new guy, so to speak."

Lexi finishes her coffee and places her mug on my desk. "Will he travel with them often?"

I let out a deep breath to face reality. "It's a possibility. But most of what he'll do will have him home within a couple of days."

"If you ever need anything, you know where to find me." She stands and picks up her cup. "I'd better get to work if I'm going to meet with Abigail for her next book on time."

"Thanks, Lex. I'll see you this afternoon."

When she leaves, I send a quick text to Enzo.

> **Me: Hope your day is going good.**
> **Miss you.**

His reply is almost instant and brings a smile to my face.

> **Enzo: Miss you, too. Wish we were**
> **still on our honeymoon. Adulting**
> **has lots of disadvantages.**

> **Me: Welcome to reality, sweetheart.**
> **See you when you get**
> **home. XOXO**

> **Enzo: Should be home for dinner.**
> **Want me to pick something up?**

**Me: Sounds good. Maddie asked to
have Soren for dinner. Make sure
you get enough for him, but not so
much that we'll be eating it for the
next week.**

**Enzo: Ha. I only made that mistake
once. How does Thai sound?**

The man knows my weakness. My mouth waters at the sheer thought.

**Me: Delicious. See you tonight.
Love you.**

**Enzo: Love you. Now let me get back
to work.** 😌

I force myself to stop thinking about Enzo and get some work done. With all the time off I've taken lately, I have plenty to catch up on. I spend the day on the telephone, touching base with clients. I even manage to read through most of a manuscript. By the time I leave to pick up Declan and Frankie from school to take them to ballet and soccer, I feel like I've got a handle on things.

Frankie and I pull into our driveway just as an unfamiliar vehicle does.

"Who's that, Mama?" Frankie asks as she hesitates to get out of the car.

"Not sure, honey. Let's find out." I leave everything in my SUV, but my keys and phone, should I need it.

By the time we get out, we see it's Enzo. *What in the world has he done now?*

"So... What do you think?" He gestures to the shiny silver SUV behind him. It's far bigger than mine, but still beautiful. As I take in the vehicle, I see it's a Toyota Sequoia, with dealer plates.

"Is it ours?" Frankie jumps up and down with excitement.

I notice he doesn't answer, but Enzo walks over and opens the passenger door. "Come on, let's go for a ride."

I have to step up onto the running boards to get into the luxurious vehicle. The seats are a soft-gray leather and it smells new. I easily relax into the seat as I watch Enzo walk around to the driver's side. *Damn, I will never get tired of looking at his sexy body.* He opens the door, meets my eyes, and gives me a knowing smirk. *Crap. Caught again.*

Frankie chatters a mile a minute about all the features she sees in this vehicle that our other car doesn't have, as Enzo pulls out of the driveway. He reaches for my hand but lets her continue. We pull out of the driveway and head toward the main highway. I learn how many cupholders, seat recliners, seat heaters as well as about a thousand other features Frankie finds in the vehicle as we drive down the road.

After a few minutes, Enzo breaks in, "So, Samantha, what do you think?"

"It's nice." I give him that. It has a lot of features. I shrug. "What do you want me to say?"

"Would you want this as your daily driver?" he hedges.

I glance around again. This car's huge. *Can I even drive a car this big? This vehicle's a beast compared to mine.* "Umm... I haven't driven it to know if I could handle this beast."

"Trust me, Sam, this is nowhere near a beast. It has a nineteen-foot radius and turns on a dime. Here, let me pull over and you can drive it."

As I drive down the road, I find that this car is magnificent. It handles like a dream. The fact that it seats seven, has a TV, and all the latest features is nice, too.

"So how much is this going to set me back?" I ask as I punch the gas in a straightaway. Holy crap. This has power!

"You'll get used to the V-8 engine, Sam. But unless you want to draw the attention of the local law enforcement, I'd lay off your lead foot," Enzo teases.

I ease off the gas and grin. "I could get used to driving this."

"Does this mean we're keeping it?" Frankie excitedly pipes in.

I glance at Enzo, who gives nothing away. "So, what are the monthly payments?" I repeat to get a straight answer.

"Nothing," he calmly replies.

Giving him my best mom tone, I glare in his direction. "What do you mean, nothing?"

"I mean, unless you completely hate it. It's already paid for."

What. The. Fuck? Who goes out and pays cash for a vehicle loaded with this many options. "Your prior job was for the U.S. Air Force, right? Not some secret agent shit or anything?"

He gives me a disapproving look. "Sam..." He glances to Frankie and doesn't say anything.

"She's heard worse," I glower, but am frustrated he's not explaining anything. "Talk."

He takes a deep breath, and slower than molasses in January, exhales. *Oh, this has got to be good.* "Samantha, you know I haven't had a lot to spend my money on over the years. I'm a simple man and live within my means. I've pretty much saved about half my money from each paycheck and invested it. Any money I got while on deployment went into that investment account, too."

"Don't you think we should've talked about this before you went out and bought it?"

"We talked about vehicles, and you said this was one you'd consider. I drove by this morning in Pops' truck and saw them putting this on the lot. I was off a bit earlier than expected and figured if it's meant to be, it would still be there. And here we are."

There's no point in arguing. He's right. But still. This is a huge purchase.

"Did you even think to run this by me first?" comes out before I can hold it in. *Crap. That sounded way snarkier than I meant.*

"Again, you had already agreed this was a vehicle you wanted. I found it, paid for it, and honestly didn't think it would be that big of a deal. I never meant to leave you out." He's quiet for a moment, then adds in a lighter tone, "By the way, I ordered Thai food. We just have to pick it up. I was dying to show you this, so I thought we could drive to pick it up."

"Being perfect isn't always polite, Enzo," I grimace and pretend to have some steam left for a fight.

"I'll work on that, beautiful." He laughs, but the look in his eyes tells me he thinks I'm being utterly ridiculous.

Men.

AS WE FINISH dinner later that evening, I look to Enzo, raise an eyebrow, and pat my belly. *It's time.* He nods in agreement and clears his throat just as Declan is about to ask to be excused from the table. "So... Guys, we have an announcement to make."

Maddie looks to Soren knowingly. By the look on his face, I'd bet he already knows what Enzo's about to say. Enzo and I have discussed that we need to tell the kids soon, but I haven't given much thought as to what we'd actually say. Enzo looks in my direction and I shrug.

"What is it?" Declan asks impatiently. He's about to go upstairs to finish his homework and I can tell he's tired, by his cranky demeanor at dinner.

Frankie's the exact opposite, her eagerness to know what's going on is almost comical. She bounces in her seat and says, "Yeah, what's going on?"

I glance to Maddie and she knowingly winks at me, smashing her mouth shut, making her lips form a straight line, just to keep from spilling the beans. I can't help but smile. She's good at secrets, but I can tell she's dying to tell this one.

Enzo reaches over to me and grabs my hand. "Well... I know that it's been an adjustment with me moving in here. But it's been okay, right?"

Both Maddie and Dec nod. Simultaneously, Maddie says, "It's the best," while Declan says, "Yeah."

Enzo nods and continues, "Since we're making changes... How do you feel about adding to the mix?"

Both Frankie and Dec stare at him in confusion, then glance at me for an interpretation. "Well, Franks," I say in a teasing tone, "I hate to break it to you, but you're not going to be the baby of the family much longer." I place my free hand around my belly and watch both of their eyes nearly pop out.

"Wait... You're..." Dec stutters.

Frankie finishes as she jumps out of her seat. "Pregnant?"

"Yes, I am." I reach out my arms to catch Frankie as she rushes in for a hug.

She places her hand on my belly and asks in wonder, "I'm finally going to be a big sister?"

"You sure are, squirt," Maddie chimes in.

"Congratulations," comes from Soren.

Enzo beats me to thanking Soren. I glance at Declan and realize he still hasn't said much. "You okay, bud?"

With a look of pure dread, he says, "Please don't let it be another girl. I can barely use the bathroom as it is." He groans in disgust. This makes the room break into laughter, with Enzo's the hardest.

Enzo pats Dec on the shoulder as he settles. "I can relate,

Dec. If it gets too bad, I know someone who can make us a bathroom all our own."

"Grandpops can build you one," Frankie announces. "Then we won't have to smell your stinkiness."

Before this gets too out of hand, I put a stop to it. "Well, there's more…"

"Yes! And you're never going to believe it," Maddie shouts over me. "Mom's having TWINS!!!"

"You have two babies growing inside of you?" Frankie's round eyes and high-pitched voice make me smile.

"She sure does." Enzo's deep voice booms and the loving look he gives me completely melts my heart.

"I won't have to share a room, will I?"

"No, Dec. We'll make the guest room the twins' room," I announce. "They'll be the only ones sharing a room. Don't worry. Your room's safe."

"What will happen when we have company?" Frankie asks.

"We're not sure yet, kiddo," Enzo answers. "Let's just get through setting up a nursery first, then we can see what happens. If we run out of space, I'm sure Pops can help us figure something out."

How does the guy always have an answer to everything?

21

SAMANTHA

AS THE YOUNG ultrasound tech moves the wand over my stomach, I look to Enzo, who's holding my hand anxiously. His eyes widen and the tension in his body shows he's on pins and needles as he stares at the screen. The rapid heartbeats echo through the small, dark room and I couldn't be happier.

I turn my attention to the screen and I see the profile of a head. The baby's fist is curled and at its mouth. I can't help the sigh that falls from my lips. I never will get used to seeing something so precious. Just before the tech moves the wand, another hand reaches out and bumps into the baby on the screen.

"That's a little freaky," Enzo whispers. "They almost look like aliens."

"Wait until you see them move," I warn.

As if they hear, both babies nearly flip upside down. They've grown so much since our last ultrasound. They're now a bundle of arms and legs. Their spines zoom in and out of focus, and if I didn't know any better, I'd say Enzo's right. I've been taken over by aliens.

The technician measures each of the babies. She identifies each part as it appears on the screen, as well as which baby it belongs to. Right now, we refer to them as Baby A and Baby B. I think it's the cutest thing ever to watch their little bodies move all over the place.

After another sudden movement on the screen, Enzo asks in wonder, "Does that hurt?"

I shake my head. "No. I only feel the big moves."

The technician interrupts with, "Do you want to know the sex of each baby?"

I look to Enzo for reassurance and he nods. Since their arrival has been enough of a shock, we think it's best to prepare ourselves for the future. "Yes. We'd love that," I eagerly state, and Enzo grips my hand tighter. I'm just as excited as he is waiting to find out, now that I know they're both healthy.

The technician moves the wand around and suddenly, there's legs and a little bottom on the screen. It goes in and out of focus for a few seconds, then she freezes the screen. "See here." She uses the pointer on the screen to bring our attention to a specific area. "See these dots here..."

"What does that mean?" Enzo jumps in as she takes several screenshots of the image.

"Congratulations. Baby A's a girl!" She takes a moment and types it onto the screen as well.

"Wow... Just... Wow," Enzo murmurs. He looks to me and I

swear I see his eyes shine as if they're filling with tears. He blinks a few times and they clear. He whispers, "I hope she looks just like you, Samantha." He bends down and presses a kiss to my temple. "I love you."

The cheery technician brings our attention back to her. "Now, let's see if we can find out the sex of Baby B."

After a few moments looking at a blurry screen, Baby B cooperates. Its bottom comes into view and I gasp, throwing my hand over my mouth. Enzo immediately turns to me. "What's wrong?"

I shake my head, pointing to the screen. "Look..."

He's silent for a couple of heartbeats and I hold my breath, waiting for his response. "Are you kidding me?" He shakes his head from side to side. "Is that what I think it is?" He turns to the technician, who nods in agreement, then to me for confirmation.

"That depends. What do you think it is?" I ask playfully.

Enzo's eyes are as round as saucers and his hand squeezes tighter against mine. "We're having a boy, too?"

"It appears so," I say, getting excited. He bends over and brushes a kiss to my lips. "Oh my God, Enzo! Can you believe it?"

LATER THAT EVENING, we gather in our family room to update the kids on their new siblings. All are eager to see the ultrasound pictures. Each takes a turn enjoying the profile pictures, not believing how big they've gotten since the last ultrasound was done. When we announce Baby A's a girl, Frankie jumps up and down. Her hoots and hollers could probably be heard by our neighbors. Her reaction melts my heart and makes me realize everything's going to be okay.

Declan, on the other hand, groans until we reveal the sex of Baby B. Then he cheers right along with Frankie. "YES!" comes out as a hiss before he turns to Enzo and grins. "Five girls in the house would be crazy."

"You may live to regret that." Maddie reaches over and rustles his hair. Then she turns to Enzo and me, sitting on the couch together. "As long as they're healthy, I didn't really care."

"My thoughts exactly, Mads," I add as I instinctively cradle my belly.

"Have you thought about names?" Maddie excitedly blurts as she pulls her feet up and settles into the oversized chair beside us.

"What about Zelma, for a girl?" Frankie suggests.

"Zelma?" *There's no way in hell I'm naming my child that. Has she been watching Scooby-Doo?*

"Or Tapanga?" Frankie shrugs.

"We're not calling our sister that, squirt." Maddie laughs. "You've been watching too much TV." Her voice turns serious and she places her hand on her chin as she thinks seriously about something for a moment. "What about... Hayley? Hayley Harper sounds cute."

"That does sound good," Enzo agrees.

We spend the next twenty minutes discussing possible names. In my mind, many more were vetoed than considered a possibility. I've read too many books or knew someone with names similar to ever consider them as a possibility.

By the time we're getting ready for bed, I think I've heard at least one hundred names for each twin. Enzo takes it all in stride. He suggests a few, but I'm pretty sure we're going to go with Lorenzo Dean Harper. He'll be the fourth son to have this family name. I'd really like to continue this tradition.

As we snuggle into bed, I lay my head on Enzo's shoulder, in that special spot I've claimed as mine. "Would you be against naming our son Lorenzo Dean Harper?"

"No, not at all." He kisses my head lightly as he pulls me closer. "I just didn't want to presume anything. As much as I love tradition, if you have your heart set on something else, I'm fine with that, too."

"Are you sure? I really like Lorenzo. Everyone I know with that name is strong, handsome, and has a big heart." My voice becomes playful by the end.

He sighs deeply. "It's not really an easy name to have as a kid, though. Kids are kind of mean. Hey... What if we called him Loren, so it's not so confusing around the house? Dad and I only had trouble when I was called by my given name."

I sit up to look him in the eye "So, you're okay with Lorenzo?"

Enzo nods and pulls me in for a kiss. It's slow and consuming. Suddenly, we're no longer interested in talking about names.

The next morning, I come downstairs to find bickering in

the kitchen. It doesn't sound too serious, but it's evident Maddie and Declan are in the midst of a disagreement. Enzo's already at work and Frankie's nowhere to be found. As much as I hate having to listen to them argue, over the years I've found when I intervene, it only gets worse. I know when to step in to stop things, but I want to see what they're arguing about before I jump in. From the tone of voices being heard throughout the house, Maddie is ticked at something.

"You're such a jerk!" Maddie shouts. "You used milk and put it back into the fridge when there was barely any left. Then you ate the last granola bar." When Maddie sees me enter the room, she shouts, "Mom, we need milk and granola bars!"

I notice Dec takes the opportunity to slink out of the room, shaking his head as he goes.

"I'll pick some up next time I go shopping," I reply.

"You need to pick me up from school today," she huffs. "Practice is cancelled and I don't wanna ride the bus," she announces like the entitled teenager she thinks she is. *I have to do this, huh.* So... this is how today's going to go. *Who peed in her cereal this morning?* I take a moment to calmly gather my wits and look to the ceiling for some guidance. *Please give me patience.* When days start like this, we are all in for a world of hurt. Maddie's a great kid, but when she's on the rampage, logical sense and reasoning go right out the window.

"I'll see what I can do," I nonchalantly counter. I've long ago learned not to engage with the enemy when she's setting up for a fight. She'll fizzle out faster if I just let it go and stay impartial.

"Ugg," she huffs and rolls her eyes. "Did you pick up that poster board for my project?" comes out in a tone that makes me cringe. *How can a fifteen-year-old sound like a toddler in an instant?*

"I didn't know you needed it," I reply.

"Mooomm! You know it's spirit week and I need to make a sign by Wednesday."

"Well, since today's only Tuesday. I'll see what I can do about getting one for you tonight," I offer, in an attempt to keep the peace.

"Grrrr..." she actually growls. *Have I just stepped into the Twilight Zone?* "I guess I'll have to wait until tomorrow," she grumbles. I swear I also hear, "I can't wait until I can drive." *If she thinks she's going to be driving with that attitude, she's got another thing coming.*

Maddie forcefully opens and shuts a few cupboard doors before I've finally had enough. "Wanna tell me what's on your mind, Madelyn Mae? Or are you going to rip every door off the hinges before school?" I arch an eyebrow and wait for a response.

"Ugh." She turns to face me, steam still flows out her ears as her chin juts in my direction. "Can't I *just* have a bad morning?" She sounds like a typical prema donna. *God, I love teenagers.*

I glance at the clock. "Well, if you want to be fit for company at school, you'll need to adjust your attitude. Soren will be here any minute. So, unless you want him to see your horns come out, you might want to rethink this fit you're throwing."

She pants, "Uh. I'm not throwing a fit."

"Sounds like one to me," Frankie states all too cheerily. I quickly step between the two of them or we might just have World War III, right here in the kitchen. I place my hands up in the surrender position as I step toward Maddie and I curtly tell Frankie, "That's enough. We don't need comments from the peanut gallery."

Frankie shakes her head, but knows better than to respond at this moment. Instead, she walks to get her bag by the kitchen table and places her lunch pail into it. Once she has her things, she walks to me and gives me a hug. "I'm walking to the bus stop. Don't forget I need to bring snacks to school tomorrow for that party. I have twenty-five students in my class and we'll need to have it there by eleven. See you this afternoon when you pick me up. Love you."

"Love you, too, Franks. Grab your brother and walk together."

Declan walks through the kitchen to grab his things and heads out the door. Before he leaves, he looks to me and whispers, "Have fun dealing with..." he looks to Maddie, who's currently brooding as she looks for something else to eat, "that."

I roll my eyes and silently mouth, "Don't you start." Then add in my regular voice, "I love you, bud. Have a good day at school."

"Love you, too, Mom."

Once Frankie and Declan leave, I use this time to grab something for myself to eat and let Maddie cool down. She's still slamming things harder than normal, but it's not worth getting into it at the moment. Eventually, she settles and sits at the table to eat in silence. *Maybe she's calmed down.*

Unfortunately, that theory's short lived as she snaps, "So you'll be there after school?"

I take a deep breath and force myself to keep a civil tone. "Yes, I'll be there."

"You need to take me driving, too. I've hardly gotten any hours in this week."

"Madelyn, you **need** food, water, shelter, and air. Everything else is a want." She starts to say something, but I cut her off, in a strict, no-nonsense tone. "If you want me to do things for you, I suggest you change your attitude and check your words."

Before Maddie can say anything, there's a knock at the door. She rushes to grab her backpack, lunch, and open the door for Soren. The little twerp doesn't even say goodbye.

When Enzo calls a few hours later and asks about my day, I groan loudly. "Are you sure it isn't a Monday? Ugg... Anything that can go wrong, has today. I started off by getting into it with Maddie, our network's down at work and the IT guys are here fixing it, and a client I've spent the last three weeks planning with decided to go in a different direction."

"I'm sorry to hear you've had a bad day, beautiful."

I dismiss his kind words and continue with my rant about my day, "I now have to leave early, pick Maddie up from school, take her to get a poster board for a project, buy Frankie snacks for a school party, and since Declan has team pictures tomorrow, I also have to take him to get a haircut. Oh... and the snarky teen had the audacity to tell me she needed to go driving today, too. As if I want to spend more time with her after our morning."

"Samantha." Enzo's deep, sexy voice is the medicine I need after a day like this. "It'll all work out. Trust me."

"I know. It's just been a crappy day," I whine.

"I actually called to let you know I'm on my way home now. We're wheels up at zero five-hundred, and from the looks of the mission, I'll be gone a few days."

I know it's inevitable he's going to be gone from time to time, but I can't help the pang fluttering through my heart upon receiving this news. *Can today get any worse?* This isn't what I need to hear right now. "Seriously?"

"Yeah, it's just a routine mission, so get that worry out of your voice, Samantha." I know he can't tell me where he's going, but from what he's told me, he's basically their transportation as well as some behind the scenes intel, so I shouldn't worry. But I obviously do. It's in my nature to worry.

He's silent as he waits for me to respond. I let out a huff. "Fine. I'm just going to miss you." I've gotten used to him being around and I sleep so much better with him here.

"I'll miss you, too, beautiful." There's silence on the other end of the line for a few heartbeats and when he breaks it, the tone of his voice is back to business. "What do you think of this... I'll pick up the kids from school. We'll take Dec to practice and then get the things Maddie and Frankie need for tomorrow. I'll even let Maddie drive, and we'll grab dinner en route."

"Are you sure?"

"Samantha." His stern voice tells me not to question him.

I look at the pile of unfinished work on my desk and glance at the clock. It would be amazing to be able to work for a couple more hours without having to worry about the kids' schedules. "Sounds good. I'll pick up Dec to get his haircut before I come home."

22

———

ENZO

WORKING for Riggs and having a family to come home to every night these past few months has been a bit of an adjustment, to say the least. I'm not used to having people to check in with. These last few days, I've put in some long hours. We joined forces with the Department of Homeland Security, so they took over the rest of the operation once we got the girl we were after. DHS has a shitstorm on their hands after what we witnessed. I sigh and shake off the action of the day.

I pull into our driveway just a little after three in the morning. I do my best not to wake Samantha and the kids. Knowing it's late, I showered the grime off at headquarters before coming home. Samantha only has a few more hours of sleep until Frankie will be up at the crack of dawn, so I leave the lights off as I enter our room. I undress to my boxers, slip back the covers, and snuggle close to Samantha. God, having her in my arms and holding her close is what I need after the week I've had.

I wake up a few hours later to the feeling of being watched. Samantha's laying her head on my chest, so it can't be her. I open my eyes to find Frankie on the other side of Samantha. Her head rests on Samantha's pillow, but her eyes are bright and a huge smile is plastered to her face.

"Hi," she whispers.

"Hi," I whisper back, suddenly worried because Frankie's in our bed and I'm only in my boxers.

"I had a bad dream. Mama said I could sleep with her since you weren't home," she explains, as if it's no big deal.

"I see that. Are you okay?"

"Yeah. I'm going to watch TV," she says, as if this is a normal occurrence. Thank God, I decided to let Sam sleep this morning, instead of my usual sexy wake-ups with her.

"You do that. I'll come down in a bit and make breakfast." After I put on some pants.

"Okay, Enzo," she whispers.

She hops out of bed and goes to the door. Before she goes out, though, she turns to say, "Oh, Mama says she needs to sleep in, so be very quiet." She rushes back to my side of the bed and hugs the part of me that Samantha's not sleeping on. "I'm glad you're home. I've missed you."

This completely takes me back and I have no idea what to say. "You, too, kiddo," finally comes out as she rushes out the door.

I feel a soft kiss on my pec, right as the door clicks shut.

"Oh... So, you're awake now," I whisper to Samantha teasingly.

She giggles and her body convulses across mine. "Yeah, I

figured if I stayed asleep, I'd get a few moments alone with you."

"Did you, now?" I tease as I roll her onto her back. She's wearing a tank that has risen over the swell of her belly and her amazing boobs are barely contained in the top. Her pajama pants have settled below her baby bump and she's gorgeous as ever.

"Yeah, I've missed you." Her husky morning voice fills me with desire.

I bend to kiss her, being careful not to put pressure on the babies as I settle between her legs with the lower half of my body. "I've missed you, too, beautiful."

After I give her a scorching kiss, I make my way down her body by peppering her with kisses along the way. I swear in the last week of my absence, her boobs have gotten even bigger. I take the time to kiss the swell of each breast before I make my way down her protruding stomach.

When I get to her belly button, which is predominantly on display, I stop for a moment. I rub my nose along her navel back and forth. I can't help but whisper, "Hey, babies. I've missed you, too. I can't wait to meet you. Your ma and I are counting down the days until you arrive." I lay my cheek along her stomach and continue, "You're gonna have the best sisters and brother you could ever ask for."

As if they were talking to me, Samantha's stomach starts to roll. It almost feels as if they are stretching to wake up for the day. I see one ripple along Samantha's upper abdomen and another in the lower half. Yes, I've seen them move before, but I'm still in awe each time. Suddenly, there's a jab at my cheek.

"Damn, are you okay, Sam? That felt strong."

She chuckles, so I know she's okay. "You and your kids do nothing halfway."

Suddenly, she gasps. "Rib," comes out as a whisper. But then a beautiful smile appears on her face. "They're happy their daddy is home."

I sigh. "It's been a long week. I'm sorry I was gone for so long. The mission took longer than expected and I was their only way out."

My team had been assigned to help break up a human trafficking ring. When we found the girl that we were hired to recover, we learned there were more. There's no way we could walk away and not recover all that were in the compound. With the help of DHS, I am happy to say twelve other women and girls were reunited with their families.

"I know. You're a rock star in the air. I've missed you, but glad you were there to bring your team home safely." *If only she knew the details.*

Suddenly, Samantha gasps and a look of panic crosses her face.

"What's wrong?" I ask, wanting to jump into action to help.

"Bladder shot," she moans. "Help me up, so I don't wet the bed."

I immediately get off the bed. She rolls to the side, then throws her legs over the edge, as if it's a well-practiced move. I reach for her hand to assist her. She still has three more months until she's full term, but she looks like she could pop sooner.

She places one hand on the swell of her stomach and the other at the base of her back. As she waddles though, I'll never tell her I'd describe her walk as that, I can't help but be in awe of the woman before me. She never complains, though I'm sure she can't be comfortable. I start to follow her into the bathroom, when I hear a light knock on the door.

"Enzo," Frankie whispers. "Do you think you can cook the pancakes I mixed up? I can't turn on the stove without you or Mom downstairs."

I glance at Samantha with a grin on my face. "Sure thing, sweetheart. I'll be right down." I grab a pair of pajama pants and a t-shirt. *The life of being a parent. Though I wouldn't have it any other way.*

"Okay," I hear Frankie say, and her feet retreat.

Samantha laughs. "Duty calls. Aren't you glad you signed up for this?" Just as I finish dressing, she waddles my way. She wraps her arms around me and says, "Thank you."

"I wouldn't have it any other way," I reply with complete honesty. I kiss her once more, then go off to make pancakes.

Once downstairs, I see Declan's already up and watching TV in the family room. He has blankets strewn about and breakfast dishes at his side. It appears as if he's been up for a while and he's completely engulfed in the show he's watching.

Frankie has the batter ready, so all we have to do is turn on the stove and warm up a pan. I cut some fruit while she focuses on making pancakes.

"How long are you home this time?" Frankie asks.

"For the next week or so, at least." I place the fruit in the bowl next to me and wash the cutting board.

"Why do you have to go away so much?" Her voice has a slight quiver and she keeps her focus on the pancake in front of her, instead of looking me in the eyes, which instantly puts me on alert and makes my heart pang. I'm not used to having people care about me so much.

Though I can't go into specifics, I think of a way to explain. "Well... sometimes people need Riggs and his team to help them. I'm the one who gets them there safely and bring them back. I don't want to go away, but I'm needed. Lives literally depend on the work we do."

"Oh." Frankie's unusually quiet for a few moments.

I do my best to let her process whatever is on her mind, but finally, I can't take it any longer. "What's on your mind, Franks?"

"Well..." She plates the pancake and makes eye contact, finally. "Dad's out of town for the next two weeks and there's this father/daughter dance." She pauses and suddenly appears shy, but quietly asks, "Will you take me?"

Suddenly, my throat is thick, and I can't speak. When I don't answer right away, Frankie stammers, "If you don't want to go, that's okay... I just...thought..."

"I'd be honored, Frankie," I croak out before she can continue with her line of thought. Then I clear my throat. "Really. Tell me when and I'll be there." I'm not the only pilot Riggs employs, so it should work out, regardless of the date.

She rattles off the date, then goes on to tell me how we will need to dress up and find something that matches one another. Ugg... I see another shopping trip in my future. I guess that's the price for having girls in my life. But when I look at the smile on Frankie's face as she gushes over the details, I know I'd make a thousand more, if she reacts like that.

Samantha joins us in the kitchen, fresh from taking a shower. Her hair is still wet, hanging loose around her shoulders. There's no denying she's over six months pregnant in the yoga pants and fitted green t-shirt she's sporting. She couldn't look more beautiful if she tried. One hand cradles the babies growing inside instinctively while the other rests at the base of her back.

Frankie sets a plate in front of Samantha at the counter as she sits on one of the barstools. "Here, Mama, have this."

Samantha looks around the counter at the toppings I have placed out and narrows her eyes as she doesn't find what she's looking for. When she starts to stand, I ask, "What do you need, beautiful?"

"Just some powdered sugar."

"I got it," Frankie chirps and Samantha sets in to buttering her pancake.

"Where's Maddie?" Samantha asks the room.

I shrug. "Haven't seen her." I dish up Samantha some of the strawberries I'd cut up for this morning's breakfast.

Samantha turns her attention to Declan. "Have you eaten, Dec?"

"I'm good," he offers as he zones back into the television show he's watching. He mumbles something else, but I don't catch it.

Once we're through eating and there's no sign of Maddie surfacing this morning, we start to clean up. Just as we're finishing, Samantha calls over to Declan, "Can you bring in your dishes from this morning, Dec?"

He completely ignores her, entranced in his show.

I wipe down the counter as Samantha tries Declan again. "Hey, Dec. Bring your dishes in. I want to start the dishwasher."

I faintly hear Declan grumble something, but he ignores her once again.

"Declan," I sternly say to get his attention.

He turns to look in my direction. "What?" he replies as he looks to me defensively.

"Your mom asked you to do something." I give him a pointed look and he blanches like he has no idea what I'm talking about.

Samantha politely repeats herself, "Can you bring in your dishes? I want to start the dishwasher."

"In a minute," Declan mumbles, then focuses his attention back to his television program.

Oh, hell no. He didn't just say that. I straighten my stance and am about to stalk over to him to give him a piece of my mind and remind him of his manners, when I feel Samantha's touch on my arm, holding me in place.

"Give it until the commercial," she whispers so that no one but me can hear.

I wait the three minutes until the next commercial, then I pointedly look toward Sam. She rolls her eyes, puts the soap in the dishwasher, then she calls across the room, "Dec, it's a commercial. Time to bring me your dishes."

He groans loudly before mumbling, "Geesh. What's the

big deal?" He begrudgingly grabs the plates and glass beside him and brings it to set on the kitchen counter. His attitude rolls off him in waves, and I'm completely out of my element. I look to Samantha, who merely shakes her head and rolls her eyes behind his back. As hard as it isn't to interfere, I'll take my lead from her. No sense in rocking the boat unnecessarily.

Declan walks back to the couch and plops down. Just as he's about to cover up with a blanket he'd tossed down, Samantha asks, "Have you finished that biography project that's due on Monday?"

"Ugg..." He flops his head against the couch hard. "I'll get to it..." *What's gotten into him today?*

"You've finished reading the book, right?" She eyes him suspiciously and I'm suddenly doubting he has much done.

A snarl rips from his throat, as his eyes shoot daggers at Samantha. "I told you I'd get to it." He lets out a huff at the end and attempts to go back to watching the show. But Samantha has other plans.

She stomps over to the television and without the remote, turns it off from behind. This causes Declan to stand quickly. Now he's face-to-face, squaring off with his mother. He may only be ten, but he's almost as tall as she. "What's the big deal, Mom? I always get my work done. Why do I have to do it right this minute?"

"Because you likely haven't even finished reading the book and it's going to take hours to do the report, not to mention everything else that's required of it."

"I'll get it done..." He juts out his chin and crosses his arms in a stand-off.

Samantha takes a deep breath, closing her eyes for a second or two. When she opens them, they are calculating and narrowed at him. "You need to start. Now. You've had weeks to work on this and you've put it off until the last minute."

"Last minute would be tomorrow," rolls off his lips faster than I would've thought.

Steam can almost be seen coming from Samantha's ears. Her fists ball and her shoulders bunch. I immediately jump into action and put myself between the two of them. "Okay, buddy," I say in an attempt to diffuse the situation. "Why don't you go upstairs and get started."

"Why should I listen to you?" Declan seethes in my direction. *Wow. He's really going to go there.* I've never seen him like this, so this should be interesting.

I straighten to my full height and look him in the eye. In a tone that usually makes grown men quake in their boots, I quietly say, "Your mother told you to go upstairs and get started with your homework."

He stares indignantly at me.

I quirk an eyebrow in his direction. "Are you going to do this on your own, or will you need some help in getting there?" This is the first time I've had to lay down the law. I hope I'm not overstepping my bounds, but the shit he's trying to pull is ridiculous.

Declan's eyes bulge for a split second, then he recovers to his glare, but he says nothing.

The tension in the room can be cut with a knife. I cross my arms against my chest and let him know I'm not budging on this issue either. He *will* be respectful to his mother. I have no idea in hell what I will do if he doesn't listen, but I'm not backing down.

After a few more death stares thrown my way, Declan huffs. "Fine!" He turns and stomps up the stairs to his room, and just before his door slams, he yells, "I used to like you."

What the hell was that? I blink a few times and look to Samantha for confirmation that this has become my reality. She simply rolls her eyes and mutters, "Welcome to parenthood. I think you've officially been inducted."

I shake my head and mutter under my breath so Frankie doesn't hear, "Good times..."

23

SAMANTHA

"WELL, I can officially say Enzo's experienced into parenthood," I huff as I sit to have coffee with Lexi in her office the following Monday morning. I'm allowed one cup a day and after the weekend I've just experienced, I'm taking it.

"Really? Why's that?" Lexi states in disbelief. There's a slight upturn of her lips and I can tell she's on the verge of smirking at me.

"For starters, Declan was a complete turd this weekend. He waited until the last minute to do his biography report and then proceeded to act like we were the bad guys for asking him if it was done."

"Sounds like a normal pre-teen," Lexi deadpans.

I tell her how Declan went all-out into complete fit mode. He refused to work on his project for the better part of Saturday, which resulted in having to spend all of Sunday completing it. Bless Enzo's heart, he actually took pity on the kid and spent most of yesterday afternoon helping Declan put the finishing touches on the poster requirements.

"I'm telling you, Lex, even after Dec was a complete ass to him, Enzo still went out of his way to help him. They didn't finish until nearly ten last night."

"Wow. That's commitment."

"I know. I was done with Dec about thirty minutes into it yesterday. He's so infuriating, I just had to walk away. Enzo didn't know what to do with himself when Dec screamed, 'I used to like you' after the start of their argument. If I hadn't been so ticked at Declan's behavior, I would have laughed at the look on Enzo's face."

"But everything worked out?"

"Yeah. Enzo was a champ and seemed to know how to handle Dec and his shitty attitude."

"Is there anything Enzo can't do?" Lexi asks, her tone sarcastic. "I mean, did you order him from make *your-fantasies-come-true-dot-com* or something? Come on... He's gotta have some flaws. No man is that perfect. Dish, Sam."

"Of course he does." I shake my head at her absurdity. Is Enzo perfect? No. Far from it. But is there anything worth complaining over? I'm not sure. Sure, he wakes up at the crack of dawn. He's almost a neat freak. I hardly have to lift a finger around him, but those aren't things to complain about. "If anything, he's too attentive."

"Oh, that's a serious problem. We should report him to Bad Husbands R Us," she scoffs.

"Ha... Ha... Very funny." I roll my eyes at her ridiculousness. "He's got his flaws, just like anyone else."

"Whatever you say, Sam."

The intercom buzzes, interrupting our conversation. "Lexi… I've got Marie on the other line. Do you want me to take a message or is this a good time?"

I nod in her direction and I get up to leave.

Lexi mouths, "We'll catch up later."

I spend the rest of the day meeting with clients via phone conferences and reading over a manuscript for a prospective client. I'm relieved to find it intriguing, and I have high hopes we'll be able to sign her. I'm just about finished for the day when I get a text from Enzo.

Enzo: What's your ETA?

Me: I'm just about to leave and pick up the kids. Why?

Enzo: I told Frankie I'd take her shopping. Meet at the school?

The thought of seeing him still has the same effect on me as when we were first dating. Butterflies zing as tingles disperse along my spine. I hope I never get over this reaction.

Me: Sure. See you in 20.

I make it there with plenty of time to spare, but somehow, Enzo's waiting for me in the parking lot. He's sexy as hell as I see him step from his Range Rover to greet me. He's dressed in dark denim, a navy Henley, and brown-leather work boots. My mouth dries at the sight of him and I have to remind myself I'm in public.

He greets me with a sexy, dimple-popping smile, as if just seeing me has made his year. I roll down my window and he lowers his head to brush a kiss against my lips. He pulls back, all too short in my opinion, and a smirk forms on his face. "Hey, beautiful. How was your day?"

"It's been good. How about you?" He reaches out to push a loose strand of hair behind my ear. The sensation of the electrical current that is ever present, sends a shiver down my spine.

"Decent. I have the next few days off. What do you think about making use of the time and painting the nursery? I'll paint it while you're at work so the strong fumes will disperse before you return home."

I rest a hand on my protruding belly and grin. "That sounds good. These guys will be here before we know it."

As we wait for the kids to get out of school, we make plans for the room. We discuss paint colors and the furniture we'll need. He says he'll stop by and pick up some samples while he and Frankie are out this afternoon. I'm sure she'll have an opinion, too. That should be interesting. Last time she picked out paint, she was dead set on pink and purple.

Later at home, I find myself lost on the internet, delving deep into my favorite social media site. Who knew looking for decorating ideas would be so time consuming? It's then that reality sets in. *Holy crap! We have to buy two of everything.*

"Well, that is the plan, beautiful. What did you think

having twins meant?" Enzo chuckles from behind me on the couch. *Shit. I didn't know he was behind me.* I turn to look in his direction and the beautiful smirk on his face has his dimple popping, which makes me lose all train of thought.

He sits beside me, placing an arm behind me to pull me closer. "Show me what you've got."

"Well, I have a few things tagged as my favorites. Let me know what you think."

As I show him my ideas, his eagerness gets the better of him and it turns into an all-out brainstorming session. All of a sudden, we're going from simply painting a room and putting some baby furniture inside, to building custom shelves that will also serve as changing tables. He insists on customizing the closet to utilize the space the best we can.

Enzo's eagerness is a sight to be seen. He's completely animated as he suggests adding on to our house to give Maddie a new room, and converting her room into a playroom for the babies since their rooms are adjacent to one another. Of course, I squash that idea like a bug. I insist the babies will be fine sharing a room. He reluctantly agrees, and I make him promise not to go overboard. Though his definition and mine of what overboard means are entirely two different things.

The next day when I come home from work, the room next to ours is unrecognizable. All the furniture has been removed, shelves are being made, and the walk-in closet now has a state-of-the-art organizer inside of it, which includes built-in dressers for each of the kids.

If I thought the room was impressive, that's nothing compared to what I see next. My jaw drops when I spot Enzo, with his shirt off, low-slung jeans resting on his hips, and a tool belt strapped around his waist. His carved, muscular back faces me as I feel my mouth go dry and all my breath leave me.

Holy freaking hell. If the kids weren't just down the hall, I'd let my fantasies run wild. *Who knew I had hot construction worker fantasies?*

"I'm happy to make all your fantasies come true, Samantha," Enzo states matter-of-factly. "Though, I'd prefer not to have company either."

Shit! Did I just say that aloud? I cover my face with my hands and laugh. "I'm blaming that on pregnancy hormones."

"If that's what makes you sleep better at night," he chides. "Though I'm pretty sure you always wanted to jump me before you were pregnant, too."

"You and your ego," I rebut.

"You love my big ego."

True. I love everything about him. But there's no point in letting his head swell.

He shakes his head as if he can read my thoughts as he reaches for my hand. "Come on, let me show you around before your thoughts get carried away."

24

———

ENZO

AS I DRIVE HOME from taking the tools back that I borrowed from Pops, I can't wash the grin from my face. I can't wait to show Samantha the finished nursery. I have kept her out since that first night, and I can't wait to see the look on her face.

Just as I'm a couple of blocks from the house, I spot a girl similar to Maddie walking briskly down the street. She keeps swiping at her eyes and it's obvious she's upset. My heart pangs as I approach, hoping it's not Maddie.

As I get within a few yards, it becomes clear, it's her. *Fuck. What's wrong with her?* I pull into an open spot just past her and rush to get out. The tears streaming down her cheeks and the blotchiness all over her face tells me she's been crying for a while. "What's wrong, Mads?"

She stops dead in her tracks and looks the other way. "I'm... fine," she mutters between breaths, "it's... Nothing."

The hell it's nothing. I've been around the block enough

times to know a woman is *never* fine. I square my shoulders and step into her path. "Seriously, what's wrong?"

"I... Don't... Want... To talk...About it," is panted out between breaths.

"Well..." Fuck. Obviously, something's wrong. I can't just leave her like this. "Are you hurt or angry?" I look her over with care, trying to assess any physical damage.

"Pissed," she croaks and relief washes through me.

"Pissed, I can handle. Come on. Get in the car." I don't wait for a response before walking to the driver's door.

I see her hesitate for a moment before walking to the passenger side of my Range Rover. Once she's in and buckled, I turn the engine over, flick my blinker, and do a U-turn.

Maddie doesn't say anything, but her breathing begins to calm. It takes a few minutes before I can no longer hear sobs coming from her chest. Whatever it is, she's pretty worked up. There's only one place I know to go when I need to let off steam and it sure isn't home.

After about five minutes of driving, Maddie looks around and finally breaks the silence. "Where are we going?"

I simply grin and state, "You'll see."

Within twenty minutes, we arrive at my intended destination. Maddie's a lot like her mom and keeps her thoughts to herself when she's upset. She eyes me suspiciously when we drive through the gates. Unlike Sam, Maddie has a filter, so I have no idea what's going on in that head of hers.

We walk into the building and head down the elevator. As we arrive at my intended destination, Maddie's eyes widen bigger than ever. Her mouth drops open and she sputters, "Wh... Wha... What are we doing?"

I walk over to my lockbox and open it. I set things down with precision so I can explain how to use everything safely when she's ready. "Have you ever used one of these?"

"No..." comes out faintly. "I can't say that I have."

"Would you like to learn how?" I eye her cautiously to make sure she wants to learn.

"Sure." She shrugs.

"Before I begin, I want to stress to you that you must always treat this gun as if it's loaded. Never point it at anything you don't intend to shoot, and keep your finger off the trigger until you're ready to shoot. That means you're aiming at your target and you're ready to fire."

Her eyes are on the semi-automatic pistol for a few moments before her eyes return to mine. "Okay."

Before I'll let her shoot anything, she needs to know how it works and the things she must do to use the weapon safely and efficiently. We discuss the frame, barrel, and action and how those components work, as well as how the features of the gun range itself works. I specifically point out the external safety and explain that it has to be disengaged before the gun can fire as well as the internal safety feature of this particular Glock. She asks questions freely and by the time I teach her how to load it and unload it, as well as make sure it's clear, I can see her eagerness growing. I show her how to load shells into a magazine, then make sure she knows how to keep her thumb clear of the slide.

"You'll only do it once if you forget this step." She smiles in response and instinctively flexes her fingers, imagining the pain. Finally, I let her practice with dummy rounds to get the feel of it before firing a live round.

Then I show her how to stand so she has a stable platform while she shoots. She laughs it off at first, but once she fires her first round, I'm sure she'll be thanking me. I point out how to line up her sights, and the importance of breathing.

"Once you have your breathing under control, take a deep breath. When you're halfway through your exhale, hold your breath, then pull the trigger slowly." I demonstrate this a few times before firing a shot.

"Okay, got it."

Finally, I gather the protection for our eyes and ears. I encourage her to use earplugs as well as the ear muffs, then we walk over to lane three and I show her how to set up. She walks me through each step I've taught her and when we've covered everything, she eagerly asks, "Can I shoot now?"

"Sure." I can't help but join in her enthusiasm. "Wait until I clear your lane, then you can fire at will."

Once I'm in lane two, I see her nod in my direction to see if it's okay. I give her the 'all clear' sign and she fires a round. She jerks slightly from the recoil, but she immediately adjusts her stance and takes aim again. Before I know it, she's emptied the entire magazine.

I enter her lane and show her how to bring her target back. I notice she actually has a decent shot. Her shots are grouped tight in the bullseye, just above the center. "Impressive, Mads."

I whistle. "If you want to have them more centered, keep your wrist firm as you fire."

She simply nods, then refills her magazine like a champ. Before I know it, she's unloaded and getting another target. After a couple more rounds, I'm relieved to see a permanent smile that's etched into her features. I'd do just about anything to keep it that way.

While Maddie's target practicing, I shoot off a text to Samantha to let her know we'd be home in a while.

Enzo: I have Maddie. We'll be home in a couple of hours.

Samantha: Everything okay?

Enzo: It is now.

Samantha: ???

Enzo: I'll fill you in when we get home.

Samantha: You'd better. LOL

I give Samantha a thumb's up in my reply and return my attention back to Maddie. By the time she's finished, she's unloaded quite a few magazines. She's rubbing her shoulders. She'll feel this in the morning. I show her how to clean up our area and put everything where it's supposed to go.

As we walk out of the gun range, we meet Ira Michaels coming in. He's met Maddie before, but quirks an eyebrow in the direction we came from. "Hey, man. How's it going?" I ask, keeping things casual.

"Just here to keep sharp." Michaels smiles. "What kind of trouble are you getting yourself into?"

"I brought Maddie to learn how to shoot and let off some steam. She seems to be a natural."

I look to Maddie to show her how proud of her I am, as a blush colors her face. She mumbles, "It was fun."

"I'm here to let off a bit of steam myself." He smirks. "Did it do the trick for you?" he asks Maddie.

"It sure did. I just envisioned the bullseye as the center of my anger, and you wouldn't believe how many times I hit it." She chuckles.

Okay... Remind me to never get on her bad side. "Wanna grab some pizza on the way home?" I still want to get to the bottom of what was bothering her. Something serious had to make her cry like that.

"Sure." She smiles like she hasn't cried a drop today. I'll count this as a win.

When each of us has a slice of pie in front of us, I choose this opportunity to find out what was wrong with Maddie. "So... What's the deal with the tears earlier?"

Maddie finishes her bite of food before groaning. "Ugg... Sophia Jones was making fun of me at school."

What the fuck could she tease Maddie about that had her that upset? "About what?" I grit out, picturing the worse-case scenario I could imagine.

"Well, Soren's at an away match today, so he wasn't able to drive me home from school." She takes another bite of her pizza.

"Okay..." still not seeing the problem with this.

"Right before school got out, Sophia started teasing me about being such a young baby and not being able to drive... Since I'm only fifteen and she's seventeen, like Soren."

"I see..." But I don't. Why would this make her cry?

"Well... then Caroline, the girl I told you about in my driver's ed class said, 'You should see the way she parallel parks. God help us all if she actually gets her license.' Everyone laughed, calling me 'curby' because I hit a curb one time. One time, Enzo. It wasn't even that big of a deal. I've never done it before and I wasn't used to driving the driver's ed car. Now the entire school is making fun of me for it. I couldn't even get on the bus. I forced myself to walk home, just so I could avoid the kids who were making fun of me." By the end, tears fill her eyes. Crap. This isn't something to cry over.

"Maddie, tell me more about Sophia. Have you fought with her before or is this a new thing?" There's gotta be more to this.

"Well, I never really knew her until I started dating Soren last fall. She used to hang out with him a lot before we started dating."

Bingo. "Well, if I had to place my bets, I'd say she's jealous of you. She probably likes Soren and wants you to not feel good enough to be with him."

She looks at me as if my head just spun around twice and popped off. "Me? You think she's jealous of me?"

"Well, why not? You're smart, beautiful, funny, and easy to get along with. You also got a great guy you're dating. Does she ever pick on you when Soren's around?"

Maddie thinks about it for a few moments. Placing her hand on her chin and looking to the sky for answers. "I guess not. It's usually just a snide comment when we're alone."

"I'm sure it has something to do with jealousy. Trust me. Girls used to do that to my high school girlfriend Vanessa when I wasn't around. But they'd be as sweet as honey if I was around. It used to piss her off." Boy, did it ever. I remember many a fight over my "so-called friends."

"Maybe..." she concedes.

"And about the thing with parallel parking... we're not going home tonight until you can do it with one arm tied behind your back," I tease at the end, making her laugh.

"If you say so." She rolls her eyes.

As soon as we finish with our meal and get a 'to-go' box for the leftovers, I take Maddie back to Riggs' place. It's the only place I know that I can set up an obstacle course for her to drive through. As we pull into the parking lot, I see Michaels and Riggs are still around. Once we get out of our vehicle, I quickly fill them in on my idea. Soon, they're both helping me create a course for Maddie to drive.

Once it's set up, I drive through it once, pointing out how to turn at specific points, to keep the cones in place. Then I sit beside Maddie as she maneuvers it. I've ridden with her a few times. I know she's a good driver, but like most fifteen year olds, she just needs practice and experience. Confidence is the biggest factor holding her back.

By the time we go through it three or four times, I actually hop out and let her drive it on her own. I want to see if she can do it without someone correcting her or warning her of things to come.

I walk over to talk with Riggs, while she drives the course.

"Hey, Harps. I heard you were in the range earlier, but I missed you," Riggs states as he leans against the hand railing to the stairs. He's balancing on one foot and the other is propped against the wall of the building.

"Yeah. I wanted to help Maddie let off some steam."

When Riggs cocks an eyebrow at me, I explain the entire situation. He nearly doubles over when I explain how I didn't have a fucking clue as to what I should do with a crying teenager who was so pissed at the world, she couldn't see straight. The gun range was a knee-jerk reaction.

"Holy shit. You may be new, but you're going to make an awesome dad. Not only will your girls know how to protect themselves, but word will get around that you regularly take them to the gun range. Half your battles will be won."

We watch as Maddie makes the last turn, then attempts to parallel park on her own. She pulls up to the car we have placed in front of the designated spot and without a single correction, she perfectly parks the car on her own.

As soon as she's in the spot, I hear a "Heck Yeah!" come from Riggs beside me and a "Omigod, I did it!" screech across the parking lot. Maddie ejects herself from the car faster than I ever thought was possible and runs toward me. I close the distance to give her a high-five, but she catches me off guard by throwing herself at me, in a gigantic bear hug. I get so excited, I pick her up off the ground and spin her around, making her squeal with delight.

By the time we settle down, Riggs and Michaels are there to congratulate her. Maddie beams with pride. After what we just witnessed, I highly doubt anyone will be calling her "curby" in the future. They each give her a high-five or fist bump and tell her they'd be happy to help her practice again anytime.

Maddie's on cloud nine as we walk into the kitchen that evening. We quickly find Samantha sound asleep on the couch, and since it's as quiet as a church mouse, I'm pretty sure Frankie and Dec are in their rooms asleep, or close to it. When Maddie sees Sam asleep, she whispers, "Thank you for an amazing afternoon." She reaches out for a hug again.

"You're welcome, sweetheart. Anytime."

Maddie turns to go upstairs, but not before she whispers, "Goodnight."

"See you in the morning," I quietly return.

When I look to Samantha, I see that she's out cold. She's curled up on her side, with one arm under her face, the other cradling the twins. Her shirt has risen, giving me a peek of her belly. I walk over and bend to kiss the swell of her stomach. I can't help but whisper, "Love you guys," as I pull away.

When I look to Samantha's beautiful face, I see she's smiling down at me. "Don't let me ruin your moment," she whispers. "I'm quite enjoying it, too."

I reach in to kiss her, too. She pulls me down to her.

Instead of attempting to get comfortable on the couch, because let's face it, there isn't room for the four of us to snuggle in this position, I end the kiss and help her to a standing position.

"So, did you peek at the nursery?" I ask eagerly.

"No, I promised I'd stay out of there until you could show me," she groans in frustration. "Will you show me now? I can't take the suspense any longer. I wouldn't even let myself go upstairs because I'd have been too tempted," she grumbles at the end.

"Oh, Samantha, what am I going to do with you?" I shake my head at her, but pull her toward the stairs, turning off the lights as we go. I make one last stop to check the front door is locked and swoop her up in my arms so we can take the stairs at a faster pace. Her pregnancy waddle is just too slow.

When we get in front of the nursery, I set her down in front of the closed door. She looks to me for permission to enter, and I nod. When she steps in, it's dark, so I hit the lights. I adjust the brightness, so she can see there's a dimmer switch.

"Ohmigod, Enzo. We'll be able to sneak in here and keep it fairly dark. I wish I'd had one of those with the other kids."

She stands in the middle of the room and looks around slowly as if she's taking everything in. I've installed white wainscoting and painted the walls a shade of blue that's apparently called Blue Birds Feather. I have no idea what nut job names paint that, but it's what Samantha wanted.

I've assembled the cribs, shelves for toys, and replaced the carpet with light gray flooring. The two-toned cribs are gray and white, matching the floors and walls perfectly. My sister came over to help me hang pictures on the walls of baby animals, as well as set up the cribs for each child. Samantha had picked out blue and gray sheets for our baby boy and the same pattern, but accents of purple, blue, and gray for our girl. We still need to get the rest of the baby gear, but the room looks as if it can be lived in, if I do say so myself.

When Samantha turns to me, her eyes shine bright and her mouth is covered by her hand, so I can't tell if they are happy or sad tears. "Did I do okay?" I ask, needing reassurance.

"It's perfect, Enzo. Simply perfect," she whispers, then throws her arms around me in appreciation. "I don't think I've ever seen a more perfect room." She reaches up on her tiptoes and I take the hint to close the gap. When her lips taste mine, she's greedy and her kiss soon becomes filled with want.

Knowing that Maddie's right next door, I reluctantly pull back to whisper, "Why don't you thank me appropriately in our room."

I don't have to say any more. Samantha quickly takes my hand and leads me to our bedroom. The minute I shut the door behind us and click the lock for safe measures, Samantha reaches for the hem of her shirt and tosses it over her head.

Not to be outdone, I do the same, then toe off my shoes as I reach for the buckle of my belt. Before I can do any more, she whispers, "Let me show you how appreciative I am for all that you do for us." She reaches out to pull me close to her. Her breath tickles my neck, sending an electric current across my body. When her lips reach mine, my body explodes with desire.

I instantly take control of our kiss and show her just how turned on I am. I fist her hair at the base of her neck and guide her mouth as it moves against mine, like I know she loves. She lets out the sexiest moan I've ever heard and she presses her body to mine. Now that she's pregnant, she can't get as close as I desire, so I lead her to the bed. Once the back of her legs presses against the bed, I guide her slowly onto her back. She quickly breaks our kiss and scoots to the center of the bed.

I follow her, kissing every part of her along the way, starting at her ankles. I kiss her waist, and as soon as I feel her writhe beneath me, I pull down the leggings and panties she's wearing, quickly letting them land on the floor. She wiggles her arms behind her, and suddenly, her bra goes flying across the room, too.

I spread her thighs apart and kiss my way along the inner seam until I reach her center. She arches her back to meet me as my tongue licks slowly across her slit, driving her wild. I reach up and press my thumb to her clit and she practically detonates in an instant. I keep up this steady rhythm until she explodes with ecstasy. I keep right with her as she peaks and comes down from her high. Seeing Samantha come apart has got to be one of the sexiest things I've ever seen.

When she recovers, she grabs at my hips and leads me right to where she wants me. *Who am I to disappoint?* I push my tip inside and allow her time to acclimate. I move in and out of her ever so slightly, feeling each and every inch of her delicious body as she takes me in. "I love you. I want you. I need you, Enzo. More... Just like that," comes out in pants as I bring her to another pinnacle of her high. Warmth spreads across her body as her body convulses once again. Her coming apart is one of the things I have come to love. I pump in and out of her at a steady pace until I know she's through her orgasm. Then I follow her into my own release, letting out a string of low curses when I finally crest the wave of ecstasy I've been riding. *Holy shit. I don't think it can get any better than this.*

25
____

SAMANTHA

BY THE FOURTH OF JULY, I feel as if I'm thirty-five years pregnant, instead of weeks. I walk downstairs, if you can call my distinct waddle walking, and catch Enzo eyeing me up and down. The fool still thinks I'm sexy, but I feel anything but. He, of course, still makes my mouth water and hasn't gained an ounce since I've met him. In fact, with each passing day, I think he somehow gets hotter. *How the fuck does that happen?*

I catch Enzo's eyes, and he's smiling wickedly at me as he shakes his head. "I haven't changed since the day we met, beautiful."

"Damn filter," I mutter under my breath.

He looks me over once again, but stops at my feet. "Uhhh..."

"What?" I say defensively.

He seems a bit sheepish as if he isn't sure how to say something. "Are you going for a patriotic look?"

"What do you mean?"

His lips turn up at the edges, as if he's trying to hold back a smile. "Well, you're wearing a red and white top, blue shorts, and two different colors of shoes."

"Are you kidding me?" I can barely put my shoes on, unless I can slip into them, let alone see them once they're on.

"Which color did you mean to put on?"

"The red ones," I moan in disgust. Now I have to go back upstairs to get them. Which, of course, means another trip to the bathroom before we can leave. The twins think it's fun to bounce on my bladder with each vertical step.

Enzo must read how I'm feeling. "Stay right here. I'll get the red one for you. Do you need anything else while I'm up there?" He points to my right foot as I slip off what I hope is the white shoe.

"No. I just need that. I'm ready to go otherwise."

He kisses me lightly on the lips before leaving the room. I use this time to gather the salads I've prepared for the barbeque at Riggs'. We'll be staying through the fireworks tonight, so I also gather my sweatshirt and travel blankets from the hall closet.

When Enzo returns, he drops to one knee, and with a formal accent, he presents the shoe. "I believe you're looking for this?"

"Why, thank you, goofball," I tease. He slides it on my foot and stands to kiss me once more.

"Don't get any ideas, buddy. We have to leave in a few minutes or we'll be late picking up the kids from Devin's."

"I know, beautiful. I'm just making the most of our time alone together. In a matter of weeks..." He places his hands around my ginormous belly. "We won't be alone much more."

"Somehow, I'm sure you'll figure out a way."

AS WE PULL UP TO RIGGS' place, the driveway is packed. SUVs and trucks line the driveway, letting us know it will be a crowded house. Enzo assured me there'd be kids here, but once we get inside, I realize it's mainly couples and a few younger children. We were guaranteed this is the place to be for fireworks, so hopefully the kids will entertain themselves. Since Soren agreed to come with us, at least Maddie will be entertained.

Riggs has a slip-n-slide set up on one side of his house. Though, at the moment, there are many more grown men than children using it, which is quite comical. Immediately, Dec and Frankie take off in that direction. Soren and Maddie head with lawn chairs in tow to a shaded area, where they will likely hang out until it's time to eat.

After we greet Riggs and his wife Stella and visit for a while, Enzo insists I sit in the shade and put my feet up. I don't put up a fight. Being on my feet is killing me at the moment. Between the heat and being a hundred years pregnant with twins, I feel as if I'm about to pop. I still have a few weeks until my due date. But I've always delivered a week earlier than expected, so I'll take the reprieve when I can. The pressure on my lower back and abdomen is crazy with two in there. But as my doctor told me a few days ago, I am not dilated at all, so who knows how much longer these two will want to incubate in there.

We find a spot on the back deck where I can take in all the action. We're next to Drew Warren and his date for the afternoon, Hannah. I spent some time with Drew at our wedding. He's quite the character and never fails to make me laugh.

"So, how much longer before those two make their debut?" Drew asks as he points to my belly.

"Not soon enough," I groan as one of them makes a painful jab to my ribs and decides to hang out there for a while. I gasp and rub my hand, trying to get them to move. But no such luck.

Drew reaches into the cooler beside him. He pulls out a bottle of beer and wipes it down with the towel next to him. Then he hands it to me. "Here."

"Warren, she's pregnant. She can't have that," Enzo snaps.

Drew sighs and shakes his head. "No shit, sherlock. I meant for her to put it on her rib cage. I'll bet you five bucks it makes the baby move."

"Seriously?" Hannah asks.

With a knowing look in my direction, Drew juts out his chin as he passes the bottle to me. "Trust me."

"What makes you so knowledgeable about kids?" Enzo inquires with a cocked eyebrow in Drew's direction. "Last I checked, you're still single and don't have any of your own."

Drew rolls his eyes. "Well, my sister had four. Every time the little booger wanted to stay in her ribs, she'd insist on getting a bottle of beer. We used to tease her on hot days when we came to her house to visit. There would always be a cold beer nearby, for just these emergencies. She claimed it worked fast and stayed cold longer than an icepack."

Hell, I'll give it a try. I place the bottle sideways, along my rib cage and sure enough, it makes the squirming baby move from my ribs. Ahhh, relief. "Drew, I think I love you."

"Hey, now," Enzo comes to the defense and gives me the most pathetic look ever, as if he wants to mark his claim.

"Oh, stop." I swat my arm in his direction. "You know I love you the most, but Drew might just have become my new best friend." *How did I not know about this beer bottle trick?* I settle into my chair and relax even further. This is pure heaven.

"You just make sure you always keep a few cold ones in the fridge. You'll be her knight in shining armor soon enough, Harps," Drew teases.

"Don't worry, Enzo. You already are," I tease in a dreamy voice, which makes his dimple pop as he smiles. My skin tingles as electric currents run up my spine from that look alone. Will I ever get immune to his sexiness?

By the time we're ready for fireworks, I've gone to the bathroom more times than I can count. The kids keep teasing me, but I kindly remind them they are to blame for this new problem as well. Having five kids will do that to a woman.

We've gathered near the edge of the clearing Riggs has set up to shoot off fireworks. As the first explosions ignite, the babies inside me jump. I reach over and grab Frankie's hand to place it on my belly. When the next firework goes off, the babies don't disappoint.

"They're moving like crazy!" Frankie exclaims. "Come feel this, guys."

Within seconds, I have about five hands placed on my belly. As soon as another explosion is heard, the babies move around like they're dancing at a disco.

"I don't think they like the fireworks," Declan announces.

"Are they going to be okay?" Maddie asks.

"They'll be fine. I promise," I say as I rub the spot that was kicked the hardest. "You did this, too, Maddie, at a New Year's display."

"Really?" she asks in disbelief.

"Sure did, kiddo. You also liked to dance to anything with a loud bass."

"No wonder you like to dance," Soren adds.

Soon, the babies settle down, and we all go back to watching the beautiful display of fireworks Riggs has provided for our entertainment. We leave right after, not only is it late, but Enzo has to work tomorrow. We say our goodbyes, and I can't help as I look at the tired kids in our car, how blessed we really are.

It's two days later that I come to find out how good we had it on the Fourth of July. I'm sitting in my office when I get a call over the intercom. Brenda's voice is full of concern when she states, "Sam... You have a Jason Riggs here to see you. Can I send him in?"

26

SAMANTHA

INSTANTLY, my body goes cold and I'm filled with dread. There's no good reason on this earth why Riggs would show up at my office. *What the fuck has happened to Enzo?* Tears suddenly fill my eyes and I'm frozen in place.

"Sam... Can I send him in?" Brenda asks again, breaking me out of my panic for the moment.

"Sure..." I somehow manage to say.

I'm still frozen to my chair and can't do anything. It feels like hours have passed and there's no sign of Riggs at my door. Finally, there's a slight tap, and the door's pushed open.

The unreadable expression he has plastered in place leaves me little hope. If I thought that was bad, the stern, "Samantha, we need to talk," has me in near hysterics. The ice that fills my veins has me trembling on the spot.

Riggs doesn't wait for me to say anything, but sits in the chair across from me on the couch. He doesn't relax, but sits on the edge as if he's going to destroy my life in a matter of minutes. "I've got some news you need to hear."

Oh. My. God. This is it. Something's happened to Enzo. Suddenly, Riggs is out of focus and I can't see his expression clearly. *I need to be able to read his expression. I have to really hear what he is saying.* I wipe at my eyes to concentrate on him, and my hand is met with wetness. Christ, I'm crying and I didn't even know it.

"Breathe, Samantha," he whispers. "You've gotta breathe."

"Okay," comes out as barely a whisper. I take in a deep breath and force myself to let it out.

"Samantha." He reaches for my hand. He can't be dead. Please, God, don't let him say Enzo's dead.

"There was a situation in the field."

I gasp and do my best to remain upright.

"Enzo's team has lost all communication after being fired at twelve hours ago."

Tears roll down my face. I don't even bother to wipe them away as I shake my head in denial. This cannot be happening.

"We're fairly certain they weren't hit, but we're unable to locate them at this time."

"Wh... What does th... that mean?" I stammer.

"They followed protocol and went radio silent. They made it to their first checkpoint, but we haven't heard from them since."

This gives me a glimmer of hope. But I still don't understand. Since I can't seem to find my voice, I stare at him, desperately waiting for him to continue.

He takes a deep breath, and in the time it takes for him to

exhale, it takes everything in me not to come out of my chair and throttle him. *Why won't he just say it already?*

Just as I'm about to find my voice, he begins again, "We're not sure if anything's been compromised, and until we have any definitive news, we'd like for you to come to headquarters. We'll be able to keep you informed of all updates, as well as provide for anything you need."

At first, I don't comprehend what this means. I replay his words in my mind until I finally realize he's waiting for me to respond. "My kids are at their grandparents' for the week in Montana. They left yesterday and won't be back for a week. Do we need to get them?"

He shakes his head. "No. I just didn't want you to have to drive anywhere or have to juggle their schedules while we wait for word on our team. I'm simply trying to make things easier on you." He does his best attempt to give me a reassuring smile, but until I see for myself that Enzo's okay, I doubt anything will comfort me much.

Riggs looks around my desk and clears his throat. "Uh... Harper's mentioned you can work from virtually anywhere. Do you want me to give you a minute to gather what you need, then we'll go to HQ?"

I look around, unaware of how to start. I doubt I'll be able to concentrate. As I stand, I get a karate kick to the bladder, so I rub my lower abdomen. "I'll just use the bathroom and we'll be on our way."

When we get to the waiting room, I notice another man with Riggs. When he reaches out his hand to greet me, I realize it's Nate Carson. We've met a few times since I've known

Enzo, but I can tell some serious shit is going down. Gone is his ever-present overzealous attitude. He pulls me into a hug as he whispers in my ear, "Everything's going to be okay."

If that doesn't freak me out, I don't know what will. A fresh batch of tears streams down my face. I don't even know what to do or say. I'm so overwhelmed with emotion, I can't think of a way to respond. *What the fuck am I going to do without Enzo?*

As we exit my office, I gasp when Sara and Lorenzo flash through my mind. "Have you notified the rest of his family?"

Riggs shakes his head. "As soon as we knew the severity of this situation, we came straight here. We wanted you to be the first to know." He looks directly at me, then turns to Carson. "Do you mind taking Sam to HQ while I stop at his parents' house? I'll meet you back at HQ in less than an hour."

Carson nods, then turns to me. "Sam, do you mind if I drive your vehicle? We rode together, so you wouldn't have to drive."

Completely numb, I state, "Sure." I rifle through my purse and pull out my keys. "I'm parked right out front." Carson gently takes my arm and leads me to the vehicle. I faintly hear one of the girls in the office saying they'll be here if I need them, but I can't be certain who voices it.

Carson goes above and beyond to help me into my SUV. When he realizes I'm unable to do much more than stare into space, I feel him buckle my seat belt around the babies and me. Then he makes his way to the driver's side, gets in, and takes me to Riggs' HQ.

Once we're on the road, he reaches over for my hand. I

hadn't known I'd been rubbing my legs until he stops me. "What can I do to help you calm down? Have you eaten recently?"

"I'm not hungry," I mumble, but I'm sure he hears me.

The entire ride to HQ, my heart aches with the thought of not knowing what's happening with Enzo. I rub my belly and hope like hell he's safe and that I'll see him soon. I can't let the reality of him possibly never coming home sink in because that's a guaranteed way for me to break to pieces. To hold myself together, I force myself to keep a cycle of thoughts repeating through my mind. *He's going to be fine. He will get through this. I won't lose him.*

It doesn't take long before we're pulling into the HQ parking lot. I find myself being ushered into a conference room by Carson. Once again, he asks if there's anything he can get me. *Besides my husband, I don't want anything.*

It doesn't take long before Sara and Lorenzo come swooping through the doors. As soon as their eyes meet mine, they rush to hug me. I'm swallowed up in their arms for an unknown amount of time. My ears feel like cotton has been stuffed in them, and I don't quite catch what is being said, but I can feel the love they have pouring from them. I squeeze them each harder to let them know just how much I appreciate them.

It's Lorenzo's deep baritone voice, thick with emotion, that finally breaks through my fog-like state. "How are you holding up?"

"As well as can be expected," I mumble.

Sara pats me on the arm and states, "I'm sure it'll be just

fine. Riggs got an update on the way here and there may have been some activity at the second checkpoint. They're verifying it now."

"What do you mean?" I ask for clarification, not sure I can let myself have hope, until I know for certain.

"I'm not really sure. I just overheard it as we arrived. They said they would come in and tell us in just a few minutes." Sara pats my arm and gestures for me to sit next to her in one of the conference room chairs.

We walk into a room and find three other women sitting at the conference room table. I faintly recognize them as some of the girlfriends or wives of the guys at the party a few days ago. I'm quickly re-introduced and reminded which man is their significant other. Instinctually, my heart reaches out to each of them because they must be in the same state as I. Other than a quick greeting, we each steer clear of the unfathomable topic as to why we've been brought to this room, waiting on pins and needles to find out more information.

After what feels like an eternity, the door to the conference room opens. This time, instead of more family members being brought together, Riggs himself enters alone. His stoic expression is unreadable. His strides are steady and he gives no indication as to which type of news he'll be delivering in just a matter of moments.

Enzo will be okay. Enzo is fine. Relax, Sam. You will get through this, runs on repeat through my head as I absent-mindedly rub my belly to comfort both my babies and myself. Their bodies twist and are just as tense as mine at this moment. As if they know there's a threat, each baby stands on alert as they stretch in what little room is left in my womb.

I keep my focus on Riggs as I feel Sara's arm wrap around my shoulders and pull me closer to her.

As soon as Riggs sees everyone's attention is on him, he doesn't waste any more time. "Thank you all for coming. I'll share and update, then I'll be happy to answer as many questions as I can." He looks around the room before taking a breath and continuing. "As you know, we've lost communication with our Delta team some hours ago, after shots were fired. As per protocol, they went radio silent and made it to their first checkpoint, which wouldn't cause alarm. But when they failed to clear the second checkpoint, we grew concerned. Their last location was a small village outside of San Salvador. I can't go into specifics of the mission, but I do know they were on their way out."

Sara squeezes my hand and Lorenzo places an arm on my back as we wait for him to continue. I feel myself tremble and I lean in heavily toward Enzo's parents for support. *I don't know what I'd do without them at this moment.*

"After several hours lapsed and they had yet to make it to their second checkpoint, we grew concerned. With their coms down and their tracking devices remaining stationary, we sent another team to get eyes on the ground for us. At this point, we are waiting for an update and we will let you know as soon as we know more."

"Mark has worked with you for years and scarier things than this has happened. Why have you brought us here?" a woman's voice whips out. "What are you not telling us?"

My eyes are drawn immediately to the icy voice sitting at the end of the table. She's a woman in her early thirties with light-brown hair. Her eyes are wild, pinning Riggs with a look that shows she's not to be messed with. I'm not sure I'd want to be on the receiving end of that glare.

Riggs exhales deeply. "Well... We wouldn't typically pull you all in on this but in this circumstance, we thought it best."

"What circumstance?" Daggers are shot in his direction again. There's a clear no BS vibe coming from this woman.

"Well... Since my team has apparently taken upon themselves to personally populate Portland, I thought it would be best to have all you expecting mothers here at one place. This way we can keep you up to date, keep an eye on you, and have a doctor on hand, if necessary." Riggs shrugs as if we should know this.

I take a closer look at the women at the table around me. Sure enough, each of us have stomachs protruding and if I had to guess, are pretty far along in our pregnancies. *How did I not notice we're all pregnant?*

Lorenzo clears his throat. "When Sara and I arrived, we overheard something about making it to checkpoint two."

"You're right. You did." Riggs nods in agreement. "It seems the team has made it to checkpoint two, but there's a mechanical failure, so they were not able to extract themselves in a timely manner."

Sara leans forward and places her arms on the table in front of her. "What does that mean?"

"We were right to send in a second team. They've made

contact and will be extracting the entire Delta team as we speak."

"So... They're... Safe?" I mutter, not wanting to have false hope, but desperately needing something to cling on to.

"They're not out of the woods yet, but within the next hour or so, we'll know if they've made it out of the hostile territory safely, and are on their way home."

Loud exhales can be heard throughout the room. For the first time since Riggs' arrival in my office, I take a full breath. There's still a weight on my chest that I know won't clear until I see Enzo for myself, but the pressure's not as deep.

"Ohmigod," I whisper in relief as I throw myself into Lorenzo's arms. Tears rush down my cheeks and my emotions are out of control.

"It's gonna be all right," Lorenzo whispers as he wraps his arms around me, giving me his strength.

"We'll know soon enough." Sara embraces the two of us and we sit here, tangled together.

When we finally break apart, Riggs clears his throat. "I'll be in command. You're welcome to make yourselves at home. I've made this conference room as well as our lounge available to you, so you won't be without the comforts of home. If you need anything, feel free to ask." With that, he walks out of the room.

Once the door to the conference room closes, Carson grabs everyone's attention. "Are any of you hungry? I'm ordering takeout and would love to get you something while we wait." He places a variety of takeout menus on the table and says, "I'll be back shortly to place the order." With that, he, too, walks out of the room.

Out of habit or perhaps it's nerves, I grab a menu off the table and peruse it. I can't for the life of me concentrate on the words printed before me. It's as if they are jumbled and in a foreign language. I'm not even sure how long it takes for me to realize the menu I'm reading is for a Thai restaurant.

The moment I do, thoughts of asking Enzo out for the first time flood my mind. I'd been so nervous and I had no idea what I was doing. I hadn't expected him to be outside my door that day. As far as I knew, he was long gone with his father and the only way I'd be seeing him again was in my fantasies. He'd taken me off guard with his deep, green eyes, sexy smile, and dimple that made me swoon. No man has ever made me react the way he does.

My heart still flutters as I recall him approaching my walkway. His complete sexiness had rendered me speechless. Of course, he'd been there to thank me for letting his dad take off for lunch. When his stomach rumbled, I'd seen it as a sign. I had no idea that one little move on my part would have set so much in motion.

There's a sudden jab to my stomach and the menu I'm resting on it nearly falls from my hands.

"You okay, Sam?" Sara reaches over to place her hand on my arm.

"I was just remembering the first day I met Enzo and couldn't believe I'd had enough guts to ask him to dinner."

"If I recall, his stomach did the asking for you." Lorenzo chuckles.

"Yeah," I say wistfully as I recall each and every moment of our dinner. I still can't believe the way he made me feel and the instant connection we shared. That evening when he dropped me off, I truly didn't want him to leave.

"I'll never forget the day Enzo came home with that suit." Sara laughs. "I knew something was up right away and I didn't even have to resort to my usual tactics to get him to spill his guts about you."

"Oh, come on, Sara. You've never had to do much when it comes to interrogating the boys. Erin... That's another story. But if there's ever a story to be told, it doesn't take you long to get it out of them."

"Ohmigoodness," Sara gasps. "Do you remember when Zane and Enzo tried sneaking out when they were in high school? Those fools thought they could actually push the car out of the driveway and we wouldn't be any the wiser."

"You're kidding me," comes out of my mouth before any further thought. *This must be interesting.*

Sara shakes her head and levels me with a stare. "You'd better believe it."

Becoming the perfect distraction for our current situation, Sara continues the story of how she just so "happened" to go out to the garage as they were pushing Enzo's truck into the driveway later that evening. She'd known they were gone and wasn't all too worried because they were together, but from what she tells me in her story, I would have paid millions to be a fly on the wall.

Stories about Enzo from Lorenzo and Sara are just what I

need to pass the time. They somehow manage to get me laughing about Enzo and the antics of his youth. I don't even realize almost two hours have passed when Riggs makes his way back into the conference room we chose to stay in.

As I look up, I realize the other women are nowhere in sight. Riggs comes and sits beside me. "How are you holding up?" Concern is etched in his voice, which puts me back on alert for Enzo.

"Is he... Do you know anything else?" I manage to mutter, all the anxiety I'd pushed away rears its ugly head and is back in full force.

Thankfully, it dies away as soon as I see relief fill his features. His eyes soften and a smile forms on his lips as he nods in my direction. "Yes. We've gotten word everyone made it out. They were wheels up hours ago. There were some injuries, but nothing sustainable. It's an estimated nine hours of flying, so they should be here late this evening."

"Is Enzo..." I take a deep breath and steady myself. "Was he injured?"

"He might have some bumps and bruises, but from the sound of it, the injuries were to someone else."

Instantly, the women I met earlier come to mind. "Ohmigod, what happened to them? Anything serious?"

"I'm not privy to specific details as of yet, but it appears as if McGowen's calf was grazed with a bullet. Nothing entered his body, but it slowed them down before they got to checkpoint two."

"But he's going to be okay?"

"Yes. There's also a medic. He's assured us he's fine."

"And nothing's wrong with Enzo?" I can't help myself by asking. *He did just say a grazing bullet wasn't a big deal after all. Is Enzo going to be covered in bruises and unrecognizable?*

"Seriously, Sam, he's fine. In fact, he's the pilot. We wouldn't have him flying if he's sustained any injuries." Relief washes through me and my chest loosens immensely. I want to scream and shout my relief from the rooftops.

Unaware of my intent, I throw myself into Riggs' arms, hugging him fiercely. "Thank you. Thank you. Thank you," I repeat into his ear. When I pull back, I find my eyes filling with tears.

"Are you sure you're okay?" Riggs has a cross between a deer in the headlights and there's a bomb about to explode expression down pat.

"Happy tears, I'm sure," Sara explains for me.

Lorenzo reaches out to shake his hand. "Thank you for letting us know." He looks to Sara and me. "Now that we know Enzo's safe and sound, we'll be able to relax some."

"Feel free to hang out here to wait for their arrival. Let's get out of this conference room, so you all can relax a bit while you wait."

Without even looking to Enzo's parents, words pour out, "Thank you, we will." There's no way I'm going anywhere until I see Enzo for myself.

A FEW HOURS LATER, Sara and I visit on an extremely comfortable couch in the lounge Riggs had let us use. Lorenzo took off to run some errands and will return before Enzo arrives.

I take a deep breath and I find myself getting sucked deeper and deeper into the cool leather surrounding me. I may need a forklift to get out of this thing, but for the moment, I simply don't care. The stress of the day has made me exceptionally tired, but I'm too wired to sleep. I absentmindedly rub my belly as my muscles turn liquid.

"Are you doing okay, love?" Sara asks as I exhale heavier than normal.

"Yeah," comes out as a sigh. "Now that I've calmed down, I think this couch may be a little too comfortable, if you know what I mean. You'll probably have to send an SOS just to get me out of it."

Her laugh reminds me of Enzo, making my heart clench in longing. "Oh, don't be silly. We'll get you out of it just fine. In the meantime, why don't you rest. You don't need to stay awake for my sake. I've got my Kindle right here in my purse and I can tell you're exhausted."

I sigh heavily. "I'm wiped, but my brain's still whirling ninety miles a minute."

"About anything in particular?"

I shake my head. "No. The moment I think I've captured it, it flies out the window."

Sara gives a low chuckle. "I was like that right before I had each of my babies."

"Really?"

"By the time Erin came around, Lorenzo swore it was a part of my nesting ritual. Did you nest with your other pregnancies?"

"More with Maddie than the rest. I had time to dote on the details. With Dec and Frankie, I think I was too busy to focus on anything but what was in front of me."

"That's completely understandable. Once these two make their appearance, I'm sure you won't have any time to worry either. I've had two close in age, but obviously not twins." Sara shakes her head before adding, "If they're anything like Enzo, I'll pray you keep your sanity."

I can't help but smile at her rolling eyes. "Oh, come on, he couldn't have been that bad."

"No, he wasn't. But he was all boy. If there was something tall, he'd climb it. If it moved, he rode it, and if it was even remotely edible, he ate it. Why one time, I had to pry dog food from his grip because he wanted to be just like the puppy we'd gotten him."

I shake my head in disbelief. "You're kidding." *Thank God, I've yet to experience that.*

"Nope." She smirks. "Parent of the year. Right here. Don't worry. It was only the one time. If I'm ever lucky enough to watch your little angels, we no longer have pets." Somehow, she manages a straight face until the end. Her downfall is when I make eye contact. Then we both erupt into fits of laughter.

"You'd better be careful what you ask for," I say when we've calmed down. "I'll be working part-time from home after my maternity leave. I may just take you up on babysitting if things get too hectic."

"Seriously, Sam, if you need me, I'm only a phone call away. Even if it's just for the chance to talk to a living, breathing human being with the capacity to respond, I'm always here for you."

As the hours tick by, I find myself losing the battle to stay awake. After a lull in conversation, I find my eyes waging a battle against gravity and losing terribly. They stay closed for longer periods of time and before I know it, I feel a blanket being thrown over me as I sleep on the couch.

The next thing I know, I hear the sound of familiar voices. "They're making their final approach." Then some silence. Since no one speaks, I figure it must be a part of the dream I'm having. Then in the distance, "How long has she been out?" from a deep, husky voice I try to recognize asks. Maybe this isn't a dream. I open my eyes to find Sara talking with Lorenzo and Riggs.

"About an hour or so," Sara whispers barely loud enough for me to hear.

I stretch and let out a big yawn. "I'm awake. What's up?"

Sara's eager eyes pin me. "Good. They're making their final approach. They should be landing in less than fifteen minutes."

Ohmigod! I can't wait to see Enzo. Instinctually, I attempt to throw myself out of the couch I've been lounging on. But these babies have other plans. I find myself stuck about halfway there. I rock myself back and try to extract myself again. This time I make even less progress. Holy crap. I think I really am stuck. *How the hell does one get stuck on a couch?*

Maybe if I scoot to the edge and use the armrest as leverage, I'll be able to stand? As I attempt to do so, I happen to look up. I find three sets of eyes staring at me with amused expressions of their face. *Great, here I am doing a beached whale impersonation and they're just watching?*

Riggs, stoic as ever, walks over without missing a beat and offers a hand. "Can I help you?"

As humiliating as it is, I reach out my hand, as it's likely the only way I'll ever get out of this couch. "Yeah. Thanks."

The second I'm upright, the weight of the babies crushing my bladder's astronomical, causing me to gasp. All eyes look to me. "I'm fine. Just pregnant," I mutter. I step toward the restroom and suddenly, the pressure increases. I take another step, determined to get to the bathroom and a gush of fluid runs down my legs. *HOLY SHIT! I just wet myself at Enzo's place of employment. This cannot be happening to me.*

A moan escapes as I do my best to look down at the mess I've made. As I turn around, I feel distinct movement from within my belly. It's sharp, and very much like an arm or leg moving across the middle. It's unlike their other movements as my skin feels tighter around their bodies.

I look to Riggs and find his eyes as big as saucers and his mouth hanging open. "Um... Sam..." he sputters.

"Oh, my!" Sara exclaims. "Your water just broke!"

"I figured it was that or she wet herself," Riggs manages to stay unflappable as he looks down at the puddle he's currently standing in.

A mixture of emotions overwhelms me. Mortification isn't quite strong enough, and panic doesn't fit either. As I survey my situation, it hits me like a brick across the face. *Holy shit, my water just broke!* I'm weeks until my due date, and Enzo isn't here. This cannot be happening! I'm not even in labor. Ohmigod... will the babies be okay?

Lorenzo's soft touch to my shoulder brings me out of my downward spiral. "Samantha, sweetheart. Are you okay?"

"Uh..." I take a moment to assess the situation. There's still fluid flowing down my legs, but at a slower trickle. It is probably one of the grossest things I have experienced, but nothing I can't live through. I haven't had any contractions, just some pressure on my lower back that's been there for days. Placing my hands on my belly feels weird. Without the amniotic fluid, they're more defined. It's almost like I can feel their actual bodies in my belly. I press tenderly along each baby as I take in their shape.

"Do you want me to call an ambulance?" Riggs pulls out his phone and waits for my response before dialing.

"I'd rather call my doctor first."

"Why don't you sit and I'll get your purse, honey," comes from Sara.

"Yes, please sit," Riggs strongly suggests as he reaches out to make sure I'm steady.

"Uh... I can't sit on that leather couch!" I scoff in disgust.

"Why the hell not?" Riggs' voice booms.

Isn't it obvious? "I'm disgusting. It's too nice and comfortable of a couch to ruin it," I argue.

"So what... Am I supposed to tell Enzo when he walks in

here, 'Dude, your wife's water broke and I'm the ass that made her sit in an uncomfortable chair?' I don't think so."

"Your water broke?" comes from the voice I've been craving to hear all day.

I turn to the door of the lounge we've been camping out in and see the sexiest man alive in the doorway. His face is a mixture of awe, wonderment, and shock. My heart melts.

IT'S BEEN A SHIT DAY. Anything that could have gone wrong, has. I've been flying for the past nine hours straight after getting shot at and having to rendezvous at another location. I'm dead on my feet and just want to crawl into bed next to Samantha and forget about this entire day.

Apparently, life has other plans.

As I round the corner to the lounge I was told my family is waiting for me, I hear Riggs' deep voice. "Do you want me to call an ambulance?" This has me picking up the pace to see what's going on. His tone is serious and a bit eerie. By the time I get to the door, I can tell Samantha's okay because she's arguing with him over sitting.

Just as I'm about to enter, the words, "Dude, your wife's water broke," register and I take in their full meaning. *Holy shit! She's going into labor?*

Needing to clarify, I ask in disbelief, "Your water broke?"

The minute Samantha turns, her rich, mahogany eyes lock

onto mine. I can see her visibly relax, just by my presence alone. I absolutely love having this effect on her.

I close the distance between us in mere strides. I wrap my arms around her and bring her in for a hug. When I pull back, she pulls in her lower lip and suddenly looks sheepish. "Yes. Just a few minutes ago."

"Have you been having contractions?" Ma interrupts. *Thank God, she is thinking clearly. I'm stuck on being near Samantha again.*

"I don't think so. There's been some pressure in my back, but lately, that's a daily occurrence."

"Have you called the on-call-doctor to find out what you should do?" I finally get my wits about me.

She shakes her head, but before she can respond, Riggs cuts in with a pointed look to Samantha, "She was just about to do that."

Samantha lets out an exasperated huff. "Great. Now we're all standing in this mess. Is there a way we could get some towels to clean this up so we don't continue to traipse through this everywhere?"

"Why don't we focus on the doctor, beautiful," I say, hoping to find out what to do next.

Samantha points to her purse next to the side of the couch that is clear from any liquids. "My phone's right there."

Pops is quicker than I can blink because he reaches out and hands it to us from a distance. I grab hold of the purse and open it for her. She reaches in and immediately calls the on-call doctor. After being on hold for what seems like an eternity, she talks to someone. The room waits on pins and needles for direction.

"Okay... Yes... No, not yet... Of course. I will see you when we get there... Okay. See you then."

She puts her phone back in her purse and a huge smile crosses her face. "Time to go to the hospital."

I'm instantly filled with about ten thousand emotions at once. I can't wait to get my family to the hospital, so I can guarantee they're safe. I'm just about to swoop them all off, until I look down at my dirt-sodden clothes. There's no way I can go like this. "Is there any way I can grab a quick shower?" I look to Samantha to judge her response first. "I promise, we will be on the road in ten. Sooner, most likely."

"Go ahead. Since I'm not in active labor, the nurse I spoke with told me to take my time and safely arrive when I can." She may have just had her water broke, but she's remaining calm and level headed. *How does she do this?*

I quickly pull her to me and plant a kiss on her lips. "I'll be back before you know it." Not wanting to waste any time, I look over to my parents. "Do you think you can walk her to our vehicle and I'll meet you out front?"

"We sure will, son." Pops smiles. "You look worse than what the cat dragged in. Get out of here and change. I want to meet my grandbabies." I hug him and Ma on my way out the door before he scolds me with, "Get movin', son."

We finally arrive at the hospital forty minutes later. Of course, Samantha put up a fight about riding in our new vehicle and ruining the seats, so I had to get plastic bags for her to sit on. Ma and Pops meet us at the labor and delivery entrance and we register at the nurses' station. Samantha keeps mentioning that she's not ready for this and all the things that are still on her list of things to do, but me being the smartass I am, just keeps telling her, "Samantha, our kids obviously don't care about the schedule. They're just ready for the world."

Once we're assigned to a room, Samantha's asked to change into a hospital gown. She asks if she can shower off the gunk and the kind nurse, by the name of Kate, offers to assist her. I pace the small space between the hospital bed and what looks like the couch I'll be sleeping on at some point. I hope to hell these babies make their entrance safely. The possibilities of unforeseen circumstances run through my mind. Thankfully, Samantha's into the room before my horrific imagination gets the best of me.

They hook her up to an IV and have monitors on her within minutes. The doctor comes in and greets the two of us. "I'm Dr. Allison. What seems to bring you in tonight?" Her warm smile and confidence puts me at ease. I reach out to Samantha's hand to find her muscles relax, too.

"Uh..." Samantha says as she sits up to shake her hand. "My water broke."

Dr. Allison does a thorough exam of Samantha. I try to wait patiently, anxious to hear what she has to say about Sam's progress.

When she's done, she explains, "Since you're at 35 and a half weeks, we're going to wait another hour or so to see if you go into labor naturally. We will induce you if they don't get things started on their own. Either way, you will be having these babies within the next twenty-four hours." She takes a step to the side toward a fetal monitor and pulls out the wand. She quickly does an ultrasound and we can still see two babies moving around. "Good. Things look good. I'd suggest you rest while you can. As you're only dilated to a three, we may have a long road ahead of us, and in this particular case at the moment, it's a marathon, not a sprint. I'll be back in a bit to check on you."

With that, she leaves the room, and Samantha and I are left alone. She couldn't look more beautiful. I reach in and kiss her tenderly. I love this woman more than life itself.

When our kiss breaks, she whispers, "I'm so glad you're here. It's been a hell of a day waiting to know if you're all right." Her eyes well up and I can tell she's about to break down into tears.

"Shhh..." I kiss her lips lightly. "I'm here now. That's all that matters." I kiss her once again and the love she has for me is felt throughout my body.

"I love you, Enzo," she whispers as I pull away.

"Love you, too, beautiful," I whisper.

There's a knock at the door and the nurse comes to check her vitals. I take this opportunity to go out to my parents in the waiting room and invite them into the room to wait a while.

My mother hugs me tight upon my arrival to the waiting room. "Oh, Enzo. I love you so much. You gave us all such a scare."

Pops joins us in a hug and adds, "Sure glad you're here."

"Sorry, Ma. I wasn't really in any danger. Plans just changed and I had to adapt. I'm so relieved I made it back before you all had to come here." I look to each of them. "Thank you so much for being here for Samantha."

"We would do that for any of our children," Ma sates, but holds my gaze as if I should know better than to say something like that.

"I know. But I want you to know how much it means to me for you to be there for Samantha. I know you love her, too. But to me, it meant the world walking in the room tonight and seeing you already there."

"Anytime, Enzo. Anytime." Pops claps me on the shoulder. "Let's go see how Samantha's doing."

Not even thirty minutes later, Samantha nearly squeezes my hand off. *Holy shit, the woman has more strength than I could've imagined.* Apparently, she'd been in labor and mistook her back pain as simple discomfort. Now she claims there's no guessing. These babies are on their way.

Before I know it, the doctor comes in and says she's dilated to a six. I feel completely helpless as she has contraction after contraction. I do my best do give her whatever she needs, even if it means I will never feel my fingers in my left hand again.

Since childbirth is the only time Samantha insists she's saying yes to drugs, a team of people soon arrive to give her an epidural. Though I want to freak out when I see the size of the needle they place into Samantha's spine, I may have to kiss the anesthesiologist because he takes the pain away from her quickly.

By the time they leave, Samantha is back to her beautiful self. She's laughing, joking, and in good spirits, considering the amount of pain she endured. We visit with Ma and Pops and I assure everyone I wasn't in any serious danger. I also take this time to call the kids and let them know their brother and sister are on their way. Samantha's parents decide they'll return tomorrow, instead of waiting the rest of the week because they can't wait to meet their new grandchildren.

I'm surprised when Dr. Allison comes in about an hour later and asks, "Okay, Mom. Are you ready to have these babies?"

"Is it time?" Samantha asks in disbelief. "This epidural's a miracle maker because I haven't felt anything."

Ma and Pops excuse themselves before things go any further.

Dr. Allison helps Samantha settle at the end of the bed and lifts the blanket covering her legs. "Yep. I'd say you're about ready."

Words cannot express my admiration for Samantha as she spends the next hour pushing with all her might. Yes, there are plenty of disgruntled curses being sworn under her breath, and her filter's off the charts for comments, but as usual, I give her a free pass. I love knowing what she's thinking. It's the best part of her. There even comes a time when she thinks she can't push any more. If I had to push a watermelon out of a lemon hole, I'd probably feel the same. But somehow, she manages to keep going.

Nothing can describe the birth of our daughter when she arrives at eleven forty-three that evening. It's a mixture of awe, wonder, and a bit of disgust when her slime-covered body finally decides to make an appearance. The scream that comes from the tiniest body I've ever seen makes me think she'd rather have stayed inside. I'm offered to cut the cord, which is the craziest thing I've done yet, then a nurse quickly cleans her up and offers to let either Sam or I hold her.

I'm suddenly overwhelmed with emotions as I take in the beauty of my daughter. She's absolutely perfect. Her skinny little hands and feet move excitedly as she enters Samantha's arms. My eyes fill with water as I bend to kiss her lightly. Life can't get any more perfect than this.

I'm taken aback when her expressive green eyes meet mine. She may only be minutes old, but the look she gives me melts my heart instantly. She looks as if she holds all the secrets of the world with her pensiveness as she checks out the room around her.

"She's so tiny," Samantha whispers and our daughter reaches out to touch her face.

"She's beautiful," comes out in almost a croak. Clearing my throat, I continue, "I love you both so much."

"We love you, too," Samantha whispers, then groans in a sound of discomfort.

"Hey, guys, let the nurses examine that bundle of joy. Baby number two's roaring to get out of here."

On cue, a nurse whisks our baby girl away.

As I put my other hand in Samantha's, a contraction hits and the doctor tells Samantha to push. As if his sister has cleared the way for him, with the first push, we can already see the head crowning. When Samantha pushes once more, his entire body comes right along with it.

I stare in disbelief as my naked son in all his glory lets out a murderous scream, much like his sister's arrival. *Holy crap. If we ever piss the two of them off together, we are in for it.* I assist in cutting the cord, then the doctor whisks him off with the nurse to get him cleaned up.

As my son is handed off, the nurse introduces her name as Rosalie. She offers to get him cleaned, weighed, and most importantly, into a diaper. Knowing both children are in capable hands, I turn my attention to Samantha.

I look at her skeptically when the doctor says push again. *What the hell is she pushing out? There'd better not be a third baby in there.* Then I see it… and suddenly, I wish I'd been looking anywhere but at the doctor and her at that moment. It's fucking disgusting.

"One more push and the remaining afterbirth will be out," Dr. Allison cheerily announces. *How can she be so upbeat after touching that?*

Immediately, I blink my eyes a few times, trying to rid myself of the sight I can't seem to unsee. I may have been in and out of war zones, watched my buddies have some near-fatal injuries, but nothing has prepared me for the strength a woman must have to go through during childbirth. Holy fucking shit. Hands down, Samantha's the strongest person I know.

I reach down and brush the hair off Samantha's forehead. "God, you're incredible, beautiful. I love you so much."

She pants as the doctor pushes down on her stomach in various places before saying, "I love you, too."

As soon as I'm sure Samantha's in the clear, I rush out to the waiting room to tell my parents our exciting news. "Everyone's perfect!" I exclaim when I see their eager faces.

They both nearly jump out of their chairs and rush to hug me.

"How's Samantha?" Pops asks.

"She's doing as well as expected, having just delivered babies. That woman is stronger than any person I know. Add to the fact that she's still smiling. I think she's a saint."

Both my parents chuckle as we make our way down the hallway to our hospital room. "I felt the same about your Ma," Pops whispers once he stops laughing.

I look to Ma and have a newfound respect I'd never known before. She's done this three times. And that was when epidurals were unheard of. This world would cease and fucking be extinct if men had to bear children.

We enter the room to find a nurse holding one of our children while Samantha has the other. They are in multi-colored pastels at the moment, so I have no idea which child is which. With them being swaddled like little burritos, all you can see are their squishy little faces and mops of golden-brown hair on top. We'll have to figure out a color system or something.

"Who've you got there?" I singsong as I reach down to the baby our nurse is holding.

"This is your son," the nurse beams. "He's quite handsome." She hands him over and I cradle him in my arms.

Ma rushes to my side. "Oh, Enzo. He looks just like you as a baby."

"God, help him," I tease as I stare into his big, green eyes. He has the most adorable thick patch of golden-brown hair that's all clean from his bath. His rosy cheeks pop out of the blanket swaddling him and his mouth is formed into the perfect little 'O.'

"Oh, hush." Ma swats at me.

"Do you have names picked out?" Pops asks from my other side.

"Yep. We sure do." Samantha draws our attention. "Let me introduce you to Lorenzo Dean Harper and Lorainne Marie Harper."

Ma oohs as Pops slaps me on the back. "You're straddling him with that name?" Pops asks in disbelief.

"Yep," I proudly say. "We'll call them Loren and Raine."

"How precious," Ma states as she walks over to see Raine in Samantha's arms. She reaches in for a hug and kisses Samantha on the cheek after doing the same to her granddaughter. "How are you holding out, Sam?"

"I'm doing as well as can be expected. I'm a bit tired, but I'm not sure we'll be sleeping much in the near future." The smile that lights up her face makes my heart clench. I don't think I can ever love her more than I do right now in this moment. She looks so natural. "Want to hold Raine?" she offers to Ma.

"You bet I do!" Ma almost squeals with excitement.

I look to Pops who's in awe of Ma holding our baby girl. "What about you, Pops? Want to hold Loren?"

He beams at me with delight and reaches for his phone in his pocket. "Can you get a picture of us?"

I stare at him in disbelief. He of all people is the one to think of a camera. I'd been so out of it, I'd missed everything.

Crap, I'm a fuck up as a father already. "Only if you do the same for us," I say as I try to recover from my earlier mistake.

We each take turns holding the babies, and several cameras have made an appearance to capture the moment. I send a picture of Sam and me holding the kids to Maddie, as well as my sister and brother. It's too late to video chat since it's nearly one in the morning when Ma and Pops decide to call it a night.

A lactation specialist comes in right as my parents are leaving and introduces herself as Piper. She assists Sam in getting the kids to nurse. To my relief, Samantha's well at ease with someone grabbing her breast and positioning it into Loren's mouth. Piper is up close and personal, and I've never seen anything like it.

"Before you know it, you'll be walking around the house, a kid on each breast and still managing to get things done," Piper teases. "You're a natural at this, Samantha." Do people really do that?

"Ha... I don't think I'd go that far, but I distinctly remember reading manuscripts and binge-watching TV series with my previous children."

One thing I'm coming to learn is there's an entire vocabulary set I haven't been privy to before having children. Words like lactation, latching on, unhooking, football position, and much more are discussed between Piper and Samantha.

I decide to make the most of my time by acquainting myself with Raine in the rocker. She's wide awake and ready to conquer the world. I undo the swaddle of blankets so that her hands are free and I can touch them. They are unbelievably tiny. Wondering what her feet look like, I unswaddle her entirely. I can't believe her feet are smaller than my thumb. When I brush my fingertips against her toes, she kicks at me and makes a cooing sound. She's still curled up like she's been in her Mama's womb and it's incredible to see the miracle of life up close and personal.

Suddenly, Raine straightens her body as stiff as a board and her face turns fire-engine-red. Did I break her? What the hell's happening. "Uh... Sam... What's going on?"

Both the lactation specialist and Sam stop immediately to see what's going on. Each are frozen in place as Raine makes a grunting sound. I immediately stand and walk to them. "What do I do? Is she okay?"

Before either of them can say anything, I feel a rumble in her diaper. She grunts again and again. My hand feels more movement in her diaper and suddenly, there's a loud farting noise that has me scared to check what's coming from that precious girl of mine.

"Um... Not it." Samantha laughs.

"Did she really just do what I think she did?" I ask in disbelief. There's no way this precious angel can sound like that.

"Let me see." I bring Raine over to her and she pulls back the top of the diaper. "Yep. You're in luck. The meconium ones are the nastiest."

I blanch at the thought. "What the hell is meconium?"

With a straight face, Samantha simply states, "It's the babies first poop and it's usually tar black and stickier than all get out to get off. They will usually only have one or two, then it will pass, and it will turn a liquid, yellowish color."

I take Raine over to the changing table, and holy shit. Sam's right. This stuff sticks to her butt like glue. It also has a sandpaper texture, so I do my best to clean her up without causing her too much fuss. My sweet girl screams like she's cursing me out the entire time. Thankfully, I'm a pro at diaper changing, so I'm able to get her settled quickly.

"Bring her to me. It's her turn to eat," Samantha directs as she gets Loren ready for a handoff. "You'll need to burp him."

Once I get Loren and Samantha settled with Raine, I move to the rocker and glide back and forth as I pat his back. Soon, a loud burp erupts in my ear, followed by a series of toots. "I see how you're going to be," I tease Loren. Samantha giggles at my response.

"Well, I'm sure he's not to be outdone by his sister." Samantha's sass is back in full swing. It warms my heart to see her at her best.

Within minutes, Loren does his best, but Raine's still the champion. I clean him up just as the lactation specialist leaves the room. Raine's nearly asleep. I offer to take her and lay her in the clear-walled bassinet next to Samantha. Samantha's awake, but it's evident she needs some rest.

"Why don't you try to get some sleep, Sam? I'll take our looky-lou here and hang with him until he falls asleep. You've had quite a day and could use the rest."

"So have you, mister." She eyes me suspiciously. "But I'm fading, and they will need to be fed before I know it." She pushes a button to make the bed recline.

I walk over and kiss her lightly on the lips. "Thank you,

Samantha. You have made me the happiest man alive today. I love you all so much."

She yawns and reaches her hand out to push the hair off Loren's face. "We make beautiful babies."

"We sure do, beautiful. Now get some rest." She closes her eyes and I walk to the rocking chair. I maneuver it with one hand, so that my legs can prop on the bench-like couch next to me.

Since the lights are dim, I grab the u-shaped pillow Samantha called a Boppy and place it on my lap. I let Loren settle down on it, so that he's facing me and I do the only thing I can think of. I tell him the story of how his mother and I met.

"One day, I came home from leave. I wanted to surprise Pops, so I went to his job site. That's the day I met and fell in love with your ma. I didn't know it then, but that one decision was the best I've ever made in my life..."

As I talk, Loren listens intently. His tiny hands wrap around my index finger and we have story time until his eyes grow heavy. When I think he'll fall asleep, I stealthily maneuver him to the bassinet and lay him inside next to his sister. I can't wait until they meet their brother and sisters. I know Maddie, Declan, and Frankie will be over the moon when they come tomorrow to meet their new brother and sister.

Not wanting to disturb either of them, I stare at my sleeping family and think to myself, life can't get any better than this.

EPILOGUE
SAMANTHA

The next December...

OUR LIFE HAS BEEN a bit of a whirlwind since the twins arrived, but we have done what we do best. Adjust and enjoy each new milestone. I'll never forget the day Maddie, Frankie, and Declan arrived at the hospital. Both Maddie and Frankie squealed and couldn't get enough of their new brother and sister, while Declan held back and waited for the commotion to be over.

When they were through, he went over to each of the twins and introduced himself as their big brother. He swore to protect them and always be there for them. I still get tears in my eyes when I think about it.

Now that the twins are five months old, they can roll over, so I can't leave them unattended for long. "Hey, Frankie, can you watch Loren while I hop in the shower?" Raine is sleeping and this might be my only opportunity to get a shower before

Enzo comes back from picking up Maddie at a friend's house. All of us are looking forward to her getting her license in February.

"Sure, Mom."

I make a mad dash upstairs, check on Raine, and get in the shower. Enzo doesn't know it yet, but we're planning a surprise birthday party for him this evening. To make things even better, his parents have invited all the kids for a sleepover. And when I say all the kids, this includes the twins. It's our first night without them. Each take the bottle just as well as breast milk. I'm stoked to have this time with Enzo. He has no clue as to what I have planned for this evening.

When I get out of the shower, I dress in my sexiest panties and matching bra. Unfortunately, it's still a maternity one, but things have come a long way in fashion since Maddie was a baby. I also put out a change of clothes I will wear for this evening. He knows we're going to dinner, but has no idea everyone else will be there. I also take the time to blow-dry and straighten my hair.

When I get downstairs, I find Maddie and Enzo home. The sight of him still sends shivers down my spine. You'd think that after a year or so, I'd be used to him entering the room. But no such luck, my heart still flutters and my mouth dries at the sight of him. Add that delicious dimple that pops when he smiles as he sees me and I'm still swooning.

"Hey, beautiful," he whispers in my ear as he pulls me in for a kiss in greeting. The tingles that race up my spine have me shivering.

"Hey yourself, handsome." I pull him closer and increase the intensity of our kiss.

In all too short of time, he pulls back. "We'd better stop, Sam."

"Must you always be so responsible," I plead.

He lets out a huff. "Someone around here has to be. Besides, we need to decorate the tree today."

"Why yes, we do. Someone's gotta hide the pickle we got in Germany," I tease. "Let's do it as soon as Raine wakes up."

Decorating the tree with two five month olds proves to be a challenge. As Maddie, Declan, and Frankie try to put up decorations, the twins have found they want to be in on the action, too, and keep rolling themselves under the tree to look at the lights. We laugh and enjoy our family the best way we know how.

"Hey, Mads, do you remember this?" Declan holds out a picture she'd drawn in a tiny frame as one of her Christmas gifts to me from school. It had just the two of them in it as stick-drawn figures.

"Oh, yeah. I drew that before Frankie was born. I think I might have been in kindergarten or preschool. What about this one, Dec?" She points out a picture of them as kids in a Christmas ornament.

As a tradition, I've taken pictures of each of the kids each year and put it into a photo frame ornament. I pull out my phone and decide if I want to keep up the tradition, I'd better take their picture.

Frankie rolls her eyes and sighs. "Why do we have to take pictures now, Mom?"

"Because I told you to," I tease. "Besides, we don't have any with the twins yet."

"Come on, Franks," Enzo encourages. "I know you've got a smile in you." He reaches over and grabs her by the waist to tickle her. She full-on belly laughs.

"Enough!" she gasps. "Enough! Okay..." Giggle. "I'll take the picture."

Each of the kids takes turns to get their picture taken as we finish decorating the tree. When it's all decorated, I ask all the kids to pose in front of it. Maddie holds Raine and Declan holds Loren. I take about twenty pictures because God knows, with five kids, if they will ever look in the direction of the camera at once.

Enzo has his phone out and takes shots at the same time. Hopefully between the two of us, we'll have a decent photo. By the time we're done decorating, it's time to go out to dinner.

I send everyone upstairs to change into nice clothes and tell them to meet us downstairs within the next half hour. Enzo and I take the twins to their room to get them ready. I'm sure to load the diaper bag with everything they will need for their trip to their grandparents. Maddie, Frankie, and Dec have already packed and have their things in the back of our SUV. They are in on the surprise tonight and miraculously haven't spilled the beans to Enzo yet.

When we get to the restaurant I'd rented out, we're immediately ushered to the back room. Maddie carries Loren and I have Raine in my arms as we enter the building. I let the kids go first and then I say, "Oh, Enzo. I forgot the bag of wipes. Can you go back to the car to get it?"

He looks at me suspiciously, but being the amazing husband he is, he simply says, "I'll be right back."

I walk into the room I've rented for this evening and see his entire family and some of our closest friends waiting. Everyone remains silent as we wait for Enzo to return. As soon as he enters the doorway, everyone shouts, "Surprise!"

Pure shock fills his face, letting me know our surprise is genuine. His eyes are wide and his mouth hangs open.

As people wish him well for his birthday with hugs and birthday wishes, Enzo eyes me. "You did this, didn't you?"

"What can I say? You know I love birthdays," I singsong.

When Enzo finally gets to me, he shakes his head and laughs our surprise off as he mutters, "I should have known something was up. You look way too good for just a night out with the kids."

Since his family swooped the babies up as soon as we arrived, I reach out to hug him. "Happy Birthday, Enzo. I love you."

"I love you more, beautiful," he growls into my ear. "I can't wait to get you home tonight." He plants a kiss on me in front of everyone.

"About that..." I whisper.

He cocks an eyebrow at me. "Yes?"

"We're not going home tonight."

"Where would we be going?"

I shrug as if it's not a big deal. "Well, since your parents offered to take *all* of the kids tonight, I thought we'd go to a hotel where you can open my other present."

His eyes darken with desire. "What kind of present are we talking about?" comes out gruff and filled with need.

"The kind you can only open in front of me. Let's get through dinner and then you'll get to see."

"Are you sure we have to wait? No one will miss us if we sneak out the back door."

"Enzo..." I nudge him. "Yes, they will. You're the guest of honor."

"Look over there." He points to his mother showing off Raine and then to his brother showing off Loren. "No one will miss us."

In the sexiest voice I can muster, I show him my final card. "If you stay through dinner and don't complain, I promise to make this one of your most memorable birthdays. I've plenty of surprises for you and it'll be well worth your while."

He pulls me to him and I feel the result of the promise I just made. He's silent for a moment as he holds me close to him. As I look him in the eye, the sexiest dimple known to mankind makes its appearance. Then he growls in the sexiest voice, making my panties wet with desire, "You've just made this the Best. Birthday. Ever!"

The End

Want more of Sam and Enzo?
Check out Mistletoe & Mayhem
Only available at:
https://amandashelley.com/books-by-amanda-shelley-2/

Want more from Amanda Shelley? Be sure to subscribe to her newsletter: https://geni.us/AmandaShelleyNL

Keep reading for a peek at **Making the Call**.
If this is your first book by Amanda Shelley, you'll be happy to know she writes primarily in one world - so this won't be the last you hear from Sam and Enzo. Chronologically, **Making the Call** is the next book in her world.

Chapter 1 - Luke

For players, girls are a dime a dozen; the coaches, not so much. I must keep my eye on the game. I've worked for this my entire life. I played college ball and was even offered a pro contract. But when a misguided tackle ended my career by blowing out my knee, I changed gears, switched my focus and spent the last six years working my ass off. I became the assistant coach to one of the best in the nation. My entire life's been devoted to learning what I can to help make my dream a reality. When Ray Carson chose to retire due to health reasons, my name was at the top of the list as his replacement. I never actually thought I'd be starting this next season as the head coach for the Rainier Renegades, a team I've always wanted to be a part of my entire life. But, in a matter of weeks, that's what's happening.

I'll never forget the day I walked into the owner's office. I rushed in to be early, unprepared to find everyone already waiting. I'd thought we were meeting to discuss the plans for summer camp. Little did I know they had something else in mind. Thank God, I'd been sitting down when I received my life-changing news.

"Hey, Luke," Mike Townsend greets, shaking my hand as I enter his office and gestures to the large conference table where I find both Tony Marcelli, our team's GM, and Ray Carson, the head coach, already sitting. "Why don't you have a seat. I have some things I'd like to discuss with you."

Instantly, my gut churns. Being under the impression we're meeting to discuss the summer camp training schedule and the logistics of getting everyone to camp, the expectant looks on each of their faces makes me think otherwise.

"Okay," I slowly draw out. "Aren't we meeting to discuss training camp?" I look from person to person already seated at the table, seeking clarification. But all of their faces remain stoic, giving nothing away. *The sorry fuckers. Couldn't they at least give me a heads-up as to what was coming?*

"We'll get to that," Mike bellows out as he takes a seat at the head of the table. He rubs a thick hand through his short, graying hair and rolls his chair forward to lean his elbows on the table. Okay, this is serious.

I take in a deep breath wondering where he's going with this. "All right."

I'm surprised to find Ray is the next to speak. "Son, you know I had a valve replaced last spring after the championship game, right?"

"How could I not? You nearly gave me a friggin' heart attack right alongside you, when I found you that day," I tease in return. Ray Carson has been my hero since I was a kid. To work with him has been a dream come true. I've followed his career since he took over for the Renegades. When I began coaching, he took me under his wings and showed me what it takes to coach a team to be champions.

Ray's gravelly voice begins an explanation, "Well," he draws in a long breath, "I thought I'd try to make it through another season, but my wife has other ideas. She wants to travel and make the most of the time we have left together." Ray looks a little sheepish, which is completely out of character for him.

"You're not going anywhere soon, Ray," I eagerly remind him. "Your doctor gave you the green light months ago, and I know you work out, so you're healthy. You have years left in you," I argue to refute his response.

"Well, I have a couple of championship rings, and more money than I could ever spend. Who knows how much time we all have left? I could be hit by a bus tomorrow, you never know," Ray states with a shrug. "You know I'm a hard-ass on the field, but when Vivian wants something, she's ruthless. I'm smart enough to give her what she wants."

Mike clears his throat. "That being said, I wanted to tell you how much we appreciated you stepping up to fill in for things last spring, while he was recovering."

"It was nothing any of you wouldn't do," I respond automatically. "Just doing my job."

"Well," Tony Marcelli interjects, "it didn't go unnoticed."

"What would you say to being the youngest head coach in the league?" Mike's deep voice suddenly fills the room.

The fuck? Did he really just say that? No fucking way. I. Am. Speechless. As my mama would say, I could catch flies with my mouth. Now that my jaw's dropped to the floor, I may need a shovel to pick it up. *Fuck... and CPR to catch my breath.* Crickets could be heard from miles away; the room is that silent as they await my response.

"Luke?" Mike says as he places his arm on my shoulder, breaking me from my trance.

"Excuse me?" I manage to get out. *There's no fucking way he just offered me the head coach position. I'm only twenty-nine years old. I won't even turn thirty until August.*

"What do you say, Luke? Do you want to be the youngest head coach in the league?"

"Seriously?" Apparently, I say it aloud.

The room fills with laughter from everyone. "I think you shocked the shit out of him, Mikey," Ray bellows out. "The boy doesn't know what to do with himself."

"I'm as serious as a heart attack," Mike says again. "No offense, Ray."

"None taken."

"Wow. That would be an honor." I finally manage to get my wits about me. "I thought it would be years before Ray retires. I love the Renegades."

"We know you do, Luke," Tony Marcelli states. "We've been thinking about this for the past few weeks, and you're the only one we want to lead this team. You stand out above the rest."

I take in another deep breath. This is certainly humbling. "Thank you for even considering me."

"Do you not want this?" Ray asks in disbelief.

"Hell, no! I want this. I'm just thinking aloud, what an honor it is to be considered in the first place. There's no way I'd pass up this offer!"

I stand and gratefully shake everyone's hand. I receive congratulations and slaps on the back as I make my way around the room. This is the job of a lifetime. I know I can do just as good of a job as Ray. I know the members of the team, and the inner workings of the Renegades, better than anyone else in the running.

"Glad to keep you around," Tony states to me as I shake his hand. "I'll have my secretary send you a new contract, and we can hash out the details later."

After another round of congratulatory handshakes that morning, we do discuss the logistics of training camp as well as some of the added responsibilities required of me in the coming weeks, since Ray will leave before camp begins. Ray had a lot more responsibilities than I did over the past few years, but I know I can handle it.

Since that meeting, my life hasn't been the same. The weeks have flown by in a blur. I'm up well before six each day. I work out on my own, eat breakfast then meet with the team by seven. I have meetings all day, work with the team during practices, and plan for the next day with my coaching staff before returning home late at night.

I prefer to get away from it all when I go out to my house on Anderson Island, but since becoming head coach, I've stayed in town more often. There's a ferry that gets me to Steilacoom, just before six thirty a.m., but I've been too tired to make the forty-five-minute commute.

Thankfully, this year's training camp went by without any major complications. Our practice schedule was rigorous, and the team feels in good shape, just coming off the championship win last season. Most of our team consists of returning players, with only a few rookies we'll test out in the pre-season games as well as some pivotal trades pushed through to help strengthen our O-line and special teams. Our hard work will pay off this fall, once the season officially starts.

To give everyone a break after our grueling schedule during summer training camp, the team has five days off before we come back at full force to gear up for the season. Many players will use this time to be with their families. It's an unspoken rule that each will continue their workout regimen on their downtime, but they don't have to be at our practice facilities for the next five days. Most of the members of our team are superstitious as fuck, so I'm sure they'll continue whatever gets them into their 'zone' as a professional athlete.

Myself, I'm looking forward to spending some time away from it all. I've been working my ass off around the clock to ensure nothing gets dropped through the cracks as the season begins. I know I need to prove myself not only to my team, but to the entire league, as I'm the youngest to ever do this. There's been a lot of hype and speculation, but I know the Rainier Renegades are ready, and I'll be there to ensure they keep the steady momentum we've built these past six years since I began working for the team.

I'm not spending the entire five days out at my home on Anderson Island, but I'll happily spend the majority of my time there. Sure, I'll review film from last season for the teams we're playing in the upcoming weeks. Since everything's digital nowadays, I can do it from the comforts of my couch, just as well as my office at the stadium. But I'll also spend time enjoying the remaining days of summer in the Pacific Northwest. There are a few projects I want to complete while I'm home, since I'll have free time to finally get around to them. The team's charity auction at the local children's hospital is the Saturday before we report back, so I must head back earlier than I'd hoped.

I pull off the ferry from Steilacoom just after four in the afternoon, and I quickly make my way to my home on the northeast side of the island. I love the land I purchased when I first was hired by the Renegades. I have a phenomenal view of the Sound as well as Mt. Rainier on clear days. I can hear the breeze as well as the water lapping against the shore when I sleep with my windows open at night. Sure, I have central air with my heat pump, but living in Washington, you don't need AC that many days of the year. Being on Anderson Island, it's nice to relax and take a break from the hustle and bustle of the city. The back side of my property is lined with trees, so I'm secluded while I'm here, which is a perk. Privacy is something I never thought was a luxury until I took this head coaching position, and my name was thrown into the limelight.

Anderson Island is the home to approximately a thousand residents. Most homes are vacation homes, so during the summer, the population raises to nearly four thousand. The island itself is just under eight square miles. It has a few restaurants and some stores if you need the basics, but if you want an item from a box store, you'll have to go to the mainland.

Thankfully, I have Evelyn, a woman who lives in the apartment above my detached garage, do my shopping and errands for me. Her young grandchildren live on the island full-time and when her husband passed away a few years back, she was looking for a part-time job close to her daughter so she could help her. I was looking for a housekeeper at the time and with my needs being flexible, it worked out for both of us. I don't have time to shop or clean for that matter and living on a remote island, it's necessary to keep things stocked up if I plan to spend any amount of time here.

Within a few minutes of exiting the ferry, I pull into the garage attached to my home and park my Mercedes next to my Jeep. I quickly unload the few things I brought with me and change into a pair of cargo shorts and a black t-shirt from back in my college days. Pulling a beer from the fridge, I prepare my dinner. I'm pleased to find Evelyn has the fixings for steak, corn on the cob, and a baked potato. Not wanting to waste time, I head to my back deck overlooking Puget Sound as well as Mt. Rainier in the distance to turn on the barbeque. Within fifteen minutes, I'm enjoying a delicious meal in complete solitude. I can already tell this is going to be just the break I needed before the season starts.

Chapter 2 - Luke

I may be on vacation, but my body's trained to wake up before the sun each day. I manage to sleep in until six, but beyond that, I might as well be wasting the day away. I get up, change into some shorts and a t-shirt, put my running shoes on, and begin to stretch. I don't have a state-of-the-art gym out here, but I do have the open road. Well, I do have a weight bench and a few free weights in a spare bedroom, but not much more than that.

I'm out the door within minutes, making my way across the island in no time. Since it's not a big island, I have a route planned that takes me along the outskirts, maximizing the amount of pavement, so I can get a good run in. The sun's bright in the sky, and the weather's warm. As I run, I take in the stillness of the island, since its inhabitants are still enjoying their Wednesday morning from the warmth of their beds. I make my way up and over hills, sharing my morning with the few deer and the birds chirping in the distance. I have one earbud in, and my favorite playlist beats out a rhythm I easily keep pace with.

Rounding the last bend, my heart clenches in my chest as I

witness a bad accident. Ahead of me, a bicyclist flies over their handlebars at the bottom of the hill. They go ass over end and skid across the pavement, to an abrupt stop. *Fuck, that had to hurt.* From the looks of it, they must've hit the large pothole on the side of the road. Their tire's now bent and twisted in an unusual shape. *Damn, they had to be cruising down this hill.* I pick up my pace to see if I can be of any assistance.

The closer I get, the more I realize it's a woman who's fallen off her bike. Thank fuck, she's wearing a helmet since her head bounced across the pavement a few times. By the time I arrive at the scene, she's sitting up inspecting the gravel embedded into her knees, palms, and elbows. *Christ, that looks awful.* Her curly brown hair spills out from her helmet, and her back is to me as I approach.

"Are you okay?" I ask, so I don't scare her.

"I'll live, but I don't think my bike will." She glances to me then winces as she pulls a large pebble from the palm of her hand. She points in the direction of her bike, and I can confirm for myself, it won't be in working order anytime soon. "Do you have a phone I can borrow? I seem to have lost mine in the wreck." I look around the area but have no luck spotting a phone. She takes off her helmet, and her brown hair springs free. It distracts me for a moment because she suddenly takes out her ponytail, shaking her locks free. God, even with dirt in it, it's beautiful. Her curly hair comes to life with each movement, catching hints of auburn in the sunlight. It's almost mesmerizing, but eventually, I remember my manners.

"Um, I live just two driveways down. Would you like come to my place to clean up, or maybe I can call someone for you? I left my phone at home this morning, so I'll have to go home either way before I can help you." I walk over to her and hold out a hand. "Do you think you can walk?"

"It'll just be easier if I come with you." She lets out a groan as pain radiates across her face. I immediately reach out to assist her into a standing position.

"Are you sure you're okay?" I ask as I steady her. She immediately begins hobbling as weight is put onto her feet. "Here, let me help you."

As if on instinct, I reach behind her back and under her knees to pick her up. Standing at her full height, she comes only up to my shoulders. She's a slender woman with curves in all the right places. If I had to guess, I'd say she's around my age, and she can't weigh more than 140 pounds. I can easily carry her to my house and get her fixed up in no time.

"Wha... What are you doing?" she stammers as I walk in the direction of my home.

"I'm taking you to my place to get you cleaned up. Then I'll come back for your phone and bike, to take you wherever you need to go," I say as I reach the entrance to my driveway.

"But I don't even know you. You could be an axe murderer for all I know."

I can't help the grin spreading across my face. She's adorable as she attempts to get stern and pin me with her ocean-blue eyes. There's a girlish presence about her, but her body tells me she's fully a woman. The short riding shorts she's wearing have crept up her thighs, and I can tell she works out regularly by the firmness of her beautiful body. Her loose tank has risen as well, revealing a toned abdomen. *She's definitely all woman.*

"Well, I'm Luke. I'm pretty sure if I were an axe murderer, the community would've found me out by now. It's a small island. I can promise you, I have nothing but good intentions. I'll let you sit out on my back deck and tend to your wounds without making you step foot in my house. I have a housekeeper, who lives in the apartment above the garage over there. So, if you'd like to have someone present, I'll gladly wake her if it'll make you feel more comfortable."

Heat creeps up her face, making it turn slightly red. *She is adorable.* "I don't think that'll be necessary. Besides, you didn't have to help. You could have just left me on the side of the road," she says as she shakes her head to hide her embarrassment. Her hair brushes my bare chest, and my senses go on overdrive. *Calm the fuck down, Luke. She's injured, and you're only helping her out.*

"What kind of company do you keep, if you think I'd just leave you out alongside the narrow road with no shoulder?" I ask incredulously.

"It was a figure of speech," she deadpans, her eyes narrowing.

"Just checking," I reply, not knowing what to say. I walk up the steps to my back deck and set her down on a lounge chair.

"Wow, you have an amazing view," she whispers as I set her down.

"It's incredible," I say before I open the French doors to go inside. "I have a first aid kit, I'll be right back."

I rush upstairs to my bathroom and return only a few

minutes later to find the mysterious woman on my porch beginning to pick out rocks from her palms. *She sure is stubborn.* "Here, let me help." I open the kit and look for a pair of tweezers. She appears to just have major road rash, but I should look things over as I help her clean her wounds. She may need a trip to the mainland to an urgent care clinic if anything needs stitches.

We spend the next few minutes cleaning out her gashes. It's just as I expected, only road rash. It'll hurt like hell for a few days, but she doesn't have any major injuries. She does her best to control her winces as I clean out each area. I try to distract her with conversation, though I'm not sure how effective it is.

"So, do you have a name?" I ask as I go through a particularly gnarled piece of skin on her knee.

Embarrassment floods her features. Her face flushes with color, and her ocean-blue eyes are suddenly hidden beneath her long lashes. "Uh, it's Dani?" she states, making it sound like a question and causing me to narrow my eyes at her. Before I can say anything, she continues, "It's short for Danika."

"Well, Dani..." I draw in a deep breath as I attack a stubborn piece of debris from her left knee. "What brings you barreling down the road this early in the morning?"

"I was trying to wake up by getting a workout in. I stayed up late last night working on a project, and I need to get into the zone, so I can continue today." A look of apprehension flickers across her face, as if she's revealed too much.

Not sure if I should pry further into what she's revealed, or let it go, I stick with a safe line of conversation. "Well, let's get you cleaned up so you can get back to it."

Dani lets out a groan, and I'm unsure if it's in frustration or from pain. "There's no way I'm going to be able to work today," she says as she shakes her head in disgust. *Well, at least she solved that mystery. Her project must be important.*

"Why is that?" I ask, genuinely interested in her answer. There's a look of determination that I don't find on many others. It's as if she's internally kicking herself for getting injured, and I'm not entirely sure why. It was obviously an accident.

Letting out a huff of breath that washes over my chest like a live wire sending electric pulses throughout my body, she states dejectedly, "I have a deadline in the next few weeks that I need to meet. There's no way I can work on my computer, when I can barely use my hands. God, I was just getting ahead, too. Nancy's going to kill me."

"Is Nancy your boss? I'm sure she'll understand," I offer, trying to show sympathy.

"No, she's my editor."

Before either of us can say anything else, Dani's distracted by the hydrogen peroxide I pour onto her knee, and she instantly gasps. "Fuck! Give a girl some warning. That shit hurts like a sonofabitch!" She lets out a low hiss, then lowers her voice as "DAMN! FUUUCK! SHIT!!!" come out in a slur of words. She takes in a deep breath and holds it, while I press on the cloth to take the sting away. I can't help my smile when I realize this sexy woman could curse a sailor out of a bar with that mouth of hers. She'd definitely give the boys in my locker room a run for their money and would certainly make them stand up and listen. I nearly lose it when she suddenly turns tomato red and covers her face with her hands. "I am so sorry," she mumbles from behind her splayed-out fingers.

"No worries, Dani. I didn't mean to hurt you." I can't help when the corners of my lips tip up. "I'm honestly quite impressed you weren't cussing up a storm when I arrived on the scene. I watched you go airborne and skid across the pavement." I can't help but cringe at the image that replays in my mind.

"God, this is so embarrassing." She shakes her head and refuses to make eye contact.

I reach my hand under her chin and guide it to make her look at me. "Dani, you have nothing to worry about. Seriously. I just want you to be okay."

When our eyes lock, I'm not sure what comes over me, but I find myself sucking in a breath to steady myself. *What the fuck was that? Focus, Luke. This isn't the time. She doesn't seem to be like a girl who is into one-night stands, and that's all the fuckin' time you have these days. And let's face it, you don't even have time for that.* I shake my head and regain control of myself. *Sort of.*

"I know," she whispers. "I do appreciate your help. Please know that."

I release my hold on her chin and try to focus on getting her left elbow clean. It only has a bit of debris in it, so it cleans up quickly. When the last of her battered body is bandaged up the best it can be, I offer her some ibuprofen to reduce the swelling and pain. I quickly make my way into my kitchen for a glass of water and the bottle of pills. Upon my return, she quickly gulps it down and rests back on the lounge chair I had placed her in.

"Would you like to sit here for a bit while I fetch your bike and look for your phone? Here, put your number into mine, so I can search for it easier." I reach my arm over, handing her my phone.

Without any hesitation, she dials her number. When she places it back in my hand, I notice she's already pressed send and hung up. "I'll be right back," I say to her as I hop off my porch and jog down my driveway.

Making the Call is available everywhere. Continue reading about Dani and Luke today! https://books2read.com/Making TheCall

ACKNOWLEDGMENTS

First, I want to thank you, the reader, blogger, and reviewer for reading this duet. There are plenty to choose from and I want you to know I appreciate you choosing mine to spend time with. I hope you have enjoyed Sam and Enzo as much as I have. They've been a part of my life for the past few years. I've spent countless hours with them. They've become like family. It's bittersweet to see their story end. I hope you have enjoyed their world as much as I have. I'd love to hear from you. You can find me on social media or at www.amandashelley.com. If you care to share your thoughts on this book with other book lovers, please feel free to leave a review at any of the retail sites or on Goodreads.

I'd like to take this opportunity to thank Amy Queau at QDesign, for creating the amazing cover of this book. She went above and beyond my expectations and even kept me sane when I found out it had to be changed. You are such a talented person and it's an honor to work with you, Amy.

To my editor, Susan Soares at SJS Editorial Services, thank you for your time and patience. I appreciated your feedback and this duet wouldn't be what it is today without your help. I'm looking forward to working with you more in the near future.

To Julie Deaton at Deaton Author Services, your proofreading is top notch. Thank you for making this as beautiful as it is. There's no way the quality would be as great as it is without your assistance.

To my beta readers, Jackie, Cara, and L.G. Thanks for all your help and support along the way. Your willingness to read and give me immediate feedback was invaluable. I couldn't have written this book without you. Some of my favorite memories while writing this book were calling or texting you and asking if you could choose your own adventure, which would you prefer when it came to twists in the plot. Thank you for being there for me and being a sounding board as well.

There are some people I'd also like to thank for special help along the way. To Andy for being my "go to" man. You answered the most random questions, but you still let me come back for more. To Curran for letting me run some hypotheticals your way to see if what I'd written was accurate. Leela, thanks for reaching out to answer my questions as well. I appreciate your help and hope you found my L&D to be accurate.

Last but certainly not least, I'd like to thank my four girls. Your love and support allowed me to finish these books, meet my deadlines, and get this published. I know you often wondered and verbally voiced why I write my books, but please know that I love and appreciate you more than you'll ever know. Thank you for letting me finish just one more page or holding that thought until I finished my sentence. I love you to infinity and beyond. Your love and support mean everything!

BOOKS ALSO BY AMANDA SHELLEY

If you enjoyed this book, you will be happy to discover Amanda Shelley primarily writes in one world. For a complete list of the series reading order as well as a chronological time line, please visit:

https://amandashelley.com/reading-order/

Mistletoe & Mayhem

Featuring Sam & Enzo from the Resilience Duet

When I met Samantha, my life flipped on a dime.

I'm still piloting missions, but no longer for Uncle Sam.

I used to think I was happy being single, but Samantha proved me wrong.

Thanks to her and our children, I'm certain I'm the luckiest man in the world.

Who knew my life could be filled with so much love, laughter, and utter chaos?

I'm looking forward to stealing some time with my wife before the holidays, but with all the mayhem of Christmas, will we be able to get away?

https://geni.us/AmandaShelleyBooks

Making The Call

Dani

As a bestselling romance author, most assume my life's glamorous, filled with combustible chemistry, and most of all,

romance. Ha! I can only wish. With a deadline looming, I've
escaped to my family's cabin on Anderson Island to free myself
from distractions. My plan's great, until a man, who could pass as
a cover model on one of my books, comes to my rescue. Is there
chemistry? Sure. Is he everything I'd look for in a guy? Absolutely.
But will my career be at risk if I give into my desire?

Luke

For a player, women line up outside the locker room. For coaches,
we're lucky to get in the game. As the youngest NFL coach in the
league, I live, eat, breathe, and even sleep football. To gear up for
this season, I return to my home on Anderson Island for a much-
needed break. When Dani literally crashes into my life, my mind's
suddenly on the sexy brunette with a sailors mouth, rather than
my team's next play. She has me dusting off another playbook
entirely, making me wonder, did I make the right call?

https://geni.us/AmandaShelleyBooks

The Boy Upstairs

I ran into Derek while trying to escape the neighbor from hell.

Instantly, we hit it off. Since he's only here for three months and the microbrewery leaves me little time for commitments, it's the perfect setup for a fling.

He's adventurous, challenges me, and he just gets me from the inside out.

With our expiration date quickly approaching, I'm left to wonder... Will my heart ever be the same without the boy upstairs?

https://geni.us/AmandaShelleyBooks

He Saved My Boy

Davis is the first guy to catch my attention since... hell, I don't even know.

Instantly, he makes me think and feel things I've forgotten existed. It has been forever since I put my needs first, so I take the chance and let him light me up from the inside out.

Our night is the kind that will ruin me for all others.

But then I get the dreaded call.

I rush out without a second glance, knowing I'll likely never see him again.

My son will always come first—Always.

Imagine my surprise when Davis walks in, and I find he's the only one who can save my boy.

This cannot be happening—*I guess it's time to pull up my big girl panties and see what happens.*

https://geni.us/AmandaShelleyBooks

Of all people, why him?

He didn't EVEN bother introducing himself, just assumed I knew him from his fame on the court.

I nearly died on the spot when our professor announced we were permanent lab partners. Between his arrogance and the constant interruption from basketball groupies, there's no way I'll survive this semester.

Sure, he's hotter than anyone I've ever seen in a science lab with his sexy blue eyes, cute dimple, and muscles for days - but I can't afford *his* kind of distractions.

Okay. Deep breath.

I can do this.

After all, it's only one semester.

Just when I think my self-control is in check, he does something to show me that he isn't the egotistical, self-centered jerk I thought he was.

How can his stupid smile suddenly make my mind melt, heart race, and palms sweat?

Our connection is consuming, and my world is knocked off kilter. It's far beyond physical attraction. He's smart, sexy, and feels like—home?

Wait, that can't be right...

Whatever it is, Vince has me breaking my rules to spend time with him.

My entire life I've prepared for meeting the wrong guys.

What the hell should I do when I find the right one?

https://geni.us/AmandaShelleyBooks

Damien: Book Three of the Perfectly Independent Series

Beautiful girls are not hard to find at Columbia River University.

The coeds on campus are great to look at but I was over that scene after graduation three years ago.

These days, outside of being part of the largest civil engineering job on campus, all I'm searching for is a decent meal and some peace and quiet. It's why I'm happy to have found what I consider a hidden gem in the diner I frequent.

All I need to do is finish this job and move on to the next by year's end.

Should be easy enough. Only when Vanessa walks up with a sexy smile and a mouth full of sass, she does more than take my order. She completely takes my breath away.

Next thing I know, I'm here every morning, making every excuse to dine with this intriguing woman. Not only is she smart and sexy, but she's laser focused on reaching the goals she's set for herself.

The more I get to know her, the more I'm convinced she's the one. I just have to find a way to get her to deviate from her perfectly laid plans and take a chance on me.

https://geni.us/AmandaShelleyBooks

The Vegas Pitch

This pitch could make or break my career.

Not only will it set a personal record for the biggest account I've ever landed, but it could set my newfound company three years ahead of schedule for expansion.

Thank god I've got Nate Bellinger on my team.

Even though I had my reservations hiring the sexiest man I've ever laid eyes on – he more than meets my expectations with his hard work and determination. Together, we've formed a solid team and play off each other perfectly.

As we wait for the final verdict, I begrudgingly take Nate up on his offer for a night on the town. After all, this is Vegas and I need to let the chips fall where they may.

Imagine my surprise when I wake up the next morning to find we've not only won the campaign, but I'm apparently married to the man I've only ever let myself fantasize about.

The kicker of it all – he has no intentions of letting me go.

But what will it mean once we leave Vegas?

https://amandashelley.com/books-by-amanda-shelley-2/

The Summer Dare

Leave it to Nana to think of everything.

After a grueling semester, I'm ready for a peaceful summer in Seaside with my sisters.

Imagine my surprise, when I'm woken by the screeching sound of a saw coming through my wall, the first official morning of break.

Not only did I come flying out of bed swinging, but I gave Ryan, the unsuspecting carpenter the surprise of his life, when I came wielding my killer coat hanger and all.

Too bad, I was only in a tank and undies and it wasn't nearly as effective as I'd hoped.

Of course, he insists he's only doing his job. Since it's Nana's last request to care for us, I can't refuse.

However, I won't let a tall, pesky, sexy as sin, know-it-all get in my way of my summer plans. I pretend I ignore him – that is until my youngest sister pokes her nose in my business and throws down a dare I can't back down from.

Kiss the next single guy who walks up to the bonfire – or explain to my sisters why I get riled up over the contractor.

When Ryan suddenly appears, I know I'm screwed in more ways than one.

Not only will my sisters learn my secret, but from the determined look on Ryan's face, I'm afraid he's eager to reveal it to the world as well.

What have I gotten myself into?

As I walk toward him, one thing is certain – this summer dare will either make or break me.

https://geni.us/AmandaShelleyBooks

The Summer Ultimatum

Watching my sister fall in love last summer gave me something I hadn't expected—hope. It gave me hope that there might be someone out there for me and hope that I might get past my misguided fears and finally let someone in.

With my help, Ryan's planning the most epic proposal. I just have to get the know-it-all musician I work with to fall in line to make it work.

Jax is wicked smart, extremely talented, and sexy as sin. But he can't see the forest for the trees when it comes to his potential. He'd rather keep playing in dive bars along the coast than take a real shot at success.

When the Seaside festival has a music competition, I present Jax with an ultimatum that will either make or break both our careers.

I've laid it all on the line, but can he?

https://geni.us/AmandaShelleyBooks

The Summer Proposal

My sisters are dropping like flies.

They're falling in love and having the time of their lives.

Don't get me wrong, I'm ecstatic for them. I love seeing them happy.

But I'm not ready for that type of commitment.

I can't even keep a plant alive, let alone find someone worthy of getting past a third date.

As the only sister done with school and single as a pringle, I have to do something fast, or I'll be my matchmaking aunt's next victim.

When Jax's drummer joins him for the summer and needs some help with his image, I make him a deal he can't refuse.

All is perfect—until I realize my summer proposal has one minor flaw.

Our relationship may be a sham, but there's nothing fake about my feelings for Finn.

https://geni.us/AmandaShelleyBooks

The Summer Arrangement

One, two, three—it's all down to me.

As the youngest and only single Lancaster, I'm eager to spend my summer in Seaside, Oregon, with my sisters. It's something I've looked forward to all year, and I'm determined to make every minute count. After all, I've only got one year before I graduate from college and have to adult for real.

However, if I want to graduate debt free, I need to work. I have a lead on the perfect summer job with the nanny agency I've spent the last three summers catering to.

I just have to win over an adorable three-year-old and convince her single dad I'm the right one for the job.

Simple enough, right?

Except when I show up at his door, I'm shocked to find he's the guy I hooked up with a few times last semester.

This cannot be happening.

I need this job. There's too much on the line to walk away. Maybe we can put the past behind us and make some sort of summer arrangement?

https://geni.us/AmandaShelleyBooks

The Summer I Found Home

Being a pilot is all I've ever known.

I served my country and I'm damn proud of my career.

But sacrifices were made, especially when it came to family.

I've missed first steps, first days of school, and first dates to name a few.

My kids grew up. They're having families of their own.

Was it worth it?

When an opportunity brings me to Seaside, I jump feet first no questions asked.

It means experiencing all those firsts with my grandkids.

With family as my focus and my guard down, I don't even see Faye coming.

She's a force to be reckoned with and has me holding on for dear life.

I thought our ship had sailed, but now that I'm home for good—I just might get more than one second chance.

arrangement?

Collide: A Sweet Romance

Falling head over heels was the last thing I expected.

Literally.

Coffee is everywhere – and more than my ego is bruised.

When the handsome stranger I plowed into calls me by name, mortification sinks in.

He rushes off to class. I run home to change, hoping to forget the whole incident.

If only I could be so lucky.

I quickly find it's a small world and Gavin Wallace is completely unavoidable. Everywhere I turn he's there. In my classes. Hanging with my friends.

I've got his full attention and I have to admit, I like it a lot more than I should.

https://geni.us/AmandaShelleyBooks

ABOUT THE AUTHOR

Amanda Shelley loves falling into a book to experience new worlds. As an avid reader and writer, sharing worlds of her own creation is a passion that inspired her to become an author. She writes contemporary romance about characters who are strong and sexy with a twist of sass.

When not writing, Amanda enjoys time with her family, playing chauffeur, chef and being an enthusiastic fan for her children. Keeping up with them keeps her alert and grounded in reality. She enjoys long car rides, chai lattes and popping her SUV into four-wheel drive for adventures anywhere.

Amanda loves hearing from readers. Be sure sign up for her newsletter and follow her on social media. Join her reader's group Amanda's Army of Readers to talk about her books and stay up to date on her latest information.

www.amandashelley.com
Readers group: https://www.facebook.com/groups/Amandas ArmyofReaders/
Newsletter: https://geni.us/AmandaShelleyNL

Goodreads: https://www.goodreads.com/author/show/
19713563.Amanda_Shelley

facebook.com/authoramandashelley
x.com/AmandShelley
instagram.com/authoramandashelley
amazon.com/author/amandashelley
bookbub.com/profile/amanda-shelley